THE
PREACHER'S
Bride

A WHISKEY RIVER BRIDES NOVEL

THERESA OLIVER

For information, contact the publisher, Hot Tree Publishing.
WWW.HOTTREEPUBLISHING.COM

EDITING: HOT TREE EDITING
COVER DESIGNER: RMGRAPHX
FORMATTING: RMGRAPHX

ISBN: 978-1-925853-36-0

MORE FROM *Theresa*

To those who have ever lost a love.
May you never close yourself off from finding it again.
But most of all, may you find peace.

CHAPTER 1

February 1871
New York, New York

"Hey, Mia!" Trent Jericho yelled from across the room as he walked into the Breckenridge Saloon. "Wanna dance?" He took off his cowboy hat, which was in sharp contrast to the suit he wore, and held it in his hand. Even though it was out of place in New York, it suited him well. He'd been a cowboy who gave it up to become a lawyer. Mia guessed that old habits died hard. Trent had been a regular for a while and was harmless. Even though he probably had money, he never flaunted it. He was down-to-earth and had never forgotten his roots.

"Trent," Mia Flynn replied as she placed her hands on her hips, taking him in. "How many times have I told you? I'll always save a dance for you."

"Yes! I was hoping you'd say that." He smiled as he placed his hat on a nearby table and walked purposefully toward her. "Just one dance, though. Then I have to go back to the hotel. I have an important case I'm arguing tomorrow."

Mia scoffed. "Why don't you buy a house instead of living in a hotel?"

He shrugged. "Not sure. I guess New York really never seemed like home to me."

"You really should get yourself a wife." Mia shook her head as she let him lead her around the dance floor. "With as much money as you spend in here—"

"Why? You offering?" he teased, raising an eyebrow.

Mia couldn't help but laugh. "Yeah, like I'd marry the likes of you!" He had always been more like a big brother to her than anything else.

He made a big show of placing his hand over his heart. "Miss Flynn, you have mortally wounded me."

Mia smiled, shaking her head. She and Trent had been friends for a long time, since she first moved to New York. "Yeah, that's what I thought. One of these days a woman's going to catch your eye—"

"And I'll run like hell." Trent took a step closer as the music came to an end. "One more dance?"

"I thought you had to go home."

He shrugged, holding out his hand. "One more dance couldn't hurt."

She pretended to deliberate as the feather in her blonde, wavy hair bobbed. She'd been a dancehall girl since she moved from Connecticut to New York three years before, after her parents died of influenza. She let out a deep breath. "Sure. Why not?" Mia was getting tired of making a living with men paying her to dance. One day she wanted to have a family of her own, but that wasn't going to happen. Not here.

A broad smile spread across his face. "Thanks, Mia. I haven't danced with a lady in a while."

Mia looked at him sharply. "You were just in here last week."

Trent raised an eyebrow. "It seems like it's been a lot longer." He towered over her as he twirled her expertly around the dance floor. "Say, have you heard from Wyatt Nash lately?" Before he left, Trent and Wyatt had been inseparable, having been best friends for longer than she had known either of them.

"Now, why would I ever hear from him? After the last mess he made in here, he can just stay where he is." Douglas, a merchant marine, had called Wyatt a cheat and had pulled a knife. He and Wyatt ended up tearing up the place, and Mia was left with the arduous task of cleaning up the mess.

"That wasn't Wyatt's fault," Trent corrected, raising an eyebrow. "Didn't he move to Wyoming like Ella?"

"Yes, I believe he did… to a town called Whiskey River." A twinge of guilt tugged at her. In her last letter, Ella had been pregnant and would have the baby soon. She and Ella had been so close—like sisters. She wished she could be there for her friend in her time of need.

"What's wrong?" Trent asked, truly concerned. He had been nice enough to her since she'd known him. Always a gentleman.

"I just wish I could be there for Ella," Mia sighed as she

looked into his eyes. "She's going to have a baby soon and, from what I understand, the pregnancy's been rough."

Trent shook his head. "That's too bad. I always liked Ella. Well, I'm sure everything will work out all right." The song came to an abrupt end. "Wanna dance another?"

"You haven't even paid me for the first two yet!"

Trent laughed as he pulled three dollars out of his vest pocket and handed it to her. "Here's for the last two and the next one."

She took the money and slipped it into the front of her dress. There had to be a better way to make a living. Being a dancehall girl paid good money, but not enough. Since Ella left, she had to shoulder all the financial responsibilities herself. While they were roommates, they rented a two-bedroom tenement and split all the bills, making it much more affordable. Now, there just didn't seem to be enough to make ends meet. She had thought of taking another roommate, but who could replace Ella?

"Mia, you're not yourself. What's going on?" Trent asked, breaking her reverie. Out of all the men who frequented the saloon, he was the best dancer. Despite their banter, Mia never minded dancing with him.

She shook her head. "It's nothing."

Trent raised an eyebrow. "Come on. It's not 'nothing.' Talk to me, little sis."

Mia let out a deep breath, and then forced a smile at his nickname for her. "It's nothing I can't handle. Times are just a little tough, is all."

A crease formed between his eyes. "Need some money?"

Trent had always been very direct. That was one of the things she had always liked about him… and she suspected one of the things that made him a good lawyer.

"No, I'll be fine." Mia looked around the nearly empty saloon. It was dead. She wouldn't be making much money tonight. "I've been taking in some sewing lately for extra money."

Trent stopped dancing immediately and took out his wallet. "How much do you need?"

"Put that away in here." She gently pushed his hand down, looking around the room. Luckily, no one was watching. "I appreciate the gesture, but I can't take your money." She shrugged. "I just need some time to figure things out." The only problem was that she had taken in all the sewing she could handle, working into the early hours of the morning, and it still wasn't enough.

"Here. Take this." He shoved a twenty-dollar bill into her hand and closed her fingers around it.

Her eyes flew open wide as she looked at the money, and then up into his eyes. "Trent, this is too much! I can't take this!"

Trent closed his hand around hers, crumpling the bill. "You can, and you will. I have no family, so what else am I going to spend it on? I already have more than I know what to do with." His shoulders lifted in a shrug. "Besides, it's only money."

"Trent, I don't know what to say," she gasped as tears came to her eyes. This would be enough to pay not only her rent, but her groceries for the entire week, too. "I'll pay you back."

"Oh no, you won't." Then he looked around and lowered his voice. "And, Mia, this is for you. Don't give the house a cut out of it."

She smiled, her eyes welling up with tears. "Thank you."

"Hey, let's have none of that." He wiped a tear away from under her eye with the pad of his thumb.

"Want another dance?" Mia asked, touched by the gesture.

Trent smiled. "Well, since I just lost that one, sure. But I'm going home after." Trent thought for a moment, and then added, "Mia, this isn't for dances. It's for you."

"I know."

Then a broad smile spread across his face. "Now, how about that dance?"

Mia laughed as she held her arms out to him willingly. Even though she knew she wasn't obligated, she gave him another dance on the house, grateful for his help. With that kind of money, she would have plenty left over for a while— if she was careful—until she could decide what to do.

As she walked up the stairs to her tenement, Mrs. O'Riley, the resident manager, came out of her apartment from across the hall, scowling as she placed her hands on her hips. Two small children clung to her skirts. She reached down and picked one up and, in one fluid motion, slung her onto her hip and took the other child by the hand. The woman's red hair was a testament to her Irish temper. "And when do ye plan on paying the rent, my dear?"

A broad smile spread across Mia's face. "As a matter of fact, I have the money right here."

Mrs. O'Riley's mouth flew open in surprise as Mia counted out the money, but quickly recovered herself. "By the way, something came for you today."

Mia's eyes brightened. "What is it?"

"A letter from Ella." She pulled out a crisp white envelope from a pocket inside her skirt and handed it to her. "So, how is she?"

Mia shrugged as she ran her fingers over the beautiful scrolled penmanship that was distinctly Ella's. "I don't know. I haven't read it yet."

"Humph!" Mrs. O'Riley huffed as she marched into her apartment, her children in tow.

Mia hurried inside her tenement and locked the door behind her. A woman living alone in New York City wasn't ideal, but it was all she could do for now. She slung her reticule haphazardly onto a side table in the living room and then looked down at the letter in her hands.

February in New York was cold and showed no signs of warming up. Mia wanted nothing more than to curl up in the rocking chair, tear open the envelope, and devour every word from her friend, but she was cold. So, she hurried to build a fire in the fireplace with what was left of the twigs in the wood box, making a mental note to have some wood delivered in the morning.

Soon, the small fire burned red, orange, and yellow, sending warmth throughout the room, so she settled in for a nice read. She picked up the envelope and looked at the return address one more time, savoring the moment. "Whiskey River," Mia mumbled to herself. What an odd name for a town. But from what Ella had told her of the friendly people there, it seemed to suit the town well.

Unable to wait any longer, she daintily tore open the envelope, revealing the contents inside.

My Dearest Mia:

It seems as if it's been longer than it has since I last saw your lovely, smiling face. This pregnancy is making me nostalgic, perhaps. Lately, I've been reminiscing about the tenement we shared, which seems a lifetime ago. But I have no regrets.

Colton is the light of my life. I have so many blessings now, so much to be thankful for: A loving husband to care for me and a new little one on the way. What more could I ask of life? I feel lucky for all that the good Lord has chosen to bestow upon me.

Now, for the town. Wyatt and Madison have settled in nicely. Of course, you know that she is the new schoolteacher and Wyatt now owns the saloon. Madison wasn't too keen on the idea at first, but they have since settled in and are happy in their new life. Wyatt cleaned up the Whiskey River Saloon since the likes of Pete McGregor, God rest his soul. Truth be told, it's probably the cleanest saloon in the county.

We also have a real, honest-to-goodness princess living in Whiskey River! Dirk Price, the owner of the livery stable, married a princess right after Christmas. I'm not sure how they met or the particulars, but they seem very happy together. She left her title behind and has settled into Whiskey River as Mrs. Gabriella Price. It has a ring to it, don't you think? Anyway, I wish them both every happiness.

Preacher Caleb Henley is struggling. The townsfolk are all worried about him and try to help him as much as they can, but he's just not the same since he lost his wife. He hasn't smiled much lately. Not that I've seen, that is. I suppose that between caring for his two small children, the congregation, and the farm, it has taken its toll on him. Colton and I continue to keep him in our prayers. I ask that you do the same. I just wish there were something more I could do. But I feel comfort in the fact that dear Mrs. Jenkins and the other ladies of the church congregation have been trying to help with the children and his house. But it's of little consequence to lift his spirits. The loss of his adoring wife, Jessica, has been a loss for us all indeed.

I don't want you to worry, but Doc Morgan has told me to rest as much as possible. Colton tells me that it's not only for my good, but for the good of the baby. Although he says nothing about it, I know he worries. I try not to complain, so as not to give him fuel for his worry.

But you, I can confide in, my dear friend. Lately, I've been feeling helpless. Colton waits on me hand and foot, never complaining. Although he has never given me cause to feel this way, I feel guilty for Colton having to shoulder the burden of the ranch and the house alone. He hired a few ranch hands, and they have been working out, which is a comfort. I just hope they continue to be of service to Colton and lessen his burden.

So, how are you? I miss you so, and wish you would consider moving to Whiskey River. The town is much, much smaller than you're used to in comparison to New York, but the picturesque landscape of the rolling mountains and the friendly, communal nature of the people make it home.

If you do decide to move here, I would expect you to stay with us, of course, for as long as you like. But if the cries of the baby in the middle of the night become too much for you, Mrs. Jenkins always has room at her boardinghouse. Alas, I know this is but a dream.

Take care, my friend. I hope this letter finds you well, and I count the days until I can see you again.

Your Loving Friend Forever,

Ella

Mia clutched the letter to her chest as she rocked back and forth, watching the glow of the fire, the only light in the room. Although it hadn't been that long since she had seen her best friend, it seemed like a lifetime.

Could she ever think of moving to Whiskey River? After all, there was nothing left for her here in New York. Ella would let her live with them for as long as she wanted, but she didn't want to intrude upon their hospitality indefinitely.

Mia let out a deep breath, considering. Even if she wanted to, she didn't have the money for train fare, and purchasing a horse and a rig would be even more expensive. Also, the journey would take weeks in what was sure to be an arduous trip across the country. No. That was out of the question.

She couldn't go, but she couldn't stay, either. The

money that Trent gave her would soon deplete, leaving her with nothing. She could continue to take in more sewing and work at the saloon, but what kind of life would that be? Eventually, she wanted to have a family of her own. Something she hadn't had in a very long time.

She rocked back and forth into the wee hours of the night, considering her options, which were slim at best, when it finally hit her. Ella had been a mail-order bride. And although she didn't end up marrying the man that she had intended to, everything had worked out well. Perhaps God did have a plan for Ella that was bigger than she knew herself.

What if she became a mail-order bride, too? After all, Ella would pick a suitable man for her, and perhaps the man Ella chose could pay for the trip.

Mia jumped from the rocking chair and dashed over to her desk, picked up the quill, and penned a letter, asking Ella if she could pick out a suitable husband for her. As she wrote, she wondered what her new husband would be like. And although she trusted Ella beyond all words, Mia just hoped that she was making the right decision.

CHAPTER 2

"Would you like me to come over tomorrow, too?" Mrs. Jenkins asked when Caleb Henley walked into his house. He hung his cowboy hat on the peg by the door, but left on his heavy coat.

Since he lost his Jessica, nothing seemed real anymore. Nothing seemed quite right. No matter how much he tried, something was missing from his life. And he knew what it was… it was her. It had only been a few months since she had passed away from consumption leaving him alone with two small children—Hailey, age two, and Shane, age four.

Most days, he tried to suppress his anger and guilt. He felt guilty for not having seen the signs, for not having taken better care of his wife. He had left her to care for the children and the house, knowing that she was ill, while he tended to the congregation and the farm, and she was also the town schoolteacher. But all along, she had insisted that she was fine. Why hadn't she taken better care of herself? Then he felt guilty again for being angry with her.

As the town preacher, he was supposed to be strong for his congregation, comfort them in their time of need, assure them that God was with them in their trials. But where was God now? Why had *He* taken his Jessica away from him so prematurely? Why didn't God take him instead?

But in his heart, Caleb knew that God wasn't to blame. He hadn't been the one to take her away. Things happened. He knew that God never turned away from his people, but why had he allowed that to happen to his Jessica?

Caleb had been going on like this for months, feeling guilty for living, feeling guilty for her dying, and missing her so badly that he physically hurt. But now it was time to take matters into his own hands. If something didn't change, he stood to lose more than his congregation. How could he continue to care for this family, his farm, and his congregation alone, and still keep his sanity?

Caleb looked at the older woman. "Are you in a hurry to go home?"

Mrs. Jenkins cocked her head to the side, her curled, silver hair causing her to look like a kind grandmother. "No, not today. What do you need, Caleb?"

He let out a deep breath. "I hate to ask, and you've already done so much, but could you watch the children for me for about forty-five more minutes or so? I have some business to take care of, and I won't be long."

She raised her eyebrows almost into her hairline. "Oh! I wouldn't mind it at all. You go do what you have to. I'll stay here with the children." Then she inclined her head toward them, playing quietly on the big oval rug taking center stage in the living room in front of the fireplace. "You take your time." She gave his arm a motherly pat.

Mrs. Jenkins reminded him so much of his mother that it was uncanny. Actually, his mother was even kinder than Mrs. Jenkins, if that was possible. But God had taken her when he was little, leaving him alone with his father, who was a preacher, too.

It seemed that history had repeated itself.

"Thank you, Mrs. Jenkins."

Caleb ran his fingers through his dark brown hair, slid on his cowboy hat, and walked out the door, pulling it closed behind him.

Caleb had left his buckboard out front with the team still hooked up in the patches of snow on the ground. He didn't have much time, so he jumped up and grabbed the reins. "Yah!" he yelled, urging the horses into a gallop. There was only one person who could help him.

Guilt filled his chest from even contemplating the idea, but he had been thinking about it for a while. It was difficult to admit, but he was having a hard time taking care of his children, being there for them and giving them what they needed. He couldn't bear the thought of his children pulling away from him and losing them emotionally. Caleb could stand to lose his congregation, but not his family. He would quit his job as the town preacher first... but there was another option.

He let out a deep breath, and it turned to steam immediately in the cold Wyoming winter air. Wasn't he supposed to put God first before everything, including his family? And the people in his congregation in Whiskey River had been so kind to him. But he couldn't go on like this; he had to do something.

And he was tired. Tired of struggling, tired of putting on a brave face, tired of just being tired.

Within minutes, Caleb pulled down the long drive leading to Colton and Ella Hill's ranch.

Colton was walking toward the house from the barn but stopped short when he saw Caleb pulling his team down his drive.

Just seeing Colton's warm smile made Caleb feel better. He just hoped that he was making the right decision for his family. For his children.

"Evening, Preacher." Colton wiped his hands on a towel. "What brings you out here tonight?"

Caleb put on the brake, stepped down, and wrapped the reins around the front bar.

It was twilight and the sun was just beginning to set, signaling the end of another day. "You got a minute to talk?" Caleb asked as he shook his hand.

Colton took off his hat and ran his hand through his long brown hair, pulled it back into a ponytail, and let it fall down his back as his eyebrows pulled together in concern. "Sure. Come on in." Colton started walking toward the house, but Caleb stopped him.

"Actually, I'd rather talk out here in private, if you don't mind." Caleb's heart was pounding at the thought of what he was about to do, but he had to do something, for better or for worse.

Colton's eyebrows pulled together in concern. "Sure. What's wrong? Something happen to one of the kids?"

Caleb shook his head. "No. Nothing like that. The kids are fine."

Colton waited patiently.

The preacher let out a deep breath. "I don't know how to begin."

Colton smiled. "Want to go sit on the porch?"

Caleb shook his head.

Colton waited, obviously giving Caleb time. Then he smiled and gave him a manly slap on the back. "Oh, come on, Preacher. It can't be that bad. Just spit it out."

"Right now, I'm not here as a preacher, but as a man. I need to talk to you about something, but it needs to stay between us… for now."

Colton nodded. "Yes, of course."

Caleb placed his hands on his hips, and then let out a deep breath. "Your wife, Ella, was a mail-order bride, right?"

Colton's smile faded. "Yes, you know she was. But Dallas King was an ass, and she fell in love with me—"

"No, no. You misunderstood." Caleb bit his lower lip as he summoned his courage. He almost dropped the whole thing and walked away, but he was desperate. "I need a wife. Someone to care for the kids and the house. Someone I can trust while I'm away. Although they've been so kind, I can't keep depending on the ladies of the church anymore." He let out a deep breath. It felt good to get it off his chest. "I was wondering if Ella might know of… a woman… that I could marry. I know it sounds crazy, but it would be purely platonic. We would have to be married for her to live in the house with me and the kids, though. But I have a spare room and she can have it all to herself." Caleb walked away to collect his thoughts, and then turned back around. "I just need some help, Colton. I'll pay for everything. She can just stay at home with the kids and take care of the house."

Colton's eyebrows pulled together in concern. "Are you sure this is what you want?"

A lump of guilt formed in Caleb's throat.

"Are you ready for this?"

"I have to be." He let out a deep breath. "Colton, it's hard to admit, but I'm having a hard time taking care of my family, being there for them, and giving them what they need. After losing Jessica, I feel that I'm going to lose them, too, and I just can't let that happen. Between trying to care for the congregation, my family, and the farm, something's got to give. I hate to say this, but I have to start putting the needs of my family first. I need someone to help take care of the children and the house while I make a living for them. Without the farm and my income from the church, we would soon be in trouble."

"What do you need me to do?"

Caleb let out a sigh of relief. "You don't think this is crazy?"

Colton laughed. "Oh, it's crazy, all right. But no crazier than anything anyone *else* in this town has done." Colton placed his hand on Caleb's shoulder and squeezed. "Caleb, you have to do what you have to do. I don't see how you've done it so far. I couldn't imagine…."

Colton let his voice trail off, not finishing the sentence. But Caleb knew full well what he was about to say: He couldn't imagine ever losing his wife like that. Caleb smiled. "I wouldn't have survived it if it weren't for my parishioners and the people of Whiskey River. I appreciate everything that everyone has done, but now I have to do what I have to do."

"Yes, you do." Colton let out a deep breath. "If I were in your shoes, I'd do the same thing. For the sake of the children, if not anything else. I know it's going to be hard for you, though. But if you're sure about this, we can go in and talk to Ella right now."

"Are you sure it's not an imposition?"

Colton smiled. "Never. Preacher, you're welcome here anytime."

"Call me Caleb," he corrected as he shoved his hands in the pockets of his trousers. He had been out making his weekly rounds, seeing to his congregation, even though the barn and the house needed tending to. But he pushed the thought quickly aside.

Colton smiled as he walked up the stairs and held open the door for Caleb. "Ella, honey! We have company."

"Oh, yes?" Ella's voice rang throughout the house, coming from the living room. "Who is it?"

Immediately, Caleb's preacher instincts kicked in when he saw Ella lying on the sofa, pale as a sheet as she attempted to sit up. "Please, don't get up on my account." Caleb sat down on a chair across from her. "How are you feeling?"

Ella gave him a smile. "I'm okay, but I feel like an invalid. Doc Morgan wants me to lie down until the baby comes." With much effort, she sat up and rubbed her belly.

"Just stay there," Caleb urged, concerned. She had been so active in the community it was hard to see her like this. For a moment, he wondered if something was wrong with her or the baby, but he forced the thought from his mind. "I won't be here long."

Ella sat up and leaned against the back of the sofa. Colton sat down beside her and slid his arm across the back of the sofa behind her. Colton's adoration for his wife was prominent in his eyes.

Ella's eyebrows pulled together in concern. "What's wrong, Reverend Henley?"

"Caleb, please," he corrected.

Ella's eyes opened wide as she looked at Colton and then back. "Are you okay?"

Caleb smiled. She was very sick herself, but here she was, more concerned about his well-being than her own. She was having a very rough pregnancy and, from what Colton said, had spent most of it vomiting. "Mrs. Hill, I hate to trouble you with this, but I wanted to know if I could talk to you about something."

"Yes, of course." Ella's eyebrows pulled together in concern.

Caleb proceeded to tell her of his plan to get a mail-order bride to help out around the house and care for his children. "My question to you is this: Can you tell me who to contact, or would you help me to find a mail-order bride?"

Ella laughed. "You're joking!"

Caleb's mouth flew open in shock as his face fell. "I… I… I'm so sorry to have bothered you with this. It was a stupid idea…." He rose to his feet and headed toward the door, his muscles tense under his jacket.

"No! You misunderstood!" Ella stopped him. "Please, come back over and sit down. That's not what I meant." A broad smile spread across her face. "You talk about the good Lord working in strange ways!"

Caleb narrowed his eyes, confused. "I'm not following you," he admitted, and sat back down.

Ella beamed brightly, bursting with excitement as she turned to her husband. "Colton, would you be so kind as to bring me the watercolor painting of Mia?"

Colton suppressed a smile as he headed into the bedroom.

Caleb wondered what was going on, but Colton was back before he could ask. He handed a small frame to his wife, and she laid it face down on her lap. "You aren't going to believe what I'm about to tell you, Caleb." She held up a letter. "I just got this letter from my best friend in New York, Mia Flynn. In the letter, she asked me if I could find her a husband. She wants to be a mail-order bride."

Caleb's eyes opened wide, unable to believe what he was hearing. "What? Why?"

"You can read the letter, if you like. Essentially, she's in financial trouble." Ella sighed. "You see, we were roommates before I left New York and we used to share the rent and expenses. It was okay for two people who were both working. But when I left, I left her high and dry."

Caleb's heart pounded hard against his rib cage, unable to believe what he was hearing. "Why doesn't she just get another roommate?"

She shrugged as she smiled. "No one was me, I guess. You see, we've been best friends for a long time. If the shoe was on the other foot, I know I couldn't replace her, either."

Caleb nodded in understanding.

"Caleb, before you agree or say anything, there's something you should know first."

He waited, listening intently.

"Mia and I worked together." Ella waited for it to sink in. "She's a dancehall girl and a seamstress."

"Caleb." Ella lowered her voice conspiratorially. "Gentlemen came in and paid to dance with us, but nothing more. It's good money, but she's getting tired of that life, just like I did." Ella bit her lower lip. "Does it make a difference? Could you still care for her, knowing that?"

"Of course I could." He shrugged. "We all come from somewhere." One corner of his lips curled up into a smile as he raised his eyebrows. "You said that she sews?"

Ella laughed. "Oh, yes! In fact, she's been sewing for ladies in New York, and she sews all her own clothes." She shrugged. "It's just not enough. She said that she would rather be a seamstress for a dress shop… or make clothes for her own family."

Caleb raised his eyebrows in surprise. "She said that?"

"Yes, she did." Ella ran her hand over the back of the picture frame. "Would you like to see a picture of her? I have a watercolor of her, but it really doesn't do her justice.

We had these done for fun when we first became roommates and exchanged them."

Caleb's heart pounded. He had just made the decision, and now everything was happening so fast.

Ella's lips curled into a mischievous smile as she handed him the picture frame.

When he turned it over, he looked into the most intriguing green eyes he had ever seen. She had blonde, wavy hair and a sweet smile. "She's beautiful." A twinge of guilt pulled at his heart. Not long ago, he had thought that Jessica was the most gorgeous woman in the world.

Ella giggled, pleased with his reaction. "She's like my baby sister."

"What's she like?" he asked, unable to take his eyes from the young woman in the painting.

"Well, she's just as nice and kind as she is beautiful," Ella replied, smiling.

Colton laughed. "But she can be feisty, too. She won't take any guff from anyone. At the saloon—"

"She's one of the kindest people I know," Ella interrupted, cutting him off, obviously not wanting to push the fact that she was a dancehall girl. Ella looked in Caleb's eyes. "Caleb, she's decent, kind, and has good morals. She only danced with men because it paid well. As you know, there are very few options for single women to make a living these days."

"I understand," he replied, unable to take his eyes from the painting.

"Does it bother you?"

He shook his head as a smile lit his lips. "Hey, if she

can help me with the children and the house, then she'll be golden to me."

Ella laughed. "Well, she's already golden to me."

"Just don't make her mad," Colton warned, obviously remembering something from the past.

"That's right," Caleb said in realization. "You all knew each other in New York, didn't you?"

"Yes, we did," Ella replied, and then rubbed her stomach.

Caleb's heart twinged. He knew that move well, remembering when Jessica used to do that when she was uncomfortable while she was pregnant. "I should go and let you rest."

Ella shook her head. "Not yet. I have a plan."

"Already?" Colton asked. "Leave it to my wife not to waste time."

Caleb laughed, his heart feeling lighter than it had in a while. "So, what's the plan?"

"Well," Ella began, leaning forward in excitement, "you can buy Mia a ticket and then she could pick it up at the train station in New York." She let out a deep breath. "You'll have to pay for everything—all of her expenses. Mia doesn't have much money."

"That's not a problem at all. I'll take care of it." Caleb thought for a moment, and then asked, "Is she good with kids?"

Ella smiled. "She loves children."

"How soon can she get here?"

A broad grin spread across Ella's lips. "I'm sure she can leave immediately. I'll send her a telegram."

"Thank you both for everything." Caleb rose to his feet. "Well, I really must go. Mrs. Jenkins has been with the kids all day. But something told me to come over and talk to you both, and now I know why."

Ella caught his hand, stopping him. "Caleb, are you sure this is what you want?"

He thought for a moment, and then nodded. "I've never been more sure of anything in my life."

"Okay, then. I'll get in touch with Mia right away." She laughed. "With so many men needing wives here in Whiskey River, I should go into business with Madame Chase, the matchmaker!"

Caleb and Colton laughed.

Caleb gave her hand a gentle squeeze. "Thank you, Ella. And if you need anything, just let me know. I'm here if you need me."

She smiled. "I appreciate that, but you just gave me the best gift of all… my best friend. If we act quickly, this means that Mia will be here in time for the baby."

Caleb smiled as he gave her hand a gentle squeeze. "I hope so."

"I'll walk you out." Colton rose from the sofa and Ella laid back down again.

When they walked outside, night had fallen, casting a blue hue over the patches of snow.

Caleb turned to Colton and asked, "Is she okay?"

Colton's smile faded as he shook his head. "I just hope that Doc Morgan is right and that it's just the pregnancy. I hope it's nothing more."

Caleb gave Colton's shoulder a sincere squeeze. "I'm sure she'll be fine. If you need anything at all, just let me know."

I appreciate the sentiment," Colton replied, "but I think you have your hands full already."

Caleb smiled as he stepped up into his buckboard. "Thanks, Colton. And be sure to thank Ella again for me, too."

"No, I should thank you. You just made her night. Mia and Ella have been as thick as thieves for years, so to speak." Then Colton's eyebrows raised in concern. "Which means you and I are both going to be in trouble."

Relief spread over Caleb. And for the first time in a long time, his laughter was genuine.

He gave Colton one last wave as he headed home, feeling better than he had in a very long time. He just hoped that he was making the right decision.

CHAPTER 3

Mia took the worn telegram out of her pocket to read it one last time before the train stopped in Laramie, Wyoming. She had taken it from her pocket, unfolded it, and reread it so many times over the past few days that creases had been etched permanently in the folds of the letter. It appeared to be years older than it was. Everything had happened so fast it was hard to believe it was real.

My Dearest Mia:

I have the most wonderful news! The preacher here in Whiskey River approached me, stating that he'd like a mail-order bride... on the same day I received your letter!

He is a good man with two small children: Shane, age four; and Hailey, age two. They are wonderful, well-behaved children who need a mother to love and care for them.

Between us, Reverend Caleb Henley has his hands full. Dealing with the loss of his wife, raising his two small children alone, and dealing with his congregation and the farm has taken its toll on him.

The reason he wants a wife is for the children, and he insists that your relationship be purely platonic. He assured me that you will be perfectly safe with him.

He has a spare room that will be yours, and he and the children will share the master bedroom.

I spoke with Caleb and he will make the arrangements for your travel. He assured me that the ticket would be awaiting you at the train station. Then Caleb, Colton, and I will meet you in Laramie when you arrive. You will need to leave New York as soon as possible, though.

Let me know if this is agreeable to you.

I cannot wait to see you, and will count the days until your arrival. Have safe travels!

All My Love,
Ella

Mia folded the piece of paper back up one more time and slipped it into her reticule as she looked out the window. She was in a shared car and hadn't gotten much rest on the journey. She let out a deep breath, exhausted from the three-day trip from New York. She mainly kept to herself, sewing, and only came out for meals. It wasn't that she was trying to be unsociable. She just wanted time to think and to get some last-minute sewing in before she arrived. On the trip, she had made a new dress, beige with tiny rosebuds, to match a light beige hat she already had. She wanted to look nice when she arrived, but didn't have much time or the money to assemble a new wardrobe prior to the trip. After she received Ella's letter, she was on the train three days later.

It hadn't taken Mia long to prepare for her trip to Laramie. As she waited on the train, Mia realized that it had not quite been a week since she had received the news that she was going to be a mail-order bride. It seemed that after she had made the decision, everything had fallen into place very quickly.

In her cabin, she slipped into the new dress she had just finished and looked in the mirror. It fit her to perfection with a fitted bodice, low neckline, and full skirt. She took out a beige modesty scarf that matched her dress, slipped it around her neck, and tucked it in place. She wanted to look good, yet proper, when she met her soon-to-be husband and his children.

Mia was going from being a single, lonely lady to having a ready-made family… all in the course of a week. She had reluctantly agreed to the relationship being strictly platonic and just taking care of the house and children. All her life, she had wanted to fall in love with a man and to have a regular family, but she had agreed to their marriage being platonic out of survival. She needed a roof over her head, didn't she? But maybe someday, they might find love together. She dreamed of Caleb being the perfect man with the perfect children in the perfect town: a ready-made family to love.

There was a loud knock on the door down the hallway, bringing her from her reverie. "Gather your things!" the steward announced as he knocked on another door. "We'll arrive soon!" He said the same lines over and again, moving down the hallway.

"Well, this is it," she whispered to herself as she looked in the mirror one last time. Her green eyes were bright, and she pinched her cheeks, giving them a little color. "There." Satisfied, she glanced around the cabin once more to see if she had missed anything. Then she slipped her reticule over her wrist and headed toward the exit, knowing the steward would get her bag.

The conductor offered her his hand. She took it and stepped gracefully down out of the train.

"There she is!" Ella yelled from the other side of the platform.

Ella's belly was protruding, but in her face, she didn't look pregnant at all. Mia was surprised at how pale she was, though. Obviously, the pregnancy had taken its toll on her. Colton stood beside his wife, beaming with pride, and on her other side stood a tall, handsome, muscular man with dark brown hair and blue eyes, holding a small, whimpering little girl with dark blonde hair while trying to wrangle a fidgeting little blond boy. They all appeared to be dressed in their Sunday best.

Ella pulled her in for a hug. "You look wonderful!"

Before she could say anything, Colton pulled her in for one of his big bear hugs. "It's great to see you again, Mia. How was your trip?"

"Good," she replied nervously and took both Colton's and Ella's hands. "It's good to see you both." Then she looked over at Caleb, who took her in with his bright blue eyes, the most beautiful eyes she had ever seen.

"Mia, this is Reverend Caleb Henley," Ella said, turning to Caleb. "Caleb, may I present to you Miss Mia Flynn."

"It's a pleasure to meet you." Mia extended her hand.

"The pleasure is mine," he mumbled, smiling. Then he handed her the little girl, now crying openly. "We have to meet the preacher here in Laramie in a few minutes."

Mia's eyes widened. "Preacher?"

"Yes. He's going to marry us."

"Now?"

Caleb let out an exasperated breath as his smile faded. "Yes. You can't live under my roof unless we're man and wife. Since I'm the preacher and, because of the children, it wouldn't be proper otherwise."

Mia was thankful that she had chosen the dress she made, which would become her wedding dress within a matter of minutes. She was about to protest, but, then again, that was what she had come there for, wasn't it? She just hoped that she was making the right decision.

Ella pulled her in for another hug and whispered, "He really is a good man, Mia. I promise."

"It's just that I thought we'd have time to get to know each other first."

"Time is a luxury I don't have at present." Caleb picked up the squirming boy, then he smiled, warming her heart. "I'm sorry for the rush, but we need to get home before dark. Are you ready?"

"I guess I have to be."

He froze, his eyes searching hers. "Are you sure you

want to go through with this?"

It was the oddest marriage proposal she had ever heard, but Mia guessed that it was the only one she was going to get. After all, they had arranged everything ahead of time and romance was out of the question… for the moment.

"Yes, of course."

He set his son down. "Wait here and I'll collect your luggage."

Then she turned her attention to the crying little girl in her arms. "And you must be Hailey."

"Papa!" she screamed, reaching for her father as she watched him and her brother walk away, huge crocodile tears rolling down her cheeks.

He was back a moment later, carrying the trunk.

"It's okay, baby. I'm right here." He walked past them with the heavy trunk, expecting them to follow, and set it in the back of the buckboard. "Hailey and Shane, this is Mia. She's coming to join our family now."

"I don't want a new mama!" Shane wailed as he stamped his foot.

Caleb scooped him up in his arms. "Now, that's enough of that."

"I'm not trying to replace your mother, baby," Mia reassured.

"Don't talk about my mama!" the boy yelled, tears coursing down his cheeks. "You didn't know her!"

Caleb looked at her apologetically. "I'm sorry, he's never acted this way before." Then he turned to the boy. "Now, I want you to be respectful of Mia. You apologize to her right now."

"No!" he yelled.

"Do you want a spanking?"

"All right," Mia intervened, not wanting the boy to get spanked on her account right after they first met. "Didn't you say that the preacher was waiting?"

Caleb let out a deep breath as he took Hailey from Mia and got the children settled into the buckboard. Then he extended his hand to help her up.

Before she took his hand, Mia turned to Ella and pulled her in for a hug.

"We'll meet you at the church," Ella whispered to her. When she pulled back, Ella wrapped her arm around Colton, who looked at his wife with adoring eyes.

After meeting him, Mia had all but given up hope that Caleb would look at her like that one day. But at the moment, she guessed that he was just as overwhelmed as she was. She quickly pushed the thought of romance out of her mind. She had made this decision, and she was going to make the best of it… for the children's sake, if nothing else.

Caleb made a clicking sound with his tongue as he shook the reins. The horses immediately started walking down the street. Mia pulled her coat around her. It was freezing out! Much colder than New York. But Mia knew she would have to get used to the weather. She looked at the children, and they were both wearing coats, as well. It was February in Wyoming, after all.

Hailey cried softly and Mia hugged her to her chest. The little girl immediately laid her head on her shoulder.

"Ssshhhh," Mia cooed into Hailey's dark blonde hair. "It's okay, baby girl."

Hailey soon quieted down, but her crying jag had resulted in hiccups.

Shane folded his arms across his chest and scrunched up his nose, sitting on the bench seat between them. "Humph!" He snuck a peek at Mia out of the corner of his eye, and then looked straight ahead.

"Straighten up," Caleb ordered curtly. Then he looked over at Mia. "I'm so sorry about this."

Mia gave the boy an encouraging smile. "It's okay. I'm sure we'll be friends in no time."

"Nope," Shane replied under his breath.

Mia was surprised at how smart he was. She knew it was probably a credit to his mother, who had obviously educated him at home. Mia's heart went out to him. Not only had he lost his mother not long ago, now he was going to be forced to accept another woman in her place. At that moment, Mia vowed to try to make it as comfortable for the children as possible.

Hailey wasn't asleep by the time they reached the church, but she was content in Mia's arms, her head resting on her shoulder.

Caleb pulled the buckboard to a stop in front of the church in Laramie and wrapped the reins around the front bar. "Here we are!" he announced happily, obviously trying to make the best of the situation.

Mia knew that it was probably just as hard on him as it was on her. After all, he recently lost his wife a few months before and was now forced to take another one. She couldn't imagine what he must be going through.

She just hoped that they were doing the right thing.

Mia waited in the buckboard while Caleb walked around and took Hailey out of her hands and helped Mia down. Then he handed back the little girl as Shane hopped down on his own accord, but Caleb quickly took him by the hand.

Mia's heart fluttered as he wrapped his free arm gently around her waist to guide her into the church. Ella and Colton were already waiting for them in front of the church when they arrived. Her friend smiled at her encouragingly as she and Colton followed them in.

A preacher was waiting, Bible in hand. "Welcome!" the preacher greeted them, a bit too chipper as he shook Caleb's hand. "So, you're getting married today?"

Caleb nodded.

"Yes, please," Mia replied aloud, her voice cracking as Hailey took in the surroundings.

The church was big and beautiful, with stained glass windows spaced strategically around.

"Well then! You've come to the right place," the preacher announced. "Right this way."

They all walked down the aisle together until they came to a stop in front of the altar.

"Here," Colton offered, reaching for Hailey. "I'll take her."

Mia smiled appreciatively as she handed her to him. Then Colton took Shane by the hand and stood off to the side. Mia hurried to take off her coat, then laid it in a nearby pew.

"Don't worry," Ella whispered. "You're doing the right thing." She cringed and placed her hand on her stomach, then sat down in the front row.

"Are you okay?" Mia asked, concerned.

Ella rubbed her stomach. "I'm fine." She gave her a smile. "Now, it's your wedding day and your fiancé is waiting."

Mia smoothed her hands over her dress, and then took her place by Caleb's side at the altar. Caleb stood with his hands folded in front of him, not even give her a sideways glance.

"Today, we are gathered before God to witness the joining of Caleb Henley and…." The preacher leaned over to her, his eyebrows raised. "What's your name again?"

She sighed. "Mia Flynn."

"And Mia Flynn," he continued, "in holy matrimony."

As Mia listened to his words, she looked over at Caleb, but he didn't look back, his expression unreadable, keeping his eyes only on the preacher.

"Do you, Caleb Henley, take Mia Flynn as your lawfully wedded wife? To love her, honor, and cherish her, for richer and for poorer, in sickness and in health, until death do you part?"

The "death do you part" struck her hard, thinking of Caleb's late wife. She imagined that it had the same effect on Caleb, as well. At that moment, she vowed to try and make the transition as smooth as possible for them all.

Caleb moved his head up and down, emotionless. "I do."

Turning to Mia, the preacher repeated the same vows.

"I do," Mia replied.

A broad smile spread across the preacher's face. "Then by the power vested in me by God and the state of Wyoming, I now pronounce you man and wife." The preacher then turned to Caleb. "You may now kiss the bride."

For the first time since they had entered the church, he looked in her eyes. He placed his hands on her upper arms. An electric current ran through her body as his lips descended upon hers in a chaste kiss. Mia was surprised by her body's reaction to this man that she didn't know. And when he pulled away, her thoughts were anything but chaste.

The preacher looked around as if it was the happiest day in the world and the most spectacular event he had ever witnessed. "May I present to you for the first time as man and wife, Mr. and Mrs. Caleb Henley!"

Both Ella and Colton started clapping.

Colton shook Caleb's hand. "Congratulations!"

The preacher said something else to Caleb, but Mia didn't hear it all.

Ella came up behind her and placed her hand on her back, claiming her attention. Mia almost cried when Ella pulled her in for a hug. "Don't worry," Ella whispered. "I know this seems rushed, but everything will work out. I know it will."

Mia bit her lower lip, fighting back tears. "Thank you."

Ella smiled encouragingly.

"Well! What do you say we all go to the restaurant to celebrate?" Colton asked, smiling, obviously trying to lighten the mood.

"We would"—Caleb took Hailey from his arms—"but I want to get the children home. I don't want to be driving back in the dark."

Colton nodded and shook his hand. Then he took a step closer. "You take care of my girl now."

Mia was touched that he thought enough of her to tell Caleb that. Back in New York, Colton had always been friendly and casual when he came into the Breckenridge Saloon. He rarely ever asked for a dance, but he had always treated her and the other ladies with respect. Mia suspected that out here in the wild, he and Ella were the closest thing to immediate family that she had. But now, Caleb and his children had just become her family, too. She went from being without any family at all to having a ready-made family all in one day.

Caleb gave him a slight smile. "I will." Taking Shane by the hand, he turned to Ella. "Thanks for everything, Ella. We couldn't have done this without your help."

She smiled. "It was my pleasure, but make sure you take care of my best friend. She's like a sister to me."

"I will. Will you two be all right driving home?"

"We'll be fine," Colton replied. "Would you like us to follow you?"

Caleb shook his head. "No, we'll be all right. Will we see you Sunday?"

"We'll try," Colton replied, "if Ella feels up for it. I don't want to leave her alone."

"No, of course not." Caleb shook his hand, and then

turned to Mia. "Ready?"

She nodded, but Ella pulled her in for another hug and whispered in her ear. "Don't worry. We'll see you soon. Mia, I know you're overwhelmed right now, but everything will work out fine. Just give it time. And if you need me, just let me know." She then bent over and held her stomach as her face scrunched up in pain.

"Ella, what's wrong?" Mia asked, her eyebrows pulling together in concern.

Ella closed her eyes tightly and Mia's heart sank.

"Ella?" Colton placed his hand on his wife's back, suddenly panicked. "Honey, what's wrong?"

She shook her head and forced a smile, straightening up. "I'm fine… really."

"Ella, you shouldn't have come. I thought the doctor had you on bed rest." Mia's eyebrows pulled together in concern. "I had no idea you were feeling so poorly."

Ella fought to catch her breath. "I wanted to come see you. I mean, you just got married."

"Everything's going just fine," Mia replied. "But you shouldn't be concerned with me. You should concentrate on yourself right now." She bit her lower lip, feeling guilty. "When is the baby due?"

Ella gave her a weak smile. "Not for another month."

Guilt filled Mia's heart. "I'm so sorry. I should have come sooner."

"Oh, hush." Ella held on to Colton's arm to steady herself. "You've had your hands full. Don't you spend one moment worrying about me." She bit her lower lip and then dug her nails into Colton's arm.

"I'll go get the buckboard." Colton looked up at Mia and Caleb. "Stay with her. I'll be right back."

"I've got her. You go ahead," Mia reassured him.

Colton rushed off.

Mia held Ella's arm, steadying her. "Ella, we have to get you to a doctor—"

"No, Mia." She grabbed her arm. "I'm fine." Then a pain gripped her stomach and she dug her nails into Mia's arm. "Uuummm!" It was obvious that Ella was trying to hide the pain. "I'm so sorry, Mia. This is your wedding day."

"Ella, don't worry about that. You need a doctor." Mia looked at her friend in concern. Ella forced another smile as she grabbed her stomach and bit her lower lip. A moment later she relaxed.

A crease formed between Mia's eyes. "Let's go back inside the church to sit down for a moment."

The fact that she didn't argue was testimony that it was more serious than Ella was letting on. "It was just a little pain. I've been having them every now and then all day. It's nothing to cause concern."

Colton pulled the buckboard up and after securing it, jumped down. He took one look at Ella and scooped her up into his arms. Then he carried her to the buckboard as Mia and Caleb followed, carrying the children. "Why didn't you tell me you were hurting?"

"I didn't want you to be concerned." Ella wrapped her arm around his neck.

Colton placed her in the back of the buckboard.

Ella looked up into his eyes and gripped Colton's arm as another pain gripped her.

"Caleb," Mia whispered. "Do you know if there's a doctor around here?"

"There's one a few streets from here on the edge of town," Colton blurted out before Caleb could answer, and then looked up at Mia. "I'm taking her there."

"Colton, I'm… fiinnnneee!" Ella yelled as a pain gripped her. "I'm so sorry! I didn't mean—" Her voice cut off as she bent over and gripped her stomach again. "Oooohhhh!" Ella groaned beside her as she grabbed her stomach.

Without saying another word, Colton held his wife as she doubled over in pain.

"Caleb." Mia grabbed his arm to claim his attention. "I have to go with them."

"Go," he ordered. Then he looked over at Colton. "We'll follow you." He hurried with the children to his buckboard.

Mia climbed in to sit behind Ella, letting her lean against her. "I have her, Colton. Let's go!"

Colton jumped into the front of the buckboard, and shook the reins hard. "Yah!" The horses leapt immediately into a full gallop and Caleb followed behind in the buckboard.

Mia rubbed Ella's arm. "Just breathe, Ella. It's going to be fine. Just breathe…."

"Don't worry, honey! We'll be there in just a minute!" Colton yelled from the front as the buckboard rounded a corner. Mia just hoped that the doctor was in.

"Yyyaaahhh!" Ella groaned as she bent over, holding tightly to her stomach as she squeezed her hand.

"Don't worry. We're almost there," Mia encouraged Ella, as the sound of the wagon and the horses' hooves pounded against the muddy road where the snow had melted off.

Colton looked over his shoulder at Ella, then turned his attention back to the road. People yelled, jumping out of the way as Colton pulled the team to a stop in front of a small white house on the edge of town. A wooden sign hung above the door that read RUFUS ALLAWAY, M.D. Colton pulled back on the brake, jumped out, and ran up the stairs. He beat on the door so hard that the frame rattled.

"Confound it!" a voice bellowed from the other side of the door. "I'm coming! Patience is a virtue!" A moment later, the door opened abruptly and a middle-aged, slightly overweight and balding man biting down on a cigar stood on the other side. "Well, what do you want?"

Colton looked him up and down. "Are you the doctor?"

"I am," the man said around his cigar. "What do you want?"

"My wife's pregnant and having pains. She's not due for another month." Colton pointed toward the buckboard where Ella was doubled over. Mia rubbed her back.

The older man rolled his eyes, perfectly calm. "Calm down. It's not the first time a baby's been born on my watch." He threw his cigar off the porch into the snow. "Well, let's not waste time. Bring her in." He was so nonchalant that Mia felt foolish for having gotten so excited. But she was sure that the doctor was used to dealing with the matter of birthing babies. It was probably an everyday occurrence for him.

Colton ran back to the buckboard, scooped Ella into his arms again, and carried her with ease up the stairs.

"Bring her in here." Doc Allaway started barking orders as they followed him into a room with a hospital bed, covered in white sheets. He rolled up his sleeves. "How close are the contractions?"

"Pretty close," Ella answered.

The doctor looked over at Mia. "Ma'am, go get some sheets from that cabinet." He motioned with his head toward a thin wooden cabinet on the wall.

Mia rushed over, doing as he asked.

"Get her a cool rag, too," Colton added when she handed the doctor the sheets. "She's burning up! I don't know why I didn't notice it before."

"Of course." Mia grabbed a washcloth from the same cabinet. A china pitcher and basin were set nearby, so Mia used it to soak down the washcloth, wrung it out, and rushed back over.

Ella fisted Colton's shirt. "Don't worry…." Another pain must have grabbed her, for she bit down on her lower lip, obviously trying to stifle a scream.

Doc Allaway took a stethoscope from a nearby drawer and wrapped it around his neck. He placed the earpieces over his ears and the bell over her stomach. A crease formed between his eyes as he listened.

"There, there," Mia cooed as she dabbed Ella's forehead with the washrag. "It'll be okay."

Without warning, Ella screamed again, raised up on an elbow, and wrapped her other arm around her stomach.

"Something's wrong!"

"Leave us." Doc Allaway looked down at Ella but was talking to everyone else in the room.

"No, I'm not going anywhere." Colton took his wife's hand.

The doctor was suddenly kind as he placed a hand on his shoulder. "Sir, I have to check my patient."

Mia waited at the door for Colton, who was obviously torn between leaving his wife at the hands of a doctor he didn't know and doing as the doctor asked.

"Mister," the doctor pointed out, peering at him over his spectacles. "I need to check your wife… now."

Colton sighed, and let Mia lead him from the room. In the waiting room, Caleb rose to his feet and the children looked up from where they were playing quietly on the floor.

Colton wrung his hands as he paced the floor.

Caleb placed a comforting hand on his shoulder. "Don't worry, Colton. She's going to be fine."

"We shouldn't have made the trip today," Colton babbled as he paced. "She hasn't been doing well. I should have—"

"Hey, hey…." Caleb stood in front of him to get his attention, interrupting his pacing. "You need to put her in God's hands. Have faith. She's going to be okay."

Colton looked as if he was going to say something more, but just sighed instead.

The doctor came out a moment later and closed the door behind him.

Colton hurried across the room and stood before him. "How is she?"

The doctor sighed. "It's a breech birth and the baby needs to be turned."

"Is there anything we can do?" Mia asked.

"Pray." The doctor walked back in and Mia and Colton followed, going to either side of the bed. "Ella," Doc Allaway began in a calm, soothing voice. "The baby's breech and needs to be turned."

Quicker than Mia would have thought possible, Ella grabbed his arm and squeezed, her eyes wide. "Doc," she panted as sweat beaded on her forehead, drenching the tendrils around her face. "If it comes down to saving me or the baby, I want you to save the baby."

"No!" Colton yelled.

Ella ignored him, her eyes searching the doctor's. "Promise me!"

He let out a deep breath.

"No! You save my wife!" Colton yelled as he started toward the doctor.

"Caleb!" Mia yelled, and he immediately appeared in the room. "Take him out of here!"

"Come on, buddy," Caleb coaxed, edging him toward the waiting room. "The doc here is going to take good care of both your wife and the baby, but he can't do his job if you interfere."

"You save my wife!" Tears streamed openly down Colton's face as he pointed at the doctor. Caleb placed a hand on his chest, holding him back.

"Colton! Let's go!" Caleb yelled, getting his attention. When Colton looked at him, Caleb added, "She's in good hands. Now, we need to get out of here, so the doc can do his job."

"Ella, I love you! I'll be right out here."

"Yaaahhhh!" she screamed in answer as another pain gripped her.

"Don't push. Don't push!" Doc Allaway instructed as he rolled up his sleeves. Then he covered her lower body with a sheet.

Mia didn't know what to do so she held Ella's hand. "Breathe, Ella. Don't push. Everything's going to be fine."

"Okay. I'm going to turn the baby now," the doctor instructed as he reached under the sheet.

Ella nearly broke Mia's hand as she screamed.

"Hold on, Ella!" Doc Allaway coaxed. "You're doing good. Don't push!"

Ella dug her nails into Mia's hand from squeezing it so tightly, but Mia said nothing. "That's it, Ella. Just breathe. I'm here for you—"

"Okay," Doc Allaway interrupted as relief washed over him. "The baby's in position now. Go ahead and push."

Ella sat up and pushed down hard as she screamed.

Mia placed a hand on her back to help her, never letting go of her hand.

"That's it, Ella!" Doc Allaway urged, sweat beading on his forehead. "You're doing just fine. Now, push one more time."

Ella screamed again as she bore down. A moment later, the sound of a baby crying filled the room.

"Ella, you're the proud mother of a baby boy." Doc Allaway laid the baby on Ella's stomach, cut the cord, and wrapped him in a small blanket.

But Ella was still screaming. "What's happening? Is something wrong?" Ella gasped, and then yelled out as another pain rocked her body.

"Miss, take the baby," Doc Allaway ordered Mia.

Mia took the baby and used the water from the basin to clean him up and then swaddled him in a blanket.

Doc Allaway smiled. "You're fine, Madame. But your job's not over yet."

"What?" Ella panted.

The doctor smiled. "There's another one."

"Another baby?" Ella sounded panicked.

"Yes, now hold still and don't push yet," Doc Allaway instructed. "I need to check you again to make sure the baby's in position."

Mia looked down at the baby in her arms. He was beautiful, with a shock of dark brown hair like his papa. Mia laid him in a nearby bassinette.

Then Mia quickly crossed the room to Ella and held her hand.

"Okay, Madame," Doc Allaway ordered, concern coloring his voice. "The baby's in position, so push! Push!"

"Yyyaaahhh!" Ella bore down once again.

"Stop! Don't push!"

"Breathe, Ella, breathe," Mia instructed as she squeezed her hand.

"Okay. Now, push!" Doc Allaway's voice was urgent. "One more time. Push now!"

She pushed again, but this time, the sound of a baby's

cry didn't fill the room.

"Is he okay?" Ella asked, her voice weak as she lifted her head.

Doc Allaway didn't answer, but quickly cut the cord and turned the baby over. Mia looked over, and the baby was blue. He held the baby up by its feet and gently swatted its bottom. He rubbed the baby all over and checked its mouth, and then held it on his arm, face down, and gently tapped its back. A moment later, the baby gasped and let out a bloodcurdling cry as a pink color washed over her.

Mia sighed in relief.

"It's a healthy baby girl," Doc Allaway announced, and then handed the baby to Mia. "She has some lungs on her, that's for sure!"

Mia cleaned up the baby girl. She was just as beautiful as her brother but was much more willing to voice her displeasure. As dark as her brother's hair was, hers was the opposite—a bright blonde. "That's it," Mia cooed as she cleaned her up and then swaddled her in another small blanket.

"Are there any more?" Ella asked the doctor.

He laughed. "No, I don't believe so." He smiled as he finished up.

"How are they?" Ella's eyes were filled with concern, her hair drenched in sweat. "Are they okay?"

Doc Allaway smiled. "Yes, they're both fine. Ella, would you like to hold them?"

"Yes, but one at a time for now." Ella held out her arms. "I don't trust myself just yet."

Mia handed her the little girl, and tears streamed down Ella's face. Then she crossed the room to the bassinette to retrieve the baby boy and carried him to his mother. Then she held him up so Ella could see him.

The doctor turned to Mia. "You can call the father in now."

A broad grin spread across her face and she handed the baby boy to the doctor. When Mia opened the door, Colton and Caleb were on their feet.

"You can come in now," Mia said to Colton.

"Is she okay?" Colton asked as he walked in.

Mia stood back, opening the door wide. "Come in and see for yourself."

When he walked in, Ella was holding one baby, and Doc Allaway was holding the other. Tears flowed down Colton's cheeks, making his eyes bright. "My God! Twins?" he asked Ella as he gently touched a baby's cheek.

The doctor smiled as he carefully handed him his son. "Congratulations, Papa. Mother and babies are just fine." As brash as the doctor had seemed when they first arrived, Mia was surprised at his tenderness now.

Ella smiled. "This one's a baby girl and the one you're holding is a boy." She waited for it to sink it.

"Oh, a girl and a boy!" Colton gushed. "What in the world—"

Ella laughed. "Yes! Can you believe it?"

"Your son is the oldest by two minutes," Mia interjected, taking in the sight of the new family, amazed. Ella and Colton had entered the clinic as a couple, and were leaving as a family. God surely did work in mysterious ways.

Tears poured openly down Colton's cheeks as he sobbed, looking down at his newborn son. "They're beautiful."

Ella placed a hand on the side of her husband's cheek. "Ssshhhh… it's okay. I'm okay, and the babies are fine."

Doc Allaway let out a deep breath. "Your wife really needs to rest now." He reached over and gave Ella's hand a gentle squeeze. "Madame, you did well. You really are a brave woman."

"Mrs. Hill. But please call me Ella." Ella smiled as she handed the baby girl to Mia.

Turning to Colton, Doc Allaway offered him his hand. "You have a lot to be proud of, Mr. Hill."

Colton shook his hand. "Thanks, Doc. I owe you everything."

"We'll settle up later." Doc Allaway smiled. "But the only thing I want you to do right now is to take good care of your wife and those two little ones."

Colton laughed as he breathed a sigh of relief. "That goes without saying."

"That's good enough." The doctor started putting things away.

"Oh, Doc?" Colton asked, claiming his attention. "I'm so sorry about yelling at you… and almost going after you."

Doc Allaway laughed, peering at him over his spectacles. "Not to worry. Believe me, I've seen worse."

Everyone in the room laughed.

Doc Allaway gave Ella a fatherly pat on her shoulder. "You can stay here until you're fully recovered."

Ella smiled. "Thank you, doctor."

"Now, get some rest."

Mia followed him into the living room, and he turned to shake her hand. "Congratulations, miss," he praised in a low voice. "You did a great job and stayed calm during the crisis."

Caleb walked up and placed his hand on the small of her back.

Doc Morgan turned to him. "Your wife did a good job in there."

Caleb smiled with pride and reached out his hand to the doctor. "Dr. Allaway, thank you for everything. I'm the preacher in Whiskey River. If you're ever in the neighborhood on Sunday morning—"

Doc Allaway shook his hand. "I'll be sure to look you up."

"Please do." Caleb's lips curled into a smile. "We could use another doctor in Whiskey River. Doc Morgan is overworked at present."

"Then what would the fine folk of Laramie do?" Doc Allaway teased, giving Caleb's shoulder a pat. "Well, if you don't mind, I'm going to check in on Mrs. Hill and then I'm going to get some sleep."

"We'll come by to check on Ella and the babies in the morning." Caleb offered him his hand. "Thanks, Doc, for everything."

"All in a day's work." He shook his hand. "It's a long drive to Whiskey River. You and the family might want to stay the night here in Laramie and then head out in the morning."

Caleb let out a deep breath. "It's early yet. We'll be fine."

Mia's smile faded. Of course, Caleb wouldn't want to stay the night and risk having to share a room with a woman he didn't know, even if she was now his wife. When she had agreed to their arrangement, she knew that love was out of the question. But she hoped that one day he might come to care for her like a husband would a wife. Well... maybe someday.

CHAPTER 4

Caleb watched as Mia looked in on Ella. Colton was sitting in the rocking chair by the hospital bed with his two children as he watched Ella sleep. After she had the babies, the doctor transferred her to a bed.

"Colton," she whispered from the doorway as Caleb looked on. "We're leaving. Is there anything else we can do before we leave?"

Caleb couldn't help but notice how beautiful Mia looked in the soft golden glow of the oil lamp. The way she pitched in and helped out during the crisis stirred something within his heart.

Mia held out her hand as Colton started to get up. "Don't get up."

"We'll be fine." Colton's voice came from inside the room. "Mia, thank you."

A smile lit her lips. "Tell Ella I'll come by to see her soon." She gently closed the door.

Caleb placed a hand on the small of her back as he looked

over her shoulder. "Let's go," he whispered. His children were asleep on the floor, tired from the long wait. By all rights, he should rent a room in Laramie. After everything Ella and Colton had done for them, there was no way they could leave them to make their own way back home alone with two infants. He sighed, knowing he had some savings, and it would be worth the expense.

He looked in at Colton. "Colton, we'll see you tomorrow. We're not leaving you here in Laramie alone."

Colton nodded, tears welling up in his eyes. It was an emotional day for him. "Much obliged."

Caleb nodded and quietly closed the door.

Mia turned to him and smiled, melting his heart. But he quickly pushed the emotion down. He had asked her to be his platonic wife, and he was determined to keep it that way.

His heart fluttered at just the simple act of touching her shoulders as he helped her on with her coat, but he quickly pushed the thought aside and turned to pick up his daughter. "Papa?" she asked sleepily.

"It's me, baby." He kissed the top of her head and handed her to Mia. Then he bent down and picked up his son. "Shane? Are you hungry?"

"Yes, Pa." Shane nuzzled onto his shoulder and then sat bolt upright and wanted down. He looked over at Mia and glared. "Come on, little guy." Caleb reached down and took his hand, and then placed his hand on the small of Mia's back. "Ready?"

"Ready as I'll ever be."

Caleb escorted her out to his buckboard and helped

her in and then slid in beside her on the other side. Shane hopped into the back.

He made a clicking sound with his mouth and the horses immediately started walking. "I'm proud of you, Mia."

A smile lit her lips. "I was so worried about Ella."

"I was, too. So was Colton."

"Thank you for getting him out of the room." A laugh escaped her lips. "He was ready to punch the doctor, and then we would've really been in trouble."

"When I pulled him out, it was all I could do to keep him from going back in," Caleb agreed. "I had to stand in front of the door to block his way."

Mia's eyebrows pulled together in concern. "Really?"

Caleb nodded. "I told him that he could do more good by praying. We spent most of the day in prayer until you came out."

Mia looked away. "When the baby girl was born blue, I thought we'd lost her."

Caleb stopped and looked into her eyes. "The baby was born blue?"

"Yes."

"You were a big help to the doctor tonight."

Mia smiled. "Thank you, but I wish I could have done more."

"You did enough." Pride shone in his voice.

As the horses plodded on through the snow, he knew that he needed to talk to her.

"Mia, I'm sorry for being so abrupt to you earlier today… at the church." He let out a deep breath. "You deserve better than how I treated you when you got off the train."

"It's okay, Caleb. I understand."

He shook his head. "No. You're a good woman, Mia, and you deserve to know what you're getting yourself into."

She looked back at Shane and then into Caleb's eyes. "I appreciate that, but I don't think that now is the time."

He inclined his head, knowing she was right.

"Caleb, I know it hasn't been easy for you and the children," she said, her voice low.

"It's been hard," he admitted as he let out a deep breath.

She let her hand drop. "Take all the time you need."

A few minutes later, he pulled the team to a stop in front of the hotel in Laramie. "Mia, I hope you don't mind us staying in Laramie tonight, but I didn't want to leave Colton and Ella… not after everything they have done for us."

"I completely agree." She gazed up at him and smiled, looking so beautiful that it overwhelmed him, but he quickly pushed the thought aside.

Caleb pulled the brake. "I'll be right back." Shane started to get down. "Come on, buddy."

Shane happily hopped down and took his father's hand. He was always following him, emulating him. It was clear that he idolized his father. Caleb just wanted to live up to it.

Inside, Caleb and Shane walked up to the front desk where a man was standing behind the counter.

"Welcome to the *Laramie Inn*!" the man behind the desk beamed, a bit too chipper. "What can I do for you?"

"I'd like two rooms please." Guilt filled his chest, not wanting to think that it was technically their wedding night.

The man turned around and pulled two skeleton keys from a peg board behind him. "That'll be $1.50."

Caleb pulled his wallet from his back pocket. The price was a bit steep but having the extra room was necessary. He didn't know her, after all, and he had his children to think about. "Here you go."

"Name?" the front desk clerk asked, ready with pen in hand.

"Henley. Reverend Caleb Henley."

The clerk wrote it down and then turned the ledger toward Caleb. "Here. Sign this, please."

Caleb picked up the pen and scribbled his name as his insides fluttered. He felt as nervous as a bride himself, although he had no idea why. She wasn't even going to be sharing a room with him. Guilt reared its ugly head once more as thoughts of Jessica and their wedding night years ago flooded his mind.

The clerk laid two sets of keys on the counter and slid them toward him. "Here you go, Reverend Henley. Upstairs to the left."

Caleb took the keys. "Thanks." Then he took Shane's hand. "Come on." Together, they walked out into the cold air. He felt guilty for leaving Mia and Hailey outside. It was cold when he and Shane went inside, but seemed to have gotten even colder in that short amount of time.

"Papa!" Hailey's face lit up and she reached out her arms for him.

"Come here, baby girl." Caleb reached over and she went immediately to him. Then he extended his hand to Mia to help her down, unable to meet her eyes. "Let's get you inside. I'll come out for your bags in just a bit."

"I'll come down with you to pick out some things from my trunk," Mia stated, "so you won't have to carry it upstairs."

"That won't be necessary. I'll need to bring it inside anyway, so no one helps themselves to your things." He walked with her up the stairs and then stopped before two rooms and opened the first door.

"Yippee!" Shane ran in and jumped on the double bed.

Caleb laughed. He set Hailey on her feet and she ran inside and jumped on the bed along with her brother. "Well, I guess this room is ours."

Mia laughed, but said nothing.

Caleb unlocked the door to the other room for her. "Here you go. I'll be up with your trunk in a bit."

Mia wrung her hands. "Thank you."

"Would you mind watching the kids for a minute while I bring it up?" Caleb asked, his voice cracking a bit. "I'll only be a minute."

"I'd be glad to." She stood in the doorway between the rooms.

"Kids, stay here with Mia and I'll be right back up."

"Aaahhh! But I want to go!" Shane wailed as he plopped down on the bed, landing on his bottom.

"No, I need you to stay here with your sister," Caleb said sternly. "I'll be right back up."

Caleb hurried away but glanced over his shoulder one more time. She had the most beautiful green eyes he'd ever seen. When he rounded the corner, he took off his cowboy hat and ran his fingers through his dark brown hair. "What are you doing, Caleb?" Never in his wildest dreams had he ever imagined that he would marry a woman other than Jessica, let alone a woman he didn't know. But he had to do what he had to in order to survive. Although he kept reminding himself, it didn't make it any easier.

Outside, white puffs of snow flurried around and then fell to the ground. Caleb was suddenly thankful that he had decided to stay the night in Laramie. Although it was a bit rowdy, especially at night, he would never have forgiven himself if anything happened to the children or to Mia on their way back home. He lifted the trunk out of the back of the buckboard and then carried it back inside the hotel and up the stairs. Mia was sitting at the small table just inside the door of his room, watching the children. She smiled as he walked past and she followed. She watched as he set her trunk on the floor just inside her room.

"I'll be right back." He hurried down the stairs. Outside, white cottony bits swirled around. He just hoped they didn't get stranded here in Laramie. Although Caleb had some cash with him, he couldn't afford hotel rooms for a week, either. "Just get through tonight and let tomorrow take care of itself," he said aloud as he climbed up into the buckboard, released the brake, and headed toward the livery stables.

After leaving the horses and his rig at the livery stable, he pulled the collar of his coat up over his neck and headed back toward the hotel. He darted inside amidst a flurry of snow.

"After the blizzard we had at Christmas, I thought we were nearly through with this." The front desk clerk smiled, leaning against the counter.

"So did I." Caleb headed up the stairs. The door to his room was still open and the children were playing happily on the bed. When Caleb stepped in, Mia rose to her feet.

"Well, if you don't need me anymore, I think I'll go freshen up a bit."

Caleb knew he should say something, but was unable to bring himself to say anything.

She smiled and then walked out, closing the door behind her.

Although he had no intention of anything else, there was no reason why they couldn't spend an enjoyable evening together. He looked over at the children and said, "Stay here. I'll be right back." As he headed over to Mia's room, he knew that she would never be his real wife, but hoped they could find some middle ground.

CHAPTER 5

After Mia closed the door to her room, she let out a deep breath. Exhausted, she walked over to the bed and plopped down, then leaned back and closed her eyes. Silent tears streamed down her cheeks. Although she knew they had agreed to a platonic relationship, she hadn't expected to feel the rejection that was weighing so heavily on her. She was used to turning men down, not the other way around, and definitely not by her husband. No, she had to steel her heart against him or she would never survive. She would open it up to the children, but not to him. He had set the rules and now she had no choice but to live by them, no matter what she dreamed.

But she couldn't help but dream of being the perfect family one day, with the children and Caleb…. But after today, she knew that dream may never be.

Knowing she was being ridiculous, Mia sat up, wiped the tears from her cheeks, and crossed the room to her trunk in search of a handkerchief. Then again, maybe she'd feel better if she washed her face.

Suddenly, there was a knock on the door, causing her to jump. When she opened it, Caleb was standing on the other side.

"Sorry for the interruption." He looked over at her open trunk, but made no effort to walk in. "Look. Why don't you leave that? I have other plans. After all, it *is* our wedding night."

Mia's eyes flew open wide. Of all the things she had expected to come from his mouth, that wasn't one of them.

He must have seen her surprise because one corner of Caleb's mouth curled into a smile, revealing a dimple on his cheek. "No. That's not what I meant. I just wanted to take you and the children to dinner in the restaurant downstairs." He leaned against the doorway, never taking his big blue eyes from hers.

Mia lowered her hands, feeling like an idiot. Of course, he wouldn't want to touch her or even come near her, even if it was their wedding night. "I'm sorry. I thought…."

Caleb raised an eyebrow, looking very attractive.

"Never mind." She wiped her hands on her dress. "Give me a minute to freshen up and I'll be right over."

He nodded once and then walked out, closing the door behind him.

She walked toward the bed, trying to keep what little she had left of her dignity. Mia sat down as tears brimmed her eyes. But she didn't have time for a good cry. She would save that for later.

Instead, she squared her shoulders and resigned herself

to make the best of the situation. Her mother would have told her as much, if she were still alive. She stood and smoothed her hands over her dress as she crossed the room to a beige china basin and pitcher with pretty pink and blue flowers along the edge, poured some water in the basin, and splashed some on her face, careful not to muss her dress. Then she smoothed the loose blonde tendrils back, slipped on a pair of beige gloves to match her dress and adjusted her hat and pinned it back into place. She pinched her cheeks and then walked out and closed the door behind her.

When he opened the door to his room, Caleb's eyes flickered with interest for a split second as he took her in, but it was so quick it caused her to wonder if she was just wishful thinking. He and the children were standing in the center of the room, their hair combed, Hailey's dress straightened. "Ready?" he asked as he lifted his eyebrows.

"Yes. Are you?"

Shane narrowed his eyes at her and then ran out the door.

"Are you sure this is a good idea?" Deep down, Mia was asking about much more than just going downstairs to dinner. "We can bring something up instead, if you like."

Caleb inclined his head in the direction Shane went. "Just give him time. He'll come around." It was almost as if he was saying it about himself too. "Let's go."

As she walked into the hallway, Hailey left her father's side and slipped her hand into Mia's, taking her by surprise. "Ready to go, baby girl?"

A broad grin spread across Hailey's face and she bobbed her head excitedly.

When they stopped at the top of the stairs, Shane was waiting at the foot with his arms folded across his chest. He looked away when he saw them.

Mia pretended not to notice.

Caleb extended his arm to her, the perfect gentleman. After she slid her arm in his, he picked up Hailey and led Mia down the stairs. They met Shane at the bottom.

"Humph," Shane grunted as he turned away, his arms still folded.

Caleb frowned as he looked down at his son. "Straighten up."

"Welcome!" A waitress approached, her face bright, a bit too chipper. "My, don't you look fine this evening. Four for dinner?"

Caleb smiled. "Yes, please."

The waitress picked up two menus. "Right this way." She guided them to a round table and set the menus down. Caleb held the chair for her to sit down. Once the children were seated, he sat across from her. "What can I bring you to drink?"

"Lemonade all around," Caleb answered without even asking her, obviously used to taking charge.

"Okay. I'll have that out to you in a minute. By the way, my name's Dolly, if you need anything."

"Thanks, Dolly." Mia opened her menu, then Hailey climbed onto Mia's lap and smoothed her little hand over her gloves.

"You like these?" Mia asked.

Hailey bobbed her head up and down. Mia observed

that she didn't say much. Losing her mother had obviously taken its toll on the girl.

"Well then, I'll have to make you a pair."

A crease formed between Hailey's eyes. "How do you do dat?"

"Make these?"

Hailey tilted her head to the side.

"I sew. In New York, I used to sew for a lot of people."

"And you danced, too," Shane added flatly.

"Shane!" Caleb scolded. "You apologize to Miss Mia right now."

Mia wondered how he knew, but she guessed that he must have overheard his father talking. Her heart sank as she wondered who else he had told. She wasn't ashamed of having been a dancehall girl, but she didn't want to be reminded of it constantly, either.

"No, I won't," Shane yelled, "because it's true!"

Caleb was about to say something else, but Mia intervened. "Yes, I was also a dancer in New York, but my favorite thing to do was to sew. In fact, I'm going to make you both some new clothes when I have the chance."

"My clothes are just fine," Shane blurted out.

"Papa, too?" Hailey asked, her eyes hopeful.

Mia smiled. Caleb looked at her out of the corner of his eye. "Yes, of course. And I'll teach you, too, when you're old enough. Would you like that?"

Hailey bobbed her head excitedly.

"She doesn't need to know how to sew," Shane retorted.

"Shane," Caleb warned.

Mia pretended not to notice. "Everyone should know how to sew. I can show you how to sew, too, if you like. Or I can show you how to make candles."

Shane's eyebrows rose. "You know how to make candles?"

"I sure do."

"It's good that you came when you did," Caleb said without looking at her. "In December, the blizzard locked down the town completely. The pass was closed and there was no way in or out."

Shane chuckled under his breath. Mia was sure that images of her freezing to death in the blizzard were going through his mind.

"I just hope we don't get snowed in now." Mia started to peruse her menu and then smiled. "But we can make the best of it if we are."

Caleb sighed. "Yes, but I don't think that it'll be necessary. This is the first snow we've had since the blizzard. It'll probably stop snowing by morning."

"Good because I don't want to be stuck here with her."

"Shane!"

"She's not my mother!" Shane got up and ran to the front of the restaurant and placed his hands on his hips.

"Shane," Mia said as she rose from her seat, hoping not to make a scene. "Please come here."

Shane planted his feet firmly on the floor. "You're not my mother, and you can't tell me what to do!"

Mia's mouth fell open in horror as they caught the attention of everyone in the restaurant.

"Shane! Get over here and apologize to Mia right now!" Caleb bellowed, rising from his seat.

A tall man with broad shoulders, wearing a cowboy hat and standing at the front smiled. "Looks like you have your hands full tonight, mister."

Finding inspiration from Shane, Hailey slipped off Mia's lap and started running around, Caleb caught her and handed her to Mia. Then Caleb marched across the room through the tables as Shane's eyes grew wide. Shane took off up the stairs toward the hotel rooms with his father hot on his heels, much to Mia's horror.

Mia forced a smile at the other patrons as Hailey started to whimper. "It's okay, Hailey." She rubbed Hailey's back in a soothing motion, trying to calm her.

Dolly approached the table and set down four glasses of lemonade. "I'm so sorry it took a minute." Mia was relieved that the waitress had avoided mentioning Shane's behavior.

"No need to worry," Mia replied as she set Hailey in a chair. But Hailey started crying and reached out for Mia, kicking her feet. Mia picked her back up and placed her on her lap.

"You must be new to town," the waitress observed in a friendly tone.

"Yes, we are. My husband lives in Whiskey River." Mia cringed at the slip.

Dolly's eyebrows pulled together as the corners of her mouth turned down. "Don't you live there, too?"

"We just got married today," Mia replied, quickly losing her patience. "What do you have for dinner? We haven't eaten all day and the children are hungry."

Dolly's eyes flew open wide. "Oh! Yes, ma'am. Ralph's fried chicken is the best."

"I'll take some, and bring her a chicken leg, too." Mia looked down at Hailey and then added, "Make it two."

"What vegetables would you like?"

"Mashed potatoes for Hailey, and I'll take whatever you have."

Hailey was crying openly now, so Mia started rocking her back and forth.

"Mashed potatoes, corn, and green beans okay?" Dolly asked.

Mia knew that Dolly meant well, but couldn't she see that she had her hands full?

"Yes. That's fine."

"Don't you ever run away from me like that again!" Caleb's voice rang throughout the restaurant as he marched down the stairs with a crying Shane tucked under his arm. "And you owe Mia an apology!"

"Never!" Shane wailed. "She ain't my mama!"

"And don't you use the word 'ain't'! Your mother taught you better than that!" Caleb looked around the restaurant, then marched toward Mia with all eyes on him. He appeared not to notice.

To her relief, the restaurant wasn't crowded. But Mia was sure that they would be the talk of the town by morning. Thank goodness they didn't live here.

"I'm so sorry about this." Caleb planted Shane hard onto a chair and then pointed his finger at him. "Sit there and don't you move!"

"Um...." It was obvious that Dolly didn't quite know what to say. "What would you like, sir?"

Besides a corral? Mia thought as she continued to rock Hailey, who was falling asleep on her shoulder.

"What's she having?" Caleb asked as he inclined his head toward Mia.

"*She's* having the fried chicken," Mia replied. The least he could do was talk directly to her.

Caleb appeared not to notice as Dolly waited, stunned. "I'll have the same, and so will he."

"No, I won't!" Shane folded his arms across his chest. "I'm never going to eat again!"

"That could be arranged," Caleb agreed.

Shane's eyes flew open wide.

"I think that'll be all," Mia stage-whispered to Dolly.

Caleb slid the lemonade aside. "On second thought, could you bring me some coffee?"

At that moment, Mia realized that she didn't know the first thing about Caleb. She realized that in the few days while she was preparing to move, she had created an image of him within her mind. The perfect man with the perfect children in the perfect town. But she had no idea who the real-live man was sitting across from her now. The man she had imagined had clearly been a fantasy she had built up within her mind.

"Yes, I'd be glad to." Dolly's eyes shifted between them. "I'll be right back." Then she left the table as quickly as she could, obviously questioning their sanity.

Mia couldn't blame her for wanting to get away. If Mia could have left, she would have, too.

"Your hair is too light!" Shane yelled at Mia out of the blue. "My mama never looked like you!"

Tears welled up within Mia's eyes, as her stomach began to tighten. "I'm not your mother, Shane, and I don't intend to take her place."

"That's it, young man!" Caleb yelled. "You're going straight to bed when we get upstairs." He turned to Mia. "I am so sorry."

Mia forced a smile, trying to will the tears in her eyes from spilling over as a lump formed in her throat. The last thing Caleb needed was a blubbering wife. "It's okay."

"No, it's not okay." Caleb narrowed his eyes at his son. "We're going to have a serious talk, young man."

"Here you go!" Dolly interrupted, setting the plates on the table filled with fried chicken, corn on the cob, green beans, and mashed potatoes topped with brown gravy.

It smelled delicious to Mia, but her stomach was so tight she wondered if she could eat. "Thank you. It looks delicious."

Dolly smiled. "I'll let Ralph know. Is there anything else I can get you?"

"No, we're fine," Caleb replied without looking at Mia.

Mia shook her head. The least he could have done was to ask her if she wanted anything, instead of answering for her.

"Well, if you change your mind, let me know," Dolly announced a bit too cheerfully, as she hurried away.

Shane started to push his plate away, but Caleb pushed

it back and then said in a low voice, "You *are* going to eat. I'm paying good money for this meal, and you are not going to let it go to waste."

"I didn't ask for it." Shane folded his arms across his chest.

"But you will eat it," Caleb corrected sternly.

Shane started to push the plate away again but stopped when Caleb glared at him.

Hailey was asleep on her shoulder, obviously having had a big day. Mia laid her across her lap and continued to rock her. She picked up a chicken leg and took a bite, but crumbs fell onto Hailey, so she set it back on the plate.

"Here." Caleb reached for his daughter. "Let me take her so you can eat."

Mia just shook her head. "No, you go ahead. I'll eat in a bit."

Caleb shrugged, and then dug into his meal.

Shane picked at his dinner, but then hunger must have taken over and he started eating with gusto.

They ate in silence, and everyone in the restaurant turned their attention back to their own conversations.

Mia took a sip of her lemonade. "So, how long have you lived in Whiskey River?"

Caleb set down his chicken thigh as he let out a deep breath. "When I found out they needed a preacher, Jessica and I talked about it and decided to move. Shane was just a baby."

"So, for about three years?"

He swallowed the bite of chicken in his mouth. "Have you

always lived in New York?"

Mia shook her head. "No, I'm originally from Connecticut. I moved to New York after my parents died."

Caleb's demeanor suddenly changed, obviously going into his preacher persona, appearing to put his own needs aside to focus on her. "Oh. I'm so sorry to hear that."

Mia smiled. "And what about your parents?"

Caleb let out a deep breath. "My mother died when I was young, and my father still lives in San Francisco."

Mia's eyes open wide. "You're from California?"

Caleb nodded. "In fact, my father still preaches there." He let out a deep breath. "When I took the job in Whiskey River, I tried to get him to come with us, but he refused, wanting to stay there and attend his congregation, saving people from the sin of greed. You know, from the Gold Rush, even though it was years ago." He took a sip of his coffee, swallowed, and then set it down. "But in his defense, people still go out there looking for gold. Greed can be very controlling."

"I'm so sorry to hear that."

Caleb shrugged. "I'm not. I have no regrets." He got up, walked around the table, and looked down at Hailey. "Here. Let me take her while you eat."

"Are you finished?" Mia asked, concerned.

He smiled. "I've had more than you. Besides, I can eat and rock at the same time."

Mia guessed that she had a lot to learn about parenting, if only for her own survival. "Thank you."

"Come here, little girl," he cooed as he scooped his

sleeping daughter into his arms. "I'll be right back."

"I'll be right here," Mia replied, relief washing over her. Her arms felt as if they were about to fall off. She was exhausted, but she wasn't about to let on to Caleb.

Caleb walked with his daughter to the front of the restaurant by the windows to talk to the man behind the counter.

Mia let out a deep breath as she looked down at her untouched food.

"I'll take it if you don't want it," Shane blurted out.

"No, you have plenty. Now, eat," Mia said, having had enough of his antics.

A broad grin spread across his face. "So, what are you going to do? Tell my father?" Although he was only four years old, he seemed to understand what was happening, and his vocabulary was extraordinary.

Mia forced a smile. "No, I'll take away your privileges."

The boy's eyebrows pulled together. "What do you mean?"

Mia's lips curled into a smile. "It means that you won't be allowed to play with your toys, and you will only be allowed to go outside to do your chores."

Shane stood so quickly that his chair fell backward, crashing to the floor. "You can't do that to me!"

"Oh, yes, I can, and I will," Mia replied softly. "Now, pick up your chair and eat. You won't get anything else tonight."

"Pa!" Shane whined as he marched across the restaurant to his father.

Leaving the chair on the floor, Mia unfolded her napkin and laid it across her lap. The lump in her throat was so large that it nearly prevented her from swallowing… nearly. Determined not to let a child get the best of her, she forced herself to eat, even though it felt like it was going to come back up with every bite.

A moment later, Caleb marched over to the table, picked up the chair, and pointed to it as he looked at his son. "Sit down and eat! And I don't want to hear any more about it!"

Tears rimmed Shane's eyes as he sat down at the table and started eating without another word.

Mia smiled as she ate. When she forced down the last bite of food, she dabbed daintily at the corners of her mouth with her napkin, laid it on the table, and then looked over at Shane. "Are you ready?"

Shane was picking at his potatoes, but had made a sizeable dent in his plate, despite his protests and antics. He looked up and smirked at Mia. "Almost."

Mia let out a deep breath. "Well, hurry up. We have to go upstairs and put you to bed."

Shane dropped his fork onto his plate, clinking loudly against the china. "I don't have to do what you say!"

"We'll see about that." Mia knew she was going to war… against a four-year-old boy.

"I think it's time to go," Caleb announced, but didn't say a word to his son. "I've already paid the bill."

She stood and reached for Hailey. "You want me to take her?"

"No, I have her." Caleb's eyes were cold. Then he looked

73

at his son. "Let's go."

"But I'm not ready—" Shane protested.

"Oh yes, you are," Caleb cut him off, and then walked upstairs, expecting them to follow.

Mia looked at Shane, and he stared back. "Shane, I know I'm not your mother, but—"

He stood, and his fists were balled up at his sides as tears spilled onto his cheeks. "Don't you dare talk about my mother!" Then he stormed up the stairs after his father.

Mia looked around, and all eyes were on her as she rose from her seat. She slowly let out her breath to keep from crying, pushed in her chair, and walked up the stairs with what little dignity she had left.

Upstairs, Caleb and the children were already in their room.

Mia could feel every muscle in her body, and her arms were about to fall off from the weight of having carried Hailey all day and not being used to it. As she opened the door to her hotel room, she tried to remind herself of the reasons she agreed to this arrangement.

Mia had just collapsed onto the bed when there was suddenly a knock on her door. She let out a deep breath and sat up. "Coming." When she opened the door, Caleb was standing on the other side. "Mia, I'd like to speak with you… alone."

She stepped back, and he walked in and closed the door. Anger welled up within Mia's chest as she waited for what was to come.

"First of all, please do not threaten my children." He ticked off the first of what she was sure was going to be a long list.

"Threaten?" Mia asked, unable to believe what she was hearing.

"Second, they are my children. Not yours."

"Now, wait a minute...."

Caleb held up a finger. When he spoke, he lowered his voice. "If my son needs discipline, then you will let me know and I will take care of it."

Mia folded her arms across her chest. "Is that all?"

He shrugged. "For now."

"Okay, now you will listen to me," Mia announced in disbelief, never raising her voice. "First of all, if I go to you for every little thing, then Shane will have no respect for me. Secondly, we are legally married now, so that makes them my children, too."

Caleb started to object, but she held up her finger, just as he had done to her.

"Thirdly, do not *ever* speak to me this way again. And fourth, if *our* son speaks to me again like he did downstairs, I will take away his privileges, which is what I told him. In case you don't know, that means that I will take away his toys, not allow him to play, and he will be allowed to go outside only to do his chores. I would never lay a hand on the child, but I will not tolerate him speaking to me like he did in the restaurant, either." She took a deep, calming breath and lowered her voice. "Caleb, I realize that you and the children are hurting, and I'm not trying to take Jessica's place, but I cannot live in her shadow. I am Mia, not Jessica. And no matter how hard I try, I never will be." She opened the door and waited. "Now, I would appreciate it if we can continue this conversation tomorrow. I'm tired from traveling."

After he walked out, she slammed the door closed behind him. She knew there were other guests in the hotel, but at that moment, she really didn't care. As she sat on the edge of the bed, alone where no one could see, tears flowed down her cheeks. After a few moments, she rose from the bed and took off her dress and hung it up. She rummaged through her trunk and found a sleeping gown and changed into it, then fell onto the bed, exhausted both physically and mentally. But try as she might, she was unable to sleep. Finally, she resolved herself to the fact that she was going to see this through, even if it killed her.

CHAPTER 6

As the night wore on, Caleb tried to sleep, but he couldn't put the events of the day out of his mind. Giving up, he sat up and scrubbed his hands across his face. Memories rushed into his mind of seeing Mia for the first time, how nervous he'd felt as he waited for her to arrive, and how his heart leapt within his chest when she stepped off the train, looking beautiful in her long coat and beige hat tipped forward on her head. Her hair was pulled up, but little tendrils had fallen down around her neck. She reminded him of spring, even though it was still winter. Seeing her for the first time, it was as if she had brought a much-needed breath of fresh air into his life.

He forced the memory of her creamy complexion and gorgeous green doe eyes from his mind, as well as how they looked at him with interest. He didn't want her to be interested, and he didn't want to be interested in her, either. The only thing he wanted was a platonic relationship.

But what he wanted seemed to be of no consequence

to his body and how it reacted to her, sending electricity through him when he touched her, his heart pounding against his ribcage when she came near.

Guilt reared its ugly head at the thought of having betrayed his wife, his lovely Jessica, by even entertaining the thought of marrying another woman, let alone going through with it. Deep down in his heart, he knew that Jessica would have wanted their children to have a mother, and for him to have someone to care for, and someone to care for him.

But knowing those things sure didn't make it any easier.

Alone, he knelt by his bed and prayed that Jessica could forgive him for making this choice, even though he felt it was the only choice he could make.

But now that the choice was made, he was determined to make the best of it.

He leaned back onto the bed and looked over. His children were sleeping peacefully, huddled together like puppies, the room illuminated only by the moonlight streaming in through the window.

Caleb rose from the bed and looked outside at the snow, blue in the moonlight. Bits of fluffy puffs were still falling to the ground, but not as heavily as it had been earlier. He pulled on his trousers and his shirt and slipped on his boots. Maybe the cold would help clear his mind. After slipping into his coat, he looked over at his sleeping children once more.

They would be fine. He wasn't going far.

"Good evening, sir," the front desk clerk greeted him as

he descended the stairs.

Caleb paid no attention as he stormed past and pushed open the front door. The blinding cold hit him harder than he had thought it would, but he welcomed it. He deserved to be slapped in the face for what he had done. Caleb shoved his hands in his pockets and walked purposefully to nowhere. He'd had no choice, since he needed someone to care for his children and the house while he supported his family.

He thought he could do it, have a platonic relationship with a woman… but then Mia stepped off the train. The moment he caught sight of her, he was done. And he hadn't expected it. Soon, he walked past a cemetery; another reminder of what he had done.

Unable to take any more, he pushed through the wrought iron gate. Even the bare trees hanging over the graves seemed to be mocking him, shaming him for his actions. Finally, he fell onto the snow-covered ground under one of the trees.

Unable to take any more, he punched the ground, no longer feeling the cold. "God, why? Why, Jessica?" he screamed at the top of his lungs as tears rolled down his cheeks. "Why did it have to be you, Jessica? God, why couldn't you have taken me instead? Damn it! You could have taken me and not her! Jessica!" he screamed as tears coursed down his cheeks, finally letting it out. He had done a good job of holding it together since he had lost her, but not now. Not ever again.

"Jessica! I need you!" he screamed as he beat his bloody fist on the ground. "Jessica, I love you. Come back to me.

Don't leave me alone. Come back!" he yelled as tears rolled down his cheeks. "Come back…."

He sobbed into his arms. He cried for Jessica… and now for Mia, who was an innocent bystander to the catastrophe that had become his life. Although she was now legally his, he couldn't bring himself to think of her as his wife… physically and emotionally… and he didn't know if he ever would. But then again, he knew he couldn't go on like this. Now that he was married, he had to find a way to let Jessica go. But how? How could he let go of his life? The woman who had made everything so perfect; who had made their house a home. And now he was going to bring another woman into it. How could he have done something so foolish? Maybe he should annul his marriage. He could give Mia enough money to stay in Laramie or perhaps travel back to New York.

But as he sat alone in the cemetery, he knew he'd never find anyone else like her. Never. But how could it ever work if he couldn't give her his heart?

Exhausted, he made his way back to the hotel.

"Sir! Your hand. Are you hurt?" the front desk clerk asked as he stormed past.

But Caleb said nothing in response as he made his way up the stairs, taking two at a time. He reached out for the doorknob of his room, and then paused, looking over at Mia's room. Then he let out a deep breath and walked inside his room.

Thank goodness, the children were still asleep just where he had left them, huddled together.

He stood watching them sleep for a long while, and then pulled the blanket up over them and tucked them in. It was cold and getting colder by the second. It was then that he noticed the dried blood covering his knuckles.

Careful not to wake the children, he crossed the room to the china basin filled with water in the corner of the room and washed his hand. The water stung as it ran over his hand. It was the first time that he felt pain. But now that he recalled, he hadn't felt any pain in a while, just the dull throbbing ache that had filled his chest since he lost his Jessica.

Caleb dried his hand, which was no longer bleeding, and hung up the towel. He decided to try to salvage what was left of the night and get some sleep and laid down beside the children, exhausted, wondering if his life would ever be right again.

Caleb was walking down the streets of Laramie when a mist appeared on the ground around him. He looked over and Jessica was standing by the same tree in the cemetery where he had just been. She walked over and sat down on a nearby bench. "Come, Caleb. Sit with me."

"Jessica, I'm so sorry...."

She looked up at him and smiled. "Please, sit with me." He did as she asked. "Jessica—"

"Shhh...," she whispered, but didn't touch him. "Don't worry. You did what you had to do."

Tears stung his eyes. "Jessica, I'm sorry...."

"Don't be." She smiled. "All I want is for you and the

children to be happy."

"Jessica, I wish it would have been me and not you."

"Don't ever say that," she scolded and then looked into his eyes. "Caleb, I'm happy... and I want you to be happy, too."

Caleb sighed. "Jessica, I miss you."

Her eyebrows pulled together in concern. "Why? I'm always with you."

Then she rose from the bench and started walking into the mist.

"Jessica, don't leave...."

She turned and smiled. "I never left."

"Pa?" Shane asked, shaking his father's shoulder. "Are you awake?"

Caleb opened his eyes and the blinding sunlight stung. Even though he hadn't gotten much sleep, he felt rested, more rested than he had in a while, knowing that Jessica was at peace.

CHAPTER 7

When Mia woke the next morning, the events of the previous day came rushing to her and she realized she'd spent her wedding night alone. "This isn't a marriage. It's a circus," she mumbled to herself. Even though she knew their relationship would just be platonic, the dream of the loving husband was nearly forgotten. She sighed as she dressed for the day, thankful for the few moments she had alone.

When she was ready, she checked her trunk to make sure her belongings were packed and threw her coat over her arm. Outside their door, she heard Shane and Caleb. She was tempted to just go downstairs and order some coffee and wait for them to come down, but she knew Caleb would need help with the children. So, she steeled herself and knocked on the door. Caleb opened it a crack.

"Good morning. Would you like some help with the children or would you like me to go down to the restaurant and wait?"

Caleb opened the door wider as he buttoned his white shirt, but not before she caught a glimpse of his tight muscled chest. "Come on in." Caleb stepped back. "The children are nearly ready. Would you mind taking them downstairs? I'll be right there. And could you order me some coffee?"

Mia smiled, glad to see that a good night's sleep had improved his temper. "I'd be glad to." But when she looked over at Hailey, her hair was a mess and sticking out in every direction. "I'll be right back with a hairbrush."

Mia went next door and got her hairbrush, two rubber bands, and some ribbon. She was going to just walk right in, but thought better of it, opting to knock lightly instead.

"Come on in, Mia."

When she walked inside, Caleb was sitting on the edge of the bed, slipping on his boots. Mia's heart fluttered, noticing how the white shirt flattered his naturally tanned skin, but she pushed the thought aside and walked over to the vanity. "Hailey, would you like me to do your hair?"

"She doesn't need you," Shane muttered under his breath.

"Shane…," Caleb warned. "Let's not get started again."

Mia ignored the jab. "Shane, after I'm finished with Hailey, I'll brush your hair, too."

"No, thank you."

"I don't think so," Caleb intervened. "Your hair's a mess and I don't have a hairbrush since we weren't planning on staying here in Laramie. So, let her do your hair when she's ready."

Shane huffed and folded his arms across his chest,

glaring at Mia.

Mia sighed, making a mental note to try to find a way to reach him. But for now, she turned her attention to Hailey. "Come on, little girl." She picked her up and set her on the dainty bench seat at the white, wooden vanity. She brushed her beautiful curls, careful not to hurt her, and then braided it and tied the pigtails off with rubber bands, adding shiny blue ribbons around the ends. When she was finished, Mia placed her hands on Hailey's shoulders and looked in the mirror at her. "Well, what do you think?"

A broad grin spread across the little girl's face. "Purty!"

Without thought, Mia bent down and gave her shoulders a squeeze, placing her cheek against the little girl's as they both looked in the mirror. "Beautiful."

Hailey jumped down off the bench and scampered off to her father. "Look!" She turned her head from side to side.

Caleb scooped her up into his arms and kissed her cheek. "You look just like a princess."

Mia patted the stool, looking at Shane. "Okay! Your turn."

"No, you're not touching me!" he shouted, folding his arms across his chest.

Mia was sure the neighbors heard.

"What was that, young man?" A crease formed between Caleb's eyes.

"Humph!" He hopped down, his footsteps heavy against the wooden floor. Then he plopped down hard onto the seat and folded his arms across his chest again and glared at her in the mirror, as if daring her to make him look presentable.

"Let's see here." Mia appraised him, trying to lighten the mood as she ran the brush through his light blond hair. A moment later, every hair was in place. "Now, isn't that better?"

He glared at her and then jumped down off the bench.

A crease formed between Caleb's eyes as his nostrils flared, obviously taking in his son's behavior. Then he turned his attention back to Mia. "Why don't you take the children downstairs to the restaurant while I carry your trunk down?"

"Sounds good," Mia replied and then took Hailey's hand. "Ready?"

She bobbed her head vigorously, her eyes wide.

"Shane?"

He let out a deep breath and then stormed out of the room.

Caleb shook his head. "I'm so sorry. It's just been so hard—"

Mia cut him off, "He'll come around." Looking into his eyes, she vowed to try and make life easier for them.

Caleb gave her a smile. "Well, I hope he comes around a bit sooner rather than later."

Mia chuckled. "He will." When she walked out the door holding Hailey's hand, Shane was sitting in the hallway on the floor.

"Ready?" Mia asked.

Shane rose from the floor without a word and headed down the hallway.

"Stay with me, Shane." Mia led Hailey down the hallway,

holding her hand. "Shane, come back here right now!" She didn't want to take a chance of being kicked out of the hotel. But then again, would it have made a difference? After their performance in the restaurant the night before, she was sure the management would be more than happy to see them leave.

After a moment, Mia gave up. She scooped Hailey up into her arms and ran as quickly as the long skirt of her dress would allow to check up on the boy. At the top of the stairs, she stopped short. Shane was standing at the bottom and smirked at her.

"Oh, no you don't, buster," Mia called down to the bottom of the stairs, attracting the attention of everyone in the room. The desk clerk's shoulders slumped, but he looked up at her and plastered on a smile. "Stop right there and don't you move!" Mia lifted her skirts and marched down the stairs headed toward him with Hailey on her hip.

A sly smile lit Shane's lips, but when he turned, he ran into someone. When he looked up, he'd ran smack dab into Colton Hill.

"And where do you think you're going, little mister?" Colton looked down at him with a grin.

"I… I was just…."

Colton laughed. "There's nothing to worry about." Colton swung him up and onto his right shoulder as Shane laughed.

"Thank you so much for catching him for me." Mia was a bit breathless from having to practically run down the stairs, afraid that Shane might run out the door.

Colton looked up at him. "You were running away from Mia?"

Shane hung his head.

"Don't do that. Mia is a good person who cares about you very much." He set him down on his feet and then knelt down to his level. "Can I tell you something, man-to-man?"

Mia bit her lower lip to suppress a smile. Shane nodded vigorously.

Colton stooped down and propped his elbows on his knees. "Gentlemen always treat ladies with kindness and respect. Gentlemen protect ladies and keep them safe, too. So, now that Mia has joined your family and since you are a man in the house, it's your job to protect her and your sister, and to always treat them properly. That means you say 'yes, ma'am' and 'no, ma'am,' too. Okay?"

Shane let out a deep breath and smiled. He obviously liked having been referred to as a man.

"Can you do that?" Colton's eyebrows rose, awaiting an answer.

"Yes, sir," Shane replied, hanging his head a bit.

But Colton placed a finger under his chin and lifted it up so that he was looking into his eyes. "Also, a man is strong. And if he always tries to do what's right, he has nothing to be ashamed of. Okay?"

Shane bobbed his head up and down.

"Thanks again, Colton." Mia tried to adjust Hailey on her hip, but the little girl was reaching for Colton.

He took her and nuzzled her neck. "It's my pleasure."

"So, how's Ella doing?"

A broad grin spread across his face. "She's just fine. Just hungry. That's why I'm here."

"And the babies?" Mia asked.

Colton grinned. "The same. Poor Ella's exhausted and the babies are hungry every few hours."

Mia chuckled. "I don't think either of you will be getting a lot of rest any time soon."

"I'm counting on it." Then he handed Hailey back to her. "Well, if you'll excuse me. I have to take Ella some breakfast before she threatens to eat the bed and everything in the hospital."

"Would you like to join us for breakfast? Then we can walk back together. We were going to come right over to check on Ella and the babies right after we ate."

Colton shook his head. "No, thank you. But maybe I'll join you for a cup of coffee while I wait."

"Of course." Mia grinned just as Caleb walked down the stairs carrying her trunk.

"Here. Let me help you with that." Colton rushed over and took one side.

"It's good to see you here this morning." Caleb adjusted his grip. Mia felt a bit ashamed for having brought so much with her. But she had been a dancehall girl and had lots of clothes. Caleb looked over at her as they passed. "Go ahead and get us a table. We'll be right back." They moved through the lobby and walked out, carrying the trunk.

Mia let out a deep breath, knowing she needed to have a long talk with him. She hadn't been told what to do in a long time and wasn't about to start now.

Mia stepped into the restaurant and a gentleman approached, carrying menus. "Joining us for breakfast?" He looked at her with interest, even though she had two children with her.

"Yes, for my husband, my children and I, and a friend. Five in all," Mia replied flatly.

The man's smile disappeared, and he cleared his throat. "Right this way, madam."

It seemed strange to be referred to as madam and to have an instant family.

The waiter laid the menus on a large round table. "Here you go, ma'am."

"Thank you," she replied, taking her seat and setting Hailey on her lap. Shane slid onto another seat without incident. At that moment, Mia was grateful to Colton for having had the man-to-man talk with him about women. It was refreshing to see a man wanting to teach a boy how to become a gentleman, even at Shane's age.

"Could I start you off with some coffee?" the waiter asked.

"Yes. Three cups please and two glasses of milk." Mia gave him a courteous smile and then turned her attention back to the menu.

"Right away, ma'am."

Shane straightened his back and picked up a menu. It was upside down but he looked so cute trying to read it.

"So, what are you going to have?" she asked Shane, enjoying him trying to act like an adult.

"Um… I'm not sure, but the pancakes look good."

Mia covered her laugh with a cough. "I make really good pancakes… and French toast, too."

Shane ignored her and went back to pretending to look at the menu.

Caleb and Colton walked into the restaurant and Mia waved them over.

"We took care of the trunk and the rig. It's parked right out front," Caleb said as he sat down beside Mia. Colton took the other seat. "Thanks for helping me with the trunk, Colton. That thing's heavy."

Colton laughed as he looked over at Mia. "It sure was."

Mia straightened. "Well, a lady needs her things."

"Yes, that's what Ella tells me."

"How are Ella and the babies?" Caleb asked.

Colton grinned. "They're doing just fine. I have to be getting back soon. Don't want to leave her with two screaming babies alone for too long."

"Isn't the doctor there?" Mia asked.

"Yes," Colton replied, "but he might be called away at any moment."

Just then, the waiter returned with three cups of coffee and two glasses of milk.

"If you don't mind…," Colton interjected, "I need two orders of pancakes to go. My wife just had twins and I need to get back to her."

The man's eyes brightened. "Well, congratulations! Right away, sir." Then he turned to Mia and Caleb. "And for you?"

"I'll have the same." Caleb closed his menu.

Shane repeated his father's actions, laying his menu down. "Me, too."

One corner of Caleb's lips curled into a smile. "Bring one for my daughter, too."

"I'll have the same," Mia quickly interjected before Caleb could order for her. "If you could please make his order first, though, it would be a big help."

The waiter smiled. "Right away, ma'am."

"Thanks for that." Colton took a sip of his coffee and swallowed.

"If you like, we can help you bring Ella and the babies back," Caleb suggested. He wrapped his hand around his coffee cup, warming his hands, and then took a cautious sip.

"I would appreciate that, Reverend." Colton smiled. "I'm not sure how we'd manage traveling with two newborn babies alone in this snow."

"Is Ella well enough to travel?" A crease formed between Mia's eyes. The scent of fresh coffee wafted toward her as she lifted it to her lips. The hot liquid rushed down her throat, instantly warming her.

Colton shook his head. "We have to go back today, no matter what. I have some cash with me, but I wasn't planning on staying here long."

"Well then." Caleb picked up the bill. "Breakfast is on me."

Colton looked at him, his eyes wide. "Now, Preacher. I couldn't let you do that."

"No, it's the least we can do after all you've done for us." A broad grin spread across his lips. "Besides, we're celebrating the birth of your children!"

"Yes, we are." Colton lifted his coffee up and Caleb clinked his cup against his.

The waiter approached with a small box. "Here you go, mister. That'll be—"

"Put it on our tab," Caleb interjected.

"As you wish." The waiter bowed his head to Caleb.

Colton shifted the box to one arm and offered his hand to Caleb. "Thanks, Preacher. You didn't have to do that."

"Yes, Colton, I did." Caleb stood and shook his hand. "We'll be over just as soon as we finish eating."

"See you then." Colton tipped his hat to Mia. "Mia."

"Give Ella my best and tell her I can't wait to see her and the babies." Deep down, she doubted that she would ever have a baby of her own. She would have to be content with mothering Shane and Hailey, and being a surrogate aunt to Ella and Colton's children.

A broad grin spread across Colton's lips. "I will." Then he headed out the door. He had so much pep in his step it was clear that he was over the moon about the birth of his children.

"Did you sleep well last night?" Mia asked innocently, taking another sip of her coffee.

"Tolerably." Caleb lifted an eyebrow as he looked into her eyes, causing her heart to flutter at just the simple gesture. By the way her body reacted to this man, she hoped to change his mind about the status of their platonic relationship, but she wondered if he ever would. "And you?"

"Tolerably." She took a sip of her coffee to hide what she

was feeling. Despite being completely exhausted, she had tossed and turned the whole night thinking of Caleb.

"Here you go." The waiter placed their plates on the table before them. "Can I get you anything else? More coffee, maybe?"

Caleb smiled. "Yes, please."

"Right away, sir." The waiter hurried away, checking on the pretty woman who was sitting alone a few tables down from theirs.

"So, tell me about Whiskey River," Mia coaxed, cutting up first Shane's pancakes and then Hailey's. "How are the people?"

Caleb's face brightened. "Well, Wyatt Nash is the new saloon owner and his wife is Madison…." He continued talking between bites as he dug into his pancake.

After the children were squared away, Mia listened as he went on about the townsfolk of Whiskey River, telling her all about them, sparing no detail. From the way he was talking about them, it was clear that he loved the town and the people in it.

"And then there's the princess…."

Mia nearly spit out her coffee. She dabbed at her lips. "A princess? I thought that Ella was just kidding."

"Nope!" Shane bounced in his seat. "Her name is Gabriella and she really is a princess!"

Caleb smiled. "That's Mrs. Price to you."

"Is this true?" Mia lifted an eyebrow.

Caleb chuckled. "Every word."

"How did she come to be in Whiskey River?" Mia asked,

intrigued, catching herself leaning a bit closer.

Caleb told her the story of how Gabriella was kidnapped and literally fell onto Dirk Price's doorstep. When he finished the exciting tale, Mia was so intrigued that she almost forgot to eat as she fed Hailey.

Caleb dabbed at his lips with his napkin. "Well, I think we'd better go before it starts snowing again."

When Mia looked out the window, the sun was shining outside for the moment. "Do you think it's safe?" Mia finished the last of her coffee and sat back, sated. It was the first meal she was able to enjoy since stepping off the train.

Caleb finished the last bite of his pancake, and swallowed. "The snow stuck last night, but not enough to keep us from going home. So, we have to go while we can." He smiled as he finished the last of his coffee and stood. "I'll be right back." He walked over to the front register to settle their bill.

Mia wished she could contribute, but she had brought little money with her. She only had a few dollars to her name. She reconciled herself to taking in sewing to make money, if they ever needed it. But for the moment, she would have enough to do with caring for the children and the household. Of course, making their clothes herself would save them a lot of money, too.

"Come here, little girl." Mia picked up a cloth napkin and wiped the syrup off Hailey's sticky hands and face. "There you go. Much better." Then she turned to her new son. "Shane?"

But he quickly picked up a napkin and sloppily wiped

his face and his hands. "I can do it myself."

Mia stood and took Hailey's hand, then pushed in her chair. Shane was about to run off toward his father, but Mia stopped him. "Push in your chair first and stay with me, please."

Shane narrowed his eyes at her but did as she said. But when she reached for his hand, he pulled away. To his credit, he walked by her side instead of running away.

After paying the bill, Caleb slid his wallet into his back pocket and turned to Mia. "Ready?"

He took Hailey from her, and held her with one arm. "Ready, baby girl?"

Caleb held the door open for Mia. Much to her surprise. Shane waited, too, instead of running ahead and jumping into the back of the buckboard. She guessed that he had taken Colton's little talk to heart. She just wished that it had been Caleb to give him the talk instead. But she knew she had to be patient with him.

Outside, snow covered the ground in a soft white blanket, but the sun shone brightly overhead. As Caleb had said, they didn't appear to be in danger of getting caught in another snowstorm on the way home. Home. She hadn't even laid eyes on it yet, but she was already coming to think of Whiskey River as her home.

Caleb offered her his hand and helped her into his buckboard, and then handed Hailey up to her. The little girl went to her with ease and sat on the bench seat between them, but Mia kept her arm around her to keep her from falling.

Shane climbed up into the back of the buckboard and sat down with his back to the bench seat, while Caleb climbed in the front beside Mia. Within minutes, they pulled in front of the little white house that served as the doctor's office and makeshift hospital at the edge of town.

"Whoa!" Caleb pulled the team to a stop, pulled the brake, and then stepped down and walked around to Mia. "Shall we?" He reached for Hailey and then took Mia's hand to help her down. Just his simple words caused her face to flush as she stepped down from the buckboard.

If he saw her reaction, he didn't acknowledge it. He offered her his arm and she took it, letting him help her through the snow and up the wooden steps leading to the doctor's office.

Caleb knocked and a moment later, the door swung open.

"Welcome!" Doc Allaway said, another cigar between his teeth. "Come on in! I suppose you're here to see your friends."

"Yes, thank you." Caleb stepped back and let Mia walk in first. "So, how's your patient doing?"

The doctor chuckled. "You mean patients. Mother and babies are all doing just fine." The doctor closed the door behind them and then walked back into his makeshift hospital.

"Mia!" Ella was sitting on the edge of the bed, fully dressed, holding one of the babies. She motioned for her to come to her and then pulled her in for a hug. Colton was standing off to the side, holding the other baby.

"How are you feeling?" Mia's eyebrows lifted in concern.

"Sore, but good." Ella held the baby up to her. "Would you mind taking Hannah for me for a minute?"

Mia smiled. "I'd be glad to." Mia carefully took the baby.

Colton's eyebrows pulled together in concern. "Caleb, would you take Blake for me?"

"Yes, of course." Caleb took the baby boy and Colton rushed to Ella's side to help her up.

"Can you walk or would you like me to carry you?" Colton asked.

Ella smiled. "Don't be silly. Just give me your arm." He helped her up and she walked slowly.

"Oh, the hell with this." Colton carefully swept her up into his arms.

Ella cringed a bit, but wrapped her arms around her husband's neck. "Colton! Your language. The preacher."

Everyone stood back, clearing the way for Colton as he carried her purposefully out the door. "Oh, I'm sure it's not anything Caleb hasn't heard before."

"Colton!" Ella objected.

"Oh, it's all right." Caleb chuckled as he walked with Mia. "He's right. It's nothing I haven't heard before."

Outside, Colton had put some blankets in the back of his buckboard so she and the babies could ride in comfort. He placed her in the back and then climbed up with her to help her get comfortable. Ella didn't lay down, but sat up, leaning against the back of the front bench seat. Then he took the baby from Caleb, swaddled him, and handed him to Ella.

"Mia, would you mind riding in the back with Ella?"

Colton asked, taking the baby from her.

Mia smiled. "I'd be glad to." Then she turned to Caleb. "Would you mind? Hailey can ride in the back with us."

Caleb shook his head. "No, not at all." Then he turned to his son. "Shane, would you like to ride with the women or with me?"

Shane scrunched up his nose. "No, I'll ride with you." He squared his shoulders. "I'm a man now." He looked over at Colton and smiled.

Colton gave him a wink.

Caleb laughed. "I have a feeling that I'm missing something."

Mia chuckled. "I'll tell you about it when we get home." She was about to give him a hug, but it felt too awkward.

Caleb gave her a smile as he helped her into the back with Ella. "I'm looking forward to it." Then he handed her Hailey, who sat down next to Mia, cuddled up close.

Once she was settled, Colton handed her the other baby.

"She's beautiful," Mia said. "You did good, Ella."

"She's just as beautiful as her mother," Colton proudly interjected.

"Well, it's obvious that both babies have inherited their parent's good looks," Mia agreed.

Caleb reached over the back and gave Mia's hand a gentle squeeze. "Will you be all right?"

Mia smiled, touched by the gesture. "Yes, of course. Besides, Ella and I haven't had a chance to catch up on our girl talk."

Caleb laughed. "Well, in that case, I'm out of here."

Then he turned to Colton. "You take the lead and I'll follow closely behind."

"Much obliged. We'll see you in Whiskey River."

"If you need anything, just pull over." With that, Caleb turned to Shane. "Let's go, son."

Shane puffed up his chest and climbed up into the buckboard on the bench seat beside his father.

When everyone was settled, they started the slow journey home. On the way, Mia wondered what she would be going home to.

***

"So, how's it going?" Ella asked when they were alone and could talk without anyone listening.

"What?"

"Between you and Caleb," Ella replied as if Mia should have known what she was talking about. "How's it going?"

"So far, so good." Mia chuckled. "Although I owe Colton."

Concern filled her eyes. "What for?"

"Colton gave Shane a man-to-man talk this morning. It was priceless."

Ella gasped. "He didn't!"

Mia laughed. "Yes, he did."

"Colton needs to learn how to keep his nose out of other people's business."

Colton looked over his shoulder. "What was that?"

"Nothing," Mia interjected. "Nothing at all." Then

she turned back to Ella. "No, he did just the right kind of interfering. Shane was running away from me when Colton stopped him. In fact, he might have run right out into the street if Colton hadn't intervened. Then he gave him a talk about the finer points of how a gentleman treats a lady." Mia chuckled. "I loved it. I just wish that Caleb had been the one to tell him."

"Just give it time." Then Ella turned her attention back to the baby boy in her arms.

"So, you're a mother now." Mia smiled, changing the subject. "Do you have enough baby clothes?"

Ella shrugged. "I have plenty. My friend Madison, Wyatt's new wife, has been helping me make them, along with the other ladies of the church. But she's been quite busy between teaching school and settling in to married life."

Guilt filled Mia at her words. "I'm so sorry. I should have been helping you to prepare. I'm afraid that I haven't been the best friend lately."

"Oh, hush." A crease formed between Ella's eyes. "You've had your hands full trying to make ends meet after I left. I'm so sorry I left you high and dry."

"Well, I think you've had enough to think about lately." She looked down at the baby in her arms as she spoke to Mia. "But let's make a deal. Let's not feel guilty. After all, life just took us in different directions."

"But you're here now." Ella smiled as a devilish look came into her eyes.

Mia could just imagine what was going through Ella's mind as she remembered the times they shared together in New York. "Yes, I am. And that means that if you need anything, let me know. I'm here to help."

"As much as I like hearing that, I'm afraid you'll be busy enough settling in to your new life without worrying about me."

Mia sighed. "I just hope that Caleb comes to accept me into his family."

Ella's eyebrows pulled together as one corner of her lips curled into a smile. "What do you mean? He married you, didn't he? If that isn't acceptance, then I don't know what is."

Mia shrugged. "I hope you're right."

Mia and Ella spent the rest of the long ride to Whiskey River talking and catching up on things after not having seen each other for so long. Soon, they came to a farmhouse with a long drive, blanketed in snow.

Ella announced, "Home sweet home."

Mia took in the wraparound front porch, and the big house with the barn in the back. "It's lovely. It suits you perfectly."

"Thank you." Ella cringed when the wagon jolted to a stop.

"Are you okay?" Mia asked.

Ella held a finger to her lips. "I'm fine, but please don't tell Colton anything. He worries too much."

Mia smiled, nodding in agreement. After all she and Ella

had been through together, it was good to see her so happy. They'd gone from single dancehall girls to married women in less than a year. The good Lord sure did work in strange ways.

"Well, this is it!" Colton stated proudly, walking around from the front of the buckboard. "Here. I'll take him." Colton took the baby boy from Ella's hands as if he were precious cargo. And he really was.

"Here, I'll help." Caleb reached for the baby and Colton handed him over.

Colton climbed up into the back of the buckboard and helped Ella to the end. Once she was ready, he jumped off and scooped her up into his arms with ease.

"Land's sake!" Ella announced, trying to brush him off. "I can walk. I'm not an invalid."

Colton shook his head and smiled, obviously enjoying the feel of his wife in his arms. "Not while I'm around. You just had babies yesterday and you need me to take care of you."

Ella just shook her head as she wrapped her arms around his neck. "If you say so, dear."

A triumphant smile spread across his lips. "Now, that's more like it."

"Oh, stop it!" Ella hit him playfully on the chest.

Colton started to walk away, but said to Caleb over his shoulder, "Wait here. I'll be right back."

Caleb chuckled. "We'll be right here." After Colton left, Caleb helped Mia down out of the wagon, each of them holding one of the babies, and then he helped Hailey down, too.

A moment later, Colton bounded down the stairs and took his daughter from Mia's arms. "Come on in, Preacher. Stay a while."

Caleb shook his head. "No, thank you. We'll help you get settled in, but we have to be getting home. I'd bet ol' Bessy is about to bust right now." When he saw Mia's eyebrows pull together in concern, he added, "Bessy's our milk cow."

"Well, while you men talk, I'm going inside to say goodbye to Ella." Mia hurried down the walk, up the stairs and then opened the door. "Ella?"

"In here!" Ella's voice came from another room.

Mia walked in the direction of her voice and stepped into her bedroom. Ella was in bed, lying on her side. "Feeling okay?"

Ella smiled. "Yes. I just need to rest."

Mia crossed the room and gave her friend a kiss on the forehead. "Take care of yourself and get some rest. I'll see you soon."

A smile spread across Ella's lips and her eyes began to close. "See you Sunday."

With that, Mia walked out and met Colton and Caleb in the living room. Hailey was holding onto her father's coattail, yawning. Mia scooped her up into her arms and Hailey laid her head on Mia's shoulder. "Ella's nearly asleep." Then she glanced down at Hailey. "And it looks as if someone else is ready for a nap, too."

"I'll be right back." Colton walked into the bedroom but was back within seconds and took the other baby from

Caleb, smiling. "Thanks for everything."

Caleb gave him a gentle pat on the shoulder. "No, thank you. What you did for us… well—"

"No need to say anything more." Colton stopped him. "What are friends for, right?"

Caleb and Mia said their last goodbyes as Colton closed the door behind him.

Mia looked over at her new son, playing in the snow. "Shane, why don't you hop up into the seat and let's go?"

Shane folded his arms across his chest. "You're not my mother, so don't tell me what to do!"

Caleb gave him a swat on the bottom and Shane's eyes welled up with tears, threatening to spill over. "Shane, I told you that we treat each other with respect… and that includes Mia. You don't have to call her Mama if you don't want to, but you will treat her with respect. And if she asks you to do something, you will do it. Understand?"

Shane bobbed his head, but said nothing as he glared at his father.

"What was that?" Caleb asked.

Shane swallowed. "Yes, sir."

"Now…." Caleb looked into his son's bright blue eyes. "Would you like to climb up into the front seat of your own accord, or would you like me to put you there?"

Without another word, Shane climbed up onto the front seat.

Caleb held his hand out to Mia and helped her into the buckboard beside Shane. Instinctively, she held out her arms to Hailey. The little girl went right to her, curled up in her arms, and laid her head on her shoulder.

Caleb climbed up onto the seat on the other side next to his son, took up the reins, and clicked his tongue. Immediately, the horses launched into an easy trot. On the way home, Caleb didn't look over at Mia at all, nor did he speak. Now that they were alone again, it appeared that he was going to speak to her only when necessary.

She reached over for Shane's hand, but he pulled away and folded his arms across his chest as silent tears flowed down his cheeks. She had hoped that Colton's talk would have sunk in and it wouldn't have come down to this, but she guessed a confrontation was inevitable. After all, the boy was being forced to tolerate another woman in the place of his mother. Her heart went out to him. She knew that he would never think of her as his mother, but she hoped that, one day, he would at least come to accept her.

Mia was lost in thought as they rode home. The rhythm of the slow trot of the horses lulled Hailey to sleep in no time, and before long, Shane leaned his head against Mia's arm as he drifted off to sleep. Then he caught himself and sat up abruptly, gave her a dirty look, and turned his eyes to the road.

Mia's heart sank. She hadn't quite known what to expect when she came here, but this wasn't it. She knew that Caleb and the children were hurting, but she hadn't expected Caleb to treat her like an outsider invading their territory, speaking to her only when necessary. She just hoped that she could get past the shadow of his late wife. She could see her everywhere. In Caleb's eyes every time he looked at her, and in the eyes of the children. She felt her presence in Shane's loyalty, in Hailey's need for a mother, and in Caleb's loyalty by only speaking to her when necessary.

This was Mia's first real relationship, and definitely not what she expected. As a child, her dreams were the same as every girl her age: to be swept off her feet by her knight in shining armor and carried away on his white steed.

Now, she knew that dreams were overrated.

Before they were married, Caleb had made no pretenses about their relationship and what he had expected from it. He needed someone to care for his children and his home, but nothing more. And that was what she had agreed to in exchange for a good home, food in her stomach, and to be treated with civility. And Caleb had done just that so far. What was there to complain about? Giving up her dream of romance was a small price to pay.

Then her thoughts went to Ella and the babies. She let out a deep breath, knowing that she would never have a baby. But right now, Caleb's children were more than enough.

Mia adjusted the quilt once more over herself and the children to keep them warm. Shane pulled away from her every time she tried to tuck the blanket in around him. But when he was shivering violently, he finally relented. She felt bad that they were out in the cold like this, but she knew they'd soon be home.

Twilight began to fall, casting golden and orange hues and long shadows across the snow. Just then, Caleb pulled the team onto a sprawling farm where a white, wooden house with a huge front porch stood in the middle of a field blanketed in snow. It looked cozy, even if it didn't quite feel like home yet.

Caleb pulled the team to a stop in front of the house. Shane jumped out of the buckboard and ran inside.

"Well, this is it," Caleb announced a bit too cheerfully. "What do you think?"

Mia jumped slightly, surprised that Caleb had finally spoken to her and was asking her opinion. "I like it," she answered, smiling. "It looks nice." It sure beat the tenement she rented in New York with Ella. But at that moment, she missed it profoundly.

Caleb smiled. "It's not much, but it's home."

"It's wonderful," she encouraged as he took Hailey from her and helped her from the buckboard.

"I'm glad you like it." He offered her his arm to help her up the stairs. "I'll put some more salt on the steps so it won't be slippery for you and the children."

She smiled. "It's fine."

He held the door open for her, but her breath caught when she walked in. Everything was in order, probably thanks to the ladies of the church. It appeared that he had tried to clean up before she arrived, but it could still use a woman's touch. It was clear that he and the children had been on their own for a while, even if it had only been for a few short months.

A lump formed in her throat as she looked around the house, although she wasn't exactly sure why. It was as if she were invading another woman's home. Jessica was everywhere.

Caleb set Hailey on her feet and Mia watched as she scampered off. Even though Hailey was little, Mia's arms felt as if they were about to fall off from carrying her. She had never been around children for any length of time before and wasn't used to carrying a little one around so much.

"Come with me and I'll show you around," Caleb offered happily. He opened the door to what she assumed was the spare room, and everything in there was fairly neat. There were some toys on the bed, but the room showed promise. "This is your room. I'm in the process of moving the children's things over to the master bedroom." He closed the door, and then walked over to what she had assumed was the master bedroom. It was a bit larger and there was a curtain hanging in the center across the length of the room, dividing it into separate spaces.

The children were already playing on the floor. Shane's eyes narrowed when he saw her, and then he went back to playing with his soldiers.

"I'll share this room with the children," Caleb announced, claiming her attention, "and you'll have the spare room to yourself."

Mia made a mental note to make cleaning this room a priority when she had the chance.

Caleb rubbed his hands together, causing his arm muscles to flex under his crisp white shirt and gray vest. "Okay, then. I'll leave you to settle in. I'll be right back with your things."

"Would you like any help?" she offered.

He shook his head as he hurried out of the bedroom.

"No, I've got it. I'll be right back."

She smiled her thanks. Well, at least he was talking to her again.

Mia looked around, not quite knowing where to begin as the muted sounds of the children playing filled the house. *Well, first thing's first,* she thought to herself. If she was going to make the house a home, she had better get started.

She walked into the kitchen. Dainty, frilly doilies lay across the countertops and on the table. She carefully folded them and opened the drawers until she found where they belonged, not to rid the house of her memory, but to open up some workable counter space.

Next, she filled two steel buckets with water that she found in the utility room off the kitchen and put them on the stove to boil. The kitchen and the house reminded her of her childhood. Making bread and baking with her mother had created fond memories that sustained her through many hard times.

Mia unbuttoned and pushed up the sleeves of her dress, preparing to wash the few dishes that were in the sink. She knew she should have changed her clothes first, but she was eager to get started in her new home. Also, they hadn't eaten anything since breakfast and she knew they must have been starving.

"Where are Jessica's doilies that were on the counters?" Caleb blurted out, stopping short as he entered the kitchen.

Mia let out a deep breath. "I folded them up and put them in a drawer." She looked at him kindly. "Caleb, I'm not trying to get rid of her. I just need the counter space."

Caleb raised an eyebrow as if he were about to say something, but then sighed. "I want you to make yourself at home here."

"Thank you," Mia replied. "And in order to do that, I'll have to move some things about."

"Yes. Do what you must." Then he turned on his heel and left the room abruptly.

As she prepared their dinner, she wondered if he would ever come to accept her. Not as his wife, but as a part of the family, at least.

CHAPTER 8

The next day, faint rays of morning sunlight shone through the window. Caleb tried to orient himself as the events of the past few days rushed into his head. Mia taking over in the house, moving Jessica's doilies. Even though she hadn't meant it as disrespect to Jessica, it was still hard to bear. He knew he had to move on with Mia, but it was easier said than done.

He remembered his dream of Jessica the night before, the night he married Mia. It seemed as if Jessica had approved and was at peace. Now, he had to find that same kind of peace for himself.

And now that he had made the choice to marry Mia, he was determined to make the best of it, although he had no idea how.

After he finished his morning prayers, he poured water into the white and blue patterned china basin and washed his face. Then he slipped on his pants, leaving his chest and his feet bare. Although he was sure it would be freezing outside, the cool air in the house felt good against his skin.

He walked past the children, sleeping soundly in their beds. He stood in the doorway for a moment, watching them sleep, knowing things were just as hard on them as it was on him.

Caleb placed another log on the fire in the living room, and warmth immediately filled the room. The fresh scent of coffee wafted through the house, and he was surprised to see Mia up and about so early.

"Good morning." Without emotion, she handed him a cup of coffee when he walked in.

"Good morning. What got you up so early?" He leaned against the counter as he took a sip. "Um… good coffee."

She smiled as her eyes went from his face to his bare chest. Then she quickly looked away, turning her attention back to the bacon she was frying on the stove. "I'm an early riser. I can get a lot of work done that way. The earlier, the better."

He looked around the kitchen and everything was in place. The dishes were washed and put away, the counters clean, and the kitchen table had been cleared off and was set with breakfast dishes. "From the look of it, you must have gotten up way too early."

She looked at him and smiled, and then her eyes went to his bare chest again. "Not that early. I've been up for a few hours."

"Looks like it. And I thought *I* got up early." He set down his coffee cup. "I'll be right back."

He walked into the bedroom and pulled on a clean shirt,

then walked back into the kitchen again, where Mia was setting breakfast on the table. "I'm sorry. It won't happen again," he admitted, referring to his walking around without a shirt.

She gave him a slight smile. "No, it's all right. Don't worry."

"Can I do anything to help?" he asked as he took another sip of his coffee, watching her work. It felt good to watch a woman work in the kitchen again. Then he turned away as guilt filled his chest, unable to believe that his thoughts had betrayed him like that.

Mia shook her head. "No, I have everything under control. Go ahead and sit down while I finish up."

Caleb's thoughts went to the night before as he leaned back against the counter, holding his coffee. "Listen, Mia. I'm sorry about what I said last night… about the children."

She just shook her head as she scrambled the eggs. "It doesn't matter."

He placed his hands on her shoulders, forcing her to look at him. "Yes, it does." He thought for a moment as he looked into her bright green eyes. "You were right. If I handle the discipline with the children, they won't respect you." He let out a deep breath. "But please be patient with me. I've been protective of the kids for so long, and I'm not used to anyone else taking charge with them—"

"Ssshhh…." She pressed her finger gently to his lips, sending shivers over his body. "It's okay. It'll work out."

He sighed. "I'll talk to Shane today. I can't believe he's been acting so poorly. It's really not like him."

"I'm an outsider, coming in and invading his territory." She let out a deep breath as she set a plate of toast on the table and looked in his eyes. "He's just being loyal… to his mother."

Guilt caused a lump to form in his throat. Caleb was tired of feeling guilty. Guilt for not being able to handle the children, his congregation, and the farm on his own. Guilt for not having taken care of Jessica better. Guilt for taking a wife out of survival.

But he had no other option. He needed his children to be cared for when he wasn't there. Losing Jessica was too much as it was. If something happened to his children because he couldn't properly care for them, he would never forgive himself. He would do anything for his family, including giving his own life.

Caleb's eyebrows pulled together as he watched her place the bowl of scrambled eggs onto the table. And now, guilt rose up within him for being drawn to her. Even if he was legally married to Mia, he was still mentally married to Jessica.

He pushed the thought aside, remembering his promise to himself to try to make the best of it. "Everything looks great. Thank you, Mia."

She shrugged as she spooned scrambled eggs onto her plate. "My pleasure. I'll try and see if I can get the house in order today."

He took a bite of his bacon. "Sounds good." He thought for a moment, and then added, "Mia, I hate to leave you alone on your first day here, but I have to visit some parishioners.

I'm so behind on my visits it's not even funny. Will you be okay with the children and the house?"

"Yes, of course," Mia replied. "Also, I was thinking that if we need extra money, I could take in some sewing."

Caleb shook his head. "That's not necessary. Let's just take it a day at a time for now."

She gave him a smile, nodding.

From her reaction, Caleb thought that she might like to work. After all, she was used to working and providing for herself. He suspected that it might be difficult for her to get used to having a man to care for her. But for now, he just wanted some normalcy to his life again and time. Time to heal. Time to move on. Just time.

"Is there anything else you'd like me to do today? Anything pressing?" she asked casually, bringing him from his reverie as she nibbled on a slice of toast.

Caleb shook his head. "No. I was just going to ask if you could get the house in order and take care of the children, but it looks as if you already have everything under control."

"Thank you." She smiled proudly and then took a sip of her coffee.

"By the way, there's plenty of food in the pantry," Caleb continued. "If you feel up to it, there are plenty of chickens out back in the henhouse."

Mia nearly spit out her coffee. "You want me to… kill a chicken?"

He shrugged, not understanding what the problem was. "Didn't you kill chickens back east?"

She laughed. "No, we went to the butcher."

Caleb frowned as he got up and placed his plate in the sink. That was all he needed, a frail woman who couldn't kill a chicken. After all, it wasn't as if he had just asked her to kill a cow. "Don't worry. The men and I slaughter the pigs and cows in the summer."

Her eyes flew open wide. "How many do you kill?"

He shrugged. "One cow and one pig per family. Then we cure the meat, smoke it, and it lasts all winter. The rest, we sell."

Mia's body went rigid. "And what part will I play in that?"

Caleb sighed. "Well, usually the women help out in the kitchen and with curing the meat. It's actually a lot of fun. A community affair." Taking in the frown on her face, he added, "Here in the country, we all pull together. We wouldn't be able to survive otherwise."

She pushed her plate aside.

Caleb shook his head, knowing that she had lost her appetite. He poured himself another cup of coffee to take with him. It was too good to let go to waste. Then he slipped on his boots and coat. "Have a good day."

"Shall I expect you home for lunch?" Mia asked, raising her eyebrows.

Caleb hated seeing the hopeful look in her eyes. He didn't want her to take interest in him. To care for him. Just caring for the children would be enough. "No." He slid on his cowboy hat. "One of the parishioners usually asks me to stay for lunch."

A disappointed look marred her features, but was

quickly gone.

Now he felt guilty for not allowing himself to care for Mia. But wasn't providing a roof over her head and food in her stomach enough? Many women would love to stay at home and care for the children while the man worked. He inclined his head, silently telling her goodbye.

"What time shall I expect you home?" she asked, stopping him.

He placed his hand on the door, but didn't look at her. "I won't be back home until later tonight." Then a thought occurred to him as he looked in her direction, but not in her eyes. "Will you be okay with the children?"

Out of the corner of his eye, he could see her nod. "They'll be fine."

He walked out, closing the door tightly behind him.

As he hitched up the team, his thoughts went back to Mia. He could tell that she was a loving, caring person, and he knew that, one day, just caring for the children wouldn't be enough. A woman like that needed someone to care for her, too. But he just didn't have it in him. That part of him lay dormant, having died right along with Jessica.

At least he would be able to make his rounds without feeling guilty for leaving the children in the care of a neighbor. For that peace of mind alone, Mia was worth her weight in gold. At least that was something.

On his first stop, he went by the Widow Campbell's house. He stopped the team out front and then knocked on her door. From inside, he could hear the methodical tap, tap, tapping of her cane against the hardwood floor growing louder as she moved closer to the door. It always took her a while to answer. "It's me, Mrs. Campbell. Preacher Henley, come to visit."

She opened the door a smidge and peered out. "Well, hello, Preacher!" Her face lit up as she opened the door wide to let him in, and then started the arduous journey back to her chair. "It's good to see you here! I'm so glad you came to visit!"

Caleb walked in and shut the door behind him. Then he took off his hat, hung it on a peg by the door, and followed her into the living room with his Bible in hand. "I'm sorry that it's been so long." He didn't want to tell her that he'd had his hands full. After all, he was there for her and not to tell her his troubles. "Is there anything I can get for you, or bring you from town?"

Mrs. Campbell hadn't been able to leave her home for a while, but she seemed to care for herself pretty well. "No, I'm fine."

He looked in the woodbin beside her fireplace. "I'll cut some wood for you before I go. Looks like your supply is running low."

Her eyes lit up as if it were Christmas morning. "Oh, thank you, Preacher! That would be grand." Then she leaned forward in her chair. "But tell me something."

"Of course, Mrs. Campbell. What would you like to know?"

She attempted to scoot her chair closer as if what she was about to say was a big secret, even though there was no one there but the two of them. "I heard you took a wife.

Is that true?"

Guilt reared its ugly head once again. He knew that the questions and gossip would fly, but he hadn't been prepared to have to field questions so soon. "Yes, it's true, Mrs. Campbell. Her name is Mia."

She slapped her leg good-naturedly. "I thought so! Mildred said that it was just a rumor, but I knew it was true! So, tell me all about her…."

Caleb bit his lip to keep from smiling. "How did Mrs. Hart get out here so fast?" He shook his head at the older women's love of gossip. But, then again, there wasn't a whole lot more for them to do in the small town.

"Oh, she rushed out here to tell me at first morning light." An innocent look came into her eyes. "In fact, she just left right before you got here. You just missed her."

Mildred Hart, her not-much-younger friend, liked to gossip as much as she did. She and many ladies in the church came out to visit and check on Mrs. Campbell. But it was known around town that Mrs. Campbell knew the best gossip of anyone in four counties.

"Mrs. Campbell," Caleb began, disapproval shading his voice, "let's have a little prayer, and then I'll go into town for you and get you what you need. When I get back, I'll cut the wood for you."

She shook her head. "Nonsense! Millie went to the general store for me yesterday." She patted his arm in a friendly way as her eyes grew wide. "Now, tell me all about her. What is she like? How did you two meet? If there's one thing I can't resist, it's a good love story. I already heard that she's beautiful."

Caleb looked up. "Yes, she is."

She snapped her fingers. "I knew it! Now, tell me all about her."

"Now, Mrs. Campbell, you'll get to meet her at church on Sunday, if you can come."

If nothing else, it might be a way to get her out of the house. Moving around had been difficult for her, so she hadn't been to church in a while.

Her eyebrows pulled together, obviously thinking. "I'll see if Millie can bring me."

"Good! I'm glad to hear it." Caleb knew that she couldn't resist the opportunity to meet Mia. "Now, let's have a little scripture reading—"

"Not until I hear a little bit about your wife." She looked at him expectantly.

"Now, Mrs. Campbell," Caleb chastised lightly, "you know that you mustn't gossip."

Her eyes grew wide in mock horror. "Preacher! I'm surprised at you." She held her hand to her chest, feigning offense. "You know I don't gossip. I'm just getting to know my neighbors, is all!"

Caleb laughed. "Call it what you like." It was still gossip, but he knew that she meant well.

"Do you think you could bring her with you for one of your visits?" The look in her gray eyes was hopeful.

Caleb sighed. "Right now, she has her hands full with the children and settling in, but you'll meet her this Sunday. We're looking forward to seeing you there."

He read a bit of scripture and, needing a little break, went out back and chopped some wood. When he had split enough to last her more than a week, he said his goodbyes and went on to the next congregation member.

Each person he visited was about the same, wanting to know about his new wife and how the children were accepting her. Each time, Caleb gave them the same answer. They could meet her Sunday at church. In fact, many of his parishioners who hadn't made it to church in a while because of the weather or bad health had all agreed to come to church Sunday. The reason? To meet his new wife. He had a feeling the church would be packed on Sunday. But if meeting his new wife brought them in, then so be it.

On the way back home later that night, he felt relieved that he hadn't had to hurry back home, knowing that the house and his children were in good hands. Maybe now there could be a bit of normalcy in their lives instead of chaos.

As he drove the team home, thoughts of Mia entered his mind. She was beautiful, kind, and although she was a city girl, it appeared that she was willing to learn and to adapt to country living. He chuckled when he thought of her horror at the thought of having to kill a chicken to fry for dinner, and he wondered how she'd fared with that, or if she had even made the attempt.

Then his thoughts turned to Jessica, remembering his dream of her. It had seemed so real. But whether it was or not, deep down he knew she would have wanted him and the children to be happy. In fact, that was the only thing that she had ever wanted their whole married life together. He felt guilty for not attending to her happiness a bit more while she was alive, although he had tried. But in the last days before her death, he had been more caught up with the church, knowing that she had everything under control with the children and their home.

Now, Caleb knew he needed Mia to care for the children and the house. There was no doubt. But he couldn't allow himself to need her, too. No. He had needed Jessica and could tell her anything. He'd confided in her about his concerns for the church and his parishioners, and she had confided in him about the children and her hopes for the future. Looking back, it was as if she had known that she wouldn't be alive to see them grow up. On more than one occasion, she had told him that he should do this or that with the children if anything happened to her. Of course, he had always brushed it off, telling her that she would probably outlive him.

Little had he known.

If he had only known, there was a lot that he would have done differently. He would have told her that he loved her more. That he needed her. But most importantly, he would have told her that she was his best friend. Not only had he lost his wife, but he had lost his best friend too.

Also, he would have taken better care of her. She had spent so much time taking care of him and the children that there seemed to be no time left for her. Yes, if he could change things, that would be the big thing he would change… the main thing… the only thing. Everything else about Jessica and their life together had been perfect.

Tears started streaming down his cheeks as the frigid winter wind blew against his face. "I need you, Jessica." He spoke aloud as he guided the team toward home. Home. That was another thing. "There *is* no home without you." Of late, there had only been a shell where they lived that they called home. Empty. Devoid of happiness… of love.

Maybe Mia could provide a home for them, but she had some big shoes to fill. Deep down in his heart, he knew it wasn't fair to compare Mia to Jessica. If things were going to work, he would have to see Mia for who she was and not expect her to fill Jessica's shoes. But could he? Could he ever look at Mia and not think of Jessica?

As a preacher, he knew he had to leave it in God's hands. But as a man, that was hard to do.

CHAPTER 9

After Caleb left, the children were still sleeping, so Mia decided to go out to the henhouse to collect the eggs and to milk the cow, knowing that, in the west, it would be the responsibility of the wife to do such things. In the city, she would have just dressed the children and gone to the market. But she had a feeling that she would be laughed out of town if she went to the general store to buy things that were plentiful on their farm.

She looked in on the children once more and they were still sleeping, so she slipped on a heavy coat and went out to the henhouse. The door to the henhouse was barely big enough for a chicken to fit through, but she crawled in as the chickens clucked and fussed and flew right at her while she gathered the eggs. A few minutes later, feathers were everywhere—even in her hair—and the chickens were very upset, but she had all the eggs in a basket that the hens had laid. Feeling accomplished, she set the basket of eggs on the counter in the kitchen, and then went into the bedroom to check on the children.

Since they were still sleeping, she walked out to the barn, found a clean milking pail sitting off to the side, and tied the cow up to what she assumed was the milking post just outside the barn. Then, she placed her hands on her hips and looked at the cow. She felt like a crazy woman with feathers in her hair and who-knew-what all over her. "Now, you and I are going to have a little talk." The cow turned around and looked at her. "After what I went through with the chickens, I don't want any trouble from you." The cow mooed. "Now, don't you look at me like that." Feeling sure that she and the cow had a mutual understanding, she began again. After setting the pail under the cow, she took an udder in each hand. But the cow kicked her, sending her flying backward into the slushy mud where the snow had melted off and people had traipsed through over and again.

Determined not to let a cow get the best of her, she set the stool beside the cow again, took an udder in each hand, and pulled. Only one little squirt of milk came out. "Well, now, that just won't do. That won't do at all!"

"Would you like some help?" a feminine voice asked behind her.

Mia jumped when she saw an older woman with curly silver hair watching her.

"Oh!" Mia attempted to smooth her hair into place. "I'm sorry. I didn't hear you come up."

The woman suppressed a smile. "I'm sorry to startle you. I'm Mrs. Abigail Jenkins. I own the boardinghouse. So sorry for the intrusion, but I heard that Preacher Henley got married, and I wanted to come over to meet you and to see if you needed any help."

Mia looked at her sheepishly. "Do you know how to milk a cow?"

The older woman dipped her head, but to Mia's relief, didn't laugh. "I do, but most folks around here keep their milk in the root cellar. The preacher may have some down there already. Now, let's go inside and get you cleaned up."

Mia put the cow back in the barn, along with the milk pail. "Thank you, Mrs. Jenkins. I guess it's obvious that I'm a city girl."

The older woman slid her arm in hers. "Believe it or not, I was once a city girl, too. Don't worry. I'll show you how to milk a cow later, if you like." She looked her over and pulled a feather out of her hair.

"I'm so sorry," Mia apologized, embarrassed. "I must look a fright."

Creases formed around Mrs. Jenkins's eyes as she smiled. "Don't worry. We've all had our moments when we were just starting out. What city are you from?"

"New York."

"I see." Mrs. Jenkins guided her toward the henhouse. Upon seeing Mia, the chickens started fussing again. "Life in the west is a bit different."

"I'd say," she agreed, attempting to brush some muck off her coat.

"Before we go in, would you mind if I show you how to gather the eggs without disrupting the hens?" Even though Mia was sure she looked funny, the older woman was kind, maintaining a straight face as she spoke to her.

Mia sighed with relief. "Yes, please."

Mrs. Jenkins showed her how to walk around the outside of the henhouse and slip her hand in through the slats. The chickens fussed a little, but weren't in a complete tizzy as they had been earlier. "That way, you don't have to go inside the henhouse to collect the eggs."

"Thank you, Mrs. Jenkins," Mia cooed as they walked toward the house. "I knew there had to be an easier way."

Mrs. Jenkins smiled. "There usually is, but we have to learn them. I guarantee you that before long, you'll be a professional at all of this." She waved her hand around dismissively.

"I sure hope so." Mia tried to smooth her dress as they approached the back door. "Would you like to come in?" Mia could see that the woman meant well, and that she wasn't there to snoop or to collect information to carry back to her friends. "Also, would you mind keeping this between us?" Mia pointed to her hair.

The elder woman laughed. "What?" she teased. "I have no idea what you're talking about."

Mia laughed. "Thank you. You're too kind."

"What happened to you?" Shane demanded as he stood in the middle of the kitchen with his hands on his hips, still dressed in his long johns.

"Go get dressed, Shane Henley," Mrs. Jenkins ordered. "You should know better than to come out here dressed like that around ladies."

Shane's eyes grew wide, and he ran off to his room

right away.

"How did you do that?" Mia asked appreciatively.

Mrs. Jenkins whispered conspiratorially, "The trick is not to show any fear."

Mia laughed, knowing that she liked this woman. "I'll clean up and will be right back."

"Take your time." Mrs. Jenkins had put a pot of coffee on the stove to brew, then realized what she'd done. "Oh! I'm sorry. I'm so used to making myself at home in the kitchen. Do you mind?"

Mia shook her head. "No, I don't mind at all."

Mrs. Jenkins smiled. "I'm sorry, but I've been helping out with the children for a while now and old habits die hard."

"That's wonderful," Mia gushed. "Actually, I'm grateful for the help. Make yourself at home, and I'll go clean up."

She disappeared into her bedroom and peered in the mirror. Feathers stuck out of her hair in all directions. It was a credit to Mrs. Jenkins that she hadn't died laughing with just one look at her. Mia cleaned up the best she could, changed her clothes, and then walked back into the kitchen.

Mrs. Jenkins already had Shane sitting at the table. He was dressed in mismatched clothes, and Mia made a mental note to make sure that the children were properly dressed before Caleb got home. She didn't need to give him any fuel as to her incompetence, although she was pleasantly surprised that breakfast that morning had gone so well. She sighed as she pushed the memories of his perfect, bare, muscular chest from her mind.

"I'll make the children some eggs," Mia announced as she walked into the kitchen. She washed and dried the eggs, and then set them beside the potbelly stove.

Mrs. Jenkins suppressed a smile. "Just to let you know, Caleb usually keeps the eggs on the counter in a bowl under a dish towel." She lifted the dish towel to reveal more than enough.

They both burst out laughing at the same time.

"I found enough eggs for mine and Caleb's breakfast this morning in a small bowl under a towel, but didn't think there were any more," Mia replied in her defense.

"Those must have been left over from yesterday," Mrs. Jenkins replied. "If Caleb doesn't do it, I combine them into one bowl when I come over."

"Thanks for letting me know," Mia replied, relieved that the woman was there to show her the ins and outs of farm life.

Hailey walked out of the bedroom wearing her nightgown, let out a sleepy yawn, and then walked over to Mia and held out her arms.

Mia scooped her up and propped her on her hip. Hailey immediately laid her head on Mia's shoulder. "What's the matter, baby girl? Still sleepy?"

She bobbed her head against Mia's shoulder and put her thumb in her mouth.

"We'll have to work on that." Mia took Hailey's thumb out of her mouth. Without missing a beat, Mia expertly cracked some eggs with one hand as she held Hailey, scrambled them, and then poured them in a hot skillet.

"So, you can cook?" Mrs. Jenkins observed, obviously impressed.

Mia shrugged. "Simple things."

"Do you know how to make biscuits?" Mrs. Jenkins poured two cups of coffee and set one on the counter beside Mia.

Mia shook her head. "No, but I used to make bread with my mother when I was little."

"Do you still have the recipe?"

Mia shook her head. "No, my aunt took all the recipes after my parents died."

"I'm so sorry to hear that," Mrs. Jenkins replied, but it wasn't the kind of crippling sympathy that so many other people were quick to give.

Mia guessed that in the west people died and experienced loss. It happened everywhere, but here they seemed to deal with it much better. She guessed that they had to in order to survive. It was just how one dealt with it that mattered. "It happened long ago."

"I'll tell you what," Mrs. Jenkins announced cheerfully. "I have some recipes that I'll bring over tomorrow, and you can copy down the ones you want."

"That would be nice." Mia smiled, pouring the cooked eggs into two bowls. "Do you happen to have a bread recipe, as well?"

Mrs. Jenkins smiled. "Yes, of course." She gave her hand a gentle pat. "I'll be sure to bring it. Here in the west, neighbors help one another."

"Thank you." Mia smiled as she set one of the bowls in

front of Shane. Then she sat down with Hailey on her lap and started feeding her.

Mrs. Jenkins carried Mia's coffee to her and set it beside her, then sat in another chair and inclined her head toward Hailey. "It looks as if she's taken right up with you."

Mia gave Hailey a quick hug. "She's my girl."

Hailey looked up and smiled.

"She is not your girl!" Shane yelled as he stomped out of the room, walked into the bedroom, and slammed the door, rattling the windows in the rest of the house.

Mia sighed as she continued to feed Hailey. "I'm sorry about that."

Mrs. Jenkins cocked her head to the side. "It appears that he's having a difficult time."

"It's just so new. I mean, I haven't even been here for twenty-four hours yet." Mia shook her head. "He's just showing loyalty to the memory of his mother. I guess he thinks I'm coming in here and taking over. And I guess I have. It's just a lot for him to handle." Mia hugged little Hailey. "But this little one was too little, really, to know what was going on at the time, so it's probably easier for her."

Mrs. Jenkins listened attentively. "She needs a mother."

"They've all been through a lot."

Mrs. Jenkins let out a deep breath. "How's Caleb handling it?"

Mia shrugged. "Not well. He won't talk to me unless it's necessary. We went to dinner last night in Laramie, and it was a disaster." Mia smiled. "I'm glad it wasn't here in

Whiskey River. The townsfolk would really have something to talk about then,"

The older woman chuckled. "Oh, pay it no mind, my dear. The princess is old news now, so your arrival and the preacher getting married out of the blue is big. But don't let it get you down. Before long, there will be someone new for the town gossips to talk about, and your marriage will be old news." She shrugged. "I guess that's how it works in small towns. Without that, no one would have anything to talk about."

Mia laughed, knowing she was right. "I know we've just met, but I feel as if I've known you for a very long time."

Mrs. Jenkins reminded her so much of her mother. Their interaction was what Mia would have imagined with her own mother, if she were still alive.

Mrs. Jenkins smiled as she patted her hand. "After you take care of Hailey, would you like me to show you how to make biscuits? It's a staple with every meal here in the west."

Mia watched Hailey scoop the last bit of egg into her mouth. "Are you full?" Hailey bobbed her head up and down excitedly. "Want some more?" The little girl shook her head, and then struggled to get down off her lap and scampered off into the bedroom. "She doesn't talk a lot, does she?"

Mrs. Jenkins shook her head. "Some. It's been hard on them all. But, now that you're here…."

"I just hope that I can be of help." Mia sighed. "That's all Caleb needs right now: a wife who is a liability and not an asset."

"And that isn't you." Mrs. Jenkins gave her hand a gentle pat. "I'll get everything ready."

"I'll dress Hailey and will be right back."

When Mia walked into the bedroom, Shane stormed out and Mia let him go, making a mental note to have a talk with him later.

Mia let Hailey pick out a dress and had her ready a few minutes later. They walked back out to the kitchen where Mrs. Jenkins had set out the flour and everything they needed to make biscuits.

After a while, the fresh aroma of homemade biscuits filled the air. But what meant the most to Mia was that Mrs. Jenkins had taken the time to teach her. It had been a while since she had a friend around, having been alone since Ella left. And with everything that was going on with Caleb and Shane, she was glad Mrs. Jenkins was there. It was nice to have a friend.

"Would you like one?" Mia asked when she pulled the tray of biscuits out of the oven.

"Don't mind if I do," Mrs. Jenkins joked as she sat down, suddenly looking tired.

"I would offer you some honey or jam, but I'm not sure if we have any." Mia set the plate in front of her.

Creases showed beside her eyes again as Mrs. Jenkins smiled. "There's some jam down in the cellar. I don't go down there unless I have to. Caleb usually brings up what I need before he leaves. As for honey, it's usually not plentiful this time of year, but Caleb has some on the counter." She let out a deep breath, as if debating whether to tell her something or not. "Jessica liked it, so he kept it in the house for her all year long."

Mia smiled. It was good to hear that Caleb had been so thoughtful of his late wife. She just hoped that one day, he might come to care for her, too. "I'll get it." She rose from her seat, thankful for the distraction. A few seconds later, she set it on the table before Mrs. Jenkins.

"Thank you." Mrs. Jenkins picked up the honey, spread it over each side of her open biscuit, and took a bite. "Now, this is what I call a biscuit!" she gushed. "I do believe this is the best biscuit I've ever had."

Mia laughed, shaking her head in disbelief. "I think you're going a little overboard, but it's very kind of you to say."

Mrs. Jenkins's eyes opened wide as she swallowed. "You don't believe me? Taste it and see for yourself."

Mia smiled in disbelief and took a bite. "Um... it *is* good," she replied, pleasantly surprised.

"See? What did I tell you?" Mrs. Jenkins beamed, and then looked at the pendant hanging from a chain around her neck. "Oh, my goodness! I have to go." She reached over and touched Mia's hand. "Are you sure that you'll be okay, dear?"

Mia smiled as she gave her hand a gentle squeeze. "Yes, of course. I appreciate you coming over. It's hard to believe that we just met. It feels as if I've known you all my life."

"Thank you. I feel the same way." Mrs. Jenkins rose to her feet. "Would you like for me to stay and help make lunch?"

Mia shook her head. "No, I'll be fine. You've done more than enough."

"I'll be back tomorrow, then." Mrs. Jenkins took her hat from the shelf, pinned it into place, and then slipped into her coat.

"Thank you for coming over. I look forward to your visit tomorrow," Mia said, smiling.

Mrs. Jenkins gave her a quick hug. "You take care, now." She sighed as she looked at her with kind eyes. "I know it's hard, but try to have patience with Caleb. He really is a good man. He's just been through a lot."

Mia nodded. "I will. Besides, I don't give up so easily."

"I'm glad that you don't." Mrs. Jenkins smiled.

After she left, Mia made the children a simple lunch of bacon and biscuit sandwiches. After lunch, they got down from their seats and hurried off to the bedroom to play.

Mia then washed the dishes, put them away, and then cleaned the living room. When she was finished, she checked on the children and they were still playing, so she went back into the living room. The rocking chair setting off to the side looked so inviting that she couldn't resist. "Maybe just for a moment." She sat down and watched the fire.

She woke with a start and looked at the clock. Three o'clock. At that moment, she realized that she must have fallen asleep. "Oh, my goodness!" she ran into the children's bedroom, and they were still playing on the floor. "Shane, go ahead and put this on." She rummaged through the chest of drawers and pulled out a shirt that matched the pants he had on.

He folded his arms across his chest. "I don't have to do what you say!"

"Oh yes you do, little mister," Mia corrected. Then she took a deep breath. "Shane, let's make the best of this and try to get along."

"You're not my mother!"

He started toward the door, but Mia stopped him. He struggled a bit, but she held on.

"Shane," she said in a soft, soothing voice. After a few seconds, he stopped struggling. "Come on and sit down beside me. I want to talk."

He let out an exasperated breath. Then, he sat down beside Mia on the edge of the bed and folded his arms abruptly across his chest.

Mia let out a deep breath. "Shane, I know that I'm not your mother."

Shane looked at her sharply.

"And I don't intend to be," Mia continued. "I mean, I'll never be able to take her place. I know that."

Tears came to his eyes as he listened.

"But I'd like to be your friend, if you don't mind."

Shane glared at her as tears brimmed his eyes. "I don't need you!"

Pain shot through Mia's chest, but she wore her best poker face. "Well, I'll be here if you ever do. In the meantime, let's just learn to get along. I know your mother's not here to take care of you, so I'd like to do that, if you don't mind."

Tears rolled down his cheeks as he hung his head.

"Hey, hey," she cooed as she pulled him to her chest.

"Shane, your mother will always be right here"—she touched his chest—"in your heart."

He began sobbing openly, so she pulled him onto her lap and rubbed his back, rocking him back and forth while he cried. Hailey looked up at her brother and scooted onto the bed beside them. Finally, his tears subsided, and he sniffled. "What should I call you?"

Mia ran her fingers through his hair. "I don't expect you to call me Mama, but how about Mia?" He looked up at her, and she shrugged. "Then, if and when you're ready, we can think of something else, if you like. Either that, or it can just be Mia. Is that okay?"

"Yes," he croaked, his voice thick with emotion.

"Shane, if I could bring your mother back, I would," she whispered as she stroked his hair. "But I'll be here for you and Hailey anytime you need me."

Shane's eyes started growing heavy. Mia picked him up, laid him on the bed, and covered him over with a blanket. She was about to give him a kiss on the cheek, but thought better of it. Hailey held up her arms and Mia swept her up. Then she laid her on the other bed, and Hailey immediately curled up on her side.

"That's a good girl." Mia pulled the blanket over her, then gave her a kiss on the cheek. "Sleep well."

As she walked toward the door, she looked over at Shane, and he curled up toward the wall, not making eye contact. Mia knew it would take time, but at least she felt they'd taken a baby step in the right direction. She couldn't come into a family and expect everything to go smoothly right off the bat.

She left the door open a crack and then walked out to the kitchen. She was pleased with the progress she had made on the house before she'd fallen asleep. The house was starting to look as if a family lived there.

"Dinner," she said to herself.

She was exhausted, but she had to get dinner on the table. So, she walked into the kitchen and opened the pantry, making a mental note to try out her new biscuit-making skills. Then she thought that country ham would go great with them, so she decided to go down into the cellar and look to see what was there.

Before she went down, she checked on the children again and they were still sleeping. She suspected that they would be down for a while, so she took a knife and a plate with her down the stairs with the intentions of only staying a few minutes.

Downstairs, she found several smoked hams, and saw the one that had been cut. She carved several slices, and was ready to go back upstairs when she heard a loud crash and then crying.

"Hailey?" she yelled as she ran up the stairs as quickly as was humanly possible.

In the kitchen Hailey was sitting on the floor with glass all around her.

"What's going on in here?" Caleb asked. Before she could respond, he walked over the glass and it crunched under his boots, ringing out in her ears as she stood stunned. He scooped his daughter into his arms and quickly looked her over. When he saw that she was all right, he turned to Mia. "Where were you?"

"I… I was down in the cellar—"

"What in the world possessed you to go down there instead of staying up here watching my children?" he demanded, and then walked over to the kitchen table and sat down with Hailey on his lap.

"I was only down there for a few seconds." Tears came to her eyes. "Before I went down, I checked on the children, and they were still sleeping—"

"At this hour?" He looked Hailey over again, and she appeared to be fine except for a few very minor cuts. "What time did you put them down for their nap?"

Anger began to replace the fear inside of her. "Three o'clock."

"Three o'clock? They should have been down after lunch!"

"Well, I didn't know that!" she yelled back. "Mrs. Jenkins was over, and she showed me how to make biscuits. We lost track of the time—"

"Well, see that you don't," he cut her off. "From here on out, you will stay up here during the day with the children. That is your primary job. If you need anything from the cellar, you will tell me, and I will retrieve it for you."

"I'm not a child, and you will not talk to me that way." She held her head high, walked calmly into the kitchen, and began sweeping up the floor. "I don't care if I *am* your wife, you will respect me at all times."

He scoffed. "You expect me to be calm when I come in

here and my daughter is sitting in a pile of glass?"

Hailey whimpered softly.

"Heavens no! And lower your voice!" She dumped some of the glass into the trash. "You're scaring her."

"Oh! I'm scaring her?" he demanded as he stood with Hailey on his hip. "I think the only thing that scared her was ending up in a pile of glass!"

"I only went down for a moment," she defended herself, placing her hands on her hips. "I had no intention of the child getting hurt."

He looked at her with cold eyes. "Well, the road to hell is paved with good intentions." With that, he marched into the bedroom and slammed the door.

Tears welled up in her eyes as she swept up the glass and dumped the last of it into the trash. Then she stomped to her bedroom and slammed the door. Two could play at that game. She paced in her room, wringing her hands. *Let him fix dinner! Let him see how easy it is to care for a house and children when you've never done it before!*

"Oh, that man is so infuriating!" she growled aloud as she paced.

The more she paced, the madder she got. Then her thoughts went to Hailey, sitting on the kitchen floor with shards of glass all around her. Tremors rocked her body as tears came to her eyes. What if something had happened to her? Mia forced the thought from her mind, knowing that she would never be able to live with herself if anything happened to the children on her watch.

For a split second, she thought of going back to New

York, but she pushed the thought quickly from her mind, determined to see this through. She sat down on the edge of the bed, tears streaming down her face, knowing that she couldn't walk away. Even though she had just met them, she had become attached to the children. She loved them, in fact. And she couldn't leave them. Not now. Not ever.

CHAPTER 10

When Caleb opened his eyes the next morning, it was dark. After seeing his child in the pile of glass and then yelling at Mia, he'd been up half the night. Guilt ran through him again, knowing he shouldn't have spoken to her that way. Deep down, he knew it had been an accident and that she would never hurt the child intentionally.

He dressed in a flannel shirt and jeans, and then put a log on the fire in the living room. Then he walked out to the kitchen, lit the stove, fixed the coffeepot, and set it on the stove. For a moment he thought of making breakfast and surprising Mia, but his stomach was too tight. Another wave of guilt threatened to crush him. Never before had he spoken to anyone that way, let alone his wife.

When the coffee was ready, he filled a cup and sat down at the table and took a sip, waiting for Mia to wake. He had thought of going out to the barn and getting an early start on the day, but he just couldn't. Mending fences with Mia was more important.

But then he remembered Mia's reaction to him telling her that there were chickens out back if she wanted to cook one for dinner, and her aversion to killing one. So, he quietly slipped on his boots and his coat and walked out to the henhouse. He found a plump chicken and took it to a stump where an ax leaned against it. After he killed the chicken and drained the blood, he brought it in and set it in the sink as a surprise for Mia. Then he washed his hands, hung up his coat, and then filled two coffee mugs this time, knowing she would wake soon.

Even though he knew it wasn't true, he felt by bringing Mia into his home—married or not—he was being unfaithful to Jessica. The whole time they had been married, he had been faithful to her and had never even thought of looking at another woman, let alone marrying a total stranger. Deep down in his heart, he still wanted to be faithful to Jessica.

"Yah!" A woman's scream brought him from his reverie. "Oh! You scared me to death!"

He looked up, having not seen Mia walk in. "I'm so sorry." He warmed his hands on his coffee mug. "I had no intention of scaring you."

"The road to hell is paved—"

"I know," he said as he let out a sigh. "Please, sit down. I'd like to talk." He motioned toward the second coffee cup.

Mia sat down and added some sugar, stirred her coffee, and then waited.

Seeing her like that in the dark with her blonde hair down around her shoulders stirred emotions within him, sending another fresh wave of guilt through him. "I'm sorry that I spoke to you that way. I've never spoken to anyone like that before in my life."

"And I'm sorry, too. I couldn't sleep last night. Flashes of seeing Hailey sitting in the glass…." Mia shook her head, unable to finish. "I promise that I'll never go into the root cellar again unless someone is there to watch the children for me."

Caleb shook his head. "No. If you don't mind, just tell me what you'd like in the morning and I'll get it for you before I leave, or when I get home." He reached over and squeezed her hand. "Please. It'd make me feel better." Her warmth coursed through his body. When he pulled his hand away, he immediately felt her absence.

Her lips formed a flat line, but she nodded her agreement.

"I have to tell you something." He took a moment to collect his thoughts, and then continued. "I was upset not only because Hailey was in danger, but because of the whole… situation." He let out a deep breath. "And that isn't your fault. I'm sorry if I took it out on you. But I promise to try to do better."

She reached for his hand. "If you need to talk, I'm here."

This time, he didn't pull away. "Thank you."

Mia pulled back and wrapped her hands around her coffee cup. "Are you making more rounds today?"

He shook his head. "No, I have to tend the farm." He took another sip of his coffee and swallowed. "The cow needs milking, the cattle fed, and so on." He looked down into his coffee mug, trying to concentrate on the chores ahead of him and not the perfect curve of her jaw in the early morning sunlight.

Mia smiled. "Being the preacher, I'm surprised that you have a farm."

"Here in Whiskey River, anyone who wants to eat has a farm." He took another sip of his coffee. "As the town preacher, I don't make much. I make the majority of my money from selling cattle and horses. Then in the summer, I plant vegetables and we sell the excess that we don't need." He felt another twinge of guilt as he realized that he'd said "we" and not "I."

Mia bit her lower lip. "Caleb, you're going to have to stop thinking of me as an outsider." She placed her hand over his. "You can talk to me."

He pulled away, knowing that she meant that he could talk to her about Jessica, but he just wasn't ready. "I know. But you don't understand how hard this is for me." He didn't tell her that, in his mind, he was still married to Jessica.

"I know. It's been hard for me, too. But if we start working together, we can accomplish more."

He could do that. Even if he couldn't think of Mia as his wife yet, he could work together with her. Somehow it made it easier and took some of the pressure off. "Yes, you're right. I'd like that. I'll do my best to try."

Mia smiled, and then took another sip of her coffee. "Me, too." Her coffee was getting cold, so she got up to get the coffeepot. "Want more?"

"Yes, please."

She filled his cup for him, then hers. Then she set the pot on the stove and turned toward the sink. "Eeeeeekkkk!" she shrieked, loud enough to wake the dead.

"Land's sake!" he announced, suppressing a smile. "Haven't you ever seen a dead chicken before?"

"Yes, of course I have!" she squealed. "But not without warning."

Caleb laughed despite himself. "After the way you reacted yesterday when I mentioned the chickens, I thought you might have an aversion to killing one for dinner. I thought I'd surprise you."

Her eyes never left the chicken. "And surprise me, you did."

Caleb laughed again. "Sorry. Next time, I'll give you fair warning."

"Yes, that would be nice."

Caleb took another sip of his coffee. He had thought of going out to the barn, but wasn't ready yet. "Come sit down and enjoy your coffee."

"I'm waiting for my heart to start beating again." She held a hand to her chest. Then she sat back down and started to relax.

"So, tell me about Connecticut. I heard it's beautiful up there." He looked into her eyes, seeing her anew.

Mia tilted her head to the side, remembering. "Yes, it is. But the winters are cold and harsh, although probably nothing compared to here, and there's not a lot of work up there for women." She shrugged. "I started taking in sewing before I left, but I didn't make enough to support myself." A smile spread across her lips as she looked into space, enjoying a memory. "I met Ella when I first moved to New York. She helped me get the job at the Breckenridge Saloon where she worked, and we became roommates. It made moving to the city much more bearable."

Caleb smiled. "So, you and Ella have been friends for a while?"

"The best. I don't know what I would have done without her. After she left, I had a hard time making ends meet." Mia let out a deep breath. "If you don't mind, I'd like to visit her sometime and see how she and the babies are doing."

"Of course. Just let me know when you'd like to go and I'll take care of the children." Caleb smiled. "Colton must be over the moon."

Mia laughed. "Colton's probably driving her crazy wanting her to rest. Knowing her, she's probably already up doing everything she did before."

Caleb chuckled. "I wouldn't put it past her. She's just as headstrong as Colton."

Mia nodded her agreement. "Yes, she is."

Mia got up from the table, taking her coffee cup with her. "Would you like some pancakes?" She looked through the cabinets and took out a bowl.

A smile curled his lips. "Where did you learn to make pancakes?"

She shrugged as she started measuring out flour and poured it into the bowl without looking at him. "My mother taught me before she died."

He gave her a slight smile, nodding thoughtfully. He wasn't the only one who had experienced loss. "Mia, would you like to make a trip into town this afternoon? I thought you could get what you need, or anything that the children might need."

Mia refilled his coffee cup as a sly smile lit her lips. "Sounds like fun. I could use a few things like buttons, thread…."

Caleb shrugged as he added sugar to his coffee. "Okay, I surrender." He got up and slipped his spoon in the sink and then whispered over her head. "It'll give the gossips something to talk about."

She laughed. "Sounds like fun."

"Besides, I'd like you to meet some of the townsfolk." He smiled, remembering her shrieking at the dead chicken in the sink. "Well, I'm going to get to work. Let me know when it's ready."

Mia smiled. "I will." Then she turned her attention back to expertly throwing ingredients together.

Caleb set down his coffee and headed toward the back door, took his hat down from a peg by the door, and slipped it on, as well as his coat. "You know, you really are full of surprises."

She chuckled. "You have no idea."

He laughed as he shook his head.

"Wwweee!" Shane yelled as he ran into the room in his underwear, skidding across the hardwood floor in his socks.

"What in the world?" Caleb asked as he placed his hands on his hips. "You can't run around here in your underwear! There's a lady present." He looked over at Mia and blushed.

Mia laughed. "Come along. Let's get you dressed." She took his hand and guided him into the bedroom.

Caleb shook his head as he chuckled. As he walked out to the barn, he laughed aloud at the memory of Mia screaming at the top of her lungs when she saw the chicken in the sink. His new wife really *was* full of surprises.

CHAPTER 11

Mia shook her head as she looked through the dresser drawers in the bedroom. "Now. Let's get some clothes on you, young man." She rummaged through the chest of drawers and pulled out a matching outfit. To her surprise, he didn't try to run away this time, and he didn't give her a hard time.

Mia slipped his shirt over his head.

"I'm sorry… Mia."

She looked in his eyes. "What for? I know running into the kitchen in your underwear wasn't the best choice, but—"

"No… I meant… I'm sorry," he stammered as a worried look appeared in his eyes.

She wrapped her arm around his shoulders. "It's okay. I understand," she said as she stroked the hair away from his face. "Hey! I have an idea. You want to help me make pancakes?"

He moved his head up and down vigorously, smiling. "Let's go."

Hailey stirred and then sat up in the bed. When she opened her eyes and saw Mia and Shane sitting on the bed, she held her arms out to her. Mia scooped her up, and Hailey laid her head on her shoulder. "Not quite awake yet, baby girl?"

She shook her head.

"Hailey, guess what? We're going to make pancakes with Mia! Wanna help?" Shane asked, jumping up and down.

Her face brightened as she bobbed her head, but she shoved her thumb in her mouth and laid her head back on Mia's shoulder.

"Shane, why don't you go play and we can make pancakes in a bit?" She stood while she rubbed Hailey's back. "Is that okay?"

He let out a deep breath. "Will you let me know when you're ready?"

"Of course." Mia smiled as she ruffled his hair. "Thanks, buddy. It won't be long."

He ran into the living room.

Mia carried Hailey into the living room and sat down on the rocking chair while Shane played quietly with his soldiers on the rug. Hailey curled up on her lap, and Mia rocked her back and forth as she stroked her hair.

"Sing," Hailey begged.

"What?"

"Sing a song." She looked up at her with hopeful eyes.

"All right." Mia thought for a moment and then began singing "My Old Kentucky Home, Goodnight," rocking her back and forth. Not having been around children, it was the best she could do.

Mia rocked her for a while, and, soon, Hailey struggled to get down.

"Let's go get you dressed now."

Mia held her hand and led her into the bedroom. Then she helped her into a pretty blue dress and brushed her long, dark blonde hair. She also checked her cuts, and they were healing nicely. She only had two—one on her arm and another on her leg. Relief washed over Mia, grateful that Hailey hadn't been seriously injured, but guilt filled her chest at the thought of what could have happened.

After Hailey scampered off, she turned to Shane, who was still playing on the floor. "Okay, Shane. Would you and Hailey like to help me make pancakes?"

"Yes!" Shane yelled as he ran out the door toward the kitchen.

"Want to help?" Mia asked Hailey.

Hailey nodded, and Mia took her hand and led her into the kitchen.

Mia pulled a chair up to the counter and stood Hailey on it. "Now, hold on and be careful," she instructed.

The little girl held onto the back of the chair. Mia got out a bowl and mixed together the eggs and milk that Caleb had brought up from the root cellar, letting Shane pour in the ingredients. Then she stirred it into the dry ingredients she had mixed together before the children woke.

She let the children stir the batter, but when it came time to pour it onto the hot cast iron skillet, Mia did that. A few minutes later, a few of the pancakes were finished and lying on a plate.

She heard a carriage pull up outside, and then voices coming from the back. Mrs. Jenkins was talking to Caleb. A moment later, Mrs. Jenkins appeared at the back door, holding a small recipe book.

"Hello, Mrs. Jenkins," Mia greeted the older woman, flanked by the children who were a safe distance from the stove. "You're just in time. We're making pancakes. Would you like some?"

"Well, maybe one." Mrs. Jenkins sat down and laid the recipe book on the table. "It looks like you have some great helpers this morning."

Mia smiled. "Yes, they wanted to help."

"We're making pancakes!" Shane announced excitedly.

Mrs. Jenkins laughed. "Yes, I see that. And you seem to be doing a very good job of it, too."

Shane smiled, and then went back to supervising the making of the pancakes.

When the last pancake was on the plate, Mia helped Hailey down from the chair and then carried the plate of pancakes to the table. The children helped, and together, they set the table. She sat the children on their chairs at the table, and then called for Caleb.

"It smells great in here," he praised when he walked in.

The children beamed.

He walked into the bedroom and came out cleaned up and wearing a clean shirt. Then he sat at the head of the table. When everyone was seated and ready, he said a wonderful blessing over the meal, thanking God for the good company of Mrs. Jenkins as well.

As Mia listened, pride welled up in her chest. When Caleb finished, she placed a pancake on each of the children's plates, passed the rest around, and then cut the pancakes up into small pieces for the children.

"Wow! Everything looks wonderful." Caleb stabbed a pancake and slid it onto his plate, and then poured some maple syrup over it. "Thank you, Mia."

Mia smiled proudly. "It wasn't just me. The children helped."

"Really?" he asked, looking at the children.

Shane moved his head up and down vigorously. "I dumped everything in, and Hailey and I took turns stirring."

Caleb took a bite. "Well, you all did a wonderful job. It's delicious." Turing to Mia, he added, "We haven't had pancakes for a while."

Mia smiled proudly, happy that she had done at least one thing right.

"I agree," Mrs. Jenkins added. "You all make a great team."

Mia smiled as she looked over at the children. "Thank you. The children really are great helpers."

"I can't stay long today, and I won't be over tomorrow," Mrs. Jenkins said as she took a bite of her pancake. "I thought I'd go over and lend Ella Hill a hand with the babies."

Mia's eyebrows pulled together in concern. "How is she doing?"

Mrs. Jenkins sighed. "She's doing pretty well."

Mia set down her fork. "Please, give her my best. If there's anything I can do, please let me know."

Mrs. Jenkins smiled. "Well, it looks as if you have your hands full with these little ones."

"I'll watch the children later so you can go over and visit," Caleb volunteered.

Mia smiled her thanks.

Turning to Mrs. Jenkins, Caleb said, "I'll stop by to check on her, too."

"Would you like another?" Mia asked as she reached for the plate of pancakes.

Mrs. Jenkins patted her plump belly. "Oh, heavens no! But that was delicious." Then she turned to the children. "If you keep this up, you'll be able to open your own restaurant and give Harrison Curry some competition!"

Mia chuckled. "Before you start naming our restaurant, I think we have enough on our hands for now."

"Oh!" Shane exclaimed. "That would be fun!"

"But next year, you're going to start school. I think that might be a bit more important," Caleb interjected.

"School? Yuk!" Shane yelled, taking another bite of his pancake.

Mrs. Jenkins laughed. "How do you know? I hear that Mrs. Nash is working wonders with the school." Then she turned to Mia and added, "She's the town schoolteacher."

"Whiskey River has just one teacher?" Mia asked, surprised.

"Here in the country, we're lucky to have her." Mrs. Jenkins shook her head thoughtfully. "There are some towns that don't even have one. They have to go miles to get an education, or be schooled at home by their mothers."

"Then we're lucky, indeed," Mia agreed as she ate the last of her pancake.

Caleb finished his off and was dabbing his lips with a napkin. "Mia, thank you. That was delicious." He slid his chair back and rose to his feet. "I hate to leave good company, but the farm waits for no man. I'll be right outside if you need me."

"We'll have everything under control," Mrs. Jenkins added as she started collecting the dishes. "Don't worry."

After they finished eating, Mia cleaned up the children and they scampered off to play in their bedroom.

"If you need me, let me know," Mia yelled after them. She and Mrs. Jenkins gathered the dishes, but set them aside when she remembered the chicken in the sink.

Mia pinched a leg in her fingers and lifted it, but then set it back down.

Mrs. Jenkins laughed. "Come on. I'll show you what to do."

They spent the morning pulling the feathers from the chicken, and then she washed it well. When the chicken was clean and devoid of feathers, Mrs. Jenkins showed her how to cut it up and gut it, and then taught her the fine points of frying it.

Mia really enjoyed having the camaraderie with Mrs. Jenkins. But after the chicken was frying in the pan, Mrs. Jenkins announced, "Well, I really must go see Ella."

"Please give her my best, and tell her I'll be by to see her soon." Mia turned over a piece of chicken frying in the pan.

Mrs. Jenkins smiled. "I will." She gave her a motherly pat on the arm. "And I'll tell her you'll be by to visit soon."

"Thank you, Mrs. Jenkins."

"Oh! I almost forgot." The older woman slipped into her coat. "I'll leave my recipes here. You can look through them and copy down what you want."

Mia's eyebrows lifted in concern. "You won't be needing them before then?"

Mrs. Jenkins smiled. "Not right now. You can give them back to me when you're finished."

"I will. Thanks, again. And if you ever need me, Mrs. Jenkins, just let me know." She dried her hands and gave her a quick hug. "So, I'll see you when I see you?"

"If not anything else, I'll see you Sunday." Mrs. Jenkins paused, biting her lower lip. "I hate to tell you this, but the preacher's wife is responsible for organizing the after-service potluck dinner."

"What?" Mia asked, panic appearing in her eyes.

Mrs. Jenkins smiled. "Now, don't you worry. Each week, the ladies bring their specialties and then we have a dance and play games with the children. We do this every week. The only thing that the preacher's wife is expected to do is to organize; tell everyone where to put everything. In the spring and summer, the men of the church bring the tables outside, and we hold it there. But in the winter when it's cold, we set everything up in the recreation hall." She tied the scarf around her neck. "But don't worry. I can help until you get the hang of it."

Mia smiled as she gave her arm a gentle squeeze.

"Thank you. I'll never be able to thank you enough."

Mrs. Jenkins pulled her in for a hug. "It's my pleasure." She shrugged. "We all could use a little help when we're starting out. Who knows? One day, you'll be the one helping someone else to learn the ropes. In the meantime, if you need anything, just let me know." Then she looked down at the chicken frying on the stove. "Well, I have to go, and it looks as if you have some chicken to fry."

"Please forgive me if I don't show you out."

She gave her arm a motherly pat. "Don't worry. I know the way."

Mia laughed. "Thanks, again. I'll bring you some chicken on Sunday."

"Be careful what you offer," Mrs. Jenkins teased.

Mia chuckled and watched as Mrs. Jenkins walked out the back door. Mia heard her say a muffled goodbye to Caleb, and a few minutes later, her carriage pulled away.

Mia turned a piece of chicken over in the pan. It was funny. She had wanted a fairy godmother as a child, and she got one as an adult. Mrs. Jenkins was amazing. Mia wondered what her story was, where her husband was, or if he had died. She figured she'd find out eventually. It seemed that now the older woman loved spending her time helping others, especially making it a mission to help out new wives and mothers.

Mia finished frying the last of the chicken, and then covered it over with a dish towel and set it on the counter until dinner. She checked on the children, and Shane waved at her from the floor where he and Hailey were playing. Mia waved back, happy with the change in Shane. She knew they had a long way to go, but she was pleased that at least the children were accepting her into the family. She had a feeling it would take a while for Caleb… if he ever accepted her at all.

After cleaning the kitchen until it sparkled, she sat down to look through Mrs. Jenkins's recipes. There were cookie recipes of all kinds, cakes, meals, a biscuit recipe, and then she came to what she had been looking for… a bread recipe. It was a simple recipe, similar to the one that her mother used when she was a child. Mia looked through the drawer of the writing desk in the living room and found some parchment paper and a writing quill and ink.

Careful not to smudge the recipe, she copied it down and then let the paper dry. As she waited, she started gathering the ingredients. Before long, she kneaded the dough, formed it into a loaf in a bread pan, and spread some oil across the top. Then she set it in a warm spot beside the stove to rise while she cleaned the kitchen. When it was ready, she popped the loaf pan into the oven. Soon, the aroma of freshly baking bread filled the house. She went back to copying down recipes.

Before she knew it, it was time for lunch. So, she made some ham sandwiches, leaving the chicken for dinner. Then she poured some fresh milk for the children and lemonade for her and Caleb. She opened the back door and stepped out onto the porch, holding the door open. "Caleb! Time for lunch!"

He walked out of the barn, wiping his hands on a hand towel as his muscles flexed under his shirt. "Be right there."

She went inside and into the children's bedroom. "Hungry?"

"Yes!" Shane yelled as he ran out of the bedroom and into the kitchen.

Hailey looked up at her from the floor.

"Ready for lunch, baby girl?" Mia asked, holding her hand out to her.

A smile spread across Hailey's face, and then she got up and ran to her. Mia scooped her up in her arms, and she laid her head on her shoulder and gave her a hug. Then she rose up and wrapped her arms around Mia's neck.

"That's a good girl," Mia cooed as she carried her to the kitchen.

Caleb watched her, expressionless, as she walked into the room carrying his child.

She set Hailey down on a chair, and then Mia set the loaf of bread and some fried country ham on the table. When Mia sat down, Hailey hopped out of her chair, ran over to Mia, and crawled onto her lap.

Caleb watched as Mia slid Hailey's plate over and started feeding her.

"You need to eat." Mia looked up at him and smiled.

Caleb picked up his sandwich and took a bite.

"So, how's it going out there?" Mia asked, inclining her head toward the barn.

"It's going well. One of the cows just calved. I was just finishing up when you called me."

Mia looked up from feeding Hailey with alarm in her eyes. "Did everything go okay?"

"Yes, both mother and baby are doing just fine."

"Glad to hear it." Mia gave Hailey another slice of bread. "You know, I could help out on the farm, too, if you like."

"Thanks. But, for now, I think you have enough to worry about."

Mia shrugged. "I could at least gather the eggs before the children wake."

"I appreciate the sentiment." Caleb downed his glass of lemonade. "But if you don't mind, why don't you concentrate on the children and the house? When you get into a routine, then we can talk about it."

"You know, I'm not used to being told what to do or to have to ask permission."

Caleb set down his glass of lemonade. "I can respect that. By the way, it was just a request."

Mia raised her chin. "Okay. I'll think about it."

Caleb laughed. "I can't imagine you out there helping with the calving."

"No, I draw the line there." Mia chuckled. "I'll leave the calving up to you."

"You drive a hard bargain," he teased.

They talked and laughed throughout the meal. *A welcome change,* Mia thought.

After lunch, Caleb pushed his chair back and placed a hand on his stomach. "That was delicious. Would you still like to go into town?"

"Yes, I would." She wiped her hands on a cloth napkin.

"Okay. Let me clean up and we can go." Caleb looked around at the dirty dishes from lunch. "Would you like some help cleaning up?"

Mia shook her head. "No, I'll clean everything up while you get ready." A sly smile spread across her face. "I don't want to take any husband of mine into town looking like he just came out of a barn."

Caleb's face fell as he walked over and set his dirty dishes in the sink.

Mia caught his hand. "Caleb, it was only a joke."

"I'm going outside to wash off at the outside pump." He rose from his seat. "I'll be back inside in a bit."

"Caleb….," Mia called after him as he walked purposefully out the back door. Would she and Caleb ever make a connection? "Children, let's get you ready."

Shane's eyes perked up, although he was trying not to show interest. "Where are we going?"

Mia shrugged. "Into town… that is, if you behave this time."

"Yippee!" he yelled as he jumped from his seat and ran from the table into the bedroom.

"And I'm picking out your clothes this time!" Mia yelled after him, turning her attention to stacking the dishes and then put the water on to heat.

After the dishes were cleaned and put away, she went to her bedroom and dressed in a light blue dress and matching hat, then slipped on her tan shoes and laced them up over her ankles. Then she grabbed her coat and walked out into the living room and laid it over the back of the sofa.

Caleb walked out, cleaned up and dressed in a crisp white shirt, gray vest, and matching gray slacks. Shane was dressed in clean jeans and a blue plaid shirt, and Hailey in a floral brown dress, with lace-up children's shoes.

"Well! Don't you look nice!" Mia took the children's coats off the hook.

Caleb crossed the room and took Shane's coat from her. "Not bad for a farmer, huh?"

Mia's heart sank. "Caleb, I didn't mean—"

"Forget it." He waved his hand dismissively and then turned to his son. "Shane, let's put on your coat. It's still cold outside."

"Come here, baby girl." Hailey walked over to her and slipped her coat on. "Now, that's better." Once the children were ready, Mia reached for her coat, but Caleb took it out of her hands.

"Please. Allow me." Caleb held the coat up for her— the perfect gentleman—and she slid her arms in. His hands lingered on her shoulders a bit longer than necessary, causing her breath to catch.

He must have come to his senses because he removed his hands abruptly. "Ready to go?"

"Yes," she replied, willing her heart to slow.

"Stay inside with the children and I'll be right back with the buckboard."

Before she could answer, he walked out the door and closed it tightly behind him. Would he ever come to think of her as anything other than a live-in maid and babysitter? She hoped that one day he would, but now she steeled her heart to him. She would be happy to give her love to the children. After all, it was little in exchange for a roof over her head and food in her stomach. Any more than that was too much to ask.

"Ready?" she asked the children, pushing the thought aside.

"Yes!" Shane yelped, jumping up and down.

"Yes, yes!" Hailey repeated, imitating her brother.

Just then, Caleb pulled the buckboard up to the front of the house with the team.

"Time to go," Mia announced to the children, finding herself caught up in their excitement. As soon as she opened the door, Shane ran out and jumped off the porch and into the back of the buckboard in just a few bounces. "Careful, now." She smiled as she reached for Hailey's hand. "Ready?"

She was about to walk down the steps when Caleb stepped down out of the buckboard. Then he stepped to the side of the porch and held up his hand. "My lady."

She smiled and took his hand as a twinge of guilt grabbed her chest. "Caleb, I meant nothing by the comment. I was only joking."

"It's all right. Think nothing of it." Caleb held her hand, causing a thrill to run through her.

At the bottom of the steps, he scooped his daughter up into his arms and nuzzled her neck as she giggled. "Ready, baby girl?"

Hailey bobbed her head vigorously.

Caleb turned to Mia. "Ready?"

"As ready as I'll ever be." She held out her hand and he helped her up into the buckboard and then handed Hailey up to her. She set the little girl down on the wooden bench seat between them.

Snow flurries started falling in white puffs from the heavens as Caleb climbed up into the buckboard on the other side. "We should go."

Mia looked around nervously. "Do you think we should? It might get worse."

Caleb smiled. "We should be fine. It will probably snow and then be done with it."

Mia sighed, hoping he was right.

"Shane, hand me the quilt and come sit between us." Caleb looked over the seat at his son. Shane handed him the quilt. Mia picked up Hailey and set her on her lap and Shane sat between them. Then Mia stretched out the quilt over them and they were on their way.

But as the horses plodded along, the snow began falling harder, until they couldn't see anything but white. Mia was barely able to make out the trees around them. She glanced up at Caleb and a crease formed between his eyes. He looked over at her, concern lighting his eyes, but said nothing.

"Why don't we sing a song?" Mia asked the children, hoping to distract them.

"Yes!" Shane perked up from under the quilt. "How about 'Yankee Doodle'?"

Mia smiled. "Sounds good."

They started singing one song after the other as they made their way through the blinding snowfall. Mia couldn't sing well, but she sang every song she knew with the children to keep them distracted. Just when she was about to run out of songs, tall wooden buildings came into view.

"We're here," Caleb announced casually, but Mia heard the relief in his voice. "Welcome to Whiskey River."

Mia breathed a sigh of relief, glad that the children would be safe.

Caleb pulled past the livery stable and a young man waved to them as they passed. Then, Caleb stopped the buckboard in front of the hotel and restaurant. "Mia, take the children inside to warm up. Go ahead and get something to drink while I take care of the team." Caleb wrapped the reins around the front pole, pulled the brake, and stepped down out of the buckboard in a few short strides. He was at her side, reaching for his daughter, quicker than Mia would have thought possible. Shane hopped down from the other side as Caleb offered her his hand to help her down.

"Yes, of course." Mia stepped down from the buckboard, taking his hand. "What would you like me to order you?"

"Coffee, please." He pulled the collar of his coat up over his neck and helped her up the stairs when the door opened abruptly, causing her to take a step back.

"Oh! I'm so very sorry, Mrs. Henley. I didn't mean to startle you," a man said, opening the door wide. "I just saw you outside and I thought I'd come help."

"Thank you, Harrison. Could you see them in while I take the team to the livery stable?" Caleb was already walking around the buckboard.

"Sure thing," Harrison said. "I'll take care of them."

"Thank you." Caleb climbed into the buckboard and released the brake. "Mia, I'll be right back."

Her lips curled into a smile as she watched him drive the

team away.

Harrison held out his hand. "The name's Harrison Curry. I'm the owner of this fine establishment." He opened the door and stood back. "Come on in."

Mia smiled. "It's a pleasure to meet you." She let Harrison help her and the children into the restaurant. Mia took off the children's coats. "When will it stop snowing?"

Harrison shrugged. "We won't be completely out of the woods until after Easter, although one time it did snow on Easter Sunday. Kind of messed up the children's egg hunt that year."

Mia smiled. "I'd bet it did."

Harrison helped her off with her coat. "But the preacher and his wife… er… Jessica… saved it, though. They had the egg hunt in the recreation hall after church." He looked at her sheepishly.

Mia smiled. "I don't mind you mentioning Jessica at all. It's okay." She patted Shane's back. "I'm glad they saved the day."

Caleb walked in and a flurry of snow blew in as he hurried to push the door closed. "What was that?" he asked as he held her chair.

Harrison smiled. "I was just telling your wife here how you and Jessica saved Easter that year when it snowed."

Caleb returned the smile. "Yes, that was Jessica's idea. She had a solution for everything."

Mia shook out her napkin and slid it across her lap as Caleb took his seat.

"Well, then." Harrison broke the awkward silence.

"Millie will be over in a bit. I'll let her know you're here."

"We're just ordering drinks. We already ate at home."

Harrison smiled. "In that case, what can I get you?"

"Coffee for me and hot chocolate for the children." He looked over at Mia. "And for you?"

She smiled, appreciating that he had asked her and didn't just order for her. "Coffee, too, please."

A broad smile spread across Harrison's face. "Okay, then. I'll let Millie know."

Caleb looked over at Mia with an appreciative smile and gave her hand a gentle squeeze.

Although he didn't say anything, his gesture spoke volumes. He seemed grateful that she hadn't shied away from mentioning Jessica. And in a way, she wished she had known Jessica. Something told Mia that she would have liked her.

CHAPTER 12

"After we finish, we'll go over to the general store." Caleb stirred sugar into his coffee.

"Will we have time?" Mia asked as concern filled her face. "I mean, the snow's really coming down out there. Shouldn't we go back home?"

Caleb took a sip of his coffee and swallowed. "No. It's not safe to leave now. We'll have to wait and see if it lets up enough for us to go back home."

Mia's eyes opened wide. "What will we do if we can't?"

Caleb gave her a slight smile. "Then we'll have to spend the night."

"There you go." Millie poured coffee into Mia's cup to freshen it and then looked over at Caleb. "Some for you, too?"

Caleb put down his cup. "Yes, please."

Millie refilled Caleb's cup and then did a double take when she saw Mia's face grow pale. "Mrs. Henley, are you all right? You look as if you've seen a ghost."

Mia cleared her throat and then took a sip of her coffee. "No, no. Not at all." Mia's voice cracked and then she took another sip.

"May I get you something else?" Millie waited, concerned as she held the pot of coffee.

"No, thank you," Mia replied, having recovered herself. "We're heading over to the general store in a bit."

A broad smile spread across Millie's face.

"Yeah!" Shane and Hailey yelled in unison. "Can we go?"

Caleb couldn't help but laugh, pleased by their reaction. It was a big deal for the children to go to the general store. "Okay, children. But just one candy stick each. No exception. Any more than that will rot your teeth."

"Yippee!" Shane jumped down and headed toward the front to look out the window.

"Don't go outside!" Mia called after them. "Wait there for us."

Millie chuckled. "Go ahead and go. I'll clean this up and you can have some more coffee and hot cocoa when you return." She leaned in and whispered, "No extra charge."

Caleb smiled. "Thanks, Millie. That's very nice of you." He reached into his pocket and pulled out his wallet. "How much do I owe you?"

Millie shrugged. "We'll settle up when you come back."

"Thanks, Millie. We won't be long." Caleb finished the last of his coffee, stood and then held Mia's chair for her.

Mia folded her napkin and then rose to her feet.

"Shall we?" Caleb helped her on with her coat and then

offered her his arm. Mia slid her arm in his, causing his heart to stir.

"You two look so cute together. Have fun!" Millie walked to the back of the restaurant to tend to another table.

"What did you mean by 'we might have to spend the night?'" Mia asked, her voice low, as she let Caleb guide her to the front.

Harrison helped Shane on with his coat as Caleb put Hailey's on her. "There you go, little mister," Harrison announced after he buttoned it up for him. "You don't want to go outside in this weather without bundling up first. It's turned into a real howler out there." Then he turned to Caleb. "We have some extra rooms. Would you like me to hold one for you?"

"Make it t—" Mia started.

"Yes, please," Caleb cut her off. After all, they were man and wife in the eyes of the town. It would look strange for them to sleep in separate rooms, and he didn't want to give the town gossips any more fat to chew. "Just in case." He looked down at Mia.

She extended her hand to Harrison. "Thank you, Mr. Curry. We truly appreciate it."

"Call me Harrison." Turning to Caleb, he added, "And don't worry about the cost of the room. It's the least I can do."

Caleb slid on his coat and hat, and then scooped his daughter up into his arms. "Much obliged, but that won't be necessary."

"No, I insist." He gave a quick glance at Mia and then

back at Caleb. "But we can talk about it later. I think it may get too bad out there even to go to the general store if you wait much longer."

Caleb clasped a hand on his shoulder. "Thanks, Harrison. We'll be back in a while."

Harrison smiled. "Have fun." Harrison inclined his head toward Mia. "Ma'am."

Mia smiled and then took Shane's hand. "Now, don't let go." Shane bobbed his head up and down vigorously, his eyes wide. Taking Caleb's arm, she let him guide her out into the swirling puffs. Neither said a word as they made their way through the blinding snow to the store.

Mia huddled close to him, nestling her face into his coat to protect herself from the snow. Within minutes, they stepped onto the covered wooden porch on the other side of the street. "Don't worry. I'll be a gentleman if we have to stay the night." Before she could answer, he opened the door to the general store as the bell on the door resonated throughout the room. Although the children would be with them, too, he thought it was necessary that he clarify it for her… and for himself.

"I know," she replied as she led Shane into the store and Caleb followed.

For a moment, Caleb wondered what she meant by that, but quickly brushed the thought aside when Mr. and Mrs. Carson stepped out from the back room.

"Land's sake! What are you two doing out in this weather?" Mrs. Carson asked, looking Mia up and down, a broad smile spreading across her face. "Well, as I live and breathe! Reverend Henley and his new bride! Come on in! I'm surprised you're out on a day like today."

Caleb set Hailey on her feet and she scampered over to Mia. "Believe it or not, it just started snowing when we left the house."

Mr. Carson crossed the room and extended his hand to Caleb. "I'm glad you all made it in one piece."

Caleb placed his hand on the small of Mia's back. "Mr. and Mrs. Carson, may I introduce my new bride, Mia. Mia, this is Mr. and Mrs. Carson."

"Mrs. Henley," Mrs. Carson extended her hand. "It is truly a pleasure."

Mia smiled warmly. "The pleasure is mine."

"Say, I'm hosting an Easter Tea for the ladies of the town the day before Easter, Holy Saturday. Would you like to come?" Mrs. Carson gave her shoulder a gentle nudge. "Anyone who's anyone will be there."

"Why yes, of course," Mia replied. "I'm looking forward to getting to know the ladies of the town. Count me in. Just let me know where and when and I'll be there."

"Wonderful!" Mrs. Carson smiled as if was the best news she had heard all day. "All of the women will be wearing their spring finery."

"Reverend, you and I and the rest of the men will have to find a way to stay far away from the clucking hens that day," Mr. Carson teased.

Caleb laughed. "You can come over to the house. I'll be home with the children while Mia's away."

"I may just have to take you up on that. Now, what can

we do for you on this fine day?" Mr. Carson gestured toward the windows where the wind was howling and snow was flying.

Everyone laughed.

"We're just here for a few things," Caleb answered and then asked Mia, "What would you like?"

"Well, I'd love some fabric...."

Mrs. Carson held up her hands. "Say no more. We have the best selection in Whiskey River. And we just got in our spring collection."

"Yes, just in time for the last blizzard of the year." Turning toward Caleb, he asked, "Would it be all right if the children have some candy?"

"There you go! Giving away all the candy again," Mrs. Carson yelled from across the room.

"Oh, never mind her." Mr. Carson waved his hand dismissively in the direction of his wife.

"Please, Pa?" Shane asked jumping up and down.

Across the room, Hailey struggled to get down out of Mia's arms and ran across the room at the mention of candy. "Pwease?" she asked, jumping up and down, imitating her brother.

Caleb laughed. "Yes, of course." Then he yelled after them as they followed Mr. Carson to the candy counter. "But remember what I said: only one each."

"Yes, Pa." Shane took Hailey's hand. "Come on, Hailey! Want some candy?"

She bobbed her head vigorously, and then let her brother lead her over to the candy counter.

"I'll be right over here," Caleb called after them and then walked over to the sacks of flour, sugar, and other household items.

As Caleb gathered the items he knew they needed, he stole glances at Mia as she looked through the fabric with Mrs. Carson. She really seemed to be enjoying herself. It amazed him that she had ever been a dancehall girl. For the short amount of time that she had been there, she was a natural with sewing and was adapting to farm life, and never appeared to be bored. It was as if she had been born to be a preacher's wife.

Caleb called out to her, "Don't worry about the price." He'd had a good year on the farm. And if it came to it, he could sell off some cattle. Both he and the children needed clothes, so the fabric really wasn't a luxury.

Mia smiled at him, causing his heart to flutter. Could he ever truly come to think of Mia as his wife? He'd married her to take care of the children and the house. Nothing more. And she had agreed to that. He quickly pushed all other thoughts aside and turned his attention back to what he had come for. He had loved once… and that was enough for a lifetime.

He picked up a sack of flour, carried it to the front counter, and set it on the floor. As he was going back for the sugar, Mia had already picked out several fabrics and it appeared that she was trying to choose between them.

"Get what you want," he told her, as Mrs. Carson started measuring off fabric. He couldn't help but get caught up in Mia's excitement as she picked out matching buttons and thread. It was evident how much she loved sewing.

And Mia seemed to get along with everyone… even Mrs. Carson. The woman came off as being too brash with many of the other women in town, but Mia looked as though she enjoyed spending time with her. Caleb was glad. Although many people were cordial to Mrs. Carson, she didn't have many true friends in town. He was glad that Mia could look past the woman's demeanor and see the good in her.

When Caleb finished, he crossed the room to Mia, hating himself for interrupting her fun. "Are you about ready, or do you need some more time?"

Mia smiled happily. "No, we're just finishing up. I'll be ready in just a minute."

"I'll meet you up front."

Her eyes sparkled as a broad grin spread across her face, causing his breath to catch.

"Ready?" Mia asked softly behind him, causing him to jump, bringing him from his reverie. "I'm so sorry. I didn't mean to startle you."

Caleb looked down at her and smiled. "No, it's okay. Did you get what you need?"

Mia laughed, sounding like bells. "That and then some. I think I'll have enough fabric and yarn to keep me busy for a while." She smiled sheepishly. "I hope you don't mind, but in my spare time, I thought I'd make an afghan."

Caleb's smile faded. "We have plenty of afghans and doilies." Jessica had crocheted doilies that Mia had put away in a drawer. Jessica had also made a few afghans. After her death, Caleb had put them away, unable to look at them every day. They reminded him too much of her.

Mia frowned. "I'll put it back, then."

Realizing what he had done, he caught her hand. "No, I'm sorry. Go ahead and get them. It's just—"

"No need to explain," Mia cut him off. "I can get the yarn later. Heaven knows I'll have plenty to do with the fabric."

Before Caleb could say more, she put back the colored skeins of yarn and then walked to the front of the store without a second look at him.

Letting out a deep breath, Caleb walked to the counter where Mr. Carson was standing with the children. "How much do I owe you?"

"Come along, children," Mia interjected. "Let's wait in the front of the store." Obviously, she didn't want to discuss finances in front of the children. Then she turned to Mrs. Carson. "It certainly was a pleasure to meet you."

"I look forward to seeing you at the Easter Tea," Mrs. Carson replied, smiling.

Mia took the children by the hand and returned her smile. "So am I. I'll see you then… if I don't see you before."

Both women giggled in camaraderie.

As Mia walked with the children to the front of the store, Shane told her all about the candy and showed her what was left of his candy stick.

"She's a kind woman," Mrs. Carson whispered to Caleb, wrapping the fabric in clean brown paper. "I like her very much."

Caleb smiled. "Thank you, Mrs. Carson. She has been

a blessing."

Mrs. Carson gave him a sympathetic nod. "I'm so glad."

Mr. Carson frowned at his wife.

It was that look, the stifling look of sympathy that everyone seemed to bestow upon him after Jessica's death, that had made losing her even harder. It had been hard enough without the continual reminder and sympathy, although everyone meant well.

"Thank you, Mrs. Carson." He tipped his hat to her. "But we really must go before we get snowed in here."

Mrs. Carson gave him a flat-lipped smile. "Yes, of course. Thank you so much, Reverend. If you need anything else, be sure to let me know." Then a broad smile spread across her face. "And be sure to bring your new wife with you. I so enjoyed meeting her."

Caleb laughed. "If I bring back my new wife, I might owe you a fortune."

Mr. Carson laughed. "Ain't that the truth!"

Caleb and Mr. Cason laugh conspiratorially.

"Thank you, Mr. Carson, for the candy." He looked at the front of the store toward his children talking to Mia as they watched the snow falling outside.

Mia looked over at Mr. Carson and smiled. "You're going to spoil them."

"Nonsense!" Mr. Carson replied. "I enjoy children." Caleb imagined a big part of it was because they never had any children of their own, so he spoiled the children of the town instead. In fact, he had become an adopted uncle, of sorts, to all the children in Whiskey River. "Be careful out there."

"We will." Caleb looked down at everything he had purchased. "Can you hold the flour and sugar for me until it stops snowing? I don't want it to get wet."

"Sure thing," Mr. Carson interjected before Mrs. Carson could object. "It'll be here when you're ready."

Caleb smiled his thanks. "I'll be right over at the hotel if you need me."

After they said their last goodbyes, Caleb walked over to Mia and placed his hand on the small of her back. "Ready?"

Mia nodded, the incident with the yarn obviously forgotten. "Bundle up, children. I don't want you to catch winter fever out there."

Caleb buttoned Hailey's coat and swung her up into his arms. "Ready to go, baby girl?"

She shook her head and Mr. Carson laughed.

"She can always stay here with us!" Mr. Carson teased as his wife slapped him playfully on his arm.

"Not on your life." To Caleb's surprise, Mia had answered before he could.

Caleb laughed. "Have a good day, and thanks again."

Mr. Carson held up a hand. "Be careful out there."

Caleb gave them one last wave over his shoulder. A huge gust of wind and snow flew in the door when he opened it. Hailey snuggled her face onto his shoulder, and he pulled Mia to his side as she held Shane's hand.

When they were nearly there, Harrison opened the door for them and pulled it closed quickly after they were safely inside. "Boy! You sure picked a fine day to come to town."

"I'd say." Caleb brushed the snow off his coat and then

slipped Shane's coat off him, while Mia took Hailey's off her. "But it looks as if we're not going anywhere until this lets up."

"Say no more." Harrison looked through some keys hanging on a peg board and pulled one off and handed it to Caleb. "Here you go. I saved our best room for you. And like I said, don't worry about the cost. It's the least I could do for all you have done for this town."

Caleb hated to do it, but he had learned long ago that rejecting someone's generosity could be insulting. "Thank you, Harrison. I won't forget this. Me and the missus could make it, but I don't want to chance it with the children."

"No need," Harrison interjected. "We have plenty of rooms available." He looked outside. "And I don't think anyone else is going to brave the weather today."

Caleb shook his head, remembering the Christmas blizzard. He had just lost Jessica and the harsh winter reflected his mood at the time. He never wanted to go through that again. "No, I have a feeling this should be the last one for the year. I hope so, at least."

"You and me both," Harrison agreed, stepping out from behind the desk. "Follow me and I'll show you to your room. You can freshen up and come down for dinner when you're ready."

Caleb offered him his hand. "Thanks for everything, Harrison."

Harrison gave him a hearty handshake. "It's my pleasure. And if there's anything you need tonight, just let me or Millie know."

"We will." Hailey rubbed her eyes and held her arms up to Caleb. He scooped her up and she laid her head on his shoulder.

"You mean we're staying in the hotel tonight?" Shane's eyes were wide.

Caleb chuckled, enjoying his son's excitement. "Yes, we are."

"Yippee!" Shane yelled as he ran up the stairs ahead of Harrison.

"Whoa! Slow down there, son." Harrison stopped him. "How do you know where to go if you pass me?"

"Shane, get back here." Caleb held out his hand for his son. "Stay with me while we're in a public place. You know better than that."

"Yes, Pa." Shane walked back to his father and held his hand, staying by his side.

Harrison chuckled. "It's okay. He's just excited." Then he said to Shane, "You want to see your room?"

"Yes, sir!"

Harrison stopped at a door and opened it with the key. "Well, here you go."

"Yeah!" Shane cheered as he ran inside, but didn't jump on the bed, much to his father's relief.

Harrison handed Caleb the key. "Again, if you need anything at all, just let me know."

"I will." Caleb held out his hand. "And thanks again."

"Any time," Harrison replied. Then he tipped his hat to Mia. "Ma'am."

She gave him a nervous smile, but he appeared not to notice.

Caleb wrapped his arm around her waist and whispered

over her head so no one could hear. "Don't worry. You're safe with me."

She raised her chin, and then walked into the room.

Caleb wondered what she was suddenly upset about but shrugged it off. Hailey had already fallen asleep on his shoulder, so he carried her inside. Mia pulled back the covers on the double bed and Caleb laid his daughter down. She hadn't had her afternoon nap, so she immediately curled up on her side, never opening her eyes.

Seeing Mia's discomfort, Caleb sat down on the edge of the bed. "Don't worry. I'll sleep in the chair. You and the children can have the bed."

Mia forced a smile. "Don't be silly. We can all share the bed and put the children between us."

Caleb raised an eyebrow. "Are you sure about that?"

Mia shrugged. "Sure. Why not? I mean, I don't have anything to worry about anyway, right?"

Caleb let out an exasperated breath. "Mia, I didn't mean—"

"I'm sorry. I shouldn't have said that. You were only being a gentleman." She looked around the room and folded her arms around her waist, taking it all in. "After all, we have an agreement and I intend to live up to my end of it."

"Mia, I'm sorry."

Shane stood in the middle of the room, looking back and forth between them.

"This is not a conversation we should be having now." Mia looked outside. "I'm sorry. I shouldn't have reacted that way."

Caleb looked at her apologetically. He was about to say that he couldn't love her in that way but decided to say nothing at all. "Are you okay?"

"I'm fine." Mia wrapped her arms around herself.

"Shane, would you like to go out and build a snowman?"

His eyes lit up. "Really?"

Mia smiled at his enthusiasm.

"Really. There's no reason why we can't enjoy the snow." Then he looked over at Mia. "Would you mind?"

Mia shook her head. "No, I don't mind at all. You both go ahead. I'll stay in here with Hailey."

Caleb's eyebrows rose. "Are you sure you don't mind?"

Mia smiled. "No, not at all. I'm a bit tired myself. Besides, us ladies could use some alone time. You boys go on."

"Well, if you insist...."

"Go." She helped Shane on with his coat and buttoned it up while Caleb did the same.

"We won't be long." He opened the door and Shane ran out. "Hey! Wait for me!"

Mia laughed as he closed the door behind him.

Caleb walked to the stairs and Shane was already down the long, wooden staircase and headed toward the door. "Shane! Stop right there." He did as his father said and waited by the front door. "I told you to stay with me. Don't ever run outside in the street. You could get run over by a wagon or a horse."

"Yes, Pa," he replied, his voice repentant for all of about two seconds. Then he grabbed his father's hand and started pulling him toward the door. "Come on, Pa! Let's go play!"

Caleb let Shane pull him out the door, and then Caleb led them to an open field behind the hotel. It was still snowing heavily, but not as badly as it had been. "So, what would you like to do first?" Caleb asked when a snowball hit him on the side of the head.

Shane ran away, laughing.

"Oh, so that's how it's going to be," Caleb teased. But by the time he made a snowball, Shane had already hit him with another.

Then an all-out snowball fight ensued until Caleb finally held up his hands. "Okay! I surrender." He stood up and brushed the snow off his clothes. By the time their snowball fight came to an end, Shane had snow in his hair and all over his coat. "You look like a snowman. Let's go inside."

"No, Pa," Shane begged. "Let's stay out a little longer."

Caleb smiled. "You want to build a snowman?"

Shane's eyes grew wide. "Sure." He looked around at the snow. "How?"

"We build it from the ground up, one step at a time," Caleb replied. "First, you start at the base...." As he proceeded to teach his son the fine points of building a snowman, he realized that relationships were like that, too. But snowmen were infinitely easier to build.

"Well, if that isn't the best snowman I ever saw." Caleb looked over to see Shane, who was now shivering.

"You m... m... mean it, Pa?"

Caleb scooped him up into his arms and set him on his shoulders. "I surely do. But now it's time to get you inside before you freeze to death."

"I'm… m… n… n… not… cold."

"Okay, but *I* am." Caleb hurried toward the restaurant as quickly as he could. "I think we need to take Millie up on her special hot cocoa. What do you think?"

"Yes!" Shane yelled. "You know what, Pa?"

"No, what?"

Shane wrapped his arms around his father's forehead in the falling snow. "You're the best pa in the world."

Hearing that from his son made everything worthwhile.

"Looks like we have some cold fellas here," Harrison observed as they walked in.

"Just a bit. We were wondering if Millie still has some of that good hot chocolate." Caleb rubbed Shane's arms over his coat and stood him by the fireplace to warm him up.

A broad smile spread across Harrison's face. "I'm sure she does. I'll ask her to get you some.

"And coffee for me, please."

Harrison waved to him over his head. "You got it."

Caleb led his son over to a table. "Feel better? I shouldn't have kept you out there so long."

"No, P… Pa." Shane shivered as his father slipped off his coat and rubbed his arms. "It was f… fun."

"I heard I had a request for my famous hot chocolate." Millie placed a cup of hot cocoa and a cup of coffee on the table. "You both need to be careful out there. Winter's nowhere near over yet."

Caleb smiled. "We got the idea."

She laughed. "Well, you can take these up to your room,

if you like. Jasmine will collect them in the morning when she cleans the room."

"Thanks, Millie."

She left them with their beverages to help a couple that had just walked in.

Caleb held the cup out for his son. "Here. Drink this. It'll warm you up."

Shane did as his father asked and within minutes, his shivering stopped.

"Now, that's better." Outside, the snow was still falling, but the sun was going down. "Hungry?"

A yawn escaped Shane's lips. "Uh huh."

Since he hadn't had his nap, Caleb knew that he would be wanting to lay down soon. He motioned Millie over again.

"What can I do for you, Reverend?" Millie asked, wiping her hands on her apron.

"Could we have a few sandwiches brought up to the room? I have a feeling that Mia and Hailey may be hungry, too." Shane's eyes were about to close, but he jerked himself awake and took another sip of his hot chocolate.

"Sure, Reverend. What would you like?"

"Surprise us."

"You got it."

"Thanks, Millie." After Millie walked away, Caleb scooped his son up into his arms. "Come on, little man. Time for bed."

"No, let's go back outside and build another snowman." He laid his head on his father's shoulder.

Caleb smiled. "The sun's almost going down. We'll have

to do it again some other time."

When he opened the door to their room, Mia was lying beside Hailey on the bed, fully clothed, and Hailey was curled up, facing her, both bathed in the faint rays of moonlight, already streaming in through the window.

"Here you go, little man," Caleb whispered, not wanting to wake Mia or Hailey. He slipped off Shane's shoes and then laid him down beside his sister and covered him up. Immediately, Shane curled up next to her and went right to sleep.

There was a soft knock on the door and Caleb opened it a crack to see Millie standing on the other side, holding a tray filled with sandwiches, coffee, and hot chocolate, looking down discreetly.

"Thank you, Millie," Caleb whispered, taking the tray through the door. "Have a good night."

Millie looked up and smiled. "You, too, Reverend Henley."

He closed the door, but when he turned around, Mia was sitting up.

"Is everything all right?" Mia asked, concern in her eyes. She looked down at the children and saw they were fine. "I can't believe I fell asleep like that."

"I can. You were tired." Caleb smiled as he set the tray on a small table with two chairs pushed up to it. "Are you hungry?"

"Maybe a little," she whispered.

"Come here and have a sandwich." He stirred two teaspoons of sugar into his coffee. Then he fixed Mia's the way she liked it and set it on the table for her.

Mia rose from the bed and sat down in the other chair at the small table. "Did you and Shane have fun?"

Caleb took a sandwich off the tray. "We built the best snowman you ever saw." He took a bite of his chicken sandwich and swallowed. "I hope it's still there by morning."

"I hope it is, too," Mia whispered, and then reached for a sandwich. "I'm glad you had a good time."

They ate in companionable silence, but he couldn't help but steal glimpses of her as the darkness of the night crept into the room. The moonlight illuminated her, casting a blue hue over her blonde hair.

Their eyes met and held, until Mia looked away. "Do you think we'll be able to go back home tomorrow?"

Caleb finished the last of his sandwich and swallowed. "Yes, we should." Caleb rose from his chair, pushed it in, and then locked the door for the night. "Well, I don't know about you, but I'm tired." He sat on the edge of the bed, slipped off his shoes, and laid down beside his son. Caleb closed his eyes, wishing Mia hadn't looked so beautiful in the moonlight, wishing he hadn't noticed, wishing he wasn't so attracted to her.

He felt a shift on the other side of the bed. When he opened his eyes, he was staring into her beautiful green eyes, her head on the pillow on the other side of Hailey. She didn't look away or close her eyes while he continued to stare, feeling the depth of her soul as feelings he hadn't felt in a while arose in his body.

"Good night," he finally said.

"Good night."

Then he closed his eyes, grateful that the children were between them, unsure what he would do if they weren't.

CHAPTER 13

The next morning the sun was shining, and Mia was grateful that they wouldn't have to stay another night. The electricity between them was palpable, permeating the air. She wondered if he felt it, too. Mia couldn't take another night of being in such close proximity to him. They made good partners and worked well together; it would have to be enough.

She hadn't gotten much sleep throughout the night and was still tired. On the other side of the bed, Caleb appeared to have slept like a baby along with the children. It was nice being together as a family, becoming a real family. Mia noticed that he was a great father and loved his family with all his heart. It was clear that he would do anything for them. His sending for her was evidence of that. And if he ever chose to love her, she knew he would give her his whole heart, too. But she dare not hope. No, she had made a bargain and she had to stick with it. It was the only way to protect her heart. After all, how could she give her heart to a man who wouldn't love her in return?

Mia tried not to watch as Caleb splashed his face with water from the china basin. She tried not to notice when he took his shirt off and shook it out, and how his muscles played under his tanned skin.

After he slid his suspenders up onto his shoulders, he turned to face her. "I'll take the children downstairs for breakfast to give you some privacy."

"Good morning," she said. There was no reason why they shouldn't be civil.

Caleb smiled. "Good morning." To her surprise, he added, "Did you sleep well?"

She shrugged. "Tolerably. You?"

"Tolerably."

Mia chuckled. "Well, from the way you were snoring, I thought you slept like a baby."

Caleb smiled. "I do not snore."

Mia burst out laughing. "Oh, yes, you do."

"Well, I'm sorry if I kept you awake." He sat down on the edge of the bed and slipped on his boots.

"Caleb, I was only joking. I like it. It's nice." In fact, Mia knew she could easily get used to it.

It appeared that Caleb was going to say something more, but Hailey sat up and stretched and yawned. Her hair was disheveled, and her eyes were still closed as she smacked her lips together.

Caleb reached down and scooped her into his arms. "Sorry, baby girl. Did we wake you?"

She moved her head up and down, her eyes still closed.

"I'll get her ready." Mia held out her arms and Hailey went right to her.

"Thank you," Caleb said and then turned his attention to waking up Shane.

Without a brush, Mia did the best she could with Hailey's curly hair, running her fingers through it and then straightened her dress. "There you go. You look lovely."

"Let's eat some breakfast downstairs, and then we'll go home." Caleb took her gently in his arms and she laid her head on his shoulder.

Mia hurried to run her fingers through Shane's hair, too, as Shane looked up at her with sleepy eyes. "Well, it's the best I can do, but you look very handsome."

Shane smiled, wavering as he stood, still half asleep.

"Ready to go, children?" He looked over at Mia. "We'll give you some privacy. I'll take the children down and get a table." Caleb slipped his and the children's coats over his shoulder and turned around at the door. "We'll wait for you downstairs."

Mia gave him a smile. "I won't be long."

He left the room, closing the door behind them.

Mia looked in the slightly distorted mirror to see that loose tendrils had fallen out from where she had pulled her hair up the day before. One by one, she took the pins out and shook her head, letting her hair fall to her shoulders. She ran her fingers through it, then pulled it up and wrapped it into a loose bun. After pinning her hat into place and smoothing her hands over her dress to brush out the wrinkles, she looked into the mirror and smiled. It wasn't the best, but she was passable.

She threw her coat over her arm, slid her reticule onto her wrist, and then looked around the room to make sure they hadn't forgotten anything. Satisfied, she closed the door behind her and made her way to the stairs. At the top, she looked around and saw Caleb and the children sitting at a table, straight ahead to the right. Caleb looked up and saw her. She smiled, but he remained expressionless as he watched her descend the stairs.

When she reached the table, he stood, pulled out her chair, and held it for her. "You look lovely."

"Thank you. It was the best I could do."

Caleb cleared his throat as he took his seat. She liked his reaction to her. Who knew? Maybe there was hope after all.

"Here you go." Millie placed a plate on the table for each of them. "Bacon and eggs. Enjoy!"

"I hope you don't mind." Caleb cut up the egg for Hailey, who was sitting on his knee. "I wasn't sure how you took your eggs, so I ordered them over medium for you."

Mia cut up Shane's egg while she talked. "That's fine. I like them fried hard, but medium is fine." Mia handed him his fork and started eating her eggs, as well.

"So, are you looking forward to Mrs. Carson's Easter Tea?" Caleb took a sip of his coffee and swallowed.

Mia smiled. "Yes, I am. Mrs. Carson seems like a very nice woman."

One corner of Caleb's lips curled into a smile. "She can be. She means well. But she sure hit it off with you."

"Oh? How so?" Mia took a dainty bite of her egg and swallowed.

Caleb set down his coffee cup. "Let's just say, be careful

what you tell her."

"Well, I think she's a very nice woman." Mia resumed eating and then turned to Shane. "So, do I get to see this snowman of yours?"

"Wait 'til you see it!" Shane crowed. "It's the bestest and biggest one ever!"

Mia smiled, enjoying his excitement. "Well, I suggest we finish eating and go out and see this creation of yours."

Shane rolled his eyes. "It's not a creation. It's a snowman."

Both Mia and Caleb laughed.

"Mia's right," Caleb interjected. "Let's eat and get back home before it decides to start snowing again."

"I think that we're through with the snow for now." Harrison walked up to their table.

"Let's hope so," Caleb agreed. "Listen. Thanks for the room last night. But I wish you'd let me pay for it—"

"Stop right there," Harrison cut him off, smiling. "I wouldn't hear of it." Turning to Mia, he added, "This man right here has given more to this town than you could imagine."

Caleb shook his head. "I wouldn't say that—"

"Well, I would." Harrison gave him a pat on the shoulder. "I'll leave you to enjoy your breakfast." He gave them one last smile and then crossed the room to greet a couple who had just walked in.

"Although it stopped snowing, it's still plenty cold." Caleb took a sip of his coffee and then looked into Mia's eyes. "Why don't you stay in here with the children where it's warm and I'll go get our things from the general store."

Mia's eyebrows pulled together in concern. "Are you sure you won't need any help?"

Caleb smiled. "No. Keeping the children out of the cold would be the biggest help."

"Yes, of course." She knew that she had married Caleb to care for the children and the house, so she had no idea why she was feeling so down. She just guessed that she needed to get back home to their routine. She could pretend a bit better there. But here at the hotel… staying in the same room with Caleb… pretending was much more difficult.

Once his plate was cleared, he rose from his seat and drank down the last of his coffee. "I'll be right back." He walked over to Harrison and took care of the bill for breakfast, and then headed out the door.

Mia giggled when she looked over at Hailey. She had more food on her face than she must have had in her stomach. "Come on, little girl. Let's get you cleaned up." After Mia finished wiping off Hailey's face and hands, she turned to Shane. "Okay, mister. You're next."

"No!" Shane yelled and then ran toward the front door, but Harrison caught him.

"Slow down there, boy." Mia could tell that it was all Harrison could do to hold him. "You need to wait for your mother."

"She's not my mother. She's Mia," Shane blurted out.

Harrison was taken aback by his comment, but held him firmly in front of him and knelt down on his level. "I know she's not your mother, boy. And I'm sorry. I only meant—"

"I know what you meant." Shane let out a deep breath.

"Just give it some time, boy," Harrison continued. "After all, Rome wasn't built in a day."

Mia quickly snatched up Hailey, along with their coats, and headed toward the door and carefully knelt down beside him. "It's okay, Shane." He had done so well, but she imagined that he wasn't prepared for moments like this. Then she thought of another approach. "Shane, would you like to show Mr. Curry your snowman?"

Harrison's eyes flew open wide, as if he had never heard of a snowman before. "You built a what?"

Shane's eyes opened in delight. "A snowman, Mr. Curry!" Then his face fell. "But we didn't have anything for eyes and a mouth, though."

Harrison gave him a smile. "Well, I think I might be able to remedy that. I'll be right back."

"Here." Mia held up his coat as Hailey stood beside her. "Let's put your coat on. Your father will be back in a minute." She wanted to tell him more, but now wasn't the time.

Shane looked at her for a moment and then relented and let her help him on with his coat.

Harrison came back a few moments later carrying a bundle of black fabric and wearing his coat and cowboy hat. "So, where's this fabulous snowman of yours?"

Shane's eyes brightened. "Out here!" He ran as quickly as he could out of the restaurant.

"Shane!" Mia rushed after him, carrying Hailey. "Shane, stay with me!" She ran out the door just in time to see him dart behind the side of the building.

Caleb was placing their purchases into the back of the buckboard and looked up, seeing what was happening. "He went that way… to the back of the building," he called after them and went back to securing the load. "I'll be there in a minute."

Mia ignored him as she ran around the side of the building after Shane. When she came around the corner, a snowman was sitting in the field to the back and side of the restaurant.

Shane was standing beside it, proud as a peacock. "See? Isn't it a great snowman, Mr. Curry?"

Harrison pretended to study it for a bit. "It's wonderful, but I have something that just might finish it up."

Shane's eyes grew wide. "What?"

As tall as he was, Harrison held the bundle down low so Shane could see. Harrison unfolded the black cloth and inside were two lumps of coal, a carrot, a red string of yarn, and a multi-colored scarf. "What do you think?"

Shane peered into the black cloth. "What is it?"

A crease formed between his eyes as he pointed to the two lumps of coal. "I thought we could use these for eyes, the carrot for a nose, the yarn for his mouth, and… where do you think we could put the scarf?"

Shane thought hard, then his eyes grew wide. "Around his neck!"

"Exactly." Harrison smiled, clearly enjoying playing with Shane.

"What are you doing?" Caleb asked, smiling as he

walked up behind them.

"We're decorating the snowman, Pa!" Shane jumped excitedly up and down.

"Here you go." Harrison gave him the bundle. "I'll let you two have the honors. After all, it's your snowman."

"Well, if you don't mind," Caleb replied.

Harrison shook his head. "No, not at all. This is something a father does with his son. I just thought it might need a bit of sprucing up, is all."

"Thank you, Harrison. I appreciate that."

Harrison stood beside Mia as they watched Shane and Caleb decorate the snowman.

"Thank you." Mia adjusted Hailey on her hip.

"It was my pleasure," he replied. "I just thought it might distract the boy a minute. Give him something else to think about."

Mia knew that he meant giving him something else to think about besides losing his mother. "Thank you."

Harrison looked over at her. "Just give it time."

She nodded in understanding, and then Harrison started adding his two cents worth on where everything should go on the snowman. To her surprise, Hailey was content to watch, obviously still sleepy.

"There." Shane reached up high to place the coal in the snowman for the eyes, but couldn't quite reach, so Caleb held him up. Once the eyes, nose, and mouth were in place, Shane turned to Mia. "What do you think?"

Mia smiled proudly. "Well, I think it's the best snowman I've ever seen."

"You mean it?" Shane's eyes grew wide.

"Sure I do."

Caleb smiled, looking into her eyes and then sobered. "I do, too, but I think it's time we go back home."

"Oh, Pa!" Shane patted his snowman, his hands red. "Do we have to?"

Caleb took his son's hands into his own and blew on them. "Yes, I do. Besides, you're freezing. We need to get you some mittens."

Mia made a mental note to make some. "Thank you, Mr. Curry, for everything." Mia held her hand out to shake his, but he raised it to his lips.

"It was my pleasure." He kissed her hand. "I hope to see you again soon."

"Hey. You're not making a pass at my wife, are you?" Although Mia knew Caleb was teasing, her heart fluttered. It was the first time that he had referred to her as his wife.

Harrison gave her a friendly wink as he playfully held up his hands. "I wouldn't dream of it."

Caleb slapped his hand playfully on his shoulder. "Harrison, here, is the most eligible bachelor in Whiskey River. All of the ladies are after him."

"Not hardly." Then Harrison stage-whispered to Mia. "Don't believe a word of it."

"Oh, I wouldn't be so sure," he teased, then wrapped his arm around Mia's waist. "Ready?"

She nodded. Caleb giving her attention felt nice.

"I'd warn you about this man, ma'am, but there's nothing to warn you about." Harrison turned to Caleb and shook his hand. "Please, come stay with us again some time. It was indeed a pleasure."

"I appreciate it, but I hope it's not because we're snowed in again."

Harrison winked. "Maybe next time, Millie or Mrs. Jenkins could stay with the children so you two can get away alone."

Caleb's smile faded. "Yes... well... we need to be leaving." He inclined his head toward Harrison. "Thanks, again."

"Please, allow me." Harrison held his arms out to Hailey and then extended his arm to Mia. "It's pretty slippery out here."

Caleb scooped Shane up into his arms and then set him on his shoulders.

Although Mia appreciated the gesture from Harrison, she couldn't help but wish it had been Caleb to offer. When they reached the buckboard parked on the other side of the street, Harrison helped her into the front and then handed Hailey up to her. "Take care of your husband. Okay? He's a good man."

She gave him a smile. "I will."

Caleb set Shane in the back and he scampered up close behind the front seat. It was safe so Mia didn't worry about him in the back, since it had stopped snowing. Caleb climbed up onto the other side of buckboard and gave Mia a smile.

"Thanks, again," Caleb called to Harrison over his shoulder as they started off toward home.

Mia waved too, glad she was able to meet some of the

people of Whiskey River. She just wished that she would one day feel like she belonged.

"It's beautiful." Mia looked out over the white landscape. The evergreens were dusted in white once again as the wind blew lightly across them.

Caleb watched the road ahead. "The sun's shining, so it won't last long. It'll melt off soon enough."

Mia smiled as she watched the landscape pass. "Yes, but it's here now. We should enjoy it before it's gone."

They rode in silence the rest of the way back, and before long they pulled up to the familiar white house with a wraparound front porch and snow-covered trees standing majestically beside it.

"We're home," Caleb announced as he pulled the team to a stop. "Why don't you take the children inside and I'll unhitch the team."

"Yippee!" Shane yelled as he jumped out of the wagon and bolted into the house.

Mia smiled, enjoying Shane's excitement. "I'll fix us some lunch."

Caleb took Hailey and set her on her feet, and then helped Mia down.

Mia took Hailey's hand and then turned to Caleb. "Would you like some help bringing everything in?"

Caleb shook his head. "No, I'll bring it in. You just decide where to put it."

Mia laughed. "That won't be a problem. I have places already in mind."

One corner of his lips curled into a smile as he reached

for a sack of flour in the back of the buckboard. "Of that, I have no doubt."

No sooner had they walked in the door, Mia took off Hailey's coat and she scampered off into the master bedroom to play, with Shane hot on her heels.

Caleb continued carting in the items, so Mia took off her coat and started fixing lunch. It seemed that the majority of what she did was cook and clean. She made a mental note to get herself on a schedule and cook some things ahead when she could to save time.

"Mia!" Hailey screamed as she ran from the bedroom. "Shane has Dolly!" Huge tears streamed down her face as if it was the worst thing in the world.

"Shane!" Mia yelled as she picked up Hailey and walked into the bedroom. Shane was hiding in the closet. "Come out here right now."

He stepped out, looking down at his feet.

Mia studied his posture and knew there was more to the story. "Shane, do you know where Hailey's doll is?"

Shane's eyes opened wide as he shook his head back and forth vigorously.

Mia let out a deep breath. "Okay. Help me find it, please."

Shane ran out of the room.

"Shane! Come back here!"

A moment later, she heard the door to her bedroom slam shut.

Mia walked over to the door and found it locked. "Shane! Open this door!"

"No!"

Hailey sniffled beside her and pulled on her skirts.

"Okay, baby girl," Mia cooed as she knelt down beside her. "Let's find your dolly. Okay?"

Hailey pulled Mia's hand, leading her toward her bedroom. Then she pointed toward the closet as huge tears poured down her cheeks. "She's dead!"

Mia's heart sank. "What do you mean 'she's dead'?" For a moment, she wondered if Hailey remembered her mother and understood that she was gone. She bit her lower lip, wondering if she should explain it to her or if she should tell Caleb.

"Shane killed Dolly!" Hailey screamed as she pointed toward the closet.

"Now, now." Mia rubbed the little girl's back. "I'm sure it can't be that bad." Mia went into the closet and lying on the floor was the headless body of a rag doll and, near it, the head. She picked it up and tried to hold the head on so as not to scare Hailey any more than necessary, but to no avail.

When Hailey saw it, she screamed and a fresh wave of tears washed over her face.

"Hailey," Mia cooed, trying to hide the doll behind her back. "I can fix it. I promise."

"R… real… really?" Hailey's eyebrows raised almost into her hairline.

Mia smiled. "Yes, really." Then, she knelt down on the floor in front of her. "I'm a very good seamstress, remember?" Mia rubbed her back in soothing circles. "I can fix it. I promise."

Hailey reached out to her, and Mia shoved the doll's

head into her pocket and scooped Hailey up into her arms. Then she carried her out to the living room. She set in the rocking chair and hid the doll under a doily on a side table beside it. Mia started rocking the little girl, cuddling with her, when Shane unlocked the door and headed toward their bedroom.

"Shane?"

He stopped and looked at her sheepishly.

"Shane, come here for a minute," she instructed, and he stepped closer. "Did you rip Dolly's head off?"

He didn't say anything at first, but just looked at his feet. Shane looked at his sister and then at Mia. "Yes, I did."

Mia let out a deep breath. "Shane, you owe Hailey an apology."

He bit his lower lip, fighting back tears. "I'm sorry, Hailey." Hailey scooted down, scampered across the room toward her brother, and wrapped her arms around him, giving him a hug.

"Shane, I'm proud of you for telling the truth," Mia praised. "But you know not to do it again, right?"

Shane's eyes brightened. "You really are proud of me?"

Mia smiled. "Yes, for telling the truth. But promise me that you won't rip off your sister's doll's head anymore. Okay?"

"I promise."

"Okay." Mia guided Hailey back to the rocking chair, set her on her lap, and started rocking back and forth. She looked at Shane, who was still standing in the middle of the floor, watching. "Would you like to rock with us?"

A broad smile spread across his face as he climbed onto her lap. Within minutes, they were both asleep for their naps. Not wanting to disturb them, she continued rocking.

It felt great to be a part of a family again. She had been alone for so long that she'd forgotten what it was like. The time that she and Ella were roommates had been the closest she had come to having a family as an adult. Now, her family with Caleb was the real thing.

As she rocked the children, she was glad they were accepting her. But she wondered if Caleb ever would. Would there ever come a time when he would think of her as his wife, as he had Jessica? Would he ever come to love her?

She knew that she could live without love, but it couldn't be all one-sided either. Seeing him with his children, she knew that he was capable of love. The love Caleb had for his children and Jessica was evident.

Tears came to her eyes as she rocked the children. Who was she kidding? Jessica was his wife, and she always would be. Mia feared that she would be living in her shadow for as long as she lived in this house with this family. She had agreed to a marriage of convenience. But as she thought of Caleb's muscled chest and beautiful eyes, she knew she was beginning to have feelings for him. But could she live in a loveless marriage?

Then as she looked down at the children as she rocked them back and forth, she knew that it was anything but loveless—at least for her.

CHAPTER 14

The next two months flew by in a frenzy for Mia: cleaning, cooking, and caring for the children during the day, and then sewing at night. Even though she had outwardly accepted their relationship as platonic; secretly, she hadn't given up the dream of it being more. Over the past few months, she had been a bit more bold with her flirtations… and Caleb had started to respond, renewing her dream of having a real marriage one day. The snow had melted off, giving way to daffodils, colorful spring flowers, and warmer days. She just hoped that spring love would come along with it. In her spare time, Mia planted a good-sized vegetable garden, while Caleb planted the wheat field. He had told her that he depended upon a good crop to make ends meet. Also, they planned to sell the excess vegetables from her garden for extra money, as well.

It was the day before Easter, and Mrs. Carson's Easter Tea was planned. Mia had been so busy and exhausted that she almost cancelled, but as the wife of the town preacher, it would have been seen as an insult. Also, she enjoyed Mrs. Carson's company.

Although the tea wasn't until one o'clock, she woke early to get ready and get the children squared away before she left. She felt a bit guilty for leaving him to care for the children alone, but he'd done just that before he married her... although it hadn't been by choice back then.

They had fallen into an easy routine of eating breakfast together as a family before going their separate ways for the day. After Caleb left to either go on his rounds as preacher or out to work on the farm, she spent her days with chores and caring for the children. Now that the weather was better, she made different dishes each week for the potluck dinners at the after-church social and dance on Sundays. It was something she looked forward to each week. She had fun trying different dishes and exchanging recipes with the ladies. The social camaraderie was something she hadn't had since living with Ella.

She looked through her closet and settled on a light blue dress with little pink rosebuds. It had always been one of her favorites in New York, and wasn't too flashy for Whiskey River. She hung the dress behind the door and then slipped into a robe.

Since it was still dark outside, she decided to take a moment of private time to take a bath before everyone woke.

As quietly as she could, she lit the stove. She looked in the utility room where the bathtub was kept and grabbed the metal buckets, filled them with water, and then set them on the lit stove to heat. While she was waiting, she took out the egg bowl and supplies to make fried country ham and eggs for breakfast.

Since Caleb was still sleeping, she grabbed the butcher knife from the wooden block and quietly crept down the stairs. After cutting off enough for breakfast, she made her way back up the stairs. When the water was ready, she poured it into the tub, filled the buckets again, and set them on the stove to heat once again. When the tub was nearly full, she carried a bar of lye soap, a wash cloth, and a towel into the utility room with her.

After pulling the curtain closed that separated the utility room from the kitchen, she let her robe fall to the floor and stepped into the tub. Then she sank down up to her neck, enjoying the warmth of the water against her skin. It wasn't often that she was able to enjoy some time alone, so she decided to savor every moment.

She closed her eyes and leaned back into the tub, relaxing, while letting the warm water soothe her tired muscles.

When she heard the curtain move, her eyes flew open.

"Oh... I'm so sorry... I was just...," Caleb stammered, his eyes wide open in shock. "I just came in for some..." Then he slipped and fell onto the floor, taking the curtain down with him.

Mia grabbed a towel laying on the side of the tub and wrapped it around her while he was flailing in the curtain on the floor, reminding her of a fish out of water. "Are you okay?"

"Ow... yes..." He held his head as he got to his feet. After unwrapping himself from the curtain, he closed his eyes and stumbled around the utility room, trying to find his way out.

Mia laughed. "I'm covered, so why don't you just open your eyes so you can see?"

His eyes flew open wide again and he looked directly into her eyes. "Yes… well… I'm so sorry… I'll be going now." With his back to her, he somehow managed to rehang the curtain, walk out, quickly pulled it closed behind him.

Mia slipped back down into the tub, letting the towel fall to the floor once more. "I'll let you know when I'm done."

"Okay… take your time."

Although she'd been startled at first, his reaction had been so comical she'd forgotten her own embarrassment. Gauging his reaction, he was going to have to say a lot of Our Fathers to get over this one.

Knowing he wouldn't come back in, she took her time bathing, enjoying the peace and quiet and time to relax before starting her day.

When she was finished, she dried off, wrapped the towel around her hair, and slipped back into her robe.

When she walked into the kitchen, Caleb was standing near the sink with his back to her, rinsing out a cup. Unable to help herself, she reached over him and opened the cabinet door. He jumped back. "Oh! I'm sorry I walked in on you. I was just putting away the soap."

She leaned back against the counter. "That's okay. The water's still warm if you'd like to bathe."

He looked at her as if seeing her for the first time and then must have caught on to her flirtations and quickly regained his composure. Caleb looked directly into her eyes, no longer nervous or flustered. "I made coffee. Want some?"

She shrugged. "Yes, I think I would."

Without breaking eye contact, he walked toward her purposefully, causing her heart to flutter. Then he reached above her and pulled a cup from the cabinet behind her, even though there were other cups in the cabinet near him. He smirked as he walked over to the stove and poured her coffee, his muscles flexing under the thin white fabric of his shirt. Then he walked back over to her and stopped just inches in front of her and held out the cup. "Here you go."

Mia gulped. "Thank you," she breathed, surprised that he was returning her advances.

Caleb looked into her eyes and then pinched a loose tendril that had fallen from under the towel between his fingers and pushed it behind her ear. Her breath quickened as his fingertip grazed her cheekbone and down the length of her jaw. Caleb leaned in, but stopped, his mouth just inches from hers and then grazed his lips across hers, inhaling her scent, looking at her through his eyelashes. He froze for a moment, but then walked away.

She let out a deep breath; her head was swimming. It was all she could do not to go to him, but she smiled as she walked into her bedroom, swooning from his nearness and their flirtatious game. She hoped this was a first step in the right direction at least.

As she dressed to go to Mrs. Carson's Easter Tea, thoughts of Caleb invaded her mind. She wondered if he really was about to kiss her and stopped himself, or if he had just been teasing her. Either way, she was surprised at the effect it had on her. Her lips curled into a devious smile, resolving to make it her mission to wear him down.

After slipping on her dress, which was fitted in the bodice to the waist and bustled in the back, she pulled her hair up into loose curls. Once her hair dried, she planned to wear a matching hat.

Suddenly, the scent of frying ham wafted toward her. Caleb must have decided to start breakfast. She squared her shoulders and then walked into the kitchen, planning to pretend that the morning incident hadn't happened.

"Good morning." She took a sip of her coffee and swallowed. "What would you like me to do?"

He smiled. "Go ahead and sit down." Then his eyes met hers, causing her heart to pound. "You make breakfast every morning. Let me treat you for a change."

Her cheeks flushed. "No, I couldn't do that. What would you like me to do?"

He raised an eyebrow, looking at her seductively. Her face turned scarlet. But this was what she wanted, wasn't it? She boldly took a step closer and brushed her lips across his. Then she let her lips travel ever so lightly across his neck and pressed her lips to his throat. In one swift movement, he swept her into his arms, backed her against the counter, and crushed his lips to hers, placing his hand on the back of her head. His breath quickened, as his lips traveled from hers, grazing his teeth along her jawbone, and then pressed his lips to hers again, as passion filled them both.

Then Mia heard the master bedroom door open and came to her senses. "The children," she whispered against his lips.

Caleb took a step back and ran his fingers through his dark brown hair, never taking his eyes from hers. She took a deep breath, allowing her a moment to clear her head.

"I'll scramble the eggs...." She started to take out a bowl, but he stopped her and looked into her eyes.

"Don't." He placed his hand over hers. "You look too nice." He cleared his throat. "Please, go sit down."

"Well, if you insist...." Then a thought occurred to her. "Caleb, are you sure you wouldn't like to come?"

"A bunch of gossipy women? Yuck!"

She laughed. "Like father, like son."

She sat at the table, grateful for the moment to gather her thoughts after the kiss. For a moment, she wondered what it had meant, but decided not to overthink it. She just planned to enjoy the day. When she looked up, Shane was staring at her. "Good morning, Shane."

"Good morning." Smiling, he hopped up into his chair, slipped a piece of bacon from the plate setting on the table, and took a bite. "You look nice today." Rolling his eyes, he added, "That's right. Today's the 'Easter Tea.'"

Surprised, Mia giggled. "Why did you say it like that?"

"A bunch of gossipy women sipping tea?" Shane said between bites. "Yuck!"

Mia laughed. "You sound just like your father."

Looking over at her, Caleb raised an eyebrow. "Where do you think he gets it from?"

Mia smiled, enjoying spending this time with the family. This was a different side of him that she hadn't seen before, and she liked what she saw… and she liked the step forward they had just taken in their relationship. "So, will you be okay with the children while I go?"

"We'll be okay, won't we, buddy?" Caleb asked his son, setting a plate of bacon, eggs, and a biscuit in front of her.

"Sure we will!" Shane smiled, taking another bite of the bacon.

She took a bite of her egg and it was cooked just the way she liked it, fried hard without the yolk broken. She took a bite and swallowed. "I like a man who can cook."

He almost spat out his coffee. "Okay. That's enough. I surrender." He smiled, obviously talking about her flirtations. "Eat your breakfast. But don't plan on doing anything that will get your dress dirty before you go. Get some sewing in, if you like."

"Wow! You're spoiling me."

He refilled her coffee cup and whispered just over her head. "Don't get too used to it." Then he kissed the top of her head and walked back over to the stove. A moment later, he set a plate down on the table filled with bacon, eggs, and a biscuit for himself, along with a bowl of biscuits wrapped in a towel.

As she ate her breakfast, she liked this new development in their relationship. She just hoped it continued. "Would you like me to pick up anything from the general store while I'm in town?"

Caleb shook his head. "No, I think we have everything

we need. That is, unless you need something."

"No, I'm fine. I don't need anything." Then she looked into his eyes. "Would you mind if I take the buckboard?"

He shook his head, not looking away. "I'll hitch up the team for you when it's time for you to go." Looking over at his son, he noticed he was still in his long underwear. "Let's get you dressed. Okay?"

"But, Pa—"

"No buts. You don't come out here dressed in your underwear with a lady present." Caleb led him into the other room as Mia finished her breakfast.

When they came back in, Shane took a biscuit from a plate that Caleb had made for him and took a bite.

Mia giggled. She got up, laid her plate in the sink, then opened a drawer and put on an apron. She was about to do the dishes when strong hands covered her own, stopping her.

"I told you not to do anything today. Just enjoy yourself." Warmth from his muscled arms filled her body as he slowly took the bucket from her hand. "Go sit down. Enjoy yourself."

"You really are trying to spoil me, aren't you?" As she walked into the living room, she was the one who was flustered this time.

Just as she sat down in the rocking chair and picked up her sewing, Hailey walked slowly into the room, wiping her eyes, still sleepy. "Come here, baby girl." Mia held her hands out to her. Hailey walked over, climbed up onto her lap, and laid her head on her shoulder.

Mia rocked her back and forth, the rocking chair creaking loudly against the floor until Hailey climbed down. Mia took her hand and led her to the kitchen table. Caleb was doing the dishes but stopped and crossed the room to Hailey.

"Morning, pumpkin." He scooped his daughter up into his arms and held her with one arm as he placed a pancake onto a plate and added syrup.

"I can feed her." Although Mia was enjoying being doted on, she was beginning to feel a bit helpless.

Caleb looked up and smiled. "Nope. Go enjoy yourself until you have to leave for the party."

"I shouldn't have gotten ready so early," Mia mumbled as she walked back into the living room. Behind her, she heard Caleb chuckle. Mia sat down in the rocking chair once more and picked up her sewing. Soon, she found herself completely immersed in making a dress for Hailey. Before she knew it, it was time to go.

Caleb walked in the front door behind her and touched her shoulder. "Mia, I've hitched the team to the buckboard for you. It's ready when you are."

"Just one more stitch." She made the last stitch and then bit the thread with her teeth, cutting it off. "There!" She held up the dress she had made for Hailey, a rose color, perfect for Easter. "All finished." She folded the little dress and laid it carefully on the table beside the rocking chair. "Now, I just need to make Shane and you each a shirt and we'll be ready for tomorrow."

"You don't have to go to so much trouble." Caleb held out his hand and helped her from the chair. "We have plenty of clothes now, thanks to you."

Mia looked into his eyes. There was interest there, but they had an agreement, didn't they? Their marriage was to be purely platonic. Then again she was the one who had made advances on him. But he didn't stop her, either. She wanted to hope for something more, but then he turned away, breaking the spell of the moment.

"Thanks for hitching up the team for me," Mia said, clearing her throat, and then slipped her reticule over her wrist. "I won't be late."

"Would you like me to drive you?" Caleb offered. "The children and I could visit around town until you're ready to leave."

Mia smiled and placed a hand on the side of his cheek. "Thank you, but that won't be necessary." She felt the intensity of his deep blue eyes and the overwhelming urge to kiss him again, but she didn't want to push it. He had taken a step forward and she didn't want to ruin it. Instead, she placed a hand on the side of his cheek. "I'll be back soon."

"Take your time," Caleb replied, not pulling away.

Unable to resist, she gave him a kiss on the cheek and walked out, closing the door behind her. Mia climbed into the buckboard and picked up the reins. "Yah!" She shook the reins and the horses leapt into a slow canter as she headed toward town.

Wildflowers now dotted the landscape, set before the mountains rising majestically to the heavens in the distance. The air was comfortably cool. The sun was shining over the earth and a gentle breeze blew through the trees. The perfect day. She just hoped the weather held out for Easter.

As she watched the scenery pass by, she smiled, thinking of Caleb. Did she dare open up her heart to him, as she had the children? When she pulled into Dirk Price's livery stable, she resigned herself to enjoy the time with the ladies and to push all other thoughts from her mind.

"Good afternoon, ma'am," Dirk greeted her after she pulled the team to a stop and put on the brake. "Going to Mrs. Carson's Easter Tea today?"

Mia smiled. "How did you know?"

He chuckled. "That's all my wife Gabriella has been talking about for months now." He offered her his hand to help her down out of the buckboard. "You ladies try not to get into too much trouble."

Mia laughed. "We'll try not to. But you know how we women are when we get together."

"Yes, lots of gabbing and tea guzzling," Dirk teased. "Have fun. And don't worry about the team. I'll take care of them until you're ready to leave."

Mia slid her reticule over her wrist and smoothed her skirts. "Thank you, Mr. Price."

"Please, call me Dirk."

"Yes, of course. Thank you." Then she headed into town, enjoying the sights and sounds of spring. The birds were singing, the people were bustling about preparing for the holiday, and excitement was in the air. For a moment, she regretted not bringing Caleb and the children along with her. She kept thinking "Caleb would like this" or "Shane and Hailey would like that." Although she was glad to get away from her responsibilities for a bit, she already missed Caleb and the children.

Before she walked into the restaurant where the tea was to be held, she squared her shoulders, determined to enjoy herself.

Suddenly, the door flew open, almost hitting her. "Welcome!" Harrison Curry greeted her. "I assume you're here for the Easter Tea, hosted by Mrs. Carson?"

"Yes, I am. Thank you, Mr. Curry."

Harrison stepped back. "Right this way." He walked to the right into a private room where several guests sat at a long rectangular table. Harrison motioned with his hand. "Enjoy."

Mrs. Carson was talking to Gabriella on her right and there was an empty place to her left. When Mrs. Carson saw Mia walk in, she stood. "Mrs. Henley, welcome! I saved a seat for you. Please, sit down." Before Mia took her seat, Mrs. Carson made the introductions, but she already knew most of them from church. "To your left, this is Ella Hill, Madison Nash, Mrs. Jenkins, and Mrs. Campbell. To my right is Gabriella Price, Kenzie Baker, Alice Stanford, Sarah Smith, and Mrs. Hart."

Mia inclined her head to each person as Mrs. Carson made the introductions and then took her seat beside Mrs. Carson.

"Well! Now that everyone is here, let's begin," Mrs. Carson announced. "I'd like to thank all of you for coming today, but first a toast." She lifted her teacup. "I hope that this tea will be the first of many and that we may take the opportunity to get to know one another a bit better when we can. Happy Easter."

"Happy Easter!" all the ladies said in unison.

They spent the afternoon sipping tea, eating cakes and Easter treats, and talking. Throughout the party, everyone congratulated Mia on being the new wife of Reverend Henley, some teasing her lightheartedly about being a newlywed. But she didn't feel much like a married woman, let alone a newlywed. To the town, she and Caleb had a good marriage. Little did they know it was a marriage of convenience.

After a while, Mia started feeling a bit like a fraud, representing herself as a married woman and a newlywed, no less, when in reality she was no more than a housekeeper and maid. She had hoped it would develop into more than that. But who was she kidding?

Mia plastered on a smile and extended her hand to Mrs. Carson. "Thank you so much for having me today. I truly enjoyed myself."

"Oh? Leaving so soon?" Mrs. Carson looked a bit disappointed.

"Yes, I have to get home to the children."

"And to your new husband," Mrs. Carson added in a friendly tone before turning to the other ladies at the table, who had been talking about Ella's twins. "I'm certain that we will be having a baby shower for Mrs. Henley very soon, too!"

"Mrs. Carson!" Mia retorted as the other ladies giggled.

"Come now." Mrs. Carson elbowed her lightheartedly. "We all know how newlyweds are."

Mia let out a deep breath, giving up. "Well, thank you for a wonderful afternoon, Mrs. Carson." She addressed the other ladies at the table, "Ladies, plan on staying after church tomorrow. It's Easter Sunday and Caleb and I are planning an Easter egg hunt." Lowering her voice conspiratorially, she added, "and make sure to bring the children."

The ladies laughed and said their goodbyes.

Mia reached over and gave Ella's shoulders a hug. "I'll see you tomorrow."

Ella smiled. "I'll be there."

Mia nodded and then turned to Madison. "Good to see you, too, Madison. I'll see you tomorrow."

Madison patted her hand. "We'll be there." Caleb had told her that before Madison and Wyatt met, she'd been hounded by a dastardly man and hardly went to church. Now, she and Wyatt never missed a Sunday.

"I'll walk with you," Gabriella said in her divine French accent. Turning to Mrs. Carson, she extended her hand, emitting a regal air, even though she probably hadn't intended to. "Thank you so much for the invitation. I'm so glad we had the opportunity to get to know all of you a bit better."

Gabriella stepped back, letting Mia walk to the front of the restaurant ahead of her.

"Have a good evening, ladies." Harrison Curry held open the door for them, and they said their goodbyes.

Mia was surprised that Gabriella wanted to walk her out.

They had only ever talked casually at church, and never on a personal level before.

"I hope you don't mind me walking you to the livery stable." Gabriella broke the uncomfortable silence.

"I know you're probably meeting your husband at the stables. Besides, I'm glad for the company."

Gabriella leaned her head to the side. "That was part of it, but I welcomed the chance to speak with you alone."

"Oh?" Mia came to a stop. "What about?"

Gabriella linked arms. "I saw that you were quickly becoming more and more uncomfortable back there." Gabriella inclined her head back toward the restaurant. "Especially when they were talking to you about being a newlywed."

Mia listened but said nothing. A lump formed in her throat. Could she tell Gabriella why? No, she knew she couldn't. Not and keep up appearances of being a happy family, or rather, a happily married couple.

Gabriella slowed their walk. "Please don't take Mrs. Carson's teasing to heart. I think sometimes she speaks before she thinks of the effect it might have on others."

"It's all right. I know she meant well," Mia replied, "but I'm so glad we've had this moment to talk."

Gabriella smiled. "Me, too."

"How are things going with you and Dirk?" Mia asked in an effort to divert the attention away from herself.

Gabriella tilted her head. "Just fine, thank you." She paused for a moment, and then asked, "Mia... may I call you Mia?"

"Of course."

"Then you shall call me Gabriella. I so like the informality here in America."

Mia nodded her agreement. "I would imagine it's been hard on you coming from another country and being thrown into the west, of all places."

"No, I love it here. Yes, it's much different than Monaco, but I love the adventure and the people... being able to be who you are and not who people want you to be."

Gabriella's words struck Mia hard. She, too, had been expected to be who people wanted her to be. It was what she had agreed to, but after this afternoon, at least they were making progress.

"Mia, I just want you to know that you can talk to me and it won't go any farther." Gabriella squeezed her hand. "And if you feel overwhelmed, please let me know and I'll be there. I know that as the preacher's wife, you must have a lot of duties."

"Thank you. I truly appreciate your concern, but everything's fine," Mia lied.

"Good. I'm glad to hear it. But I'm here for you, should you ever need to talk. Believe me, I know how hard adjusting to a new life can be." Gabriella linked her arm with Mia's again and resumed walking. "You've been thrown into a ready-made family, and in the prestigious position of being the preacher's wife. Although you make it look easy, it's a lot to live up to, which is something I know about." She patted Mia's arm. "My parents died when I was very young and I was raised by my uncle,

Charles III, Prince of Monaco." Gabriella gauged her reaction. When there was none, she continued, "That said, it was understood that one day I would marry a man of my uncle's choosing for the good of the monarchy."

Mia pulled her to a stop. "But you and Dirk are so happy."

Gabriella nodded. "Yes, we are. But I had the courage to choose my own life, instead of just accepting what was. When I met Dirk, I knew what I wanted." Gabriella bit her lower lip and continued. "Mia, don't be afraid to live your life on your own terms, no matter what women like Mrs. Carson and others say." She looked into her eyes. "After all, we only get one life. Live the life you want and make it the best life imaginable." She inclined her head. "*I* have."

Mia pulled her in for a hug. "Thank you so much, Gabriella. And I'm glad you found the path that made you happy."

Gabriella smiled when she pulled back. "Find yours, too."

"I will."

As they walked back to the livery stable, Mia knew she was right. She had to live her life on her terms, and not worry about what others thought. But it was easier said than done.

★★★

On the way home, thoughts of Caleb and their relationship was wearing on her, so she decided to put it out of her mind and concentrate on the scenery instead. The many colors of spring brightened the horizon. Mia vowed to use some of the colors for the Easter eggs she planned to dye with the children. Since it was still light out, she pulled the team over to the side of the dusty road, then walked out into the field and picked some lovely wild flowers in varying shades of purple, yellow, pink, blue, and red.

She also picked some maple bark and sassafras, as they would make a good brown and a reddish color for the eggs.

Her grandmother had shown her how to make dye from items in nature when she was a child.

After she collected what she needed, she headed back to the team and was on her way. "Yah!" She shook the reins and the horses began a slow trot. As she drove home, she couldn't help but think of Caleb and how flustered he had been that morning. She flushed, thinking of him seeing her naked in the bathtub and taking the curtain down. Then she thought of the kiss. Maybe he was taking the next step forward with her, after all. Then she thought of his kindness that afternoon, of him not letting her do anything for fear of mussing her dress and smiled, wondering what the future held.

CHAPTER 15

Caleb was waiting on the porch, leaning against the wooden post with his hands in his jeans, when he heard the buckboard and team coming down the long drive. His lips curled into a smile as he skipped down the steps and walked around the team to her side. "Did you have fun?"

Smiling, she took his hand and he helped her down. "Yes, I did. Mrs. Carson made sure that many of the women in town were there."

Caleb chuckled. "Oh, I have no doubt of that." As they approached the front porch steps, he pulled her to a stop, debating his words. "Listen, I need to speak with you about something."

"Oh?" Her smile faded.

"This morning, I—"

"Ssshhh….." She placed her finger on his lips as her heart sank. He regretted having kissed her. "Please, don't say it."

"I'm sorry. It was my fault." He bit his lower lip and

then let it out. "I shouldn't have walked in on you like that. I shouldn't have kissed you—"

She started to walk past him, a look of pain in her eyes. "It's okay."

Caleb stopped her, enjoying the feel of her soft arms in his strong hands a bit too much. "No, it was my fault. I should have known—"

Mia placed a finger gently to his lips again, causing his heart to pound. "It's okay. Let's just let it go."

Caleb let go of her arms and took a step back. "Yes… okay…."

"Where are the children?"

Overwhelmed by her beauty and her scent, it took a moment for Caleb to find his voice. "In the bedroom, playing."

"Okay. I'll get dressed and fix us some dinner." Mia started to walk inside, but Caleb stopped her again.

"Mia?"

"Um?"

He smiled. "You look beautiful."

A soft shade of rose colored her cheeks as she turned her head slightly. "Thank you, Caleb." Then she looked into his eyes. "We'd better go in now. The children…."

Caleb cleared his throat and ran his fingers through his hair. "Yes… right…." He opened the door for her and watched her walk in. It was all he could do not to follow her into her bedroom.

After she closed the door, he went into the kitchen and put some coffee on to boil. "Get a hold of yourself, man," he whispered to himself, trying to clear his head of Mia.

He had thought of her all afternoon while she was away. Her in the bathtub, her wet hair falling over her shoulders and then standing in the kitchen in her thin robe, showing her curves. It had been all he could do not to ravage her. But he owed her and Jessica more than that.

It was strange. The more time he spent with Mia, the more attracted he was to her, the more his heart connected with hers. Sighing, he remembered the dream he had of Jessica the night he married Mia. Jessica wanted him to be happy, but he pushed the thought aside. How could he give himself, heart and soul, to Mia when he'd already given everything to Jessica?

Mia walked out a few minutes later, dressed in the same work dress she had made when she first arrived in Whiskey River. Even though it wasn't nearly as fancy, she was still beautiful. She looked over at Caleb. "Want to help us dye Easter eggs?"

A smile lit his lips. "You know what? I think I will."

"I'll go get the children." She gave him a smile as she disappeared into the bedroom.

Shane ran into the room a moment later, sliding across the floor in his socks. "Yes! Easter eggs!"

Caleb watched as Mia made the dye: Red from cranberries, brown from tree bark, yellow from buttercups, purple from violets, and green from grass, just to name a few. Soon, she had filled several cups with a vinegar-dye solution in different colors. It was amazing to watch her work. "How did you learn to do that?"

Mia looked up. "Make Easter egg dye?"

Caleb helped Hailey carefully place an egg into the red dye solution. Instantly, the egg started to change color.

Mia smiled. "I used to make Easter eggs with my grandmother when I was young."

"I want to help!" Shane jumped up and down, clearly excited.

"Here you go." Mia handed him an egg and then helped him place it carefully into the purple solution.

They worked for the next hour making Easter eggs.

"Here we go!" Mia placed the egg plate onto the table as he and the children looked on.

"Can I eat one?" Shane asked. Hailey bobbed her head in agreement.

"No, you'll have to wait until tomorrow after church at the social." Mia pulled out a few of the cracked eggs from the pot. "There are a few cracked ones that we can't dye. Would you like one?"

"Yes, please." Then he turned to his sister. "Want one, Hailey?"

Hailey looked up at her brother with wide eyes. She adored Shane, and whatever he did she was sure to try.

"How many do you have left?" Caleb asked as he peered over the edge of the pot.

Mia pushed playfully on his chest. "You're as bad as the kids." Then she reached in and pulled out two eggs and gave him one. "Shane, Hailey, you do it like this…." She gave the children each a peeled egg and, before long, they were all sitting at the table, eating the leftover hard-boiled eggs.

Mia had obviously suspected that the children would want some, so she had saved some back, telling everyone that they were "cracked" and couldn't be used for Easter eggs, but Caleb knew better.

Caleb smiled, his heart swelling as he watched her with his children. Never would he have thought that another woman could care for them the way that Jessica had. Yet, here she was. Mia had brought some much-needed sunshine into their home. She was wonderful with the children, and his heart was slowly changing toward her. Was he falling in love with her? Was Mia feeling it, too? But then he thought of Jessica....

Caleb pushed back his chair and stood. "Well, if you have everything under control in here, I'll go out and feed the cattle and check on the crops."

"I'll start dinner." She started cleaning the dry yolk off the children's faces.

Outside, the birds were singing their evening song as the sun lay low in the sky. He found himself hurrying to feed the cattle and the horses, and then he walked out to check the wheat field. Little green sprouts had pushed their way up through the soil. He loved this time of year. It was a time of renewal, of new life, of second chances. A time when the earth started anew.

Could he ever come to think of Mia as his wife? His real wife? He let out a deep breath as he walked along the field. At the back of the field, some deer were grazing. He made a mental note to spread some hair clippings around the field the next time Mia cut their hair. The scent would keep the deer away. He just hoped that this year's crop was a good one. He hadn't sold much cattle so far and bringing Mia here had eaten away at his savings. But once he sold off the wheat this summer, his savings should be restored. He just prayed that God would bless them with a good crop.

He picked up a blade of grass and put it between his teeth and resumed walking. He and his family had received many blessings, the biggest one was Mia. She'd blown into their lives like a cool breeze, bringing hope with her.

They had a rough start but now had settled into a routine. And somehow, despite his protests, she had wormed her way into his heart. He admired how kind she was with the children. Before she came, Shane had started to rebel, but she had dealt with him with patience and had turned him around. And Hailey loved her as her mother. It hurt him that she would never know her real mother, but Mia had willingly stepped in and had filled the void for her.

Mia was actually the perfect preacher's wife, having taken on her duties with ease. It had been rough on her at first, managing the varied roles, but soon she had settled in. Now, it was as if she had always been a part of the town and a part of his family.

As soon as he walked back into the house, the scent of biscuits and fried chicken wafted toward him. Mia was finishing up in the kitchen. It was all he could do not to walk up behind her and kiss her neck, but he pushed the thought from his mind. "Um… smells good." He hung his hat up on the peg beside the door and then ran his fingers through his hair.

Mia looked around and smiled. "Go wash up. It's almost ready. I'm setting it on the table now."

Caleb washed up at the outdoor pump, then went back inside to his bedroom and dressed in a clean, dark blue shirt, leaving it untucked. He pulled off his boots and left them under his bed, knowing he would be in for the night. He loved walking around in the house in his bare feet. When he was a child, he would have gone all summer with no shoes, if his parents had let him.

He headed into the kitchen, and Mia was taking the biscuits out of the oven. "Can I do anything to help?" he asked.

Mia slid the biscuits into a bowl lined with a towel and wrapped them up. "Here. Set this on the table for me." Her eyes never met his.

Had he imagined the incident this morning? Maybe she wasn't interested. His heart suddenly sank, although he had no idea why. Was it because he had kissed her? "I'll get the children."

She placed the last chicken leg onto an already piled-high platter.

Caleb watched her for a moment and then walked into the living room where the children were playing with their toys. "Ready for dinner? It's time to eat."

Shane whooped as he ran into the kitchen with Hailey hot on his heels. Mia had already prepared a plate for each of them and set them on the table at their place settings.

Mia took her seat, shook out her napkin, and spread it across her lap. Then she folded her hands and looked into

Caleb's eyes, melting his heart. "Would you like to say grace?"

Caleb smiled. She didn't return the smile and he didn't know why it bothered him. He let out a deep breath and said the blessing over the meal, thanking God for the bountiful food and company.

As they ate, the children prattled on, but Mia was quiet.

"Tired?" Caleb asked.

"A little." She picked up a chicken leg, took a dainty bite, and swallowed. "I'm sorry. I seem to have a lot on my mind."

"Oh?" He stopped his fork, halfway to his mouth. "What's wrong?" For a moment, he thought that maybe she was thinking of their encounter this morning, too. He had practically thought of nothing else all day.

She shrugged, but never looked into his eyes. Then she set her fork down. "After dinner, I'm going to go to bed early, if you don't mind. I'm tired and we have a big day ahead of us tomorrow."

He gave her a slight smile. "Don't worry about anything. I'll bathe the children and will do the dishes."

Her eyes met his, causing his heart to pound. "No, I couldn't leave you with everything to do. Thank you for taking care of everything all day and not letting me do anything."

Caleb shrugged as one corner of his lips curled into a smile. "After the children are in bed, I'm going to take a bath, too."

Mia chuckled and resumed eating. "Is the curtain okay?"

She took a bite of her mashed potatoes and raised an eyebrow.

Caleb was glad that they were able to laugh about it. "Yes, it's no worse for wear. After you left, I also drained the tub and rinsed it out."

"Thank you." She chuckled, obviously thinking of him falling down and getting wrapped up in the curtain after seeing her in the tub. Try he as he might, he hadn't been able to look away. He was too stunned, not expecting to walk in on her like that.

"Well, I'll be sure *not* to walk in on you." She chuckled as she took another bite of her chicken.

Caleb nearly choked on his chicken.

"Are you all right, Pa?" Shane asked as he stopped eating.

Caleb cleared his throat and took a sip of his lemonade. "I'm fine, thank you."

Mia giggled as she continued eating.

After dinner, the children scampered off to the bedroom to play and Mia started stacking the dishes. Caleb walked up behind her and was tempted to pull her into his arms but thought better of it. Instead, he placed a hand over hers, enjoying the fresh scent of her hair.

"I'll do this." He took the plate from her, a bit slower than necessary. He felt her hand tremble as she pulled away and turned around, her face just inches from his. She held onto the counter as she looked into his eyes, obviously anticipating his next move.

But all Caleb could do was to look into her eyes.

After what seemed to be an eternity, she moved away and smoothed her hands over her dress. "Well, I think I should go to bed. I'll see you in the morning."

Caleb smiled, hating himself for not being able to take it farther. "Mia, I...."

"Ssshhhhhh...." She placed a hand on his cheek and looked into his eyes. "No need to explain." With that, she hurried from the room.

He was going to tell her that he couldn't do that to Jessica, that he needed time. But she knew. As he stood in the kitchen alone, intoxicated on Mia's scent, he had no idea if he would ever be able to take it farther with her.

After he finished the dishes, bathed the children, and took a bath himself, he walked outside into the moonlight, knowing he wouldn't be able to sleep. Caleb sat down on the edge of the porch and watched the moon as the wind blew through the trees and across the grass and wildflowers. This truly was God's country.

What was he going to do about Mia? Maybe he shouldn't do anything. After all, he had what he wanted, someone to care for the children while he made a living. Should he risk losing everything again by trying to take it further with Mia? As he sat on the porch in the moonlight, he didn't think he could.

★★★

Caleb woke before dawn, and the moonlight was still shining in through the windows. He slipped into some jeans and a shirt and walked out into the kitchen.

"Mia? Are you all right?" Caleb froze, taken by surprise to see her there.

Mia's hands were wrapped around her coffee mug and her head was bent down. She looked up at him, just now seeing him. "Oh! I'm sorry. I didn't know anyone else was awake." She got up and poured herself another cup of coffee.

"I just woke up."

She held up the coffee pot. "Would you like a cup?"

He took a cup from the cupboard. "I'll get it."

She nodded and sat back down.

Caleb poured his coffee. "What are you doing up so early? Couldn't sleep?"

Mia smiled. "No, I made some candy for the children… for Easter." Mia gestured toward a plate sitting on the table filled with hard sugar candy, beside the Easter eggs.

Caleb smiled as he sat down at the table with his coffee. "That's very nice of you. Is there anything I can do to help?"

Mia shook her head. "No, I think that's just about it."

Caleb took her hand. "Thank you so much for everything you do. I truly appreciate it."

Mia slowly removed her hand and placed it casually on her cup. "It's my pleasure. After all, I'm part of the family now, am I not?"

Caleb smiled. "Yes, of course."

"Well…." Mia rose from her seat. "I'm going to get ready before the children wake." She set her cup in the sink. "I'll be right out." She headed into her bedroom, leaving him alone with his thoughts.

"What are you doing?" Caleb mumbled to himself under his breath and then walked into his bedroom to get ready for church. The children were still sleeping, curled around each other like puppies, huddled together for warmth and comfort. They were his life and he would do anything for them… including marrying a woman he didn't know.

But he was lucky it had been Mia. She was wonderful, kind, and she loved his children. Why, then, was he pining for her love, too? Wasn't her loving his children enough?

He pushed the thought aside. After what they had been through, his children deserved a good Easter holiday.

Caleb slipped into the gray trousers that Mia had made for him weeks ago, a medium blue shirt, and vest that matched. Then he pulled on his black boots that he kept shined just for Sunday service and looked in the mirror. He brushed his dark brown hair, determined to enjoy this day and to make it as special as possible for his children.

Satisfied, he walked over to where the children were sleeping and shook Shane's shoulder. "Shane, honey. Time to wake up. It's time for church. Happy Easter."

Shane's eyes flew open. "Easter?"

Caleb smiled. "Yes, son, and it's time to get ready for church."

"Easter!" Shane yelled and then ran out.

He heard Mia laugh from the kitchen and Shane talking to her animatedly.

Caleb looked down, and Hailey rubbed her eyes and then reached up to her father.

"Come here, baby girl." Caleb picked her up and she

immediately laid her head on his shoulder. "Someone's not quite awake yet," Caleb announced as he walked into the kitchen and sat down at the table, where Shane was already eating.

Mia was standing by the stove, flipping over a piece of bacon, wearing a lovely blue dress, covered by an apron.

"Would you like me to do something?" Caleb asked, carrying Hailey.

"No, thank you." She motioned toward the table with the fork she was holding. "Go ahead and sit down. I'll have everything on the table in just a bit."

Caleb smiled, enjoying the way that Mia took charge. She had come a long way since she came to live with them, since they were married. It was still difficult to imagine she was his wife, although she fit into the family perfectly.

"Here you go," she chirped as she set a bowl of scrambled eggs on the table, along with the plate of bacon and a bowl of biscuits wrapped in a towel. She set two plates in front of him. "Would you like to feed her, or would you like me to?"

He shook his head. "No, go ahead and eat. I'll take care of her."

Mia sat down at the table and folded her hands. "Would you like to say the blessing?"

"Yes, of course." Caleb set down his fork and said a prayer over their meal, thanking God for the good food and fellowship, and the hands that cooked it. "Amen."

Mia smiled, but said nothing as she started to eat.

Suddenly, Shane noticed the plate of hard candy on the table. "What's that?"

"Oh!" Mia's eyes opened wide as she placed a hand on her cheek, looking at Caleb. "I didn't put it there. Did you?"

Caleb shook his head, playing along. "No, it wasn't me." He shrugged. "But it looks like a surprise was left for you since it's Easter morning."

"Wow!" Shane reached for the candy, but Mia put up a hand to stop him.

"You need to eat your breakfast first."

"*Then* can I have one?"

Mia smiled, inclining her head toward Caleb. "Well, you'll have to ask your father."

Shane looked hopefully at his father.

"Maybe just one piece…."

"Yippee!" Shane hurried to eat his bacon and eggs.

Caleb laughed. "Whoa! Slow down there, son. I don't want you to get a belly ache from eating too fast."

"Yes, Pa," Shane replied, eyeing the candy.

Hailey took a piece of bacon and Caleb set her on his lap. As she ate, she slowly began to wake up.

"Well, let's hurry and eat," Mia instructed. "We don't want your father to be late for service."

Everyone hurried to eat as Caleb looked at her appreciatively. His new wife truly was remarkable. He pushed the thought aside and finished eating while feeding Hailey.

When they finished breakfast and had a piece of candy each, Mia brought out the children's clothes and Mia and Caleb hurried to dress them. Hailey was in a light blue dress and Shane in gray trousers, a matching vest, and a light blue shirt that nearly matched Caleb's clothes.

When everyone was ready, Mia placed a clean dishtowel into a basket, placed the brightly colored eggs inside, and then covered them over with another towel. "I'll be right back." She came out of her bedroom a moment later, wearing a light blue hat that matched her dress.

"Ready?" Caleb asked.

"I'll keep the children inside while you hitch up the team."

"Thank you."

"Will you need any help?"

Caleb chuckled. "What? And mess up that pretty dress of yours?" He gave her a wink. "Not on your life."

She blushed as she lowered her eyes, turning her attention back to the children.

"I'll be back in a minute." Within minutes, Caleb drove the buckboard around to the front of the house and put on the brake. Then he jumped out and skipped up the stairs, taking two at a time, excited for the holiday. He flung open the door. "All aboard!"

Caleb looked down at his daughter, who was holding Mia's hand. "Time to go, little girl. Ready for Easter?"

"Yes!" Shane yelled as he ran out the door.

Hailey bobbed her head vigorously. Caleb chuckled as he picked her up and swung her into his arms. Then he held his arm out to Mia. "Ready?"

She slipped her arm in his. "Yes, sir." Mia was only kidding around, but he liked the sound of those words on her lips.

On the way to the church, the sun shone brightly through the canopy of trees, spring leaves budding, along with a gentle breeze blowing through the buds and wildflowers.

"Why don't we sing a song?" Mia suggested, smiling as she looked over at Caleb.

"Yes, why don't we?" It had been a while since they were able to laugh together as a family. Guilt started to raise its ugly head, but this time he pushed it down, determined not to ruin the day. "So, what do we sing?"

Mia thought for a moment and then replied, "How about 'Oh! Susanna'?"

"Perfect!" He started it out.

"I come from Alabama,
With my banjo on my knee,
I'm going to Louisiana,
My true love for to see;
It rained all night the day I left,
The weather it was dry,
The sun so hot I froze to death,
Susanna, don't you cry."

Then they all joined together on the chorus:

"Oh! Susanna, Oh, don't you cry for me,
I've come from Alabama
With my banjo on my knee."

They continued to sing it at the top of their lungs all the way to church. If anyone saw them, they would have thought they'd lost their minds, but Caleb didn't care. It was a wonderful nonsense song with a catchy tune, fun to sing.

And he wanted this day to be wonderful for the children… something good to remember.

As usual, they were the first ones to arrive at church. Before she went in, Mia gave his hand a gentle squeeze. "Good luck."

Caleb squeezed her hand and watched as she walked away with the children.

"You two look good together."

Micah Morgan, the town doctor, was standing there. Caleb offered him his hand. "Thanks, Doc. It's good to see you here."

Doc Morgan shook his hand. "Well, I have no patients in my hospital right now and, so far, there are no emergencies, so here I am."

"I hope you find another doctor soon. I know it's a lot for you, being the only doctor around these parts."

Doc Morgan smiled. "From your mouth to God's ears."

"Yes, indeed."

Just then, Dirk and Gabriella Price pulled up in their carriage and Dirk helped her down.

"Mrs. Price, it's so good to see you doing so well." Doc Morgan reached out and squeezed her hand. "How's the shoulder? Giving you any trouble?"

She leaned her head to the side. "Sometimes. But it's fine, for the most part." Although Caleb didn't know the details, it was common knowledge that Gabriella had been shot during a skirmish by thieves who wanted to hold her for ransom to her uncle, Charles III, Prince of Monaco.

"But we're not here to talk shop," Caleb said. "Doc

Morgan, I want you to enjoy yourself today and try not to worry about work."

Dirk smiled. "Yes, indeed. But don't worry. I take good care of her."

"I can see that." Doc Morgan smirked. "But if the injury ever gives you trouble, Mrs. Price, just let me know and I'll give you liniment to help."

Just then, other parishioners walked up.

"Happy Easter, Reverend." Doc Morgan clasped his shoulder and then let it go. "We'll go on in so you can greet your other parishioners."

"Happy Easter." Caleb gave him a manly slap on the shoulder and watched as he, Dirk, and Gabriella walked inside.

Caleb greeted the other members of the congregation and many of the ladies carried baskets with colored eggs just as Mia had.

Then, Millie Martin and Kenzie Baker rode up in a buggy.

"Millie, it's good to see you here." Caleb smiled as he shook her hand. Kenzie had become a regular since she arrived in Whiskey River, but Millie rarely attended. "I'm surprised that Harrison let you out long enough."

Millie smiled, adjusting the basket of Easter eggs on her arm. "I told Harrison that I wasn't going to open this morning so I could attend services. I haven't had a day off in a while, so he shouldn't complain. But between us, I really don't mind working. Keeps me out of trouble…" Then she looked over at Kenzie and smiled. "… and out of Kenzie's shop. I could spend my whole paycheck in there if I don't watch it."

One corner of Caleb's lips curled into a smile. "Did he? Complain?"

Millie shrugged. "He tried, but I still got my way. I also told him that he needs to hire another girl."

Caleb's eyes almost bugged out of his head. "So, is he?"

"It's looking good."

Then Caleb turned his attention toward Kenzie. "How's business, Miss Baker?"

Kenzie extended her hand, palm down. "Please, call me Kenzie." Her voice was a cross between an Irish brogue and a British accent. Her strawberry-blonde hair was pulled up under her hat.

"If you insist, Caleb replied, shaking her hand.

"I do." Kenzie gave him a smile, satisfied. "And business is booming. If your wife is ever interested in picking up some work, let me know. I've seen your clothes and she does wonderful work."

Caleb smiled. "I'll tell her. I think she has all she can handle right now, but I'm sure she would appreciate the offer."

Kenzie tilted her head to the side. "Well, if she ever changes her mind—"

"I'm sure she'll let you know." Organ music began to play, signaling that the service was about to start. "Well, if you'll excuse me…."

"Say no more." Millie held up her hand. "Happy Easter, Reverend."

He bowed his head slightly. "Happy Easter."

After they went inside, Caleb closed the door and the walked to the altar and signaled to Paul, the organist, th it was time to begin the service. Excitement was in the a as everyone stood and Gabriella led the congregation in th first song.

Caleb gave a sermon about Jesus dying on the cross but focused on His resurrection and the true reason why the holiday was celebrated. Throughout the service, Mia sat in the front row with the children, smiling as she listened and participated. Shane and even little Hailey tried to participate, as well.

"And be sure to stay for the egg hunt after service. Happy Easter!" Caleb announced, bringing the service to a close. Then Paul and Gabriella launched into the closing song.

Caleb stood in the back, thanking those who came an weren't staying. Caleb watched as Mia organized the eg hunt. Most of the adults hid the eggs while the childr remained inside with the other adults. After the last egg hidden, the children and adults began hunting eggs toge

"May we, Pa?" Shane asked, his eyes wide.

"Yes, of course!" Caleb crouched down in a run position, as if he were ready to start running to find the "But not if I find them first!"

"Yippee!" Shane ran off.

"Be sure to bring the eggs back to me!" Mia ye him.

Mia and Caleb hunted around for eggs wit Soon, the baskets of all of the families were fille

After the egg hunt, the children started pla

while Mia, Mrs. Jenkins, and the other women of the community organized the buffet. Even Mrs. Carson joined in the festivities.

"Well, children," Caleb announced at the end of the day after the last parishioner had left and the last table put away, "it's time to go."

"Do we have to?" Shane's mouth opened wide in a big yawn.

Caleb laughed. "Yes, we have to." Hailey was wobbling on her feet as she held Mia's hand. He swept her up into his arms and she immediately laid her head on his shoulder. He looked over at Mia. "She'll be out before we get home."

Mia smiled. "Or sooner."

Caleb knew that Shane was tired. Instead of climbing into the back of the buckboard of his own accord, he stood by the side of it yawning. "Come on, little fella." Caleb picked him up and set him in the back. They'd had a busy day and neither of the children had taken a nap.

On their way home, the sun was lying low in the sky. "It'll be dark soon," Caleb observed.

"Yes, it will," Mia replied, looking out over the colorful landscape stretched out before the majestic mountains rising in the distance. "This is so beautiful."

"God's country," Caleb agreed, looking into her eyes. "Did you have fun today?"

"Yes, I did."

Caleb chuckled under his breath. "I think Mrs. Carson even had a good time. You are so good with her."

Mia smiled. "She's a nice lady." Her eyebrows pulled

After they went inside, Caleb closed the door and then walked to the altar and signaled to Paul, the organist, that it was time to begin the service. Excitement was in the air as everyone stood and Gabriella led the congregation in the first song.

Caleb gave a sermon about Jesus dying on the cross, but focused on His resurrection and the true reason why the holiday was celebrated. Throughout the service, Mia sat in the front row with the children, smiling as she listened and participated. Shane and even little Hailey tried to participate, as well.

"And be sure to stay for the egg hunt after service. Happy Easter!" Caleb announced, bringing the service to a close. Then Paul and Gabriella launched into the closing song.

Caleb stood in the back, thanking those who came and weren't staying. Caleb watched as Mia organized the egg hunt. Most of the adults hid the eggs while the children remained inside with the other adults. After the last egg was hidden, the children and adults began hunting eggs together.

"May we, Pa?" Shane asked, his eyes wide.

"Yes, of course!" Caleb crouched down in a runner's position, as if he were ready to start running to find the eggs. "But not if I find them first!"

"Yippee!" Shane ran off.

"Be sure to bring the eggs back to me!" Mia yelled after him.

Mia and Caleb hunted around for eggs with Hailey. Soon, the baskets of all of the families were filled.

After the egg hunt, the children started playing games

together in concern. "I don't know why so many people have a problem with her."

"Because she's not so nice to everyone, but she seems to like you. Who knows? Maybe you can soften her and help her to make some new friends." Caleb chuckled. "This was the first time that she and Mr. Carson have come to church in a while. Maybe they'll start coming regularly again. It'll help her to feel like a part of the community."

Mia smiled. "When we can, I'd like to have her and some ladies from the church over for tea. Maybe it will help."

Caleb shrugged. "Maybe. And you can have your tea party anytime you like."

"Thanks, Caleb." She thought for a moment, watching the scenery pass. "Did you have a good day?"

Caleb looked over at her and smiled, his eyes meeting hers. "One of the best." And Caleb knew it was true. It truly was one of the best days that he had ever had.

CHAPTER 16

Throughout the rest of spring and halfway through summer, Mia had spent most of her days working in the garden when she wasn't working inside, cleaning, baking, or sewing. She, Caleb, and the children had fallen into a routine once again. Over the last few months, Mia had been so busy working that she hadn't had much time to think of Caleb and their arrangement. In fact, she'd become content. Mia had accepted the fact that if this was all there would ever be between them, then she could live with that. She loved the children and steeled her heart against loving Caleb. Since he had walked in on her that time in the bath and kissed her, then apologized, she hadn't pushed it. Her heart couldn't take it.

Hailey played nearby with her doll while Shane played a Civil War game on the other side of the field. Mia didn't really approve of it, but there were worse things he could be doing. Besides, boys loved to play war games, and she would rather him get it out of his system now. Although she was grateful for the military who protect their country, she couldn't imagine her son ever going off to a real war.

Mia paused to watch the children play. It was funny how love was. Since she had married Caleb, she had come to think of Shane and Mia as her own and could never think of having to live without them.

She couldn't even conceive of what Caleb had gone through when he lost Jessica. No one should ever have to lose their spouse so young. But unfortunately, sometimes that was part of life. She had no idea what she would ever do if something happened to Caleb.

Pushing the thought aside, she resumed her work in the garden. In the distance, Caleb was tending the wheat field. It hadn't rained in a while and she feared that they would lose their crop. But Caleb had been working hard to save the wheat field, and she had been working to save the garden, carting buckets of water to keep the plants watered. It was a big job to water just the garden, but was impossible to water the field, as big as it was. She just hoped it rained soon.

Mia worked until the sun was high in the sky and sweat poured from her brow into her eyes and down her cheeks and neck. When she looked out over the field to wipe the sweat from her brow, Caleb was still hard at work. She sensed that this crop was more important to their survival than Caleb had let on.

"Children! Let's go inside and have some lunch." Mia stood, her back aching from bending over, weeding for so long. Then she walked over and picked up Hailey, who was growing bigger by the moment. "Shane, stay here. I'll be right back."

Mia walked around the wheat field, careful not to walk through it. Caleb had worked long and hard on it and she wasn't about to do anything to destroy it. The July sun was beating down on the ground, creating a haze over the land. When she was parallel to Caleb, she caught his attention and he motioned for her to come over.

Mia waded through the tall wheat while Hailey brushed her hand lightly over the tops, letting it tickle her hand. "Caleb, it's pretty hot out here. Let's go in and I'll fix us some lunch."

Caleb didn't stop working, but looked up. "No, you go ahead. I need to do a bit more out here first."

Mia let out a deep breath. "Caleb, it's hot and you haven't had anything to eat or drink for a while. Come on in for a bit, then you can come back out here when you're rested."

Caleb wiped the sweat from his brow on the back of his sleeve. "Mia, I can't. We haven't had any rain for a while and if we lose this crop…."

"What?" Mia placed a hand gently on his arm, claiming his attention.

Caleb looked down, taking a moment to gather his thoughts, placing his hands on his hips. "Mia, if we lose this crop, we'll lose everything."

Mia felt her eyebrows pull together in concern. "What are you talking about? I thought we were doing okay. What happened?"

Caleb let out a deep breath and started walking toward the edge of the field.

Mia rushed to catch up with him, but carrying Hailey, she couldn't move as fast. "Caleb, wait up! We need to talk about this." Caleb stopped short, causing Mia to run into him. He turned around and waited. "Caleb, whatever it is, you can tell me about it. I'm your wife, after all."

"My wife?" Caleb bit his lower lip as he walked away. "Never mind."

Mia knew better than to follow him. She knew she should have given him a few moments to calm down. It was the first time that he had ever snapped at her. But she pushed the thought aside and ran after him as Hailey started to cry. "Caleb, wait!"

"Do you really want to know what happened?" Caleb turned on his heel. "Bringing you here ate into my savings, and then I had to spend money on a hotel. We spent a fortune on material and supplies at the general store. Do I need to go on?"

Mia staggered back as if she'd been slapped. "For one thing, you needed a wife… or a live-in babysitter and housekeeper, or did you forget?"

"Yes, you're right." He twisted around to leave. But instead of letting him go, Mia caught his arm, bringing him to a stop. He looked at her and waited.

Mia's heart fell. She hated herself for what she was about to ask, but she had to know. "Caleb, you don't regret bringing me here, do you?"

Caleb let out a deep breath, but said nothing.

"Okay, that's all I needed to know." Mia walked ahead of him, but Caleb stopped her.

"Mia, I didn't mean that—"

"Oh no?" She wheeled on him, her eyes flaring. "Well, I'm sorry if bringing me here depleted your savings. And I'm sorry if making clothes for you and the children depleted your savings, too. I have a little money left from when I first came here. It's not much, but I'll give you what I have."

"Mia, no—"

She held up a finger to stop him as Hailey cried openly. "I'll take a job with Kenzie Baker at the *Ladies Dress Emporium* and I will pay you back every dime."

"Mia, I'm sorry—"

"And another thing," Mia cut him off, on a roll now. "Bringing me here was *your* idea. So, don't you ever throw it up to me again."

With that, she turned and walked through the field, tears stinging her eyes. By the time she took a few more steps, she was crying just as hard as Hailey, so hard that it took her by surprise when Caleb grabbed her arm and wheeled her around. Before she could object, his lips crashed down onto hers as heat and passion filled her body. He took Hailey from her arms, never breaking the kiss. Mia tried to push back, but Caleb held her tightly with one arm, his lips crushing hers, preventing her escape. She pushed onto his chest again, but he held her until she melted into him and returned the kiss.

When she realized what was happening, she took a step back, her eyes wide with disbelief. "What was that? You set the rules before I came here, or don't you remember? After all this time, I pushed my feelings aside and have honored your wishes. And now that I'm mad, your solution was to kiss me?" She looked directly into his eyes. "I don't understand you."

She headed toward the house. "Shane! Come in for lunch!" she called after him. It must have sounded harsher than she meant it to, but either way, he must have known she meant business because he ran right in without argument.

In the kitchen, she poured the children some lemonade. Shane was silent as she started slamming around pots and pans, preparing to make lunch. Caleb walked in carrying Hailey, but she ignored him, continuing her tirade. He set Hailey on a chair. Suddenly, strong, muscular arms wrapped around her from behind, holding her as she cried.

He just waited until her tears slowed to a whimper.

"I'm sorry," Caleb said in her ear, his voice merely a whisper. "I shouldn't have said that. It was wrong of me."

Mia wiped her eyes. "And the kiss?"

"I didn't mean what I said."

Mia knew that he had avoided the question. "That's what I thought." She went back to fixing lunch, this time without slamming the pots and pans.

"Stay here. Shane, watch your sister," he said to the children and then took her hand and pulled her outside onto the porch, away from the children. "Mia, you have to give me time—"

"Look," Mia began again, "you set the rules before I came here, and I agreed to follow them. Sure, it was hard at first, but we fell into a routine. I've reconciled myself to the fact that there will never be anything more between us.

But you can't do things like kiss me unless you mean it. You can't play with my heart like that unless you're sure—my heart can't take it." She placed a hand on his cheek. "Caleb, I know you still love Jessica and you always will. I care about you and I love the children, but I can't allow myself to love you unless you return it. So, please, don't change the rules unless you're prepared to deal with the consequences."

With that, she walked into the spare room, her bedroom, knowing he'd already shattered her heart into a million pieces. She just hoped she could survive living with Caleb Henley. He alone had the power to break her for good, for she had already fallen in love with him. Even though she had told herself not to love him romantically, her heart had a mind of its own.

She laid down, knowing that she had left him to care for the children for the rest of the day and night. But she was exhausted and needed some time away from him to mend her heart. Why was he changing the rules now? Of course, he would never forget Jessica, nor would she want him to. Jessica was his past, and Mia wanted to be his future. But she couldn't take their relationship further unless he could give her his heart, too. And she sensed that might not be for a very long time, if ever.

Tears streamed down her cheeks as she tried to reel in her emotions. The kiss, the passion she felt for him still lingered on her lips. He was a wonderful man, the best man that she had ever met, but he was a man who could never, would never, give her his heart.

★★★

Bang, bang, bang!

Disoriented, Mia opened her eyes.

It was dark.

A flash of lightning struck outside the window, lighting up the whole room.

"Mia! I need you!"

Bang! Bang! Bang!

This time, the banging on the door was louder.

"Caleb, I'll be right there!" Mia yelled through the door as she slipped into her robe.

"Mama!" Hailey wailed, causing Mia's heart to jump.

"I'm coming, baby!" Mia didn't bother to tie up her robe. She flung the door open and Caleb was standing in the doorway, soaking wet. "What's wrong? What's happening?"

"Watch the children. I'll be right back," Caleb yelled as he ran out the back door.

"Caleb, be careful!" Mia yelled after him, just as lightning flashed in the distance. She watched him for as long as she could and was surprised when he ran through the rain past the barn toward the back field. The rain outside was beating hard against the earth, flooding the ground. "The wheat field…." Mia's heart nearly stopped as tears came to her eyes. "Come, children. Kneel down. Let's pray." She wrapped her arms around the children and, together, they prayed that God would protect Caleb, their crop, and the vegetable garden that would be a source of their own food and income for the upcoming year. For what seemed like an eternity, they never stopped praying until Caleb walked slowly back in.

"Caleb! You're drenched to the skin." Mia jumped up and ran to get him a towel. When she ran back in, he was standing in the open door, frozen in place as the children stared. Mia walked slowly over to him as a flash of lightning illuminated the night behind him. "Caleb… what is it?"

"The crop… it's gone."

Mia bit her lower lip as tears rimmed her eyes, threatening to spill over. "Oh, Caleb… no." She walked toward him, her eyes never leaving his. Lightning flashed again, casting his image into silhouette. Thunder crashed behind him, rattling the house, causing the children to shriek.

Caleb pulled back and ran his hand through his hair, dazed as he scrubbed his hands over his face. Then he knelt down by the children on the floor. Hailey reached up to him and he scooped her up into his arms and then walked to the back door. The lightning continued to flash outside as he bounced his baby girl and rubbed her back absentmindedly, watching the storm roar outside.

Mia let out a deep breath and then reached for Shane and he went right to her. For the first time, she picked him up, sat down on the rocking chair, and started rocking, stroking his hair.

No one said anything more as they waited, the only sound was the rocking chair squeaking methodically against the floor between thunder bursts and lightning strikes.

"Mia, are we going to die?" Shane asked, his voice low.

Mia lazily stroked his hair, rocking him back and forth. "No, honey. We're not going to die." Mia pushed back his hair and kissed his forehead. "Your father and I will protect you."

As Mia continued to rock, she noticed Shane was trembling. Caleb was still looking out the back door, swaying back and forth as he held his daughter. Even though they had lost everything, there was still hope. She decided to remind him.

In a low voice, Mia started singing "Life Let Us Cherish."

> *Life let us cherish, while yet the taper glows,*
> *And the fresh flow'ret pluck ere it close*
> *Why are we fond of toil and care*
> *Why choose the rankling thorn to wear*
> *And heedless by the lily stray*
> *Which blossoms in the way*
> *Life let us cherish, while yet the taper glows,*
> *And the fresh flow'ret pluck ere it close*
> *When clouds obscure the atmosphere*
> *And forked lightnings rend the air*
> *The sun resumes his silver crest*
> *And smiles adown the west*

With Hailey asleep on his shoulder, Caleb turned and walked into his bedroom and closed the door. Mia continued to sing, but stopped when Caleb walked back out into the living room. He stopped in front of Shane and looked down at his son, his eyes not meeting hers. "I'll take my son."

Mia looked into Caleb's eyes. "Caleb, I—"

"I don't want to talk about it," Caleb cut her off. Without another word, he walked into the bedroom, and closed the door behind him.

Mia rocked for a bit, humming the tune softly, wondering what would become of them now. At that moment, she had never felt more alone.

CHAPTER 17

Caleb woke early the next morning to the pitter-patter of rain against the roof. Luckily, it had slowed to a normal rain and was no longer the hard, driving rain that it had been the night before. The children were still sleeping, so he quietly slipped on his jeans and a flannel shirt. Then he sat on the edge of his bed and pulled on his boots.

He let out a deep breath, knowing he needed to assess the damage. There was no time like the present.

As he walked past Mia's garden, the watermelon and tomatoes lay open on the ground, and the tall corn stalks lay flat, ruined. He would look at it closely later to see what could be salvaged. Some of the tomatoes, watermelon, and vegetables were ripe and unharmed, but most of it would have to be tilled under and left to rot for the next planting season. They would be doing well to have enough vegetables to last them through the winter, let alone to be able to sell any.

Caleb continued walking through the rain and came

to the wheat field. Stalks of wheat lay flat on the ground, beaten down by the rain. He walked out over the field and nothing, not one stalk, was left standing. Rage filled his chest as he bent down and picked up a broken wheat stalk.

"Why?" he screamed up to Heaven. Tears rolled down his cheeks as he fell onto his knees. "First you take Jessica, and now you take my crop? Why? Am I being punished for something?"

As a preacher, he knew better than that. But as a man, it was hard to accept.

"I'm sorry…," Caleb cried as his fingers dug into the ground, "for whatever I've done to deserve this, I'm sorry."

Suddenly, he felt a hand gently touch his shoulder. Caleb looked up to see Mia. He quickly brushed the tears from his cheeks and rose to his feet. "What are you doing out here? Go back inside."

"Caleb, it's not God's fault," she said, her voice merely a whisper.

He wheeled on her. "Then why did he do it?"

"Caleb…" Mia reached out her hand to touch his arm, but he pulled away, so she folded her arms across her chest. "Caleb, God did not do this… and God didn't take Jessica, either."

"What?" He took a step forward. "Yes, God did take Jessica. And now, He's taken it all."

A weak smile appeared on her lips as she shook her head. "Caleb, God hasn't taken it all. You still have the children… and you have me."

He scoffed. "Really? I really have you?" His voice

dripped with sarcasm.

A hurt look came into her eyes. "You could, if you'd let me in." She walked to him with her arms out, but he turned around and headed toward the house, leaving her standing alone in the field.

Caleb hadn't meant to hurt her. He knew that this wasn't God's fault, and that Jessica's death wasn't His fault either, but who else was there left to blame? He should have taken better care of her....

All of a sudden, he heard footsteps running up behind him, the wheat crunching beneath her feet. Mia grabbed his arm and turned him around. "Now you listen here, mister. I will not let you give up! We're down, but we're not beaten. After the children wake, I'll go into town and will talk to Kenzie Baker about taking in some sewing."

"No wife of mine will ever work—"

"Caleb Henley!" Mia placed her hands on her hips. "If we work together, and with God's help, we can accomplish anything."

"If only I'd not spent the money, then we'd be fine."

"On what?" Mia's eyes flared. "On bringing me here?" When he didn't answer, she continued. "Well, I'm here now and I'm going to go to work. I'm sure Miss Baker will let me work from home. And with what you earn as a preacher—"

"I don't make a lot." He let out a deep breath. "I made my money mainly from selling cattle and the wheat crop." He motioned toward the field flattened down behind him. "But now that's gone."

"So? Then let's keep what we'll need and we can sell off

the rest of the cattle. It's too much for one person to handle, anyway." A faraway look came into her eyes as she planned. "We'll keep Bessie for milk for the children and another female and a bull. We can sell off the rest. We can also sell off a few horses, too. Then when we're on our feet again, we can rebuild. Together, we'll be on our feet in no time. By this time next year—"

"By this time next year?" Caleb scoffed. "We have to survive in the meantime! I have to provide for my children and for…." He left what he was about to say unfinished.

"Well, pardon my language, but you, sir, are an ass." She took a step closer to him and placed her hands on her hips. "From here on out, I plan to carry my weight around here and will bring in money to contribute."

"Mia, you do contribute. You care for my children—"

"*Our* children!" Mia spat out, shaking her head. "You just don't understand, do you?" She pointed toward the house. "I love those children as if they were my own. And since I married you, they are. And I will lay down my life for them just like you would." She pulled her shawl around her, calming herself. "I'm going inside. The children will wake soon." Then she looked into his eyes. "And you, sir, will have to swallow your pride. I've worked before and I can do it again." With that, she turned on her heel and stormed off toward the house.

Caleb knew he shouldn't have said those things to Mia. She had been good with the children and the house. And she was right. He was the one to make the decision to spend the money to bring her there. As he walked slowly toward the pasture to assess the cattle, he tried to picture what the past six months would have been like without her. Sure, he would have money in his savings, but he wouldn't have her. He scoffed. He didn't have her now. But who's fault was that? He had been the one keeping her at arm's length.

When he made it to the pasture, the rest of the cattle were no worse for wear, except for the loss of two and a small calf. Luckily it was still raining, keeping the dead cattle untouched by flies and wild animals. He headed toward the barn, retrieved the butcher knife along with several clean gunny sacks, then headed back. He spent the rest of the morning carving the cattle where they lay, salvaging what he could, and thankful for the surprisingly cooler weather after the rain. He would deal with the carcasses later so as not to attract wildlife looking for a free meal. Once the sacks were filled, he headed back to the butcher table in the barn and finished the process. One cow would be more than enough to keep the family fed for the upcoming year. He hoped Mr. Carson would be interested in buying the rest.

When he walked inside, the children were dressed and sitting at the table, eating lunch. Butchering the cattle had taken the whole morning.

"I'm going into town," Caleb stated flatly as he carried the carved meat down into the cellar. When he walked back up, Mia folded her apron and laid it on the counter.

"We're going, too."

"I'm going alone. You stay here with the children."

"Come on, children. We're going into town." Mia ignored him.

"Yeah!" Shane whooped as he ran into the bedroom.

"Shane come back here!" Mia yelled after him. "You need to wipe off your hands. They're sticky." Mia wet down a clean rag and wiped off Hailey's hands and face.

"Do I have to?" Shane yelled as he staggered back into the room, dragging his feet.

Caleb let out a deep breath. "Yes, you have to. We're leaving in just a minute." He stomped out the back door and headed toward the barn. Once the buckboard was in place, he hitched up the horses, one by one. When everything was ready, he loaded the wrapped meat in the back of the buckboard. It took four gunny sacks for just one cow. For a moment, he thought of just going into town alone, but Mia and the children were waiting on the front porch, bundled up in their overcoats. Hailey had a scarf tied around her head and Shane was wearing his cowboy hat to protect them from the rain.

The look on her face told him that she had anticipated that he might go without them. She was obviously having none of that.

Caleb was too tired and mentally drained to argue.

When he pulled the team to a stop, Mia walked swiftly to his side and handed Hailey up to him before he could jump down. Once Shane was in, Mia hurried to the other side while he was settling Hailey in. He reached over to help her up, but she didn't take his hand. Once she was seated, she set Hailey on her lap and then looked over her shoulder at Shane. "Are you okay back there or would you like to ride up front with us?"

Shane stood, holding onto the back of the bench seat. "No, I'm fine."

"Sit down before you fall down." Caleb was in no mood for his shenanigans. "And don't look in the gunny sacks."

"Yes, sir," Shane replied and did as his father asked.

After a while, Mia broke the silence. "Why did you want to go into town this morning?"

Caleb bit his lower lip. "We lost two cows last night, and the meat was still good. Mr. Carson buys his beef from me for his family every summer and he hasn't bought his yet. I'm taking the extra meat into town to see if he'd like to buy it. The rest will be plenty to last us all year."

A crease formed between her eyes "Are you sure the meat was still good?"

"It was still raining enough to keep the flies away and the bodies were still warm."

Mia bit her lower lip. "While you talk to Mr. Carson, I'll take the children with me to *The Ladies Dress Emporium* and will talk to Miss Baker."

Caleb let out a deep breath. "You really don't have to do that, you know. You work hard enough as it is."

"And you don't?" she challenged.

Caleb turned his attention back to the road. "Mia, I really don't want to argue with you."

"Then I'm going to speak with Miss Baker, and that's that." Mia looked out over the landscape. Rain drizzled over the land and was overcast, blocking out the sun. As hot and dry as it had been just the day before, now everything was nearly flooded. "At least we don't have to worry about not getting enough rain anymore."

Caleb narrowed his eyes, not in the mood to laugh. Then he turned his attention back to the road.

"I'm sorry. I was just trying to lighten the mood."

Caleb looked over at her and sighed.

Mia appeared to ignore it. "How was the rest of the cattle?"

"Still standing." Caleb watched the road without really seeing it. "I'll ask Ellis Smith or one of the other local ranchers if they want to buy them." He looked over at Mia. "We can't afford to feed them."

Mia looked as if she was about to say something more, but must have thought better of it and looked away.

"You shouldn't have come," Caleb announced flatly. "All I need right now is for you or one of the children to come down with influenza."

"Caleb, that's enough."

"Well, you should have listened to me and kept the children home."

Mia let out a deep breath. "You're sounding like a spoiled child."

Caleb's head snapped up and his eyes flared.

"Look. Let's just get through this crisis first."

"Before what?"

Mia looked straight into his eyes. "Before we make any other decisions."

Caleb didn't know what she was talking about, but he had a good idea. "Well, if you're going to leave, you may as well do it now."

Mia glared at him. "Stop it."

"What?"

"Pushing me away."

Not wanting to argue, Caleb turned his attention back to the road. Soon, the familiar sights of Whiskey River came into view. Caleb rode past the livery stable and pulled the team to a stop in front of the general store.

"I'll be right back." Mia scooped Hailey up into her arms and headed off toward *The Ladies Dress Emporium.*

Caleb walked to the back and slung two gunny sacks over his shoulder. "Shane, stay here with these two sacks for just a minute." He knew no one would bother them, but this was his livelihood and his family's only source of survival. He wasn't going to take the chance.

"Yes, sir." Shane climbed over the seat and into the back of the buckboard.

"I'll be right back." Caleb walked up the wooden stairs of the general store.

"Yes, Pa."

Caleb smiled at his son. Mia was right. He really did have a lot to be thankful for.

The bell on the door rang loudly, alerting the storekeepers. "I'm surprised to see you out on a day like today," Mr. Carson chirped loudly, wiping his hands on his white apron. "What can I do for you?"

Caleb stopped in front of the counter. "I hate for the short notice, but I was wondering if you'd be interested in buying some beef from me. I have two more sacks full of meat in the buckboard."

"Well, I wasn't going to buy our beef for another few weeks...."

Caleb let out a deep breath. "I lost two cows last night in the storm, and I can't use all the meat." He shrugged. "Since you usually buy a full cow from me every year, I thought you might be interested."

Mr. Carson's eyebrows rose. "How much do you have?"

"A whole cow." Caleb shifted his stance under the weight. "Shane is outside with the other two sacks, so I can't stay. Also, the meat has to be cured right away. I just thought I'd give you first shot at it before I go over to Harrison across the street."

Just then, Mrs. Carson walked out from the back room and Caleb's heart fell. He'd rather deal with Mr. Carson any day of the week than Mrs. Carson. She could be a hard woman at times. "Morning, Preacher. What are you selling?" She placed her hands onto the counter and straightened her shoulders, going into her business persona.

Mr. Carson sighed. "Go in the back, Myrtle. I've got this."

Mrs. Carson's mouth opened as she placed her hands on her hips. "I most certainly will not! This is business and I handle the buying—"

"Some of it," Earl Carson corrected. "And I'm handling this." Then he turned to Caleb. "Leave the meat and tell the boy to come in. We'll work something out."

Caleb bit his lip to keep from smiling as Earl stared down his wife. He was probably the only man on the planet who could handle Myrtle Carson. She stared back at him for a moment, huffed, and then walked over to the fabric. Although she pretended to busy herself with straightening the bolts, Caleb wasn't fooled. She was listening.

Caleb went outside and grabbed the other two gunny sacks, straining under the weight. "Come on in, son." Back inside the store, Earl was still standing behind the counter.

"Now…," Earl began again, "I don't have a lot of extra cash on hand.…"

They haggled a bit over price. Once they came to an agreement, Mr. Carson scratched his head. "I don't have that much cash on hand right now, but I'll tell you what I can do. I'll give you half now and store credit for the other half."

"You will not!" Mrs. Carson interjected, placing a bolt of fabric onto the table a bit too hard.

"Stay out of this," Earl warned.

"I will do no such thing!"

"That's okay." Caleb started walking toward the door. "I don't want to be the source of any marital discord. I'll just go across the street to the restaurant and see what Harrison can do for me."

"Myrtle, let me handle this, unless you'd like to eat chicken all winter!"

Mrs. Carson started walking toward him until Mr. Carson held up a hand to stop her. "We would have had the cash on hand, had you not made a show in front of the town with that Easter Tea of yours! Now, go back to your work or go to the back and let me do business, woman!"

"Humph!" Mrs. Carson stormed off into the back, out of

sight and slammed the door closed.

Mr. Carson turned to Caleb and smiled as if nothing were amiss. "Now, is that favorable to you?"

Caleb sighed thoughtfully. "Could you do three-quarters down and the rest on store credit?"

Mr. Carson smiled as he held out his hand. "You have yourself a deal, Preacher." Then he smiled at Shane and lowered his voice. "Is it okay with you if I give the boy some candy?"

Shane's eyes brightened, having heard the offer.

Caleb smiled. "Yes, of course."

"Yeah!" Shane jumped up and down.

Caleb laughed. "You're going to spoil him."

"Now, you can't spoil a child with too much love." He turned and pulled a jar of candy sticks from the shelf. "Here you go, boy."

Shane looked sheepishly at his father.

Caleb smiled. "Go ahead, son."

Mr. Carson held the jar down low for Shane so he could pick out the one he wanted himself.

"What do you say, son?" Caleb coaxed.

"Thank you, Mr. Carson."

Mr. Carson smiled and then turned to Caleb. "I'll be right back. We don't keep that kind of cash out here." He walked into the back.

Sudden relief washed over Caleb, knowing this would help them through the rest of the summer. Now, for the rest of the year....

"Did you lose anything else?" Mr. Carson asked as he

counted out the money.

Caleb let out a deep breath. "My crop is gone."

Mr. Carson's eyes opened wide. "Your wheat?"

Caleb sighed. "The whole crop." Then he smiled, putting on a brave face. He just wished he could have done the same earlier for Mia. "But things will work out."

A look of pity came into Mr. Carson's eyes—a look that Caleb hated. "Tell your wife to bring by any extra eggs she has, and I'll buy them from her. Also, when she makes butter or cheese, tell her to make enough for me, too." He leaned forward conspiratorially and motioned with his head in the direction his wife had stormed off. "She can't make cheese or butter for squat."

"I heard that!" Mrs. Carson yelled through the closed door.

Caleb laughed as he held out his hand to the balding older man. "Thanks, Mr. Carson. I'll let her know."

Mr. Carson shook his hand. "And call me Earl."

"Will do… but only if you call me Caleb."

Mr. Carson laughed, straining from the weight of the gunnysacks filled with beef when Caleb handed only one of them to him. "Yes, but only outside of church."

Caleb tipped his hat to Mr. Carson. "Have a good day." Then he raised his voice as his lips curled into a mischievous smile. "And you have a good day, too, Mrs. Carson."

The door cracked open and Mrs. Carson stuck her hand out and waved a handkerchief. "You, too!"

As Caleb walked out, he couldn't help but think of the Carsons and what a strange couple they were. But somehow, it worked for them. He guessed that was what couples needed to do… find common ground where they both could be happy.

The rain had slowed, nearly stopping. He and Shane waited for Mia and Hailey in front of the store. Feeling much better, he looked down at his son and smiled. "Us men spend a lot of our time waiting on the womenfolk, don't we?"

Shane let out an exasperated breath as he placed his hands on his hips. "We sure do."

Caleb laughed. He looked up and spotted Mia walking through the drizzling rain, carrying Hailey. Her hat was wilted and her hair drenched, along with Hailey's. "Any luck?"

"Miss Baker is swamped with work. She said that she would deliver the dresses that she'd like for me to work on herself after it stops raining."

A broad smile spread across Caleb's lips. "No need. Mr. Carson bought the beef and also said that he would buy your extra eggs and butter. He'd also like to buy some cheese the next time we make it. And this afternoon—"

"Cheese?" Mia asked, raising an eyebrow. "I don't know how to make cheese."

Caleb smiled. "It's easy. I'll show you."

"Caleb, after our discussion this morning, I'm keeping the job." Mia didn't even smile.

Caleb knew he deserved it. After all he had said, he knew he brought this on himself. "But you don't have to work."

She looked into his eyes. "Yes, I do."

He let out a deep breath. "Mia, I'm sorry—"

She looked him square in the eye. "Let's go home."

Mia started walking toward the buckboard and Caleb followed. Through the restaurant window across the street, Millie looked up from wiping a table and waved and Mia returned the wave. But there must have been something in Mia's expression that Caleb couldn't see, because Millie's smile faded and she went back to wiping off the table.

This time, Caleb walked around to the passenger side of the buckboard, took Hailey from Mia, and then offered her his hand to help her up. She took it, sending chills over his body, and stepped up into the buckboard. He planned on a mail-order bride. He hadn't planned on falling for her.

As they drove home, the rain finally settled into a light drizzle. Even so, by the time they got home, the children were soaked through. "Whoa!" Caleb pulled the team to a stop and put on the brake. Then he hopped down and hurried around to the other side. Once Mia shoved Hailey into his arms, she didn't wait to take his hand and climbed down on her own. "Mia—"

Mia spun around. "Caleb, don't worry. I got the message loud and clear this morning. I'm here to take care of the children and the house and nothing more." Tears started pooling within her eyes, threatening to spill over. "I'm sorry you had to spend the money to bring me here. I promise I'll pay you back every cent as soon as I can."

"Mia, I didn't mean to say—"

"You knew exactly what you were saying."

Caleb stiffened. If she was going to play that game, so

was he. "Fine. Go inside and take care of the children. I'm going over to the Smiths' or the Stanfords' to see if either of them will buy the cattle." He climbed up into the buckboard and took off the brake. "I can start over in the spring."

"*You* can start over," Mia repeated, as if willing the words to sink in. "Well, be careful." She reached for Hailey and the little girl went right to her.

Caleb watched as she walked purposefully into the house with the children, remembering when he told her to leave if she was going to go. And actually, she had been right. He was pushing her away without even realizing it. He just hoped that they could work it out before it was too late.

On the ride to Ellis and Sarah Smith's ranch, he could only think of Mia and what he had said that morning. In retrospect, he'd been cruel, blaming her for the depletion of his funds when it had been his idea to bring her there. Although he counted on paying for her train fare and the preacher to marry them, he hadn't counted on staying at a hotel or the extra meals. But he had no right to blame it on her.

The bullets of rain pelted down harder than before. He pulled the collar up over his neck and pulled his hat down. Caleb was glad when the Smiths' ranch came into view.

Relieved to be out of the rain, he knocked on the door and heard footsteps clicking against the wooden floor on the other side of the door. When it opened, Mrs. Smith's eyebrows rose almost into her hairline. "Why, Preacher Henley! You're soaked through and through! Would you like to come in?"

Caleb took off his hat. "No, I'm so sorry to intrude, but is Ellis busy?"

Mrs. Smith pointed toward the corner of the house. "He's out in the barn. You can go on back, if you like."

Caleb slipped on his hat and tipped it toward her. "Thank you, ma'am." He jumped down off the porch and walked toward the barn.

Ellis Smith stepped out from inside, wiping his hands on a rag. "Why, Preacher Henley! What brings you here?"

"I'd like to talk to you about a business matter. Are you busy?" Caleb asked, shifting his weight.

Ellis looked at him for a moment, concerned. "Come on in out of the rain and we'll talk." He motioned toward the barn.

Caleb smiled. "Thanks, Ellis."

Inside the barn, Ellis wiped his face with the hand towel. "What seems to be the problem, Preacher?"

Caleb took off his hat and hit it against his leg, knocking off the rain. "I was wondering if you'd like to buy my herd."

Ellis froze. "Your herd?" He walked over and stood in front of him. "Are you sure about this?"

Caleb sighed, looking out the barn window and stared over the pasture. "Yes, I'm sure." Any other man would have taken advantage of the situation and would have stolen his herd when he found out that Caleb was in financial straits. But he knew that Ellis would never do that to him. "I lost my crop last night," he admitted honestly.

Ellis gasped behind him.

Caleb turned around. "So, I need to sell my herd. Also, it's just gotten to be too much, trying to do it all. And I can't afford to hire a hand to help me out."

Ellis threw down the piece of straw he had between his teeth. "I'm so sorry to hear that. I hate to see you get out of the business."

"I am, for now." Caleb smiled. "But come next spring, who knows? I might get back into it again."

Ellis clasped his hand on Caleb's shoulder, man to man. "Why don't you think about it first. Give it a few days. You might change your mind."

"To tell you the truth, I'm tired. I need a break and I'll have enough on my plate with cleaning up the farm and preaching."

Ellis sighed. "I'll talk to the church counsel and see if we can give you a raise." He smiled. "I'm ashamed at what we pay you. You're a good preacher and you've built up the church to what it is today. You deserve more."

Caleb gave him a weak smile. Although more money for his duties would help, he hadn't become a preacher for the money. "That's okay. I know the church can't afford much."

"I'll tell you what I can do." Ellis shoved both of his hands into his pockets. "I can buy half of the herd and I'll talk to Stanford to see if he'll buy the other half. If he agrees, we'll work it out between us. We'll offer you a fair price. I promise."

Caleb shook his hand. "I know you will. That's why I

came to you. Thank you, Ellis, for everything."

"I'll let you know by tomorrow." Ellis smiled as he released his hand.

Caleb slipped his hat back on. "I can't tell you how much I appreciate this."

"Give the Missus my best." Ellis walked him out.

"I will. Mia will be happy for the sentiment."

When he got home, Caleb noticed that Mia was up working into the wee hours of the night. It was obvious that she was determined to pay back every nickel that Caleb had spent on her, just as she had promised. Guilt raised its ugly head for having said that to her. He just hoped that she could come to forgive him… one day.

CHAPTER 18

Ellis worked it out with Cole Stanford, a single local rancher, and the two of them bought Caleb's herd. Caleb was sad to see the cattle go, but relieved at the same time. He had been stretching himself for too long, trying to care for his family, parishioners, and farm. It was nice to have more time to commit to his family and parishioners. In addition, the church gave him a raise. It wasn't much, but it helped.

It was now September. The long, hot summer months had ended, and fall would soon be upon them. When Caleb wasn't tilling up the soil, preparing for the next year, he spent his time woodworking.

"Here you go." Mia handed him a glass of lemonade, bringing him from his reverie. He had been working in the barn, finishing up his latest project: a crib for Dirk and Gabriella. Dirk had been so elated at the news that they were having a baby that he was beaming, telling everyone and anyone who would listen. With the extra time, Caleb had taken in jobs for the community. "Almost finished?"

Mia asked, yawning.

"Nearly." Caleb nodded, sanding down the crib. Even though it was September and had cooled off, it was still hard enough work to work up a sweat, but it was fun. It also gave him time to think.

"It looks beautiful," Mia said, running her hand over the crib. "You did a wonderful job."

Caleb's heart swelled with pride. "It's not finished yet but will be within the next few days."

Mia sighed. "Well, don't stay out too long. It's getting late."

"I won't." He looked down at the crib. "I'll be in to kiss the kids goodnight in just a bit."

"Okay." Mia pulled her shawl around her shoulders as she headed toward the door.

"Mia?"

"Yes?" Turning, her eyes were bright in the light from the kerosene lamp.

He put down his sanding block. "Mia, thank you for pitching in since you've been here. With your help, we'll be well equipped to handle the upcoming winter months." He walked over to her and looked into her eyes. "You've been a blessing to us all."

"Thank you, Caleb. That means a lot," she replied, blush coloring her cheeks. "I'll see you inside."

"I'll be in soon."

Caleb watched as she walked away. After working long and hard every day making bread or the meals, cleaning the house, and raising the children, Mia spent her nights sewing.

On many occasions, Caleb walked out into the living room to find Mia asleep in the rocking chair with a dress on her lap that she had been sewing for Kenzie Baker. He loved watching her sleep. She always looked so content. Seeing how she cared for the children and the house, and the way that she had chipped in to save the family, he couldn't help but admire her.

When they could afford it again, he vowed to get her a new-fangled sewing machine. He had heard that they saved a lot of time. Although they were getting on their feet, he couldn't quite afford a sewing machine yet. But maybe one day.

Streaks of orange, pink, and red marbled the evening sky, creating a beautiful ending to a lovely September day.

Exhausted, he summoned his strength and split some wood for the night. With winters in Wyoming, it was necessary to spend a lot of time splitting wood to prepare for the upcoming winter.

After he gathered the wood, he carried it into the house, wondering why it was so dark. He didn't think he had been out there much longer after Mia had come out, but when he looked around, Mia had fallen asleep in the rocking chair with his children cuddled up on her lap, asleep as well. She must have taken time out from her sewing to spend time with the children.

Still holding the wood, he watched them sleep as something stirred inside of him. Being careful not to wake them, he quietly put the wood in the wood box, put a log on the fire, and then went outside to wash up at the outdoor pump, vowing to take a proper bath later. Although the days were still warm, it was beginning to cool off at night.

After washing up, he went back inside and took his shoes off by the back door, not wanting to soil the clean house and ruin Mia's efforts. In the bedroom, slipped off his dirty shirt, and put on a clean white shirt and denims. He didn't bother to tuck it in, and he left it open at the neck.

Feeling refreshed, he lit candles throughout the house, in the living room, and two tapered candles in long-stemmed glass holders on the kitchen table. While in the kitchen, he peered at the stove to see what he could make for dinner. He was pleasantly surprised when he found fried chicken on the counter under a dish towel, and mashed potatoes on the stove, kept warm by the pilot fire, along with fresh bread. He smiled, knowing that she must have killed a chicken herself. Caleb went down into the root cellar for a can of tomatoes and stewed them with bits of Mia's fresh bread. He set the table with four place settings and put the meal on the table, then put water on to boil for a bath for the children after supper.

Careful not to wake Mia, he took Shane and Hailey from her one at a time.

"Papa?" Shane asked when he woke.

"Ssshhhh," Caleb cooed as he led him and Hailey into the kitchen. "Let's not wake Mia. She had a busy day."

Shane smiled as he sat down at the kitchen table along with his sister. Caleb fed them dinner, and then sat and enjoyed watching his children.

"Aren't you going to eat, Papa?" Shane asked as he took

a bite of his chicken thigh. "Yum… this is really good."

Caleb chuckled. "It looks good, but no. I'm going to wait for Mia."

"Yes, Pa," Shane replied, and continued eating. Caleb tore Hailey's chicken into small bites for her, but she ate her mashed potatoes by herself without issue. Over the summer Hailey had turned three and become much more independent, feeding herself and trying to do everything that her older, now five-year-old brother did. They were growing up so fast. Caleb knew that Jessica would be proud.

When the water was heated, he poured it into the tub, repeating the process until there was enough water. After they finished eating, he bathed the children and dressed them for bed. They said their prayers, and he put them in bed and told them a bedtime story. Then he kissed them both good night and pulled the door almost closed, leaving it cracked open.

In the living room, Caleb noticed that Mia had slept through it all. She must have been very tired because usually, she was a light sleeper. He didn't have the heart to wake her just yet, and he didn't want to eat without her. So, he sat in the rocking chair across from her and watched her sleep. He couldn't help but think of how caring and accepting she was of his children. And Mia really was beautiful. Her blonde hair looked golden in the candlelight. The way her jaw curved to her slender neck was lovely, and her body was perfect, with curves in all the right places.

"Mia," he whispered, hating himself for waking her. He waited for a minute, and she continued snoring lightly.

"Mia, wake up. It's time for dinner."

He reached out and gently touched her cheek with the back of his hand. "Mia," he whispered.

She didn't stir, and it was getting a bit chilly, so he put more wood on the fire. Warmth immediately filled the room.

Caleb walked back over to her and decided to try one more time. "Mia, time for dinner."

She finally opened her eyes.

"Wake up, sleepyhead," he teased as he knelt at her feet and looked up at her.

She looked at him and smiled, and then jumped with a start. "Oh, my goodness! Where are the children?"

Caleb smiled. "Don't worry. They've been fed, bathed, and put to bed."

"Oh!" She sat up and looked around, panicked. "How long have I been asleep? The last thing I remember was rocking the children—"

"Don't worry about it." Caleb rose to his feet and extended his hand. "Are you hungry? The fried chicken looks great."

Mia looked at him, confused. "You didn't eat yet?"

He shook his head as a smile lit his lips. "I was waiting for you." When she hesitated, he added, "I heated everything up, but it's going to get cold again if we don't eat soon."

She smiled as she took his hand, rose to her feet, and let him guide her to the table. Mia's eyes opened in surprise. "Everything looks great." She slid the cloth napkin across her lap as he sat down beside her. "I'm so sorry—"

"Ssshhhh...." He pressed a finger gently to her lips.

"It's okay. You've been working really hard… too hard," he observed as he took her hand. "Mia, I can't tell you how much I appreciate it."

Remembering what he said to her after they had lost the crop, he reached for her hand, determined to make things right between them. "You've been working so hard. No wonder you fell asleep." When she had received her first paycheck from Kenzie Baker, she had insisted it was to pay him back. But he had told her to keep it, feeling horrible for having thrown it up in her face. But after she kept insisting, he had finally agreed to her buying groceries, fabric, yarn, and the like. Secretly, he felt horrible about her having taken a job. She worked hard enough in the house and with the children, after all. And after the sale of the cattle, they didn't need it as badly as they had before.

She smiled and looked down at his hand in hers.

Caleb slid the napkin across his lap. "So, shall we?"

"Yes, let's."

He said the blessing, and then added, "Let's eat."

She giggled, causing his heart to soar. Then she spooned some mashed potatoes onto her plate along with a chicken breast and he did the same.

Then he sliced the bread. "Everything looks delicious."

Blush colored her cheeks.

Caleb took a bite of a chicken leg. "This is delicious. Mia, you really outdid yourself."

She smiled as she buttered a slice of bread. "Thank you."

"I made it while the children were playing."

Caleb nodded. "Speaking of children, you're great

with mine."

"You mean *ours*," Mia corrected, throwing down her napkin. "Caleb, when will you start thinking of me as part of this family? They are *my* children, too." She rose from her seat, but he caught her hand.

Caleb smiled appreciatively. "I'm so sorry, Mia. You're right. I'll try to do better."

Reluctantly, she sat down and turned her attention back to her food.

"So, what did you do for the holidays in New York?" he asked, knowing the holidays would be upon them soon enough.

She shrugged. "This past year, I spent it alone. I worked on Christmas Eve, and then I was off on Christmas morning. I spent most of the day sewing."

He took another bite of his chicken leg and a moan involuntarily escaped his lips.

Mia let out a deep breath and leaned back against the back of her chair. "Caleb, may I tell you something?"

He put down his fork. "Yes, of course."

Mia smiled. "Caleb, what you said to me… throwing the money you spent up to me—"

"I'm so sorry about that," Caleb cut her off. "I should never have said those things. Can you ever forgive me?"

"That depends."

"Upon what?"

"It depends upon if you'll ever say it to me again." She let out a deep breath and sat back. "Caleb, you can't say things like that… ever… even when things get tough. We need to get past how we met." Mia leaned forward and gave his hand a gentle squeeze. "We have to be a team… to work together."

Caleb understood. "Mia, you're right. You've become a vital part of this family." He took her hand and bit his lower lip. Then he looked into her eyes. "I'm so sorry, Mia." At that moment, he had an overwhelming urge to kiss her, but instead, he rose from his seat and pulled her to her feet. "May I have this dance?"

She giggled, taken by surprise. "Why, yes, sir," she teased, giving him a slight curtsy. "I would be delighted."

There was no music, so he began to sing "Aura Lea."

> *"When the blackbird in the spring,*
> *On the willow tree,*
> *Sat and rocked, I heard him sing,*
> *Singing Aura Lea.*
> *Aura Lea, Aura Lea,*
> *Maid with golden hair;*
> *Sunshine came along with thee,*
> *And swallows in the air."*

Mia looked at him, her eyes wide. "I didn't know you could sing."

Caleb smiled. "There are a lot of things you don't know about me."

Her lips curled into a smile. "Well, we'll have to do something about that."

She drew closer, sending electricity through him. He spun her around, and then started singing again as he swung her around the room. He couldn't believe she was so light on her feet. She really was a great dancer. A few moments later, he ended the song with a dip.

Caleb held her as she leaned back, and was tempted to kiss her slender neck and then her cheek and lips. Instead, he lifted her and spun her around and set her on her feet and bowed as she curtsied. Moving a strand of hair away from her face, he placed his hands on the sides of her head and lightly brushed his lips across hers as her hands rested on his arms.

"Good night, Mia," he whispered as he looked in her eyes. Then he touched her cheek with the back of his hand and smiled. "Thank you for the dance."

Emotion filled Mia's eyes. Caleb wasn't sure what it was, but it hadn't been there before. "Good night."

He walked into the bedroom, pushed the door closed, and leaned his forehead against it. Seeing her like that, so beautiful and vulnerable, it was all he could do to walk away. A twinge of guilt filled his heart, but this time, it was a different kind of guilt. It was the guilt of not seeing her as his wife… until now. The guilt of taking a wife and then not being a good husband to her.

He knelt by his bed and folded his hands. "Jessica, I have feelings… for Mia. I never thought I could feel anything for any woman other than you, but… something about her calls to me. She's great with the children, and I know she loves them. I hope you understand, but I need her. Please forgive me. It doesn't mean that I love you any less, but I think I'm ready to open my heart again. I love you, darling, and I always will, but I love her, too." -

Then he sat on the edge of the bed, not wanting to sleep, energized at the revelation of giving in to his feelings for Mia. Until this point, he hadn't realized how much effort he had exerted, fighting his love for her. Now, it was as if a weight had just been lifted from his heart.

Caleb swore he heard the rocking chair going back and forth against the hardwood floor. Unable to resist, he walked out to check on her, and she was sewing once again.

"Mia, you really should go to bed," he gently scolded, smiling as he watched her work. "It's getting late."

"You go ahead." She smiled. "I'll go to bed in a few minutes."

A smile spread across Caleb's face. He shoved his hands into the pockets of his jeans. "Well, don't stay up too late." He walked back to the bedroom, touched by the gesture. He turned around and whispered, "Good night, Mia."

She looked up and smiled. "Good night." She gave him a slight wave and then went back to her sewing.

When he walked back into his bedroom, he no longer felt guilty at all.

Caleb couldn't help but admire Mia's independence. In one way, she reminded him so much of Jessica, and in another way, she was nothing like her at all. It was time he stopped comparing her to Jessica and start seeing her for who she was instead.

One morning there was a nip in the air and Caleb knew that autumn was right around the corner. It was early September and, although it was still warm in the day, it was slowly cooling off during the night. When he walked out, Mia was sitting in the rocking chair, sewing by the firelight, and didn't see him come in.

"You're going to hurt your eyes, sewing in this light."

"Oh!" Mia quickly put away what she was working on.

"When do you sleep?"

She laughed. "Oh, I sleep. Don't worry."

He took a step forward. "Make sure to take care of yourself. You're working too hard." He let out a deep breath. "Mia, I—"

"I'm fine," Mia cut him off, smoothing the skirt of her work dress as she rose to her feet.

Somehow, the words tugged at his heart. That was exactly what Jessica used to say before....

"So, what would you like for breakfast?" she asked, interrupting his thoughts. "I already made coffee."

Before he could object, she jumped to her feet, beating him to the kitchen. Then she poured him a cup of coffee, added sugar, and handed it to him. He took a sip, and it was just the way he liked it.

Then she poured one for herself and sat kitty-corner from him at the table. "So, what's on the agenda for today?" she asked a bit too cheerfully.

He smiled at her enthusiasm. "Since it's early, I thought I'd show you how to milk a cow. That is, if you're up for it?"

A broad smile spread across her face. "Really?" She raised an eyebrow doubtfully, looking as if she was about to say something more, but then she must have remembered something and her face fell. "What if the children wake up while we're out?"

He shrugged. "If we go now, we'll be back in before they wake."

The grin returned. "Let's go, then."

Caleb hurried to slip into his coat, and then helped her on with hers. They walked outside into the brisk morning air as streaks of purple and orange swiped across the sky. He walked into the barn and stopped in front of Bessie's stall. "She's the most even-tempered."

"Good to know." Mia's eyes widened as she looked at the cow.

Caleb laughed. "Come on. I'll show you." He hooked a lead strap to the cow's halter and then led Bessie out into the hallway. "First, we tie her to the milking post." He smiled at Mia. "We don't want to have to spend the morning chasing her down in the field."

"I thought cows usually grazed in the fields."

Caleb smiled. "Well, she'll run from us if she thinks we want her."

Mia laughed.

Caleb shrugged, took out a milking stool, and placed it beside the cow's udders, which were bulging with milk.

"Does it hurt her when she's not milked?" Mia asked, concerned.

"Yes, that's why she has to be milked twice a day. We get

enough milk from her to supply our milk, as well as cheese, cream, and butter." Then he rubbed his hands together. "First, you need to warm your hands. She'll kick you when your hands are cold."

Mia giggled. "That explains it."

"What?" Caleb asked.

Mia shook her head. "My first morning I was here, I tried to milk the cow, but had no luck."

Caleb chuckled, wishing he could have seen that. "After your hands are warm, you take an udder in each hand…." He proceeded to show her the fine points of milking a cow. Once milk was streaming steadily into the bucket, he stepped back. "Here, you try."

She sat on the stool, warmed her hands, and pulled. The cow jumped. "Oh my!"

Caleb laughed. "That's okay. Just pull and twist at the same time, but gently."

She tried again, and milk shot directly in her face.

Caleb burst out laughing, and then handed her a rag. "Don't worry. It's happened to all of us."

"Let's try this again." Mia pulled on an udder and milk accidentally sprayed all over Caleb. She laughed. "Oh, I'm so sorry!"

"Oh yeah?" he asked.

She giggled and jumped up from the stool, causing it to fall over. Bessie mooed in protest and stepped aside as far away as the lead strap would allow. Mia ran into the yard laughing and Caleb chased her. He caught her around the waist and then swung her around as she laughed. As he held her, their faces came close together and they both suddenly became serious. Caleb reached up and brushed a strand of hair away from her face. His hand lingered on her cheek and she leaned into it. As he looked into her eyes, his heart pounded as her breath quickened. Caleb leaned in and crushed his lips to hers as he ran his hand through her hair. She returned the kiss, wrapping her arms tightly around his neck. Then he lifted her off her feet as his lips explored hers. Finally, he set her down on her feet. Placing his hands on her cheeks, he gave her one last sweet kiss. "I think the children might be awake now," he whispered against her lips. Then he pulled back, hating to release her. "I'll finish up out here."

Mia smiled, rubbing her arms as she walked toward the house. She gave him one last look over her shoulder, smiling, and then continued inside.

A chill ran through him as Caleb watched her walk into the house. He took off his hat and ran his fingers through his hair, gathering his senses. He shook his head to clear it and chuckled as he went back to milking the cow. "I'm in big trouble. Yes, I am." Even though they had been married for a while now, he still didn't know if he was ready to give her his heart. But maybe he was closer.

CHAPTER 19

"I know! Let's sing a song," Mia chirped as they rode along, on their way to church.

"Yeah!" Shane stood in the back of the buckboard, holding onto the back of the seat. Hailey sat between Mia and Caleb in the front. "What do you want to sing?"

"How about 'Yankee Doodle'?" Mia asked.

"Yankee Doodle, Yankee Doodle!" Shane and Hailey shouted at the same time.

They sang at the top of their lungs all the way to church. Then they passed by a river, visible from the road.

"I never noticed the river before."

Caleb smiled. "That's Whiskey River. The actual river that the town was named after."

"Really?" Mia asked, intrigued. "I thought that the town was just named Whiskey River. Not that it was named after an actual river."

Caleb chuckled. "Yes, some miners came through here and loved the countryside. When they saw the river, they thought it flowed like they always hoped whiskey would. Hence the name. Then families began to move in and the miners moved on to California in search of gold. Mrs. Jenkins and her family were one of the founding families."

Mia's eyebrows pulled together in concern. "Family?" For as long as she had known Mrs. Jenkins, she never mentioned having a family.

"Yes, she was married, but her husband died when he went off to fight in the Civil War… or at least that was what she thought had happened to him since he never returned."

Mia sighed, understanding. "I could never imagine losing a spouse like that."

"It's not easy." Caleb gave her a weak smile.

Mia's eyes opened wide. "Oh, Caleb! I'm so sorry. I wasn't thinking—"

"It's all right."

They rode in silence the rest of the way, each lost in their own thoughts. Mia wished that Caleb would come to think of her as his wife now, but she had no idea if he ever truly would. But maybe there were heading in the right direction.

Before long, they pulled up to the beautiful stone church. The leaves on the trees surrounding it were starting to change color. It appeared that the whole countryside was teeming with life but would soon fall into slumber. It was as if the stone church had just sprouted up out of the earth, then God had planted grass and flowers around it and had set snow-capped mountains in the distance for good measure.

"It's beautiful." Mia looked at the church, amazed. "No matter how many times I've seen it, it still looks lovely."

"Yes." He looked at the church with pride, pulling the buckboard to a stop. "The church was the first permanent structure in Whiskey River." Caleb smiled as he scooped Hailey up into his arms. Then he helped Mia down and placed his hand on the small of her back as they headed toward the church.

Soon, they were greeted by a few other parishioners who were waiting for them.

"My, my!" Gabriella gushed at the sight of the family, standing by Dirk. "Don't you look nice today!"

"Thank you. More of Mia's creations," Caleb announced proudly. "She stays up late nearly every night sewing…." He looked over at Mia. "…Which I've been meaning to talk to her about."

"Kenzie is delightful, isn't she?" Gabriella's eyebrows rose, obviously knowing that Mia had been sewing for her.

"Yes, she is. She's such a nice lady… and funny, too."

"Well then," Gabriella linked arms with her as they walked into the church, "would you care to come for afternoon tea this week? Perhaps Wednesday at one o'clock? I'll invite Kenzie, too, if she's free. We can have some girl time—" She looked over at Dirk and Caleb. "—away from the men."

Mia giggled. "I'd like that."

"Good!" Gabriella smiled. "I'll see you then."

Mia and the children took their places in the front pew as Gabriella approached the organist. People began filing in, and the women of the church greeted her, talking about their latest recipes or styles, and they all commented on the

Henley family's outfits.

When Ella and Colton came in carrying the twins, she motioned for them to come up front again. It had quickly become their tradition to sit in the row behind Mia and the children.

"Ella," Mia gushed, pulling her in for a hug. "I'm so glad to see you this morning. The babies are getting so big!"

Ella sighed. "They're a handful. What I wouldn't give for a good night's sleep."

"You and me both," Colton agreed. Then he beamed at his son in his arms. "But they're worth it."

Mia reached over and gave Ella's hand a squeeze. "I'll come over one day this week and will watch the children so you can take a nap, if you like."

Ella smiled. "You don't have to do that. I'm fine."

"I'm serious." Mia shrugged. "Besides, we haven't had a chance to catch up on some good old-fashioned girl talk."

Ella laughed. "Well, since you put it that way…."

They both laughed.

"How's tomorrow?" Mia asked. "I'll bring the children with me, if you don't mind. We can all play while you sleep."

"Sounds good to me."

"Well, well!" Mrs. Jenkins chirped as she pulled Mia in for a hug. "Don't you all look marvelous?"

Mia smiled.

"How's everything going?" Mrs. Jenkins asked.

"Better."

She gave her hand a gentle squeeze. "I'm glad to hear it."

She leaned in conspiratorially. "But if you need anything, I'm here for you."

After they lost the crop, she had worked hard and used her money to help support the family. When she had told him it was to pay him back, he wouldn't accept it. So, she told him it was to help the family, to buy groceries and material. Over the past few months, things had gotten better.

The elder woman smiled. "Well, if you need me for anything, just let me know."

"I'm fine now, but I'd love it if you'd come over just to visit." Mia returned the smile. "Maybe we can have some coffee."

"I'd like that," Mrs. Jenkins replied, and then they both noticed Caleb approach the pulpit. "Well, I must take my seat. I'll talk to you after the service."

"Sit with us," Mia insisted, patting the seat beside her.

Mrs. Jenkins shook her head. "Oh, I couldn't."

Mia smiled. "I insist."

"Well, if you insist." She and Mia giggled.

Mia loved having Mrs. Jenkins sit beside her and the children during the service.

Caleb gave a wonderful sermon and Gabriella sang beautifully as she led the church in song. Gabriella could have been a professional singer somewhere in Europe if she had wanted to. But here she was, happy as a lark in Whiskey River. It said a lot for the town.

Mia loved watching Caleb capture the attention of the congregation. But most of all, she loved seeing his love of God so prominent in his sermon. It inspired her to be better… to be a better person. Something stirred inside of her as she watched him.

After the service, she took the children to the recreation hall and started organizing right away.

A band started playing as women brought in their specialties, each greeting Mia and setting their dishes where she directed them. She quickly took over, no longer feeling like an outsider, struggling to fit in.

"Excuse me." Caleb cleared his throat behind her, and then took her hand. "But could I borrow my wife for a bit?"

Her heart fluttered at his words as the ladies around her giggled.

Caleb led her out to the dance floor and spun her around. They effortlessly launched into a waltz, capturing everyone's attention.

"I didn't realize you could dance so well," Mia commented as he guided her expertly around the floor.

"I learned in college," Caleb replied, never missing a step. He looked into her eyes. "But my dancing skills pale compared to yours."

Mia blushed, but held her head high as all eyes were on them. When the song ended, he leaned her back in an elegant dip as everyone clapped. Then Hailey and Shane ran up and they all danced together.

After dancing for a while, they took a break to eat. Everyone sat on the floor against the wall or in the chairs that were available. Mia ate until she couldn't eat any more. Each dish was more spectacular than the last.

After they had finished eating, Caleb asked her if she

would like to go with him to play with the children outside. She quickly agreed.

Watching him play hide-and-seek and tag with the children stirred her heart. Despite everything else, he really was a great father.

"Here, I'll take her." Caleb held his arms out for his daughter. It was the end of the day and Hailey had curled up on her lap.

Mia shook her head. "No, I have her. Go have fun." Mia carried her inside, sat down on a chair, and Caleb followed.

He reached over and kissed his little girl's forehead. "We'll be going soon. I'll help the men break everything down and put it away, and then we can go." He looked into Mia's eyes. "Is that okay, or would you like to leave now? I can take you and the children home and then come back."

Mia shook her head as she smiled. "No, we'll be fine."

She looked over at Shane, and he was yawning and rubbing his eyes, as well. He would probably fall asleep on the way home.

Home. It was a small word that meant so much.

It was almost dark when they got home, and both children were asleep, tired from their full day. Mia carried Hailey and Caleb carried Shane inside and they put them straight to bed, since their bellies were full and they had missed their naps. Then they walked into the living room, leaving the door cracked open.

Mia covered her mouth with the back of her hand as she let out a big yawn. "Well, I think I might try and get some sewing in." She took Caleb's hands in her own. "Thank you for today. It really was wonderful." She turned to walk over to what had become her rocking chair, but Caleb held fast to her hand.

"Would you like to sit with me for a while by the fire?" Caleb asked.

Mia smiled. "Yes, of course."

"I'll get us some coffee if you'd like to make yourself comfortable." He disappeared into the kitchen before she could say anything.

"Would you like some help?"

"No, I've got it."

She threw some pillows on the floor by the couch on the oval area rug, sat down on one of them, curling her legs under her skirt, and watched the fire. The flames burned in orange, red, and yellow tongues, lapping at the log. It was mesmerizing. She was so exhausted from the day's work that she caught herself nodding off when Caleb entered the room, carrying two coffee cups.

"Here you go, love," he breathed as he handed one to her. She was suddenly wide awake, her heart fluttering. *Love?* He sat down beside her. Up close like this, she noticed how his muscles played under his shirt, evidence of his hard labor over the years. Remembering the first morning when he walked out without a shirt, she knew that his stomach was just as tight, but she pushed the thought quickly aside as their agreement came to mind.

"Thank you." Mia looked in her coffee cup as she held it with both hands. "Caleb?"

"Um?" he asked, looking up from his coffee as he

propped his elbow on the sofa, and lifted his eyebrows. He was so handsome, with the sharp contrast between his dark brown hair and blue eyes, that it took her breath away.

"I was so proud of you today. Watching you preach. Watching you with the children. Watching how you chipped in with the men of the congregation so easily, not afraid to roll up your sleeves." She looked into his eyes. "You might not want to hear this, but I'm proud to call you my husband."

A smile lit his lips, but his eyes never wavered from hers. "I like hearing that." He looked away, and Mia's heart sank, thinking that he was going to let her down easily, but then he looked back into her eyes. "Mia, I'm proud of you, too. The way you pitched in and took in sewing so we could get on our feet. We're okay now, so you don't have to do that anymore. You've been working too hard."

Mia looked into the fire, watching as the flames lapped at the wood in varying shades of yellow, orange, and red. "I wanted to pay you back…" She looked into his eyes, sincere. "…for what you spent to bring me here." She hated to bring it up, but since the day in the field, him spending the money to bring her there bothered her.

Caleb had a sharp intake of breath. She turned to look at him and he placed a finger under her chin. "Mia, I'm so sorry that I ever said that to you. That day in the field, I was hurting and I took it out on you, which was completely unfair. Please, forgive me."

She started to turn away, but he wouldn't release her gaze.

"Mia, you've become a part of this family. You've been

wonderful. The community has accepted you, and so have my children. Thank you. I have no regrets about marrying you and I don't want you to have any, either."

He slid his hand gently on the side of her cheek and into her blonde hair as he looked in her eyes, searching for acceptance. Then he slowly leaned in and pressed his lips to hers, sending shivers throughout her body and filling her heart. As his lips moved with hers, it was as if her body knew his, as if it recognized him as hers.

He pulled away a moment later, looked into her eyes, and then wrapped his arm around her and pulled her to his side. She watched the fire as she laid her head on his shoulder, enjoying the warmth of his body so close to hers.

Then Caleb placed his hand on the side of her face once more. "I'm tired, so I think I'll say good night." Caleb looked in her eyes, over her face, and then pressed his lips to hers once more in one last, sweet kiss.

Heat rushed through her body, and she was tempted to take the lead and deepen the kiss, but thought better of it. Mia knew that this was hard for him. "Good night, Caleb."

She felt his eyes on her as she rose from the pillows and walked toward her bedroom… alone.

After she closed the door, she leaned her head against it, wondering what she was doing. She had finally accepted what they had, and he was changing the rules. Now, she was as confused as ever, having no idea what he wanted from her, what he expected. Could he ever truly give his heart to her and leave the past behind?

★★★

Mia woke early the next morning, still wondering if they would ever become a true husband and wife. But last night was a step in the right direction.

As memories of the night before rushed through her mind, she wondered what he wanted from her now. When she became a mail-order bride, she had accepted that it would be a life devoid of romance. But now, did he want her as his real wife?

Although she knew she was probably reading too much into it, she decided to catch Caleb before he left. Mia knew she could never leave the children, but staying there was tearing her apart. She was more confused than ever and needed some time to think.

At church, she'd made plans to visit with Ella. Mia thought that maybe it would help to take her mind off her own problems and focus on helping Ella and Colton. Even though Ella's children were getting bigger, Mia knew she could still use some help. She was ashamed of herself for not having visited more often than she had.

Mia looked outside and it was still dark. Just a few streaks of red and purple threatened to break the midnight sky. Maybe Caleb was still here. She hurried to dress and rushed out, hoping she wasn't too late.

When she walked out, Caleb was sitting at the kitchen table, sipping his coffee. "Good morning," he greeted her, smiling. But his smile slowly faded when he saw the expression on her face.

Mia pretended not to notice. "I hope you don't mind…." She crossed the room and slipped into her coat. "But I made plans to see Ella today. Don't worry about the children. I'll take them with me."

Caleb rose from his chair. "How long will you be gone?"

"I'll be home in time to make dinner." She adjusted her hat. "Would you mind taking us? I'll have Colton drive us home this afternoon."

"Yes, of course." His voice was thick with emotion. He downed the last of his coffee and then looked into her eyes. "Are you all right?"

She shrugged. "I hardly know."

"I'll keep the children today."

"Then I'll take a horse, if you don't mind."

He took a step toward her. "Is there anything I can do? Anything I can say?"

She shook her head as she took a step back. "No, I just need a day."

He took a step closer. "For what?" he asked casually.

She bit her lower lip as her eyes welled up with tears. "Caleb, when I came here, I knew the rules. I knew what you expected. Now, I have no idea."

One corner of his lips curled into a smile. "Is that so bad?"

She took a step back. Standing so close to him, inhaling his intoxicating scent, was confusing her. "Yes, it is." Tears welled up in her eyes, threatening to spill over. How could she tell him that he had the power to shatter her heart into a million pieces? "Caleb, you can't keep playing with my heart. Last night—"

"You don't think I'm an honorable man?" He looked down, placing his hands on his hips. When he looked up, his eyes flared.

"No… that's not what I meant at all…." He had her so confused that now she was even confusing herself. "Caleb, I don't want to sound selfish, but I just need a day to think things through."

"Okay." He reached down beside her for his boots, slipped them on along with his coat, and headed out the back door, letting it slam closed behind him. A few minutes later, she heard the sound of horses' hooves shuffling in the snow at the front of the house.

She followed him outside and stepped down off the porch. "I'll be back before dinner," she reminded him.

Caleb handed her the reins.

She said nothing more as she swung up into the saddle. "Kiss the children for me."

A crease formed between his eyes, but he said nothing.

"Hup!" she ordered as she leaned forward in the saddle. The horse launched into a moderate canter. She looked behind her one last time. Caleb was standing out in front of the house, watching her leave.

What was that all about last night? She had been in love with him for quite some time. Against her wishes, she had tried to stick to their agreement… to be a mother to his children and to clean the house, but to keep her distance from him. And up to this point, she had done a good job of protecting herself. The time with him last night sitting on the floor by the fire had been just a taste of what she truly wanted but had reconciled herself never to have. She was deluding herself thinking that he was falling in love with her, too.

On the way to Ella's house, she welcomed the time to think as tears ran down her cheeks. She couldn't live in a one-sided marriage. She couldn't give him her heart while he still withheld his.

Alone for the first time and not wanting to go over to Ella and Colton's house too early, she decided to go for a ride. It would give her time to think. She thought of the river and pointed the horse in that direction, hoping she remembered the way.

When she got there, she slowed the horse to a walk. Mia slid off, holding tightly to the reins, and walked as the horse followed her down to the edge of the river. The horse dipped its head down into the water. Unable to hold back, she wrapped her arms around her waist, trying to hold herself together, and collapsed to her knees as sobs wracked her body. How could she have fallen in love with a man who could never love her in return? And it wasn't even his fault. His intentions had been clear from the beginning. But last night... last night had changed everything.

After she regained control of her emotions, Mia bent over and saw her reflection in the water. She was a wreck. She couldn't let Ella see her this way. Mia sat down on the river bank and let the horse graze on the tender grass at the water's edge. She sat for what seemed like hours, watching the river flow by at a lazy pace as the wind blew softly through the trees. Whiskey River was truly a magical place.

Feeling better, she splashed her face, washing away the tears. Then she cupped her hands and took a drink, feeling the cool water pour down her throat.

"Good girl," she cooed as she patted the horse's sorrel-colored coat. "Ready to go?" To her amazement, the horse bobbed its head frantically up and down. She mounted the horse, then took off in the direction of Ella and Colton's house.

By the time she arrived at their house, she felt better. She slid off and took the reins, ready to lead the mare to the back, but Colton walked out onto the front porch.

"Welcome, Mia!" Colton called out to her as he skipped down the stairs. "It's good to see you." He pulled her in for a one-armed hug and took the reins from her with the other hand. When he pulled back and saw the expression on her face, his face fell. "What's wrong?"

She shook her head as she quickly dabbed at her eyes. And here, she thought she looked presentable. "I'm okay."

He grabbed her shoulders, forcing her to look in his eyes. "Are you sure? What happened?"

"Nothing." She quickly put a smile on her face. "Please, don't tell Ella. I came over to help. Not to burden her."

"Mia, we're here for you if you ever need to talk."

She inclined her head. "Thank you, but I'm fine… really." She held up both hands. "Do I look better now?"

He pulled her in for another hug. "You look fabulous. Now, you go inside and visit with my lovely wife while I take care of your horse."

"Are you sure?"

A broad grin spread across his face, clearly a proud papa. "Absolutely! Go have fun with Ella and my children."

Mia laughed. "Your children? Did Ella have anything to do with it?"

"Maybe a little bit," Colton agreed as he walked her horse toward the barn. "I'll be inside in a bit."

"I'll tell Ella."

Colton laughed as he disappeared with the horse around the corner, headed toward the barn.

"Ella?" Mia asked as she walked into the house and closed the door gently behind her, and then headed through the living room and into the kitchen.

"In here!" Ella called out just as Mia walked in. Her face lit up as soon as she saw Mia. "Well, hello! How are you doing today?" Ella was sitting at the table, breastfeeding one of the babies, covered with a lightweight blanket.

"Great!" Mia replied, smiling when she saw her. And it was true. She was feeling much better now that she saw Ella. She looked into the crib setting in the kitchen. Hannah's blonde curls covered her head as she held her hands up to Mia, waving them. "Well, hello, baby girl," Mia cooed as she lifted her out of the crib. Then she turned to Ella. "What would you like me to do?"

Ella handed her the baby boy. "Here. I'll trade you. I need to feed her, too."

"It'll be my pleasure." Mia took Blake with one arm and handed Hannah to her with the other. As blonde as his sister was, Blake was just the opposite with dark brown hair that curled around his neck. They looked so much like their parents that it was uncanny. As they swapped places, the babies reached for each other and touched hands. It was the sweetest thing Mia ever saw. She sat Blake down and gently patted his back to burp him.

"My, my, it's amazing how much they've grown! Have they started walking yet?"

Ella switched sides and began breastfeeding again, and then covered up with the light blanket once again. "No, but they're crawling everywhere. They're growing too fast."

Mia smiled. "They'll be running before you know it." She continued patting his back and, a moment later, she was rewarded. "Feel better?"

The baby cooed in answer. "Da, da, da, da!"

"Whoa!" Mia's eyes opened wide and then looked at Ella. "He's talking?"

Ella smiled proudly and rolled her eyes. "Just 'da, da.' He has Colton wrapped around his little finger." Then she looked down at her daughter adoringly. "They both do." Ella watched Mia for a moment, rocking the baby. "You know, you look great with a baby."

Mia laughed without humor, turning her attention back to the baby in her arms. "Oh, I don't know about that."

"What's wrong?" A crease formed between Ella's eyes. "You don't want to have children?"

Mia let out a deep breath, enjoying rocking Blake. "Yes, of course I do."

"Well, then. What's wrong?" Ella asked as she placed

the baby on her shoulder, fixed herself, and started burping the baby girl.

Mia shrugged. "Well, I already have two."

Ella's daughter let out a big burp. "That's a good girl!" she cooed.

Mia rocked Blake and watched as he shoved his fist into his mouth.

"Mia, I know you," Ella said as she rocked Hannah. "What's wrong?"

Mia looked down at the baby. "Last night, Caleb kissed me… I mean really kissed me."

"Oh?" Ella leaned forward, clearly intrigued. "And that's a problem?"

Mia nodded.

"What's going on?"

Mia bit her lower lip in an effort to fight back the tears. "Ella, when I agreed to be his wife, he stipulated that he wanted a platonic relationship and I agreed to it. But now, he's changing the rules. I had no trouble protecting my heart before, but now…." She let out a deep breath, keeping her tears at bay. "Ella, he could never give me his heart—"

"And you're in love with him," Ella cut her off.

Mia bit her lower lip. "Yes, I am. Somehow… last night… he broke through the walls I had built around my heart." She let out a deep breath and then looked into Ella's eyes. "I'm in love with him, even though I tried not to be. But what if he's not in love with me? What if he could never love me?" She shook her head absentmindedly back and forth. "I can't live in a one-sided relationship."

"Mia, he can come to love you," she cooed. "Just give him time."

"I know. I have."

"It might take a long time."

"I know," Mia repeated. "But what if he never comes to love me... the way I love him? He could easily break my heart without knowing it. And I can't expect him to love me."

"Mia, I'm sure he already loves you." Ella adjusted the baby in her arms. "Have you talked to him?"

"I brought it up when he asked what was wrong this morning and he didn't say a thing."

"Mia, he may not love you the way he loved Jessica," Ella replied, "but you can love people differently—"

"I know that." Mia let out a deep breath. "I'm sorry. I shouldn't have brought it up."

Ella shook her head. "Mia, don't say that. You can talk to me about anything. You know that."

Mia gave her a weak smile. "I'm not meaning to complain. I love the children. At first, it was hard with Shane. Losing his mother has really taken its toll on him." She paused at the memory. "But now, we get along fine. He doesn't call me Mama, but I don't expect him to."

"Besides going to church, what do you do together as a family... to have fun?"

Mia shrugged. "We started making breakfast together every morning. No matter what is happening that day, Caleb and I get up early and make breakfast together for the family."

"Well, that's something!" Ella encouraged. "Just give it time."

Mia noticed that the baby in her arms was sleeping, but she kept rocking.

"You're not thinking of leaving him, are you?" Ella asked as she rocked Hannah.

Mia shook her head. "I couldn't leave the children… no matter what happens with Caleb."

Ella sighed. "Mia, you said you love him, right?"

"Yes. Of course, I love him. He's kind, funny, wonderful with the children, handsome…."

"Okay then," Ella replied. "Don't you think that he might think the same things about you?"

Mia shook her head.

"Mia," Ella cooed, her voice sympathetic. "He's probably showing you that he loves you every day, without actually saying the words."

Mia shrugged. "Well, how about I make us some lunch? What would you like?"

"Mia, I know what you're trying to do." She looked down and the baby had fallen asleep in her arms. "Okay, I'll let it go… for now. But I'm here when you're ready to talk."

"Please, don't tell anyone."

"I never do."

"Thank you, Ella. I promise I didn't come over here to burden you."

Ella laughed. "Burden me? Never!"

Mia chuckled as she put Blake down in the cradle. "I'll tell you what. I'll put the babies down for a nap and I'll keep them out here with me while you rest." Mia kissed the top of her head when she reached for the baby in her arms. "You go lay down and take a nap while I make lunch."

Ella kissed the baby before Mia took her and then stood. "Well, if you insist."

"I do, Mama. Now, go! Get some rest." Mia carried Hannah over to the crib and laid her beside her brother. They curled up beside each other immediately, like puppies huddling together.

"Okay." Ella headed toward her bedroom, but turned back to Mia. "Wake me when lunch is ready."

Mia smiled. "I will."

"Mia?"

"Yes?"

Ella chuckled. "I thought you might not want to have children after witnessing me give birth."

Mia laughed, and then shook her head. "No, I haven't ruled it out. I still want to have more children… even though I already have two."

Ella laughed. "Good night."

"I'll see you in a bit."

With that, Ella disappeared around the corner. She heard a door close a moment later.

As Mia started cooking lunch, she thought of Caleb's children. She would always think of them as hers… no matter what happened between her and Caleb.

CHAPTER 20

The next day, Caleb woke up early and went out to the kitchen to start the coffee. He considered making French toast, but thought better of it. Mia had spent the day at Ella's house the day before, and when she came in, she didn't say anything all through dinner. Then she cleaned the dishes and helped dress the children for bed. The only thing she said the whole time was good night before going straight to her bedroom and closing the door.

Since it was morning, he hoped that she felt better and that things could go back to… well… if not normal, then *their* normal.

Mia came out of her bedroom fully dressed. Instinctively, Caleb wondered if she was going to stay away the whole day again. "I'll start breakfast in just a minute," Mia announced as she checked on the children, and then left the bedroom door cracked open. "What would you like this morning?" she asked as she walked past him and into the kitchen, not looking at him.

"Anything you like," he growled. It was Jessica all over again. But Jessica left involuntarily; Mia was leaving willingly of her own accord. He went to the back door, threw the contents of his coffee cup outside, and then set it on the table. Without another word, he slipped on his hat and went out to the barn. He didn't want to go far in case Mia decided to leave again.

Inside the barn, he leaned against a post. Yesterday, she'd begun to distance herself from him… from them. He turned around and punched a board in the barn wall. His hand started bleeding, but he felt nothing.

He wondered why Mia had started pulling away from him. Maybe she didn't love him. It was obvious that she loved his children, but what if she didn't love him? It was the only explanation he could manage.

Caleb let out a deep breath as he grabbed the wheelbarrow and shovel, then walked over to a stall. When he was angry, that was what he did… shovel stalls. It was a safe way to get his anger out. Physical activity always helped him when he was frustrated, and this time was no different.

Now, he had changed the rules and had fallen in love with her. But he still loved Jessica, didn't he?

Caleb was mad at himself for thinking that he could marry a woman for convenience, to marry a woman and not fall in love with her. How could he have done this to himself? To her? Mia had walked into this situation with her eyes open, into his home with an open heart. She had been content to love his children and he did a good job of keeping her at arm's length. And they were doing just fine… until he changed everything.

He couldn't blame her. After all, he had been in love with Jessica for years. Loving another woman felt like a betrayal. But now, he realized that he loved Mia and that he needed her, but did she love him?

Caleb washed up and then walked inside, determined to talk to her. To try and salvage what was left of their marriage, of their relationship.

When he walked in, he was relieved to see that Mia was in the kitchen, washing the breakfast dishes. "We need to talk."

"About what?" she asked casually, rinsing a dish.

He looked around. "Where are the children?"

She motioned toward the bedroom. "Playing in their room."

He took her by the hand and started pulling her through the house. "Good. They'll be all right for a minute while we talk."

"Caleb…," Mia replied, trying to keep up as he pulled her out the front door and onto the porch. "Caleb, you're scaring me."

Outside, he left the door open. Then he let go of her hand, skipped down the stairs and onto the front lawn.

"Caleb—" Mia followed him slowly down off the porch.

He held up a hand, cutting her off. "I need to say something and it's not going to be easy." She waited, not saying a word. "I'm sorry about the other night. I ruined everything."

She let out a deep breath. "Caleb, what are you saying?"

Tears welled up in his eyes. "Mia... when I kissed you the other night... I shouldn't have. Everything was working, and then I ruined it."

She crossed the lawn to him and placed her hand on the side of his cheek, forcing him to look into her eyes, but he pulled her hand down. "Mia, I can't give you what I want to give you."

She raised an eyebrow. "And what's that?"

Caleb let out a deep breath. "My heart."

"Oh." She waited for a moment, and then asked, "Would you like me to go?"

He shook his head. "No, I don't want you to go."

"Then, what do you want?"

She waited for a minute, but he said nothing.

"I see. Well, when you figure it out, let me know." Without another word, she walked into the house, leaving him standing on the front lawn... alone.

CHAPTER 21

The next day, Mia woke, realizing that it was Wednesday, the day she had promised Gabriella that she would come over for tea with her and Kenzie Baker. She wondered if she should go, but thought that it may do her and Caleb some good to have a little time apart. She dressed and walked out into the kitchen, and Caleb was sitting at the table.

"Good morning," Mia said. "Want some breakfast?"

Caleb didn't look up from his coffee.

Mia bit her lower lip and then pulled a skillet out from under the kitchen cabinet. "I promised Gabriella that I would go over to her house today for tea at one o'clock. Will that be a problem?"

In one swift movement, Caleb rose from his seat and set his coffee cup by the sink. "No. No problem at all."

Her heart pounded within her chest as she watched his muscles play under his shirt, but she forced herself to look away.

Then he walked over to the back door and slipped on his

cowboy hat. "I'll be out back, doing chores. Let me know when you're ready to go." Without looking back at her, he walked out back, letting the door slam loudly behind him.

Mia finished washing the breakfast dishes and then cleaned the rest of the house. She needed to work off some energy, so she got down on her hands and knees and scrubbed the floors. When she was finished, the house was clean from top to bottom. She looked around, assessing her work, and she was proud of what she had accomplished. Then she looked over at the clock. Eleven o'clock.

Mia looked in on the children and they were playing quietly on the floor of their room. Shane looked up and smiled, and then went back to his game of war. She fixed a quick lunch of bacon sandwiches from fresh bread that she had made that morning.

She hurried into her bedroom and dressed appropriately for tea in a pale pink dress, then donned a matching hat. When she came out of the bedroom, Caleb was sitting at the kitchen table with the children and look up.

Mia slid her reticule over her wrist. "Would you like me to do anything before I leave?"

Shane looked up. "You look pretty!"

Mia gave him a weak smile. "Thank you, Shane."

"Caleb?"

"No, we'll be fine." Then he looked up with dead eyes. "Would you like to eat with us before you go?"

Mia shook her head. "No, I'll eat at Gabriella's."

Caleb turned his attention back to his sandwich. "I hitched up the team for you. The buckboard is waiting out front. What time will you be back?"

"Before four. I won't be long."

"Have fun." Then Caleb turned in his seat to look out the kitchen window.

Mia fidgeted with her reticule for a moment. "Caleb, I don't have to go—"

"No, as the preacher's wife, you do." His head snapped back to look into her eyes. "You can't make promises without intending to keep them."

Mia staggered back as if she'd been slapped. She had a feeling that he was referring to the promise she had made to him instead of the one she made to Gabriella. "Caleb, I've kept my promises...."

Caleb rose from his seat and stood in the doorway, looking out the backdoor. "Just go."

"Caleb, don't push me away." His words hurt her worse than she had thought they would.

He wheeled around to face her. "Well, I'm not the one leaving."

Hurt suddenly turned to anger as she looked into his eyes. "Yes, you are. You already have." Then she turned around and walked out, slamming the door behind her. "Oh, that man is so infuriating!" she muttered with clenched fists as she marched toward the buckboard.

"Oh, I am?"

She wheeled around, and he was standing on the front porch, leaning casually against a post.

"What do you want from me?" she screamed as hot, angry tears coursed down her cheeks. "What do you want?"

Caleb let out a deep breath and then walked down the steps and wrapped his arms around her, letting her cry on his shoulder as he rubbed her back. "Honestly... I really don't know."

Mia nodded against his chest and wiped away her tears when she pulled back. Then she looked into his eyes. "Caleb, I can't keep going on like this."

He let out a deep breath. "I know."

She stared at him for a long while and then placed her hand on the side of his cheek and looked into his eyes. He took her hand and helped her up into the buckboard without another word, then stood on the porch and watched as she drove away.

The sun shone brightly, beating down upon the earth as she headed toward Gabriella and Dirk Price's house. Tears streamed down her cheeks as she rode on. Since she was alone, she let them fall freely. Somehow, she instinctively knew that it was over; she'd fallen in love with him and he obviously wasn't in love with her... and probably never would be. She would wait forever for him if he wanted her to, but he had no idea what he wanted. Maybe they could go back to the way things were. But then again, they had been balancing on a knife's edge for quite a while... for far too long. She was kidding herself to think they could go back to the way it was.

Thankful for the moment of peace, she listened to the birds sing as the wind blew softly through the trees, creating a wonderful symphony. The snow-capped mountains rose in the distance and verdant trees dotted the base. Someday, she would love to go there to see the top of the mountain. But deep down inside, she knew she never would.

Soon enough the trees parted, and the Price ranch appeared ahead. It was a lovely cabin with a large wooden front porch that stretched across the front of the house. Various trees were around it, creating a beautiful landscape. It was as if God had planted a seed and the cabin had sprung up in between them.

As she pulled down the drive, she stopped in front of the house beside Kenzie's buggy and put on the brake. Then she dabbed at her eyes to make sure she was presentable. She didn't want anyone to know that her world was falling apart. At least, not yet. She climbed down and smoothed a hand over her dress. Satisfied she was presentable, she walked up the steps and knocked on the front door.

When it opened, Gabriella was standing on the other side. "Mia, I'm so glad you came! Come on in. Kenzie is already here," she greeted her in her rich French accent.

"Thank you." Mia came into the living room and the kitchen table set to the left, creating an L shape, the connector between the two rooms. "Gabriella, I love your home. This is so charming."

Gabriella beamed. "Why, thank you. I made a lot of the decorations."

Mia looked around and noticed the crocheted doilies that

adorned the tables and the afghan on the back of the couch. "The afghan is beautiful."

"You like it?"

Mia nodded.

"Dirk's grandmother made it for him long before I came. I just love it." Gabriella beamed. "It's the most beautiful piece in the house."

Mia noticed a cross-stitched portrait of a house in what appeared to be a winter landscape. "Is that a picture of this cabin?"

Gabriella smiled. "Yes, it is. I made it for Dirk last Christmas, our first Christmas together."

Mia ran her fingers along the edge of the frame. "It's lovely."

"Thank you," Gabriella purred, leading the way into the dining room where Kenzie was waiting.

"Hello, Kenzie," Mia greeted her.

Kenzie gave her hand a gentle squeeze. "Hello! I'm glad you came."

A pale blue tablecloth with a lovely spring flower pattern adorned the table. A beautiful wildflower bouquet set in a glass flower vase took center stage on the table. "Gabriella, everything's lovely," Mia gushed, looking at the china tea pitcher and the delicate plates of teacakes and cookies.

"Thank you." She smiled as she sat down kitty-corner from Kenzie. Mia sat down on the other side. "So, shall we begin?"

"Yes, of course," Kenzie replied.

Gabriella carefully poured the tea and set it down onto

the table. Then, she took a teacake and passed the plate.

They spent the afternoon laughing and talking about lighthearted topics, sipping tea and eating a variety of the little homemade pastries.

"So, how are things in town?" Gabriella asked Kenzie and then took a sip of her tea.

Kenzie laughed. "Hectic, lately!" Kenzie took a dainty bite of a cookie and swallowed.

"So, has business been that good?" Gabriella asked.

Kenzie inclined her head toward Mia. "Yes, thanks to this lady sitting here." She raised her teacup to Mia, took a sip, and swallowed. "But that's not what I meant."

Mia's eyebrows pulled together in concern. "What do you mean?"

"The last wagon train going east just came into town and they're staying in Whiskey River, buying supplies and preparing for the trip." Kenzie shrugged. "It's good for business, but very hectic, trying to fill the orders before they leave while keeping up with my regular customers, too. But I'm not complaining, mind you."

"Wagon train?" Mia asked as she casually took a sip of her tea.

Kenzie smiled. "Yes, this is the last one going east before winter hits. Otherwise, the weather will be too rough to make the journey, unless by train."

Mia took another bite of her cookie to hide her interest. "So, when is the wagon train leaving?"

"Tomorrow." Kenzie took a sip of her tea. "Then the town will get back to normal again."

"Who's going with them? Anyone I know?" Mia asked as she took a bite of a tea sandwich filled with egg salad.

Kenzie shook her head. "No, probably not. Mainly some young people, wanting to start a new life away from the west, or people who found life too rough out here wanting to go back east."

Gabriella set down her tea cup and it clicked against the china saucer. "Why so interested?"

Mia shrugged. "Just curious. I've never seen a wagon train up close before. I've only heard about them."

Kenzie laughed. "Well, if you go into town now, you'll see one up close."

Then Mia looked over at Gabriella and smiled. "So, I heard you have some good news! How far along are you?"

"I'm about five months along."

"You're hiding it very well." Kenzie smiled, setting down her teacup. "So, what does Dirk think about this?"

"Dirk's so excited he's telling anyone who will listen," Gabriella beamed and then turned her attention to Mia. "So, are you and Reverend Henley wanting to have more children?"

Mia nearly spit out her tea, almost choking.

"Oh! Are you okay?" Gabriella perched on the edge of her seat, ready to help.

Mia held up her hand as she coughed into her napkin. "So, when are you due?" Mia took a sip of her tea, avoiding Gabriella's question.

Gabriella sat back in her chair but was still concerned. "I'm not due until Christmas."

"Christmas?" Kenzie squealed. "That's fabulous!"

Mia smiled. "What a wonderful Christmas gift!"

They spent the next hour helping Gabriella make plans for her new baby and picked out baby names, while Mia secretly formulated a plan of her own.

CHAPTER 22

When Mia came in the front door that afternoon, Caleb was waiting in the living room as the children played in the bedroom. He honestly hadn't thought she would come home until after the children were in bed, although he wasn't quite sure why. When she left, it had just felt so final… even though she was only going to an afternoon tea with friends.

"Well, I'm glad you're here." Caleb sounded bitter even to his own ears. "After this afternoon, I wasn't sure if you were coming back or not."

"What made you think that? I told you I would be back in time for dinner." Mia glared at him. "What would you like me to make?" Mia walked into the kitchen and slipped on an apron.

"No, don't worry. I was planning on making dinner," Caleb replied abruptly, following her.

Mia looked over and steaks were setting on the counter, ready to cook. "Then I'll make the potatoes."

"No, I'll do it," Caleb replied as he took the pan out of

her hand.

Mia took off her apron and threw it onto the counter. "What is this, Caleb?"

"Why, whatever do you mean?" His voice dripped with sarcasm as he lifted a gunnysack filled with potatoes from the pantry and threw them onto the counter.

Mia folded her arms across her chest. "Caleb, I'm sorry that I've been a bit distant lately, but I've had a lot to think about."

He threw his hands up in the air. "And you don't think that I haven't? I've been doing nothing but think!"

"Stop yelling...."

"Why?" he yelled as he looked at her. "I've been screaming on the inside for a very long time!"

"Why didn't you tell me?" Mia demanded. "Instead, you pull back every time you start to get close."

He looked her up and down. "No wonder I'm pulling away! You've been distancing yourself from me ever since the other night!"

Tears sprang to her eyes as she ran outside to the front yard.

Caleb let out a deep breath as he held onto the counter. Then he pushed away and followed her outside. Mia was kneeling on the ground and her shoulders were shaking. She was crying. Caleb bit his upper lip as he watched her with his hands on his hips, realizing that he had done this. He hadn't even let her get in the door before he'd started in on her. This wasn't him.

He walked over and placed a hand gently on her shoulder.

"Mia, I'm sorry. Come on in and let's talk about this."

"No!" Mia whipped around, tears streaming openly down her face. "You don't want to talk! In fact, those were the first words that you said to me in days!"

Caleb threw his hands up in the air again. "You really want to do this out here… in the yard?"

She swiped a hand across her face. "I don't want to argue in front of the children."

"Oh, that's rich." He turned to face her. "You haven't even been around the children much this week!"

"Stop it, Caleb!" she yelled as tears streamed down her face. "You don't love me, and you don't have to. I was doing a good job of keeping to our agreement, as you had asked. I loved the children but protected my heart from you. And then everything changed! I don't even know how you feel! If you love me, then you have to tell me. I can't live in limbo." She let out a deep breath, trying to calm herself. "I understand that you lost the love of your life. I can't even begin to imagine what that would be like, but you can't do this to me. You can't keep torturing me." She rose to her feet. "You can't have it both ways."

Caleb froze, watching her with his mouth open, knowing what she said was true. "Mia, I've tried—"

"You've tried?" Mia screamed. "You haven't tried at all! I've been the only one trying!" She let out a deep breath. "Caleb, we were fine. We had an agreement and I could live with it. But then you kissed me, and everything changed." She took a step closer to him. "Caleb, I realize that I may be making too much of it, but I've thought about it and I'm not the kind of person who can be… casual. Caleb, I'm asking you. How do you feel… about me? You can love more than one person."

She waited, but he couldn't say the words and he didn't know if he ever could. He knew he wasn't being fair to her, but how could he tell her how he felt without feeling as if he was betraying Jessica?

"That's what I thought." She stormed into the house and he heard a door slam shut.

Caleb placed his hands on his hips as he looked up at the darkening sky and then let out a deep breath. How could he have done this? Maybe the best thing was to let her go. He walked into the house and knocked on her bedroom door. "Mia, come on out. Let's talk."

She was crying on the other side of the door.

"Mia, I'm coming in." When he heard no answer, he opened the door and found her sitting on the edge of the bed with her head buried in her hands. Caleb knelt down on the floor in front of her. "Mia, you're right."

She raised her tear-streaked face until her eyes met his.

"I haven't been fair to you… and I'm sorry." She stood and crossed to the other side of the room, folding her arms across her chest, and he sat on the bed. "Mia, let's talk."

She shook her head. "You don't want to talk. You just want to yell."

Caleb stood. "I'm sorry about that." He moved toward her, but she took a step back.

Tears sprang to her eyes once more. "Caleb, you don't have to forget Jessica. She will always be with you… in your heart. But you can't hold on to her so tightly that you won't let anyone else in."

Anger suddenly filled his chest. "Jessica has nothing to do with this."

"She has everything to do with it." Mia shook her head. "Caleb, you have to be able to find a way to move on."

"I am moving on."

"No, you're not." Tears ran slowly down her cheeks. "And as long as you hold on to her so tightly, how can there be a chance for us?"

Caleb let out a deep breath. "There is no us." He paused for a moment, and then walked out, closing the door behind him.

★★★

Caleb went into the kitchen and finished making dinner. During dinner, Shane asked where Mia was and Hailey asked for Mama. Caleb lied, telling them that she wasn't feeling well, although he was tempted to tell them that she wasn't their mother. Their mother had died. But he just didn't have the strength, and he could never be that cruel.

The night wore on, and he was sitting by the fire, drinking a cup of coffee, when Mia came out of her room. Her eyes were glossy from crying as she wrung a handkerchief in her hand and headed straight for the children's bedroom. She froze at the door as she peeked in before entering.

Caleb waited as he took another sip of his coffee and listened. There was no noise. He knew that she wouldn't harm his children, but he stood and moved slowly toward the door, and then pushed it open.

Mia was sitting in the rocking chair, with her back to the door, watching the children sleep.

"Mia?"

When she spoke, her voice cracked. "Caleb, before you say anything, hear me out. I'm too tired to argue."

He waited, saying nothing.

She cleared her throat as she watched the children. "There's a wagon train leaving to go back east tomorrow. It's the last one of the year before winter hits… and I'm leaving with them."

Caleb gasped. Although he had been expecting it, it was still hard to hear. "I'll take you into town tomorrow." His voice was heavy with emotion.

She shook her head. "No, I'll ask Colton to take me in the morning. If you take me, it'll be too hard."

Tears welled up in his eyes. "I'll go ask him now." He cleared his throat and tried again. "You take care of yourself."

She nodded as she continued to rock back and forth.

He let out a deep breath as he placed his hand on her shoulder and gave her a gentle squeeze.

Mia reached up and placed her hand on his.

Then he pulled away, picked up his boots, and walked back into the living room to slip them on. It was late, but he needed to get out of the house and he knew that Colton wouldn't mind him coming over at this hour. He saddled up his white stallion as he tried not to think of Mia and how his life had crumbled yet again… as tears ran slowly down his cheeks.

CHAPTER 23

"Mia?"

Bang, bang, bang!

When Mia woke, it was dark. She tried to orient herself as she slowly opened her eyes.

Mia's bedroom door suddenly flew open and hit the wall with a bang.

She sat up and caught her breath, wide awake, recognizing Caleb's voice. "What's wrong?"

"The barn's on fire!" he yelled as he ran out her bedroom door.

Mia rushed out of the room, dressed in her nightgown.

"Stay here!" Caleb yelled, and then headed back out, headed toward the barn.

Outside, flames were visible inside the barn. "My God!" She darted into the master bedroom and the children were still sleeping. She shut their door and then rushed outside as quickly as she could.

Caleb led a horse out of the barn with a blanket over its

eyes. Then he let it go and it hurried out into the field. "I thought I told you to stay inside!"

"The children are safe, and you need help!" she yelled as she jogged into the barn, and he followed.

Caleb quickly wrapped a blanket over another horse's eyes and led it from the barn.

Mia did the same, working with Caleb to save what they could. "We'll need the milk." She hurried over to ol' Bessie's stall.

Mia unlocked the stall door and tried to lead her out, but the cow felt the heat and pulled back. Mia grabbed a lead strap and hooked it to her halter and quickly wrapped a horse blanket over her eyes. She finally got her out of the stall and was leading her toward the barn entrance when a beam crashed down on her, knocking the wind out of her and pinning her to the ground as bright orange and yellow flames blazed around her. She tried to push the beam off, but it was too heavy, and she was too weak. Dazed, she willed herself to stay conscious.

"Mia?" Caleb's voice echoed into the barn, frantic. "Mia, where are you?"

She heard him in the distance and she wanted to yell back, but she couldn't force her eyes to stay open. It was becoming more and more difficult as each second passed.

A moment later, she opened her eyes and her heart jumped. Caleb was standing on the other side of the beam, looking down at her.

"Mia!" The moment he saw her, he took off his shirt and patted the log, putting out the flames. Then he bent down and tried to push the beam off her, but it was too heavy. He took a saddle blanket and patted the beam to put out the flames and threw it down. Bracing himself against the stall, he used his foot and pushed with all his might.

Tears fell onto her cheeks. "Caleb, go! Save yourself!"

He shook his head as he pushed hard against the beam, but it wouldn't budge. "I'm not leaving you!"

She shook her head, coughing. "Caleb, you have to think of the children! They can't lose you, too! Now, go!"

"If you think for one minute that I'd leave you here to die, then you don't know me very well." He pushed the beam with all his might, straining with the effort. But, this time, it moved... a little. "Yah!" he yelled as he kept pushing with his feet, and this time, it fell off her. "Come on." He bent down and scooped her up into his arms with ease, then carried her a safe distance from the barn and laid her on the ground. Then he ran back in the barn.

"No, Caleb!" Tears rolled down Mia's cheeks as she fought to stay conscious. "Caleb!"

What felt like an eternity but was only a moment later, he collapsed onto the ground beside her.

Mia looked over at him. "Are you all right?"

"Yes, I'm fine." Caleb laid his arm over his forehead, coughing. "I had to save ol' Bessie. We need the milk... for the children."

Mia started laughing as she coughed, although she wasn't sure why. It just struck her as funny.

Caleb looked over at her as if she were crazy at first, and then started laughing, too.

"What about the other animals?" The fresh air was sharpening her senses, clearing her head, helping her to become more alert.

"We got them all out," he breathed, coughing, trying to catch his breath.

"Were they hurt?"

Caleb let out a deep breath. "Some had a few burns on their hooves and legs, but they're no worse for wear. I'll put some liniment on them and they'll be fine. If I need to, I'll get Doc Morgan to look at them later."

Mia guessed that there were no veterinarians in these parts, so Doc Morgan probably took care of the animals, too.

Mia looked around, disoriented as her head pounded. "Where are they?"

Caleb rolled over and opened his eyes, trying to catch his breath. "In the back fields or in the neighbor's fields, away from the flames. We'll round them up later." He thought for a moment, and then asked, "Are you okay?"

"My head hurts and my arm is burnt. But other than that, I'm fine." She looked over at him as he sat up. "How about you?"

"I'm fine." Caleb propped himself up on his arms, still breathing heavy and coughing. "Let me see your arm."

Reluctantly, she held it out to him.

He looked at it and frowned. "We need to put some lard on that. It'll soothe the burn and will take out the sting."

After that, they sat in silence, making sure the fire stayed contained, watching the barn burn down as flaming beams hit the ground.

***

As the sun rose over the snow-capped mountains, it became a gorgeous riot of color with the turning leaves. In the morning sunlight, she could see some of the animals in the distance, but she wouldn't be there to help round them up. As they watched the barn burn down, Caleb had said nothing. At that moment, she knew she would have stayed… if he only asked.

Mia let out a deep breath as she rose to her feet, exhausted. She would have plenty of time to sleep on the journey. Looking over her shoulder as she walked toward the house, Caleb just sat on the lawn watching what was left of the barn smolder… lost in his own thoughts.

CHAPTER 24

As Caleb watched the embers burning over the ground where the barn once stood, the best he could tell, the barn must have been struck by lightning or perhaps one of the bales of hay spontaneously combusted, even though it was early October. He wasn't completely sure, and he resolved himself to the fact that he might not ever know. As he looked around, his thoughts went to Mia trapped inside the barn. He let out a deep breath. What would he have done if she had died? When he'd looked around and she hadn't come out of the barn, he remembered thinking that he couldn't lose her, too... not the way he had lost Jessica.

Maybe now she wouldn't leave. Maybe now they could have a second chance. After all, wouldn't she stay to help him rebuild? It might buy him a little time....

As he looked out over what was left of the barn, he realized there wasn't much more that he could do out here, and he was exhausted. He headed up the slight incline toward the house. When he opened the back door, Mia wasn't making breakfast, and the house was quiet.

He walked through the kitchen and into the living room, heading toward the bedroom where the children were sleeping, but stopped. When he looked toward the front door, his heart fell. Mia was sitting in the rocking chair in the living room, packed and ready to go, looking beautiful in a purple dress and matching hat. She must have cleaned up while he was outside. "What's this?" He'd been sure that she would change her mind, that she would stay.

He heard the sound of horses and a buckboard pulling up out front and knew it was Colton.

"Colton's here." She stood from the chair, fiddling with the reticule in her hand.

His heart sank as he noticed the curve of her jaw and slender neck, her perfect body, the golden hue of her hair, committing it all to memory. He turned away to hide the tears forming in his eyes. "I'll help you with the trunk." Then he went into the bedroom where the children were still sleeping, unaware that their world was about to change yet again.

When Caleb carried Mia's trunk outside, Colton jumped down out of the buckboard, a crease forming between his eyes. "What happened?"

Caleb placed her trunk in the back of his buckboard. "The barn burned down last night."

"My God!" Colton exclaimed. "And the animals?"

Caleb let out a deep, exhausted breath. "Some have minor burns and smoke inhalation, but we got them all out."

Colton looked over at Mia standing on the porch.

"Are you sure you want to do this?"

Caleb couldn't look.

"Yes." Her voice broke, breaking his heart, as well.

Colton looked over at Caleb and raised an eyebrow, but said nothing.

Caleb gave him a manly slap on the shoulder. "Well, I guess you'd better get going." Then he turned to Mia as tears filled his eyes. "Take care of yourself."

She nodded. "You, too."

Unable to take any more, Caleb walked around the corner of the house, where what was left of the barn was still smoldering. Soon, he heard the buckboard and Colton's team pull down the long drive, fading in the distance until they were gone.

Then the memory of thinking her dead rushed through his mind again, coupled with her leaving for good, his heart heavy with utter despair. He looked into the orange- and yellow-streaked morning sky and nodded.

The children were still sleeping and Caleb needed a minute. He walked over to the family cemetery, found Jessica's grave and looked at the hard, marble headstone, so unlike Jessica. "Jess, as you probably know, I almost lost Mia last night. I could accept her leaving me of her own accord a thousand times over, but I could neverose her through death the way I lost you. And now she's gone. But I want you to know that if she'll have me, I'd like to be her husband now—her real husband. I don't just need her for the children and the house. I need her for me. I love her, Jessica. Although I loved you with a fierceness unlike any

I've known before, the love I have for her is different, but unmatched as well. It has taken over my heart, and I never even realized it… until now. Jessica, if you can hear me, please give us your blessing and help me to get her back. But know that I love you, darling, and I always will."

With his mind made up, he ran into the bedroom and dressed quietly. If he hurried, he might just be able to catch her.

He slipped on a shirt and then ran outside to gather the horses as quickly as he could and hitched them up to the buckboard. After he pulled it out front and put on the brake, he jumped down and rushed into his bedroom, where the children were sleeping. "Shane, Hailey. Time to wake up."

Shane sat up and rubbed his tired eyes. "Why?"

"Because we're going after Mia." Caleb grinned, ruffling his hair.

Shane's eyes opened wide. "She left?"

"Yes, and I'm going to get her, but we need to hurry."

Shane jumped out of bed and Caleb grabbed a clean change of clothes for him and Hailey.

Hailey was sleepy, yawning when he started to dress her and her eyes opened.

Shane jumped up on the bed beside them. "Hailey, you want to go get Mia?"

She bobbed her head frantically, although she obviously had no idea what was happening. But she would follow Shane to the ends of the earth.

Once the children were dressed, he scooped Hailey up into his arms. "Let's go, Shane," he said over his shoulder to his son.

"Yeah!" Shane ran out of the house and jumped up into the back of the buckboard.

Caleb set Hailey on the seat next to him. She smiled happily and clapped her hands.

As they headed toward Whiskey River, Caleb hoped he wasn't too late.

CHAPTER 25

Mia dabbed at her eyes but tried to hold it together as she rode with Colton to Whiskey River, after she said a tear-filled goodbye to Ella. She had hoped that Caleb would ask her to stay, but he didn't. He just stood there, watching as she left. Images of the children passed through her mind as the horses plodded along the dirt road. She hated leaving them, but they weren't her children, not really, although she couldn't love them more if they were. Tears rolled down her cheeks as images of them ran through her mind... images of Shane playing war in his room while Hailey played with her doll... images of laughing with them at breakfast, the closest they had ever come to being a family... images of Shane yelling at her, then coming to love her... images of Hailey calling her Mama.

Then she remembered Caleb's broad, bare, muscular chest the first morning after she came to live with them and then again in the barn when he had taken off his shirt to put out the fire on the beam... the curve of his mouth when he was amused... the sound of his laughter... Caleb greeting his parishioners happily and then preaching from the pulpit... the look of warmth in his eyes. She committed it all to memory, for she knew she would never come to love anyone else the way she loved them.

"Are you sure this is what you want?" Colton asked her, breaking the silence.

She shook her head. "No, but he didn't ask me to stay, either."

Out of her peripheral vision, she saw Colton nod. "A man can ask every day without saying the words."

Mia burst into tears. Suddenly, a handkerchief appeared before her eyes. "Thank you. But please, don't make it any harder than it already is."

Colton sighed beside her. "Mia, he's a good man."

She inclined her head in agreement. How could she tell Colton that Caleb would never love her the way that she was hopelessly in love with him?

Thankfully, Colton said nothing more.

A few minutes later, they pulled into town. Since she had lived there, Mia had never seen the town so full of life. The Whiskey River General Store was bustling with business as people walked in and out of the store and the restaurant.

Colton pulled the team to a stop in front of the restaurant. "Are you okay?"

"I'm fine." Mia squared her shoulders, quickly swiping her hand across her cheeks.

Colton sighed. "Stay here for a minute and let me talk to someone... maybe there's a family who will let you ride with them." He waited a moment, obviously giving her a moment to change her mind. When she didn't say anything, he interrupted the silence. "I'll be right back."

Colton started off, when she heard the sound of another buckboard riding up into town behind her. Mia thought she was dreaming when she turned around and saw that it was Caleb and the children. Colton suppressed a smile and stopped when he saw what was happening.

Caleb pulled the team to a stop in front of her as the horses snorted loudly, pawing at the ground. Caleb handed Hailey down to Colton. Shane hopped down, but Colton caught his hand, stopping him.

Caleb rushed over to Mia and held her hand, helping her down from the buckboard. "Mia, don't go."

"We'll be right over here… if you need us," he whispered and walked casually onto the porch of the restaurant with the two children.

Caleb never took his eyes from Mia. "Mia, I've been a fool. Please, don't go."

Tears welled up in her eyes as she shook her head. "Caleb, I can't keep going on this way… the way we have. I can't be just a caregiver for the children and a maid… not after the other night." She bit her lower lip. "Not anymore."

"And I don't want you to." Still holding her hand, he looked down and then into her eyes. "Mia, I've been such a fool. I love you and I want you to be my wife… my real wife. I'll move the children into the spare room this afternoon."

Mia frowned. "But what about… Jessica?" She hated herself for asking, but she had to know. She meant what she said. She couldn't go back to the way it was… the way it had been.

Caleb took her hands into his own. "Yes, I love her, and I always will."

Mia's face fell as her heart broke into a million pieces. She knew that he would never get over the death of his first wife. How could she expect him to?

"But I love you, too."

Mia's eyes snapped up.

Caleb let out a deep breath. "I said goodbye to her, and I explained it to her… in my own way. Yes, I will always love her, but I love you, too. Wasn't it you who said that you can love more than one person?"

She smiled through her tears.

"Mia, when you ran into the burning barn last night and didn't come out.…"

Colton gasped from the porch, holding Shane's hand as he held Hailey.

"I thought I'd lost you… forever." Caleb bit his lower lip as he looked away and then back into her eyes. "I don't know what I would have done if I had lost you like that. Please, I beg you.…" He got down on one knee as he held her hand. "Be my wife… my real wife this time. I promise to put no other woman before you, and to love you for all the days of my life."

Tears streamed down her cheeks as a smile spread across her face. "Yes. A thousand times, yes. And I promise to honor, cherish, and love you… for as long as we both shall live."

Colton smiled. "You may now kiss the bride."

Caleb laughed as Mia blushed. Then Caleb's lips descended upon hers. Passion filled them both as she wrapped her arms around his muscular back. When he pulled back, his eyes never left hers as he spoke to Colton. "Colton, I'll be over to speak with you later, but we're going home now."

Colton raised his hands in surrender. "Hey! I saw nothing."

Mia smiled. "Caleb, when I was a little girl, I always dreamed of my knight in shining armor riding up to rescue me. I never thought he would already be my husband."

Caleb shook his head. "No, I haven't been… until now. But I promise to honor and cherish you for as long as we both shall live." He repeated their wedding vows, this time meaning every word. "And I promise to honor my vow to you as your husband, and to give you my whole heart… forever."

Although they were already married, she felt that they were now truly married as he helped her into his buckboard.

Colton walked over with the children.

"Thank you, Colton, for everything. Sorry for the trouble." Caleb took Hailey from his arms and handed her up to Mia and Shane climbed into the back.

Colton smiled. "No trouble at all. What are friends for?"

Caleb shook his hand.

"Hey! Let's not forget her trunk." Then Colton looked over at Mia and gave her a wink. "A woman has to have her things."

Mia smiled. "I already have everything I need." And at that moment, she knew she was right. A loving husband and a beautiful family was all she had ever wanted.

★★★

Mia snuggled into Caleb's side, holding Hailey as they drove back to the house. For the first time, she felt that they were actually going back to their home. Caleb leaned his head against hers as she curled her arm around his, and then he raised her hand to his lips.

When they reached home, he wrapped his arms around her and his lips descended upon hers again, a silent promise of his love. Then he got down, took Hailey, and helped Mia from the buckboard. She linked her arm with his, about to go inside with her new husband.

"Wait, my wife." Caleb pulled her to a stop as she giggled. "There's something I haven't done yet." He opened the door and let Hailey and Shane go first and they scampered off. Then Caleb scooped Mia into his arms and carried her into the house. "I haven't carried you over the threshold yet."

Mia laughed as she wrapped her arms around his neck, enjoying the feel of his broad shoulders under her touch, knowing that at long last, they were finally home… together.

Then they heard the sound of horses' hooves and a carriage pull up out front. Turning, they saw it was Mrs. Jenkins.

"Mrs. Jenkins!" Mia exclaimed, happy to see her. "I'm so glad you came."

"Well…," Mrs. Jenkins said. "Word spread around town. Colton Hill stopped by to tell me, and then I had George go around to some of the neighbors."

Mia's eyebrows rose, knowing that everyone in town had been busy with the wagon train. Colton must have told everyone in town after she left with Caleb and the children. "Did the wagon train leave?"

"Yes." Mrs. Jenkins chuckled. "Mr. and Mrs. Carson are happy as larks with the extra money they made. They practically sold out of everything in the store." Mrs. Jenkins smiled as she held out a covered dish she had been holding. "Here you go. Since I knew you may not have time to cook, I brought something over."

Caleb smiled as he took the dish. "Thank you, Mrs. Jenkins. We could never repay your kindness."

"Oh, think nothing of it." She waved her hand dismissively.

Mia smiled, feeling content, despite everything they had lost. Somehow, with Caleb's love, it didn't seem to matter. "Thank you, Mrs. Jenkins. Please, stay and eat with us."

"I'd love to, but please call me Abigail."

Mia smiled. "That might be hard to do. Old habits die hard."

Mrs. Jenkins smiled. "Yes, they do"—she looked over at Caleb—"but people can change." Then she took the children by the hand. "I'll take the children inside and will organize the food."

"I'll help," Mia replied.

"No, you and Caleb stay out here and greet everyone.

I'll take care of everything inside." Then she looked down at the children. "Come along. Let's get you two something to eat."

Caleb smiled. "Thank you, Mrs. Jenkins."

Mia watched Mrs. Jenkins take the children inside, while Caleb walked toward the remains of the barn to assess the damage. There was nothing left of the barn but ash. All the embers had finally died out, leaving a charred mess in their wake.

The townsfolk started coming by to help with the cleaning, give emotional support, and brought over food. Mia was amazed by the generosity and concern of everyone. By that afternoon, it seemed that practically everyone in town had come by to offer their help or to express their concern.

Mia held onto Caleb's arm. "It appears that everyone in the town has come by today."

Caleb smiled as he gave her hand a gentle pat. "Here in Whiskey River, we all pull together in times of need." Caleb looked over at the house and smiled as he pulled her in for a hug. "Well, at least it didn't get to the house and everyone is safe."

"We can always rebuild," Mia agreed as she looked into his eyes.

"Of course we can." Out of the corner of his eye, he saw that Wyatt Nash and Harrison Curry were walking toward them. "Wyatt. Harrison. Thanks for coming." Caleb shook their hands.

Wyatt, dressed in a white shirt, gray vest, jeans, and a black cowboy hat, motioned toward the men that were standing around.

"Wyatt, thanks for coming." Mia walked toward him and stretched out her hand.

He reached out and shook her hand. "We've talked about it and we came to a decision." Wyatt smiled mischievously. "What are you doing this Sunday after church?"

One side of Caleb's lips curled into a smile. "Why? What do you have in mind?"

Wyatt shrugged. "We thought that instead of having our usual get-together after church, we'd like to come here and have a barn raising. We can go to church for the service, and then we'll all come over here after." Wyatt looked in his eyes. "That is, if it's okay with you."

Caleb let out a deep breath. "Wyatt, everyone, we appreciate the gesture. I can't ask you to do that."

Wyatt laughed. "You didn't ask. We volunteered."

Harrison shook Caleb's hand. "Here in Whiskey River, we all pull together."

"Besides, we can always use an excuse for a dance," Wyatt teased.

Mia's eyebrows pulled together.

Eyeing her confusion, Wyatt clarified, "After the barn raising, we'll have a dance."

Mia's smile broadened. "I'm surprised that you'll be able to raise the barn that fast."

Harrison laughed. "This isn't our first rodeo, little missy." Then he looked at Caleb. "So, what do you say?"

Caleb shook his hand and clapped him on the back. "I say thank you! We really appreciate this."

Harrison smiled. "Hey, we're a community." He shrugged as he looked over at Wyatt. "And you and your family are one of us."

★★★

True to his word, Caleb moved the children out of the main bedroom and into the spare room that night. They spent the rest of the week settling in as a family and getting ready for Sunday.

"Caleb, I'd like to go to the general store today," Mia announced after breakfast one morning when the dishes were put away. "I'd like to get some things for Sunday."

Caleb smiled and gave her a quick peck on the lips. "Only if we get something for you, too."

She reached up on her tiptoes and gave him a quick kiss on the cheek. "Thank you. I'll get the children ready." Then a thought occurred to her. "Did you have anything else planned for today?"

He shook his head. "No, I was just going to spend the day with my lovely wife and family."

Mia laughed, glad for the change. The past few days had been wonderful. The marriage that she had dreamed of with a doting husband and wonderful children had come true. Since the day he had professed his love, everything had changed. True to his word, Caleb had become the best husband that Mia could have ever wanted. When he had decided to give her his heart, he gave it all.

A few minutes later, the family was on their way to town in the October morning air. They sang songs along the way and soon Caleb pulled the team to a stop in front of the Whiskey River General Store, pulled the brake, and wrapped the reins around the front bar.

"Yippee!" Shane yelled as he jumped out of the buckboard.

"Don't touch anything!" Caleb yelled as his son darted into the store.

"Oh, Caleb. He's just excited."

"Yes, but if he eats too much candy, then he'll be up all night." Caleb adjusted Hailey in his arms.

"You mean *you'll* be up with him all night," she teased.

Caleb laughed. "Yes, *I'll* be up with him all night." Caleb offered his wife his arm, and Mia took it, feeling his muscles under his coat. "Listen, when we go in, go ahead and get whatever you want."

Mia smiled as she hugged his arm. "Thanks, but I'll only get what I need, which consists of thread, buttons—"

"Okay, okay!" Caleb opened the door for her. "I surrender!"

"Well, hello! What brings you into town today?" Mrs. Carson greeted them as they walked in. "I'm so sorry to hear about your barn, but we're looking forward to seeing you on Sunday."

Mia grinned. "I hope you're planning on coming over to our place after church. The town's planned a barn raising party. There will be a dance afterward."

A broad smile spread across Mrs. Carson's face. "We wouldn't miss it for the world." She pointed to her husband, who was stocking a shelf behind the counter. "Mr. Carson has been talking about it all week."

"Is it okay if they have a candy stick?" Mr. Carson asked, ignoring his wife.

"Please, oh please!" Shane and Hailey chimed together, jumping up and down.

Mia looked at Caleb.

"It's up to your mama," he replied, ignoring Mrs. Carson when her mouth flew open.

"Please, oh please?" Shane and Hailey both begged Mia.

Mia let out a deep breath. "Go ahead. But just one each. Don't eat too much."

Mr. Carson beamed. "Here you go," he cooed, handing each of them a candy stick.

"Now, what do you say?" Mia asked.

"Thank you!" both of the children chimed together, and then ran over to Mia to give her a hug.

Hailey reached up, wiggling her fingers, and Mia swept her up into her arms. "What's the matter, baby girl?"

Hailey wrapped her arms around her neck. "Thank you, Mama."

Mia smiled as she kissed her new daughter on the cheek. "You're welcome, but Mr. Carson is the one you should be thanking."

Mr. Carson laughed. "They already did."

But Hailey didn't remove her arms as she looked in Mia's eyes. "I love you, Mama."

"I love you, too," Mia replied, and then kissed her cheek. "Now, go play with your brother for a minute. I'm going to make us all something special."

Mrs. Carson dabbed at her eyes as she watched. "I'm so glad to see that you're all adjusting so well," she whispered.

"Thank you." Mia walked over to the fabric shelf containing bolts of fabric in many different colors.

"Are you looking for anything in particular?" Mrs. Carson asked.

Mia let out a deep breath. "Just some fabric to make the family some outfits. Since it's October, this may be the last time I'll buy fabric for a while before the weather gets bad. Do you have anything new?"

"How about this?" Turning, Mia saw that Kenzie was pointing to a bolt of fabric. She was smartly dressed and wore a friendly smile.

"That's lovely!" Mia gushed.

Kenzie smiled. "I think it would look nice on you."

"You're coming to the barn raising at our place this Sunday, aren't you?" Mia asked. Since she had started working for Kenzie, they had become fast friends. Mia could never think of Kenzie as her employer.

Kenzie chuckled. "Yes, of course." A sincere look came into her eyes. "I'm so sorry to hear about your barn."

"Thank you," Mia replied. "We're just glad no one was hurt."

"Now, let's get down to business," Kenzie announced. They spent the next half hour comparing fabrics, and before they left, Kenzie had helped her pick out enough fabric for two outfits for each member of her family.

"Aren't you getting anything for yourself?" Mia asked, waiting while Mrs. Carson measured off the lengths of fabric for Mia.

Kenzie smiled. "No, I get my fabric from a supplier out of Cheyenne. I came here for vegetables." Then she leaned in conspiratorially. "But I never could resist fabric shopping."

They both giggled.

Mrs. Carson smiled. "You've made excellent choices."

"Thank you," Mia replied, and then picked up some matching thread and some dainty buttons, along with some men's buttons, to go along with it.

"Well, it's been lovely chatting." Mia looked around for Caleb, who was speaking with Mr. Carson and entertaining the children.

"It's been a pleasure. By the way, I have another dress for you to sew for me, if you like." Kenzie extended her hand, and Mia shook it.

Mia smiled. "Actually, I've decided not to continue working for you, if you don't mind. I was going to come by the store to tell you. But I wanted to thank you for everything."

Kenzie pulled her in for a hug. "No, thank you for all your help." She pulled back and looked into her eyes. "You were a blessing. But if you should change your mind—"

"You'll be the first to know," Mia finished.

Kenzie paid Mrs. Carson for the vegetables.

"Thank you, Miss Baker," Mrs. Carson gushed. "Please, come again."

Kenzie smiled. "Oh, you can count on it. Have a good day!"

Mia spent the next few nights sewing for the children after they went to bed. She would have made an outfit for Caleb, too, but there wasn't enough time. She made a mental note to make him one before the next Sunday, though. She wasn't going anywhere.

Saturday night, Caleb entered the living room and leaned against the door facing, smiling. "Coming to bed?"

Mia smiled, enjoying herself. "Not just yet. I'm almost finished."

Caleb smiled. "May I see?"

She shook her head as she smiled. "No, not yet. I want it to be a surprise."

Caleb tapped the door facing. "Have fun, but don't stay up too late."

"I'll be there in a minute."

As she watched Caleb walk away, she knew that she had everything, that her dreams had just come true.

EPILOGUE

Mia got up early and walked out of the bedroom and into the living room Sunday morning. It was a bit chilly, so she put a few pieces of wood on the fire. It was November and the frigid winter weather had already set in. Within minutes, long tongues of red, orange, and yellow flared, lapping hungrily at the wood, filling the house with warmth. Then she went out to the kitchen and put on some coffee. While it was brewing, she tiptoed to the rocking chair in the living room and checked the clothes she'd made for the children. Today was the day of the barn raising and dance, and she wanted her children to look good. Although she knew Shane would be out playing with the other children before the day's end, at least he would look good for church.

"Good morning." Caleb walked out of the bedroom, shirtless. "You look great this morning."

"So do you," she said, and then pulled him in for a hug, enjoying the feel of his broad muscles under her fingertips.

He patted her back, and then whispered into her hair.

"Do I smell coffee?"

"Yes, you do. I'll pour us some."

He nodded. "So, how late were you up last night?"

She shrugged. "I'm not sure, but I got everything finished."

"Mia, thank you for all the hard work you've been doing," Caleb praised, taking the coffee she offered him. "But be sure to get some rest and take care of yourself, too."

She smiled, thankful for the sentiment. "I will."

"So, French toast?"

She laughed. "I think we have enough time."

Caleb slipped on a shirt and, together, they fixed breakfast. When they were nearly finished, the children came out, rubbing their sleepy eyes. They were delighted when they heard that their parents had made French toast and scampered quickly to their seats at the table.

After their family breakfast, which had become a ritual once again, she and Caleb cleaned up the children and dressed them in their new clothes. Hailey's dress was pale pink with little blue buds and matched Mia's to perfection. Shane's clothes matched his father's. A crisp white shirt, dark gray vest, and matching trousers. Mia then combed Hailey's hair, and then pulled it up high and tied it off with a coordinating pink ribbon. Then, she pulled her hair up, pinned the curls in place, and added a hat that went perfectly with the outfit.

"Well! You all look wonderful!" Caleb said to his family. The children giggled, and then he gave Mia a kiss on the cheek. "You look gorgeous."

She blushed. "Thank you." She raised an eyebrow mischievously. "And you look very handsome."

He laughed, and they all slipped on their coats, piled into the buckboard, and headed off to church.

When they arrived, she walked with the children to the pew in the front row and Caleb greeted the parishioners, as usual. She looked around, and Kenzie was shaking Caleb's hand. Then she spotted Mia and walked over to her.

"Good morning!" Kenzie greeted Mia happily.

Mia pulled her in for a hug. "Good morning!"

Kenzie leaned back and took in the children's clothes. "Well, well! Don't you all look nice! I love the clothes!"

Mia grinned as a sense of pride filled her. "Thank you." Then she gave Kenzie another hug. "I'll see you after church."

Kenzie nodded, and then crossed the church to talk to Gabriella.

Mia went on to greet Mrs. Jenkins, Madison and Wyatt, and more. This Sunday morning, the church was packed. Caleb gave a wonderful sermon, thanking God for all the blessings and people in their lives… and for the wisdom not to take those people for granted.

Mia knew that he was right. Even though their barn had burned down, it didn't matter. What mattered most was that they had each other. She had a lot to be thankful for, the top one being… a family. In her heart, she knew she would always love them and would never take them for granted.

After the service was over, the congregation headed over to their farm. When they arrived, the men got to work right away raising the barn, while the women set up the food outside on tables and long boards stretched between sawhorses.

Later that night, there was a brand-new barn where the old one had stood, just as good as the one before. When everything was finished, people pulled out their instruments and started playing, while couples swirled expertly around the floor.

Mia saw Ella and Colton standing off to the side, holding the babies and motioned them over.

"Ella, come sit over here with me." Mia indicated some wooden folding chairs.

The men had brought the chairs from the church, along with some tables. The ladies of the church came over and gushed over the babies, observing how much they had grown.

Everyone was there—Gabriella and Dirk, Madison and Wyatt, Kenzie, and so many other people that she knew. Whiskey River really was a place of community and family, where everyone looked out for and helped each other. Mia felt very lucky to be a part of it.

"Would you like to dance?"

When Mia looked up, Caleb was smiling as he held out his hand. She took it. "I'd love to."

"What were you thinking about just then?" Caleb asked as he led her out onto their new barn floor.

Mia smiled as she let her husband lead her. "I was just thinking of how lucky I am to be a part of this community here in Whiskey River."

He smiled. "I'm the lucky one… to have you as my wife."

Mrs. Jenkins had been holding the children back, giving them a moment alone. When she let them go, and they ran out onto the dance floor with them. Mia and Caleb scooped them into their arms and they continued dancing.

Shane struggled to get down, and Caleb set him on his feet. But instead of running away, he tugged on Mia's skirt to attract her attention. She bent down low and looked into his eyes.

"Could I dance with you… Mama?"

Mia was momentarily taken aback, but then handed Hailey to her father and took her son's hands. As they swayed to the music, Caleb and Hailey swayed beside them. Then Shane looked up at her and smiled. "I love you, Mama."

Tears came to her eyes as she replied, "I love you, too, son." She looked in Caleb's eyes, misty with tears. "I'm lucky to have this family." Mia smiled as the four of them danced together.

"We both are," Caleb agreed as he spun her and his children around the dance floor.

The night was magical as the stars began to make their appearance in the darkening sky. And Mia knew it was true. They *were* lucky to have each other, and to be a part of the wonderful community of Whiskey River.

NOTE FROM THE AUTHOR

I hope you enjoyed meeting the townspeople in the fictional town of Whiskey River in *The Preacher's Bride* (Whiskey River Brides, #4). Thank you for reading, and please consider leaving a review. The story continues with *The Banker's Bride* (Whiskey River Brides, #5) when Dallas King sends for another mail-order bride and finally meets his match. Other stories will follow—ten in all—featuring the habitants of Whiskey River, new characters and old favorites alike. I hope you enjoy the town and the people in it as much as I enjoyed writing it. Thank you for spending time with us in Whiskey River, and I look forward to sharing more books with you.

If you have any comments or suggestions for future books, I'd love to hear from you! You can email me at theresaoliverauthor@gmail.com. Happy reading! ~ *Theresa*

ACKNOWLEDGEMENTS

First of all, thank you to my husband who understands my need to put pen to paper.

To my children, who are forever a source of inspiration.

To Becky Johnson and Hot Tree Publishing who first believed in this series. Thanks for taking a chance. You're the best!

To editors and beta readers who helped to make this book so much better than it originally was: Justine Littleton, Olivia Ventura, Randie Creamer, Tina Moran, Casey Ford, Kristen Mitchell, Rebecca Gilbert, and all of the other wonderful editors of Hot Tree Publishing who touched my manuscript and helped it to shine. Special thanks to Randie Creamer, who talked me off the ledge and helped to organize my script into something I can really be proud of. Also, special thanks to Liv, who challenges me to think out of the box, in an effort to make my manuscript the best that it can be.

To Genevieve Scholl, my first editor. Thank you for always believing in me and my work! You seriously rock!

But most of all, thank you to my fans! For it is because of you that I can do what I love to do… write.

ABOUT THE PUBLISHER

Hot Tree Publishing opened its doors in 2015 with an aspiration to bring quality fiction to the world of readers. With the initial focus on romance and a wide spread of romance subgenres, Hot Tree Publishing have since opened their first imprint, Tangled Tree Publishing, specializing in crime, mystery, suspense, and thriller.

Firmly seated in the industry as a leading editing provider to independent authors and small publishing houses, Hot Tree Publishing is the sister company to Hot Tree Editing, founded in 2012. Having established in-house editing and promotions, plus having a well-respected market presence, Hot Tree Publishing endeavors to be a leader in bringing quality stories to the world of readers.

Interested in discovering more amazing reads brought to you by Hot Tree Publishing? Head over to the website for information:

WWW.HOTTREEPUBLISHING.COM

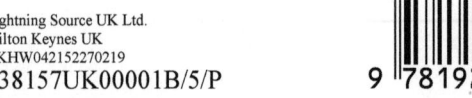